# Rockwell

## The Storm Testament VI

# Rockwell

## The Storm Testament VI

# Lee Nelson

Council Press
Springville, Utah

ISBN 13: 978-1-59955-096-1

Published by Council Press, an imprint of Cedar Fort, Inc., 2373 W. 700 S., Springville, UT, 84663
Distributed by Cedar Fort, Inc., www.cedarfort.com

LIBRARY OF CONGRESS CATALOGING-IN-PUBLICATION DATA

Nelson, Lee.
  Rockwell : storm testament VI / by Lee Nelson.
    p. cm.
  ISBN 978-1-59955-096-1 (alk. paper)
  1. Rockwell, Orrin Porter, 1813-1878--Fiction. 2. Mormons--Fiction. I.
Title. II. Title: Storm testament VI.

  PS3546.E4675R63 2007
  813'.54--dc22
                          2007026685

Cover design by Nicole Williams
Cover design © 2007 by Lyle Mortimer
Edited and typeset by Lyndsee Simpson Cordes

Printed in the United States of America

10  9  8  7  6  5  4  3  2  1

Printed on acid-free paper

To Richard,
who never seems to let
life's setbacks get him down.

# Prologue

Ike and I spotted the smoke before our horses reached the top of the ridge. Ike was the escaped slave who had come to the Rocky Mountains with me in 1838, later to become a Goshute chief. We were riding west along the foothills of Mt. Moriah in west central Nevada.

We were on an errand for a friend, Elizabeth Roundy, who was staying at the Porter Rockwell ranch on Government Creek at the south end of Skull Valley. Orrin Porter Rockwell had died the previous summer, and Elizabeth was trying to assemble his history. Much of it she had obtained from Rockwell while he was living, from personal interviews. Now she was interviewing those who had known the old gunfighter. She had asked Ike and me to run over to Ely and escort a widow named Polly Hatch back to Government Creek. The woman had agreed to come with us on horseback. What this widow knew about Rockwell that wasn't already known was not clear. I only knew that Elizabeth was determined to spend some time with this woman, and Ike and I agreed to bring them together.

It was early fall, 1879. Ike and I were taking a shortcut through the higher foothills of Mt. Moriah, hoping to spot some big mule deer we had heard were in the area. That's when we saw the smoke.

We approached the top of the hill carefully, wanting to see who was making the smoke before they saw us. Occasional bandits still roamed the vast wilderness areas of Nevada, and even though the Indian conflicts of the sixties had pretty much been resolved, roaming bands of renegade Indians still made trouble for whites from time to time.

In addition to seeing smoke, we could hear yelling and high-pitched whoops and hollers, like those of drunken cowboys engaged in a wild horse roundup.

What we saw upon reaching the top of the hill, however, was totally unexpected. There were cowboys, all right. Three of them were gathered around a fire where earlier they had apparently been branding calves. A small herd of cows with large fall calves was grazing randomly through the nearby sagebrush. The cowboys' horses were tied to juniper trees.

A naked Indian child was running away from the cowboys, scampering through the tall sagebrush like a frightened rabbit. The three men were yelling and waving their hats after the child. I began to think that perhaps the child had stolen something, but the cowboys were making no attempt to catch it.

Then I noticed two more children, also naked, on the ground by the fire. Their hands and feet were tied together. When two of the cowboys grabbed hold of one of the children, it began to kick and squirm. The two white men sat down by the fire, stretching the child out between them, one holding the hands, the other the feet. The child was face down, its face and belly in the dust.

It wasn't until the third cowboy knelt beside the fire that I realized what was happening. The third man was checking a branding iron. They were branding the children. The child we had seen scampering through the brush had apparently been let go by the cowboys after they had finished branding it. Now they were getting ready to brand the next child.

I turned to ask Ike if he thought we ought to interfere. He had already made his decision. As his big buckskin gelding lunged into a full gallop, Ike jerked his .50 caliber Sharps rifle from his scabbard. Loosening up on the reins, I allowed my horse to follow. The cowboys were just getting ready to apply the brand as we galloped up. Their reaction to Ike's drawn rifle was an interesting one.

"Don't shoot the little heifer," said the cowboy with the branding iron, apparently thinking Ike was going to shoot the child. "She ain't done no harm. Just want to brand her so everyone'll know she's a Wine Cup squaw when she's all growed up."

I had heard of the Wine Cup Ranch, one of Nevada's largest, but I didn't think the ranch ran cattle this far south. Had our meeting been a more friendly one, I would have asked the cowboys why they were in the area, but Ike had business more urgent than idle conversation.

When he growled, "Gimme dem pistols," the cowboys finally realized he was pointing the big buffalo gun at them.

"Tell yer nigger to put up his gun," the cowboy with the branding iron said to me.

"He ain't my 'nigger.' " I grinned and then added, "He's a Goshute chief, and if these are Goshute children, you men are in a heap of trouble."

"Gimme dem pistols," Ike growled a second time.

"Ain't no law 'gainst branding Injuns," protested one of the cowboys. Ike glanced back at me, apparently wondering if the cowboy was telling the truth.

I told him I wasn't aware of any law against branding Indians. Then I added—and perhaps I shouldn't have—that I wasn't aware of any laws against branding white men either.

"Gimme dem pistols," Ike repeated again, this time bringing the heavy rifle to his shoulder, aiming it square at the chest of the man holding the branding iron. The click seemed louder than usual as Ike cocked back the hammer.

The man dropped the branding iron, undid his gun belt, and tossed it toward Ike. The other two men let go of the girl and removed their gun belts too. The girl rolled away, her hands and feet still tied.

Without removing his eyes from the three cowboys, Ike said something to the children in Goshute. Excitedly, they began chattering back at him. I couldn't understand any of the conversation; still, I dismounted and sliced the lashings that bound their hands and feet. Without lowering his rifle, Ike maintained a careful watch on the three cowboys.

As soon as I had set the little girl free, she scampered out of sight into the sagebrush. The boy ran over to Ike, keeping a close eye on the three cowboys.

"We're hands from the Wine Cup Ranch," said the man who had held the branding iron. He said it as if that information alone should be enough to make Ike put down his rifle and retreat. Ike did neither. He was not through with the cowboys, not yet.

"Me Goshute chief. No like white men dat brand Injun children," he said.

"They were on Wine Cup land," argued the cowboy. He then repeated the earlier comment about there being no law against branding Indians.

Instead of continuing the argument, Ike said something in Goshute to the boy. The child looked in astonishment at the three cowboys, then up at Ike, grinning from ear to ear and nodding that he was in full agreement with whatever Ike had said. I had my hand on the butt of my pistol, just in case the cowboys tried anything.

I didn't know what Ike and the boy were talking about until Ike ordered the three cowboys to drop their trousers. When they refused, Ike said something to the boy, who immediately removed the bridle from the nearest horse and sent the animal galloping off through the sagebrush.

Again Ike ordered the cowboys to drop their trousers. When they continued to hesitate, the boy went over to a second horse and began removing the bridle. He stopped when the cowboys began to pull down their trousers. Ike kept his rifle pointed at them, the hammer still back. Ike ordered the men to stretch out, face down, on the ground. Reluctantly, they obeyed. "You'll never get away with this," hissed the leader. "A Wine Cup posse will hang you for this."

I thought Ike was carrying the matter too far. Freeing the children was enough. But Ike had lived with the Goshutes for many years. They were his people now. They had taken much abuse from the whites. Maybe his courage and this drastic measure would make other white men think twice before abusing Goshutes. On the other hand, he might just infuriate the whites and cause increased persecution of his people.

When the angry cowboys were stretched out on their bellies, their tender buttocks glistening white and smooth under the midday sun, the boy removed the branding iron from the smoking coals. Even in the sunshine, there was an orange-gray glow to the Wine Cup insignia.

All it took was a nod from Ike and the boy stepped over to the nearest cowboy and slapped the branding iron against the lily-white skin.

Though the cowboy screamed out a string of profanities, the boy held the iron steady as a cloud of greasy, sweet smoke filled the air. Apparently the boy had seen cattle and horses branded and knew exactly how to do it, except perhaps he pushed a little too hard, holding the iron there a moment too long. But he received no criticism from Ike.

As soon as the boy was finished, he returned the smoking iron, which had lost its red glow, to the fire. Ike remained quiet as the cowboys continued to curse and complain. The boy branded the second and third cowboy as thoroughly as he had the first. When the boy finished, Ike sent him over to unbridle the two remaining horses. The wounded cowboys protested, but Ike only mumbled something about them being too sore to ride anyway. After the horses had galloped off, the boy gathered up the trousers and carried them to Ike, who tossed them into the fire.

A few seconds later we were galloping off to the west, following the trail the two Indian children had followed a few minutes earlier. Ike had returned his rifle to the scabbard and was carrying the Wine Cup branding iron in his hand. The boy was riding behind Ike, his little brown arms clinging tightly to the black man's thick waist

——◆◆◆——

After rounding up the Indian children, Ike set out to find their parents, whom he suspected had taken up hiding in the rugged mountains to the south. I went on to Ely to keep our appointment to pick up Mrs. Hatch. Ike said he would catch up with me and the woman on our way back to Utah. We figured the branded cowboys wouldn't give either of us any trouble since they would be headed north toward the home ranch. We would be out of the area long before they could attempt any kind of retaliation.

As I continued the journey alone, I had a lot of time to think about the branding of the three cowboys. I wasn't really concerned about revenge from them. The Wasatch Front settlements of Utah where I lived were a long way away. And Ike, in his wanderings with the Goshutes, would be almost impossible for the cowboys to find.

What concerned me was the provocative manner in which Ike handled the situation. It was taking a long time to bring peace to this wild land, the kind of peace where people could come and go from place to place without fear for personal safety or fear of livestock and property being stolen.

Almost certainly, those cowboys and possibly their friends at the Wine Cup Ranch would seek revenge; if not on Ike and me, then someone else, perhaps another band of hapless Goshutes. If Ike had merely freed the children and then reported the incident to the nearest legal authority, swearing out a complaint against the cowboys, there would have been less chance of retaliation.

On the other hand, the law would probably have done nothing to the cowboys. After all, the children were Goshutes, and Ike was black. What chance did Indians and a black man have against the Wine Cup Ranch, even within the confines of the law?

The cowboys had been wrong in branding the children. Ike had been right in stopping them. His methods had been severe, but no more severe than what the cowboys had been doing to the children.

I wondered what Porter Rockwell would have done in such a situation. He had received much criticism for his methods of keeping peace. Too often, his critics claimed, he sent individuals to their Maker without allowing due process to determine guilt or innocence. If published reports were true that he had dispatched over a hundred men without due process, it seemed likely that he might have judged some in error and sent them unjustly to the grave. There was a good chance Rockwell would have been tougher on those cowboys than Ike had been. Ike had not killed anyone.

I wondered if Rockwell had really done all the things legend said he had done, if the man was as large as the legend. I wondered about his stormy romances in Nauvoo, the shooting of former Missouri governor Lilburn Boggs, and Rockwell's role in the controversial but hushed up battle of Bear River, the largest Indian massacre in the history of the American West. I remembered the promise Rockwell had received from Joseph Smith that if he would not cut his hair, he could not be harmed by bullet or blade. Had he really shaved off all his hair to make a wig for a widow in San Francisco? Why? And if he was as devout in his religion as some claimed, why did he drink so much, especially in later years?

I was looking forward to escorting Polly Hatch back to Government Creek. She would know a lot about Rockwell. She had been in California researching what he had done there, both in San Francisco and in the gold fields during the gold rush of 1849. She had also known Rockwell when both were young in Jackson County, Missouri.

—————

My stay in Ely was a short one. Polly Hatch had her saddle bags packed and her bedroll ready when I arrived. She was eager to get to Government Creek. After feeding me a quick mid-morning breakfast, she showed me to the stable, where I saddled her riding horse and loaded her gear on a packhorse. A few minutes later we were on our way. I wasn't in Ely more than two hours.

Polly was thin but by no means frail. Though she was in her mid-sixties, with gray-streaked hair and a mildly wrinkled face, her blue eyes were bright and intense. She had a quick smile and a hearty laugh, and from the way she dressed I didn't guess I'd have to baby her along. She wore blue denim trousers, a well-worn leather jacket, and cowhide boots. Her medium-length hair was tied back with a bright red scarf. Before getting on her horse, she buckled on a pair of mean-looking Mexican spurs. Polly Hatch was no ordinary woman. I was looking forward to the trip.

We didn't talk much at first. We just relaxed and enjoyed the eagerness of the horses to cover the miles. My horse was obviously pleased at turning around to head back home. Polly's horse was just glad to get out of the stable, and the packhorse wasn't about to be left behind.

That night we camped just south of Taylor Peak, near the top of Connor Pass. For supper we finished off a lunch she had packed for us. I told Polly about Ike and the Indian children, that I guessed we would meet up with him the next day and travel together back to Government Creek. She had a lot of questions about me and Ike and what we had been doing, but when I asked her about Rockwell, she seemed reluctant to talk. I didn't push.

The next day, travel was more difficult. A chill northwesterly wind brought in a bank of gray clouds. With the sun gone, we pulled our coats tightly around us, pushing ahead most of the day. In the wind and cold, talking was difficult, so we mostly remained quiet. Polly didn't complain about the cold. I was grateful for that.

By afternoon, with the temperature continuing to drop, I became fearful of getting caught in a snowstorm and began looking for shelter. I remembered a cave Ike and I had found low in the foothills of Mt. Moriah. Not only would the cave offer protection from the storm, but it would also be an easy place for Ike to find us. We headed straight for the cave, reaching it by late afternoon, just as snowflakes were beginning to fall. I quickly set to work unsaddling the horses and staking them out for the night as Polly walked up the slight incline to check out the cavern.

It wasn't until I carried the saddles up to the cave a few minutes later that I discovered we were not alone. Polly was in eager negotiations with a squat, well-fed Indian. As I entered the cave, she was handing him a nickel, which he immediately slipped between his teeth and tried to bite in half. I suppose he was making sure she had not given him a counterfeit wooden coin.

Satisfied the nickel was genuine, the brave bent down and picked up a dead cottontail rabbit, handing it to Polly. She turned to me, announcing proudly that she had purchased fresh meat for supper. She handed me the rabbit to clean while she began unpacking her things.

The Indian explained in broken English that he was a Paiute, and that his name was Turtle Runner. I resisted the urge to laugh.

I skinned the rabbit, removing its head, feet, and tail. I scooped out the entrails, leaving them in a pile just outside the mouth of the cave. After placing the cleaned rabbit on a smooth rock, I gathered wood and sticks for a fire, which I started just inside the mouth of the cave, where it would have some protection from the falling moisture but wouldn't smoke us out.

By now the snow was thick and heavy. Though the horses were less than fifty yards away, they were difficult to see. The wind had stopped.

Turtle Runner watched me work but made no effort to help. He also showed no intention of leaving. I had hoped he would be on his way after receiving his money for the rabbit, but with the storm it appeared he was planning to spend the night with us.

Soon there was a blazing fire, warm and comforting against the falling snow. The rabbit was strapped to a long stick, which I began turning when the underside began to sizzle. The Indian was totally occupied with watching the cooking rabbit. I guessed he was a lot hungrier than we were. My mouth began to water as the aroma of roasting meat filled the cave.

The rabbit wasn't large. In fact, it was very small and wouldn't provide much of a meal for one person, let alone two.

And now that Turtle Runner had obviously decided to stay, we were faced with the prospect of dividing it three ways.

When I mentioned to Polly that we ought to think about cooking something else because there wouldn't be much rabbit after it was divided three ways, she seemed surprised that I intended to share with the Indian. But instead of saying anything to me, she marched over to Turtle Runner and announced in loud, deliberate pigeon English that the rabbit was ours, and he would have to find something else to eat.

I expected a protest from the hungry Indian. After all, he had caught the animal. Yes, he had sold it to Polly, but since he was sharing his cave with us, it seemed only proper we should share our rabbit with him.

But Turtle Runner offered no protest. When Polly finished making the situation clear to him, he simply turned and walked toward the entrance of the cave. For a second, I thought she had hurt his feelings and he was leaving. I didn't try to stop him.

But Turtle Runner had no intention of leaving. Just outside the entrance of the cave, he stopped and bent over, picking up the discarded remains of the rabbit entrails, skin, feet, and head.

Returning to the fire, he deposited his treasure on the glowing coals beside the sizzling rabbit, now a glistening golden brown.

The aroma of roasting rabbit was soon replaced with the stench of burning hair and flesh.

About the time Polly and I began to eat the rabbit, Turtle Runner popped the first foot into his mouth.

There was a loud crunching sound as he ground it up, singed fur and all, finally swallowing with one deliberate gulp. When the feet were gone, he wolfed down the crispy entrails.

Last, he rolled the blackened head from the coals. After letting it cool for a few minutes, he carefully removed the charred ears and happily pushed the entire skull into his mouth. With bulging cheeks he began to chew, the crunching skull making more noise than the feet had made. He didn't spit out anything, except a few little rabbit teeth.

When Turtle Runner finished eating, he wiped his mouth with the back of his hand. Then, with a contented grunt, he stretched out on the floor of the cave and went to sleep. He had no blanket, only a pair of dirty elk-skin leggings and the fire to keep him warm. Soon he was snoring, his face as innocent and content as a baby's.

Polly and I watched the sleeping Indian for a long time. Then Polly said, "In a way he reminds me of Rockwell." I had no idea what she meant. Rockwell was a feared and respected lawman and gunfighter, a legend in his own day. He was nothing like this fat Indian, content with a bellyful of rabbit guts. I didn't say anything; I just waited for her to continue, glad she finally seemed willing to talk about Rockwell.

"It disgusts me to see that Indian eat the insides of a rabbit," she continued. "Yet, if I lived like he does, if I faced the same hunger and sensed the same desperate need for nourishment, maybe I could enjoy a rabbit head too. At least I would be able to appreciate and accept how he could enjoy eating those things."

"What does all this have to do with Rockwell?" I asked.

"Many are disgusted at what he did."

"You mean the killings?"

"Yes."

"Over a hundred, they say."

"I doubt it was anywhere near that," she said. "Still, he killed people. And for a man who took his religion seriously, that is a hard thing to understand. I think the judgments of society he receives will become more harsh as we become more civilized, more removed from the way of life that not only allowed but demanded people like Rockwell do what they did."

We were both silent for a while, she giving me time to think over what she had said. It made sense. Still, I wasn't sure I understood or grasped the full depth of what she was trying to say. The Indian, like Rockwell, saw life from a different perspective. Therefore, both are difficult people for the rest of us to understand.

"He wasn't always that way," she offered. "I knew him in Jackson County before he had killed. He was different then. He was afraid to fight."

"Not Porter Rockwell," I objected.

"Do you want to hear the real story?" she asked.

"Sure," I said, not wanting to sound too eager.

"Why not," she said, mostly to herself. "Don't feel much like sleeping with that Indian so close. The snow may keep us here a long time, so there's plenty of time to tell the whole story.

"When I first met Port," she began, "he and his father were building a ferry on the Big Blue River in Jackson County. He was young and strong and eager to please. He had a tall bay with four white stockings that he thought was the fastest horse in Missouri. He was barely eighteen, just beginning to shave. And he was looking for a wife. I was sixteen and desperately hoping he might notice me. But he only had eyes for Luana Beebe. She lived in Independence . . ."

That's how it began, Polly Hatch telling me her version of the Porter Rockwell story before she met with Elizabeth Roundy at Government Creek. I kept the fire going all night, and she narrated the events surrounding Rockwell's life in Missouri, Illinois, and Utah.

What follows in this volume is the same story, as I remember it. In several places, however, I have added detail that I picked up from others who knew Rockwell. Whether he was a hero or a villain— I'll leave that for you to decide.

# Chapter 1

Port's mood was gray like the cold November clouds, and he wasn't sure why. An icy north wind was blowing the last of the yellow-gray leaves from the oak and hickory trees. But he didn't think the cold and the threat of a first snowfall had anything to do with the empty, chilled feeling that was causing actual pain somewhere deep inside, in a place he couldn't touch.

No, it couldn't be the weather. Actually, the icy north wind felt refreshing against his sun- and wind-tanned face. He wasn't cold, buttoned tightly in a buffalo hide coat, with a badger-skin cap pulled over his ears, and his hands almost hot in rabbit fur mittens.

Port was of medium height and build, with wide, muscular shoulders and a thick bull neck. His hands were not calloused from farm work; they were slender but strong. His face was ordinary, except for the thick, straight eyebrows and the piercing steel-gray eyes radiating vitality and a marked intensity.

And it wasn't the place that made him feel black. He was standing in what he thought was one of God's most beautiful creations. He was knee-deep in grass no longer green, but yellow-white from the cold winter air. He stood in a gentle saddle between two hills, looking north across a vast rolling sea, the lush frozen meadows of the Missouri prairie. In the distance, the Big Blue River wound like a giant silver snake through the lush valleys of Jackson County, hugged closely on both sides by thick forests of cottonwood, maple, butter wood, and pecan, the trees gradually thinning as the ground rose to meet the vast, undulating prairie.

Far away, almost at the end of his vision, the Big Blue lost itself in the lazy waters of the brown Missouri, the longest river in North America.

Soon it would be too dark to shoot, and he would be going home. The hunt had been a successful one. The back of his wagon contained a respectable pile of feathered, gray lumps spotted with fresh blood—nearly a hundred passenger pigeons shot by Port in an afternoon of hunting.

He looked to the west to make sure the gray cloud was still approaching. It was. It wasn't a storm cloud but birds, thousands of passenger pigeons.

Port checked his rifles, all three carefully loaded with double portions of black powder and bird shot. Anybody could aim into a flock of pigeons and shoot one or two down. That didn't take skill. In fact, it was hard to miss. There were so many.

To make pigeon shooting a profitable business was a different story. Port could get four cents for each dead pigeon at Wilson's store, a mile west of the Big Blue crossing. But the cost of lead, powder, and wadding each time he fired his rifle was about three cents. This didn't leave a very good profit, even if he hit a pigeon with every shot, and few people could do that. The trick was to hit the dark spots of the flock where as many as five or six pigeons could sometimes be brought down with a single firing. Port figured he was averaging about three birds per shot, netting him ten cents after expenses.

Port had been selling birds to Wilson's for nearly a month. He was eighteen and had moved to Jackson County earlier that fall with his parents and sister, Electa. Several hundred Mormon families had moved into the county that year, but while most were buying virgin land for farming at the going rate of $1.25 an acre, Port and his father had elected to start a ferry on the Big Blue. With the ferry located twelve miles west of Independence, the Rockwells figured the growing number of settlers in the area, plus the westward migration, would provide them a good business for many years to come.

Having run out of money before the ferry was finished, Port had gone to shoot pigeons. All that was left to purchase was one thousand feet of new hemp rope and two iron pulleys, on order at Wilson's store. Today's catch of pigeons would just about finish paying for the rope and pulleys.

With the ferry almost complete and paid for, Port wondered why his mood was so black. He thought back over the events of the day, and he wondered if his conversation with the young Missourian earlier that morning could have anything to do with his mood.

The handsome young man, mounted on a fine sorrel, had stopped to chat with Port as the latter was securing a sideboard to the ferry.

"Then you must know Luana Beebe," said the youth upon discovering that Port was a Mormon.

"Nope," Port said, putting down his hammer, wiping the sweat from his brow, and looking up into the face of the young man who had introduced himself as Willard Sweeney.

"She's a Mormon," Sweeney added.

"From the Big Blue district?" Port asked, wondering why he hadn't heard of this Luana Beebe. Though he hadn't been in Missouri long, he'd certainly been there long enough to scrutinize every unattached Mormon female who crossed his path.

"No, Independence," the young stranger said. "Prettiest woman I ever saw, even if she is a Mormon. A face, young and innocent, like an angel, but a body like a woman—if you know what I mean." The stranger looked at Port and winked. Then he jerked his horse around, urging it into a gallop down the road toward Independence.

Standing by his wagon, waiting for the pigeons, Port wondered if his black mood had anything to do with Luana Beebe. Though he had never met the young woman, knowing there was an unattached, beautiful Mormon female being courted by a big-mouthed gentile had triggered new, unfamiliar feelings.

He had been thinking about this Luana Beebe all afternoon and already had a clear picture in his mind what she looked like. She was certainly the most beautiful young woman in all Missouri, a woman vulnerable to the likes of Willard Sweeney, a woman needing protecting.

The problem was that she was twelve miles away. There wouldn't be a natural opportunity to meet her until spring conference in April, several months away. Port didn't wonder what her personality, her likes and dislikes, might be like. He knew only that he had to meet her before it was too late, and April conference was definitely too late. For all he knew, Luana and Willard might be married by then.

He wondered if part of the dark feeling inside was jealousy. He wondered how it was possible to have such a longing to see a woman he had never met. It didn't seem rational, or even possible. But he couldn't deny what he felt. Conference seemed like four years away, not four months. He couldn't just wait until April to meet Luana Beebe.

Then it occurred to him that perhaps it wouldn't be necessary to wait so long. By noon the next day he would have the new rope and pulleys in place. His father would be on hand and eager to operate the new ferry. By early afternoon, Port could be on the road to Independence.

Suddenly the dark feeling was gone. He felt happy. He felt like jumping in the air and kicking his heels together, but he didn't, knowing the movement might cause the approaching pigeon flock to change its course. These new feelings for Luana Beebe didn't make any sense, but he couldn't deny how he felt.

Realizing the pigeons were nearly upon him, Port raised his rifle to his shoulder, aiming carefully toward the darkest part of the flock. Carefully, he squeezed the trigger. Four or five birds fluttered helplessly down from the sky. Before they hit the ground Port had the second rifle to his shoulder, squeezing off a second shot. By the time he had fired the third weapon, the frightened flock was out of range.

He reloaded one of the guns in case a straggler or two came along. Then he began walking toward the dead birds. He hadn't gone more than a step or two when he noticed an approaching bird. It wasn't a straggler following the departing flock; instead, it was coming back from the flock, leaving the perceived safety of the other birds. It continued in a straight line toward Port. He raised the loaded rifle to his shoulder but didn't fire when the pigeon came within range. It was an easy shot, but something—perhaps the curiosity as to why the bird was returning—kept him from shooting. Perhaps it was angry at him for shooting its companions. Perhaps it would attack him like birds sometimes attack eagles and hawks for invading their nests.

When the bird came within range, Port could tell by its dark, glossy color that it was a male passenger pigeon. It didn't attack. Instead, it circled several times and then landed beside one of the fallen birds, a female.

Port lowered the rifle from his shoulder, watching the pigeon more closely. It strutted around its dead companion, occasionally cooing, again and again nudging its fallen mate with its beak, trying to wake the bird up so it could fly away.

"Go away, little dove. My gun is loaded," Port whispered to the live pigeon. It remained by its companion.

"She's dead. Your life is in danger. Return to the flock," Port continued. The bird remained.

Port wondered if a pigeon could really love another that much. It didn't seem possible, but he didn't know how else to explain the bird's behavior.

The gaiety of the previous moment was gone. There was a deep sadness surrounding the place, a sadness he knew would remain as long as the bird remained. And the pigeon didn't seem to have any intention of leaving.

Port quickly picked up the rest of the birds and tossed them into his wagon, leaving the dead female so as not to interrupt her companion's fearless vigil. He climbed onto the wagon seat, wondering how a bird could love so much, wondering how dangerous loving could be. The male bird had no business returning to its fallen mate. Its return defied all survival instincts. Could love wield more power than the need to survive? Apparently it did in the case of this poor pigeon.

Port wondered if human love was like that. Maybe he should wait until conference to meet Luana Beebe. He wouldn't want to do anything stupid like that poor pigeon. Perhaps he should proceed more carefully. But conference was still too long to wait. He would be cautious, but he would go to Independence tomorrow. Tomorrow Luana Beebe would meet Orrin Porter Rockwell.

# Chapter 2

Instead of hitching up the wagon for his trip to Independence, Port saddled Bill, a three-year-old bay gelding he had purchased from Cyrus Ward, a well-known horse breeder in Independence.

Upon reaching the Big Blue the previous fall, Port had walked into Independence to buy a horse. The Rockwells had sold their animals before leaving Ohio, the cost being too high to transport livestock on the rivers. They decided to replace the animals once they reached Missouri.

With a long rope coiled over his shoulder and four twenty-dollar gold pieces in his pocket, Port began his search. Several inquiries directed him to the residence of Cyrus Ward, the most successful horse breeder in the area.

As Port approached the Ward place, he noticed a well-fed, middle-aged man chasing a beautiful bay gelding around a small pole corral. Several black children were perched on the fence, watching the man's unsuccessful attempts to capture the frightened animal.

Whenever the angry man managed to corner the horse, it somehow managed to plunge away from him. Once when he got the rope around its neck, it reared and shook the rope free before the man could tie the knot. Swearing, he threw the rope on the ground.

Having learned from one of the children that the man was Cyrus Ward, Port entered the corral.

"Let me fetch him for you," Port said, unraveling the rope in his hand and forming a loop. The red-faced Ward stepped back against the fence, catching his breath and nodding for the young stranger to proceed.

Port caught the colt with his first throw. The animal stopped and turned toward the young man. Except for a slight quiver, it remained still, its head high and ears forward. Port approached at a slow, relaxed pace, talking quietly to the animal. The horse made no attempt to get away as Port stroked its neck gently yet firmly.

After securing Ward's rope around the neck and removing his own rope, Port stepped back, drinking in the details that made the horse desirable—the sloping muscular hip, the straight back, the pencil neck, the barrel chest, the perfect markings, including four white stockings and an even blaze down the center of the face. The dark, alert eye was as clear as glass. The ears moved nervously back and forth. Port sensed an intensity of spirit but no meanness. From the earlier movements about the corral, he knew the animal had superior athletic ability. Still a young horse, it was tall—almost sixteen hands, he guessed.

For as long as he could remember Port had wanted such a horse—tall, perfectly marked, and athletic. It was the kind of animal a general would ride into battle. Port led the animal over to Ward and handed him the lead rope.

"Thanks," Ward said. Port dropped his rope on the ground and offered his hand. The two men shook hands and introduced themselves. Port explained he was a Mormon moving from New York to the Big Blue district.

"Probably need a horse," Ward said. "Interested in buying this one?"

Port could hardly believe his good luck. Of course he was interested. He would give anything for such an animal. He was careful, however, to conceal his feelings. He had traded horses before and knew the unwritten rules of the ultimate poker game—the horse trade.

"I'm looking for a good saddle horse," Port admitted. "But an animal that can't be caught isn't much good in a country where the fences aren't built yet."

"How much will you give me?" Ward asked.

Port felt a wave of excitement. Ward had brought up the subject of price too soon. The man was more eager to sell than the young man had supposed.

Port knew better than to be the first to mention price, which was a sign that one was eager to deal. Instead, he asked, "What you got to have for him?"

"What's he worth to you?" Ward responded, realizing he had appeared too eager, beginning now to play the game himself.

Port figured the horse was a real bargain at seventy to eighty dollars, but he wasn't about to tell Ward that.

"What's a horse worth that can't hardly be caught in a corral?" Port asked. "You tell me."

"How about fifty?" Ward asked.

Port was delighted at the price, but didn't say anything. He wondered if perhaps something was wrong with the horse, something in addition to being hard to catch. The price was too low.

"A horse that hard to catch might have something else wrong with him," Port offered.

"I could get a hundred dollars for him tomorrow in St. Louis, and you know it," Ward said, beginning to appear gruff.

"Then why are you willing to sell him to me for $50?" Port asked.

"Because I just wasted an hour trying to catch him, and I don't have the time to go to St. Louis, not in the middle of the harvest."

Port sensed the man was sincere. He also sensed Ward was in a hurry to get back to work—another advantage for Port. He reached in his pocket and retrieved two twenty-dollar gold pieces.

"I've got forty dollars. Didn't plan on spending that much," Port offered, extending his palm so Ward could get a good look at the gold.

"You'd be stealing him at fifty," Ward said. "I can't let him go for forty."

"Can't go fifty," Port said as he reached down to pick up his rope. He returned the two gold pieces to his pocket. "While we're getting settled on the Big Blue I'll think it over," Port promised. "Maybe I'll come back in the spring."

"I'll have sold him to someone else by then," Ward protested.

"Then I'll buy another. If not from you, from someone else," Port said simply. "Plenty of horses for sale."

He turned and started toward the gate, hoping Ward would call him back. Ward remained silent. Port resisted the urge to look over his shoulder to see what Ward was doing. He opened and closed the gate and proceeded toward the road. Ward remained silent. The children remained still, looking back and forth at Rockwell and Ward.

Port was beginning to think he had made a mistake when Ward finally called to him. "Forty, on one condition."

Port slowly turned around and re-entered the corral.

"What's the condition?"

"I raise a lot of colts. Can see you're a good hand. After you get settled, how about green breaking a colt for me?"

"A deal," Port said, extending his hand and fighting to subdue the enthusiasm he felt for having obtained such a fine horse so cheaply. Port gave the two gold pieces to Ward, who in turn handed Port the lead rope to the horse.

"What's his name?" Port asked, turning to his new horse.

"Bill, after an old buck slave. Died the same week the colt was born."

"Never seen a horse named Bill before," Port responded, stroking the horse's neck. "I like it." He began leading his new possession toward the gate.

"If you'll hang around a minute, I'll run to the house and get you a bill of sale," Ward said, beginning to hurry toward the log home.

"Wait," Port said. "One more question. Still don't know why you sold him so cheap. Is there something else wrong with him? Now that he's mine, I suppose you can tell me."

Ward turned back, grinning.

"Can't bridle the S.O.B." were his only words as he turned back toward the house. Port laughed out loud at his good luck. He had been worried that there might be something seriously wrong with the horse. The bridling problem would be easy to fix.

Upon receiving the bill of sale, Port hurried toward the river, eager to show his father the fantastic horse he had purchased for only forty dollars.

Training Bill to allow himself to be bridled was easy, taking only a few days. The technique was simple. After haltering and saddling Bill, Port would take the lead rope between the animal's front legs and up the side of the horse, where he secured the rope with two half hitches to the saddle horn. Then he would proceed with the bridling. Whenever the horse jerked his head to avoid the bit, it jerked the stiff hemp rope against the tender skin between his front legs. Once the horse was bridled, Port left the rope secured to the saddle horn, occasionally reaching for one of the horse's ears. Whenever he tried to jerk away, the horse felt the pain of the stiff rope between his front legs. After a few days, Bill no longer resisted being bridled.

It took longer to make the horse easy to catch. Upon reaching the Big Blue, Port built a pole corral for Bill, but he did not feed or water the animal inside the corral.

Every day Port cut an armload of the tall Missouri prairie grass and piled it at the base of a nearby tree. For Bill to eat, he had to be caught and led to the feed. To drink, he had to be caught and led to the stream. It didn't take Bill long to associate eating and drinking with being caught. After two weeks he was eager to push his nose into the halter whenever Port entered his corral.

Bill responded just as well to the rest of his training. Within weeks he was spinning to the right or left at the slightest touch of a rein to the side of his neck. He could plunge into a full gallop, then sit down and slide to a halt. He didn't need coaxing with spurs to jump a four-foot pole fence or swim the Big Blue. When Port wasn't working on the ferry or shooting pigeons, he was with Bill, becoming prouder of the fine animal every day.

Occasionally he would give the young horse his head, letting him run at top speed down the dirt road toward Independence. Bill felt fast, and though Port had not yet tested him against another horse, he strongly suspected he might have unwittingly stumbled onto one of the fastest horses in Missouri. Soon the day would come when he would find out. He could hardly wait.

But today he was going to Independence to meet Luana Beebe, and he was going to ride Bill. He wanted to make the best possible impression on the young lady, and Bill would help do that. He hoped Luana would be out in the yard when he arrived, so her first impression would be of him astride the magnificent animal.

# Chapter 3

It was early afternoon when Port finally got away from the Big Blue and headed east toward Independence. He was riding Bill and leading his father's black mare, which was carrying a bulky load lashed tightly to a packsaddle. Just before leaving, the thought occurred to Port that it might help his cause if he were to present a gift to Luana Beebe. No sooner had the thought entered his head than he knew exactly what he wanted to give her.

It was about a two-hour ride to Independence, but Port set out at a trot that would enable his horses to cover the distance in an hour and a half.

The storm that had been threatening the day before had blown away, leaving a clear, blue November sky. A chill still hung in the air, but the afternoon sun was warm. It would be much colder coming home after dark, but Port hadn't thought that far ahead.

Gradually, his pace began to slow down. It wasn't that the horses were getting tired and couldn't maintain the faster pace. Port was beginning to have second thoughts about his eagerness to meet Luana Beebe, a total stranger. It wasn't that he didn't want to meet her. What bothered him was what he would say to her once introductions were made.

Back in New York he had always avoided direct contact with females his own age. They made him feel awkward, so he stayed away. He had usually been too busy with farm work to attend social gatherings, though he attended church regularly.

Port had never been gifted with words. He didn't even know how to read and write, which left him at a definite disadvantage among the Mormons, who were constantly reading the Book of Mormon and discussing it with each other. Because he didn't read, Port usually remained quiet during discussions.

Furthermore, he had no desire for book learning. He liked to do things with his hands, like build rafts, hunt, farm, and work with his horses. He wanted nothing more, except the companionship of a good woman. He realized he knew little of Luana Beebe, but from what Willard Sweeney had told him, he had a strong feeling that destiny was bringing him and Luana Beebe together. Still, he was beginning to feel more and more foolish the closer he got to Independence. What was he going to say to her?

Port slowed the horses even more. He kept wondering what he would do if she shunned him or his gift. Perhaps he shouldn't give such a nice gift at their first meeting. Perhaps he should have waited until conference, where he could see at a distance what she looked like before he went courting.

By late afternoon, just a few miles from Independence, Port had just about decided to turn back. He was sure he had been foolish to rush into this thing so quickly. He had almost convinced himself he needed more time to think things over.

That's when he heard someone call his name from behind. He turned to see Willard Sweeney gallop up on his sorrel mare. For an instant, Port felt guilty. After all, Willard had told him about Luana, and now he was competing with him.

"How's the ferry business?" Willard asked, his voice friendly.

"Got it going this morning. Half a dozen customers before I left."

"What brings you to Independence?"

"Taking some stuff to a friend," Port said evasively, nodding toward the loaded pack horse.

"Good-looking bay you're riding. Looks familiar."

"Got him from Cyrus Ward, here in Independence."

"The one he couldn't catch?"

"That's the one," Port responded, glad Sweeney was thinking about something other than why Port was going to Independence.

"Can he run?"

"Think so, but I haven't raced him yet. That'll come soon enough."

"Want to race?" Sweeney challenged.

"Can the mare run?" Port asked, carefully eyeing the sorrel. She was a tall, long-legged animal, like his bay.

"Won everything at the Fourth of July celebration last year," Willard boasted. "Fastest horse in Jackson County." His buttons were about to burst. "Got five bucks says she can outrun your bay."

"Didn't bring any bettin' money," Port responded. His business with Luana Beebe was more pressing, though he'd rather be racing. "Let's do it sometime next week. Will you be over to the Blue?"

"Now might be a bad time for me too," Sweeney said. "I'm expected at Luana Beebe's for supper."

Port gulped. His face turned paler. What was he going to do now? He didn't say anything.

"Remember Luana Beebe?" Willard asked. "I told you about her yesterday at the ferry." Port nodded, still silent.

"Yessir, prettiest woman in Jackson County," Willard resumed enthusiastically. "When I was visiting her yesterday, she bent over to pick up a ball of yarn and I saw clear to her belly button." Both young men were quiet for a minute. The paleness of Port's face was quickly replaced by an unnatural flush.

"Plan on marrying her?" Port asked guardedly.

"Shoot, no," Willard replied quickly, like he had already given the subject a lot of thought. "She's a Mormon. Got queer beliefs."

"Maybe you forgot I'm a Mormon too," Port responded.

"Ain't going to marry you neither," Willard said. Both laughed.

"But I'd sure like to get her alone in the dark where I could get my hands under her dress," Willard concluded with finality.

Port could stand no more. No one could talk about his Luana that way and get away with it. It didn't matter that he hadn't met her. As far as he was concerned, Willard had already breached what Port thought were a woman's sacred rights to privacy and decency. Willard had to be stopped.

Port took a hard look at Willard. The young man, with his wavy black hair, dark eyebrows, and friendly smile, was more handsome than he remembered. Much more so. He was taller than Port, with broad shoulders and muscular thighs. Port wondered if he could lick Willard in a fair fight, concluding that he would probably be hard-pressed to come off with a win. All he knew for sure was that he had to keep Willard away from Luana. How he might do that, he wasn't sure. But he had to try.

"I'm calling on Luana Beebe today too," Port said. "Maybe you can show me the way,"

This time Willard reined in his horse.

"You wouldn't dare horn in on me," Willard challenged.

"Already have."

"But you've never even met her."

"I will today."

"If we both show up, neither of us will get anything."

"All right by me."

"Let's fight," Willard challenged, whirling his horse around to face Port. Willard looked confident. Port didn't think he could win. He had never been in a real fistfight. He didn't count the scuffles with his brothers and friends on the farm in New York. Port's throat was dry. He felt a little sick.

"The winner visits Luana. The loser goes home. What do say?" Willard demanded.

The two fierce young men glared at each other for what seemed a long time to Port. He didn't want to fight, but neither did he want to retreat. Suddenly he had an idea.

"Let's race for it," Port challenged. "My bay against your sorrel. Loser goes home, leaves Luana alone."

"You got yerself a race," Willard bellowed.

"About a half mile?" Port asked, no longer any emotion in his voice.

"Fine with me."

"I'll tie the pack horse to a tree," Port explained. "We ride back a half mile to start. The first one to the pack horse wins." Willard nodded his approval. Port dismounted, tied the black horse to the nearest tree, and then began to remove Bill's saddle.

"What are you doing?" Willard demanded.

"Taking the saddle off. Like to race bareback."

For a moment Willard seemed confused. He had never seen anyone, except Indians, race bareback before. He wasn't sure if he should object or not. On the one hand, the horse without a saddle would have the advantage of carrying less weight. On the other hand, there was a greater chance Port would lose his balance and fall off.

Willard offered no further objection as Port removed the saddle and placed it beside the packhorse. Port had raced enough in New York to know his horses could run faster when he rode bareback. He wasn't sure the advantage had as much to do fewer pounds as with the weight of the bareback rider being further forward, closer to the withers. He only knew that when he rode bareback, his horses ran faster, if he could stay on. With Luana's future at stake, he had to give Bill every possible advantage.

Port crawled upon the bareback horse. Bill's back was wet from being under the saddle all afternoon. Without speaking, the two young men headed up the road to a point they agreed was about a half mile away.

The sorrel mare was prancing sideways, sensing a race was about to begin. Bill, on the other hand, was walking calmly, not understanding that his speed was about to be challenged. Port wished he could tell Bill what was about to happen. If only horses understood English. It wouldn't take Bill long to figure out what was going on once the race began, but if the race was close, those first few seconds of uncertainty could make all the difference. Port tightened his legs, hoping that through pressure he might communicate to the horse that something very exciting was about to happen.

When the riders finally turned to face the finish line, Port grabbed a handful of black mane with his left hand, making sure he had a firm hold. Once the horses were running he wouldn't need the mane, but during those first four or five leaps as the horses accelerated from a standstill to a full gallop, he would need to hold on tight to keep the horse from lunging out from under him.

With the mane firmly in his grasp, Port looked over Willard.

"Ready?" the Missourian snarled. Port nodded.

"Go!" shouted both of them simultaneously.

As Port had feared, the sorrel mare got off to a much better start and was two or three jumps in the lead before Bill realized what was happening. But the bay caught on quickly. Through his legs and the reins, Port sensed a sudden increase in intensity, a burst of energy. The natural competitive spirit of the horse had awakened and was taking over. The head went lower, the nose reached out a little further, and the well-tuned muscles seemed to be bursting with energy and strength.

By the time the horses reached full gallop, the mare was several lengths in front, spraying Port and Bill with stinging particles of dirt and rock. Port leaned further forward, the mane whipping his face. Bill was no longer falling behind, but feeling more powerful with every stride.

"Hiya!" Port bellowed in the deepest, strongest voice he could muster. For a moment, totally absorbed in the excitement of the race and drinking deeply of what he thought the true stuff of life was made of, he forgot Luana. This was living. "Hiya! Hiya!"

By the halfway mark, Bill had nearly caught the streaking sorrel. Willard looked over his shoulder once and applied his rawhide whip to the mare's rump. The whip had little effect. The mare was already giving her all. But that was not enough.

Bill was gaining on her with every stride, passing her well ahead of the finish line. The bay won by nearly two lengths.

*Wow! What a horse!* Port thought as he reined in the bay. How much faster would he get with a little experience? And Bill was only three years old! Fastest horse in Missouri.

Willard didn't stick around as Port dismounted and saddled Bill.

"I'll tell her you're sorry you couldn't make it," Port shouted after Sweeney as he rode away.

"You haven't seen the last of me!" the Missourian shouted as he rode out of sight.

# Chapter 4

After the horse race Port still felt reluctant about going to see Luana, but now that he had won visiting rights from Sweeney, he felt compelled to follow through, regardless of his fears and uncertainties. Not only had he earned visiting rights by winning the race, but he also felt he had saved Luana from the clutches of a lustful villain. She was in his debt. The only problem was she didn't know it, and Port had no idea how he might explain the situation to her.

Upon entering Independence, Port's first pleasant thought was that he might not be able to find the Beebe home. But the first man on the street knew the exact location and gave Port clear directions.

It was almost dark when Port reached the Beebe residence, a comfortable wood frame house on a large lot. A log barn stood behind the home, and an assortment of fruit trees was scattered about the yard. Since the Beebes had just arrived in Independence the previous summer, it was obvious they had purchased the home rather than building a new one as most Mormons were doing.

Slowly Port dismounted, tying both horses to the hitching rail. He could see no one near the home or barn, but lights in the glass windows told him the Beebe family was home.

Removing his felt hat, he ran his fingers through his short, sandy hair as he walked toward the door. He had washed his hair that morning. It still felt clean. He rubbed the side of his face to see if it was still smooth from an early morning shave. It was.

Racing Willard Sweeney had been fun. This was not. He wished he were home. But it was too late to turn around. His palms were sweating.

With his hat in his left hand, Port raised his right fist to the door to knock. He hesitated. It wasn't too late to turn around and head for home. No one had seen him, not yet.

But after winning the race and turning away Willard, he couldn't turn back. He knocked. He was unaware of the excess adrenaline in his system. The thick pine door shuddered on its hinges.

"Don't have to beat the door down," cautioned a middle-aged man with spectacles and gray, receding hair as he quickly pulled the door away from Port's thundering fist.

"May I speak with Luana?" Port asked, his voice faltering.

"And who might I tell her is calling?"

"Orrin Porter Rockwell."

"From around here?"

"The Big Blue." Port nodded to the west, the direction of his home.

"You're a member of the Church, then."

Port nodded that he was, noticing that Mr. Beebe was looking down at his hat, which during the brief conversation had been rolled up into a ball. Quickly, Port moved the wad of felt behind his back.

"What business are you in, young man?" Beebe asked as he ushered Port into a small parlor, motioning for the nervous young man to be seated.

"Got a ferry on the Big Blue. Started operations today. Charge twenty-five cents for wagons, ten cents for horses and cattle, a nickel for people. Business is good." Port could hardly believe he had said so much. Maybe this wasn't going to be as bad as he had thought.

"Is your father named Orrin too?"

"Yes, sir."

"I've heard of him. Aren't you from Palmyra? Friends of the Prophet Joseph?"

"I chopped wood and picked berries to help pay for the first printing of the Book of Mormon," Port answered. He could tell that this last bit of information had won him the respect of Mr. Beebe, who was about to ask another question when he was interrupted by a female voice calling from the next room.

"Was that Willard at the door?"

"No," the father said. "A Mr. Rockwell to see you."

Port's stomach was in a knot as Luana entered the room. In appearance she was everything he had imagined her to be, perhaps more. She had a beautiful, girlish face, and a full, womanly figure. She was an attractive young woman by anyone's standard.

"Mr. Rockwell, my daughter Luana," Mr. Beebe said.

"Pleased to meet you," Port responded. The girl made a graceful bob with her knees to acknowledge the introduction. The young man before her was neither tall nor handsome. His clothes and manners were plain. Yet there was unusual intensity in his gray eyes. After a brief—perhaps too brief—survey of her visitor, she turned to her father.

"I wonder where Willard is," she said.

"He won't be coming tonight," Port responded.

"Are you a friend of Willard's?" she asked, turning back to Port.

"Not exactly, but I ran into him this afternoon, and he won't be coming."

"Why not?"

"He lost a horse race." Port didn't want to be talking about Willard, and he wasn't sure where the conversation was taking them, but he didn't know what else to do, except answer her questions.

"Did he get hurt?" she asked, raising her hand to her mouth in alarm.

"Nope."

"Then why isn't he coming? I don't understand what you're saying."

"We were riding together toward Independence," Port began, hoping desperately he could keep his wits about him and get the story right. "Willard said he was coming to see you. I said I was too."

"Excuse me," Beebe said, deciding it was time for him to leave the room. Port wasn't sure he felt any better being alone with Luana. He sensed she was annoyed with him, at least with the news that Willard wasn't coming.

"He wanted to fight," Port continued.

"You didn't hurt him."

"No. We raced instead. It was agreed the winner would see you, and the loser would go home."

"And you won?" Luana asked. She seemed surprised that Port had won and also annoyed that the two young men would race for visiting rights without consulting her in the matter.

"Yes, I won," Port said.

"Now that you've paid your visit and collected your spoils, I suppose you can go."

"I guess so," Port said. He yearned to tell her how Willard had insulted her womanhood, how the race had been a contest to protect her honor. But such things were too personal to talk about. Port turned toward the door, starting to put his hat on but deciding against it when he remembered how he had wadded it into a lump. He felt foolish. Why hadn't she been flattered that two men had fought, had raced for her hand?

"Good-bye, Mr. Rockwell," she said, when he finally opened the door. He turned and faced her.

"I brought you a present," he said matter-of-factly.

"A what?"

"A gift."

"How strange. We had never even met until this evening."

"I heard a lot about you from Willard," he explained. "I just wanted to give you something."

"What is it?" she asked. Port sensed she was beginning to soften toward him.

"It's outside, on the horse. Come with me. I'll show you."

Luana hesitated. At first she hadn't liked this strange young man. Yet he had just won a race against the fastest horse in Missouri for the privilege of visiting her. And he had brought her a present. She wasn't sure if she should feel flattered or frightened.

She grabbed her shawl and followed Port into the night.

Luana watched cautiously as the young man untied and removed a large bundle from his black packhorse. Dropping to his knees, he carefully spread out on the ground what appeared to be a thick blanket.

"What is it?" she asked.

"A wool quilt, stuffed with the down of 978 doves," Port said. "Actually, there weren't that many. Some had so much blood on them that we threw them out."

Luana was speechless. Down quilts were rare and very expensive if purchased in a store—especially the quilts stuffed with the feathers of wild pigeons or doves.

"Did you make it?" she asked.

"Shot the pigeons," Port answered. "Mother put it together. Finished it last night. She said it was for me, but I wanted to give it to you." He began to roll it up.

"Thank you," she said as he handed her the quilt.

"Guess I'll be going now."

"Where?"

"Back to the Big Blue."

"Have you had your supper?"

"Don't reckon I'm very hungry."

"We had a place set for Willard, and since he's not coming, would you stay?"

"Yes'm," Port said. He followed Luana back into the house.

# Chapter 5

On February 2, 1832, in Independence, Missouri, Porter Rockwell married Luana Beebe in the first Mormon wedding in Jackson County.

During December and January, when not courting in Independence or operating the new ferry on the Big Blue, Port had been busy constructing a small, one-room log cabin on the banks of the Big Blue. That's where the young newlyweds moved in. Their earthly possessions included the cabin, a down quilt made from the feathers of over nine hundred doves, a tall bay horse named Bill, and half interest in the Big Blue ferry.

About midmorning on one of the first warm days in March, Port found a spot where the sun had warmed a sideboard on his ferry. He stretched out on his belly like a lazy cat sunning itself in a window sill. One arm fell loosely over the edge, allowing his fingers to dangle carelessly in the cold river water.

Port dozed, not thinking about anything in particular, just enjoying the first really warm spring day. While the rest of the young men his age in the Big Blue Mormon colony were busy preparing the soil to plant crops, all Port had to do was wait for paying customers to come along in need of a ferry.

Suddenly, he was aware of an unnatural rock to the boat. The water at the river's edge was smooth as glass. Someone or something had stepped on board and was sneaking up on him. Port waited, his fingers still dangling in the water, trying to appear unaware of the intruder. While trying to present no visible change in behavior, his muscles were slightly tense now, ready to spring into action and do whatever was necessary, should the intruder try anything.

The next instant, Port felt the firm heel of a boot against his ribs, pushing him toward the ferry's edge. Instantly, his right arm clenched like a vise on the sideboard of the boat. At the same time he twisted his muscular body against the thrust of the boot. As Port looked up, he saw Luana playfully pulling away from him, her surprise foiled. He continued to roll in her direction, getting his feet under him, lunging, and catching her at the knees before she could leap to shore.

Ducking his shoulder into her slender waist and pulling her arm over his head, he was able to get her weight upon his back and lift her off her feet, encouraged rather than discouraged by her squeals of protest.

Walking to the edge of the boat, he held her, kicking and squirming, over the icy spring runoff water.

"You wouldn't dare!" she squealed.

Port resisted the temptation to throw her into the icy water. He rather liked the feel of the warm, lithe body squirming upon his shoulders—the soft breasts against his back, the firm thigh against his arm.

He still found it hard to believe at times that this beautiful young woman was his wife, that she was his to share his bed and cook his food. And she seemed to enjoy being his woman as much as he enjoyed having her. He had never dreamed life could be so good.

Instead of throwing Luana in the river, Port slowly let her slip to her feet, holding her close and firmly planting his mouth on hers as her toes touched the wooden planks. She responded in kind, making a contented, humming sound. Suddenly, she pushed him away.

"Time for your reading lesson," she said.

He tried to ignore her, tried to pull her back to him. But she was rigid, resisting. Finally, he let go.

"A man can't get along in this modern world without being able to read," she scolded.

"I can read the sky when a storm's coming," he responded. "I can read the river—where it's shallow, where it's deep, where the back currents are, even where the most fish are hiding out. I can read a horse's eye, knowing if the animal wants to kick me. I don't need to read books too."

"But you do," she said brightly, "and I am going to teach you how, if it's the last thing I ever do."

"My father didn't learn to read, nor his father before him," Port said. "Can't see as I need it either."

"Porter, I'm going to teach you to read, and that's that," Luana said.

Though Port still didn't want to learn to read, he wasn't about to put up much of a fight if this beautiful woman was so determined to teach him. Maybe she would read him some love poems, maybe some of the Songs of Solomon from the Bible. With Luana as the teacher, maybe learning to read wouldn't be much of a chore.

Suddenly, Port was aware of someone calling from across the river.

"Looks like a paying customer," Luana commented, looking with Port across the water to see a well-dressed stranger on a beautiful black horse, waiting to be ferried across the river.

"Want to lead the mare while I go over and pick him up?" Port asked.

"Sure," Luana responded, leaping to shore. She untied the old black mare and began leading it up the path along the river's edge. The mare was harnessed to a long rope that through a system of pulleys enabled the horse to pull the ferry back and forth across the river by walking up and down the bank. When the mare was led upstream, the raft was pulled to the opposite bank. When the mare was led back to the launching platform, the raft was pulled back to the near bank.

Port could operate the ferry by himself if he didn't want to ride on the raft with his passengers and their animals. To help on the raft, he needed someone else to lead the horse up and back. Sometimes he wondered if a dog could be trained to lead the horse, responding to voice commands shouted from the raft. Then Luana and his father wouldn't have to help so much. He was on the lookout for a smart dog.

These were the thoughts that occupied his mind as the ferry moved slowly toward the opposite shore. The smartly dressed man had dismounted from the black horse in preparation for boarding the ferry.

"Good morning to you," Port said, as the ferry bumped into shore. The handsome stranger responded in kind. He was a middle-aged man, alert and intelligent-looking, with a healthy head of wavy hair and a warm smile. Porter liked the friendly stranger.

Port pushed a long pole into the soft mud on the river side of the ferry, wedging the craft tightly against the bank. When the stranger had led the nervous horse on board, Port pulled the pole out of the mud and signaled for Luana to lead the mare back to the launching platform. As she did so, the raft began to move.

" 'Bout time someone put a ferry on the Big Blue," the stranger said. "Can't say I ever enjoyed getting wet, especially when the water's so cold. Is business good?"

"Very good," Port responded. " 'Tween the migration and the Mormons, expect a grand summer."

"Understand there's over a thousand Mormons in Jackson County," the stranger said.

"Only about nine hundred," Port said. "But more are coming, lots more. Maybe another thousand this year."

"Why so many?"

"Joseph says Jackson County is Zion, the gathering place for the Saints. That's what Mormons call themselves."

"Any niggers coming with them?"

"Some free ones, maybe. But not many slaves. Joseph teaches against slavery."

"But Missouri is a slave state."

"The Mormon Church is not a slave church."

"A thousand more this year," the man said, changing the subject. "That's a lot of votes."

"Lot of what?" Port asked, not understanding.

"Votes, like in the ballot box."

"You a politician?" Port asked, as the raft bumped into shore. He steadied the craft with the long pole while the stranger led his horse onto the bank.

When Port jumped to shore, the stranger extended his hand.

"Please excuse me for not introducing myself," he said. "The name's Lilburn Boggs, lieutenant governor of this great state. And who might you be?"

"Porter Rockwell, sir. Pleased to meet you. The ferry fare is five cents."

Boggs reached into his pocket and handed Port a dime, telling the young man to keep the change.

"I'll tell you a secret if you'll keep your mouth shut," said Boggs after he had climbed onto the black horse. "Someday I'll be governor of the state of Missouri. You just wait and see."

"I will," Port said.

Boggs tipped his hat to Luana, who was standing beside the black mare about ten yards off. Then he pulled his horse around and galloped up the road. Port liked the stranger and hoped he would indeed become governor of Missouri. He turned to Luana, who was just standing there, hands on hips, a bright smile on her face. He hoped she had forgotten the reading lessons but didn't think she had.

# Chapter 6

"At first the Mormons in Jackson County sincerely believed they would get along with their new neighbors," Polly explained, somewhat of a sidebar to the Rockwell narrative. We were finishing up the last of the rabbit. The half-naked Indian, Turtle Runner, was sleeping soundly on the bare ground. Outside the cave, the snow was still falling. The horses were standing silent, their backs to the storm, patiently waiting for the night to pass. Melted snow ran in long, straight rivulets down their sides and legs.

"After all, the Mormon Church was only three years old," she continued. "There was no history or precedent of persecutions, other than some of the resistance Joseph Smith had met in founding the Church and getting the Book of Mormon published. Many thought that initial opposition was a result of the Church being so new. It would be different in Jackson County, they thought. The hard-working, family-centered Mormons would be good citizens, respected and loved by their neighbors.

"Such was the feeling until W. W. Phelps published an article in the new Mormon paper, the *Evening and Morning Star,* about 'free people of color.' The direction of the article was clear. The Mormons were opposed to slavery, not a popular stand in a slave state like Missouri.

"Many Mormons wanted to believe they were being persecuted for their religious beliefs. That was not the case, at least not at first. Taking away a man's slaves was taking away useful, productive property that enabled him to make money. The Missourians didn't want anybody messing with their slaves, particularly not an idealistic religious group that controlled lots of votes. If the number of Mormons continued to grow, soon they would outnumber the old citizens. Mormons would control the elections. They could vote out slavery and anything else Joe Smith decided to do away with.

"The old citizens were concerned, and the more they got together and talked about the Mormon situation, the more serious it seemed.

"The Mormons were getting large blocks of good land, sparking a real estate boom. Land was already approaching the outrageous price of three dollars per acre. The old citizens could no longer afford to increase their holdings. What good was it if the land you already owned was worth more if you didn't want to sell?

"The Mormons were clearing the land and shooting the game. The deer, elk, and wild pigeons were becoming more scarce. At the rate things were going, Missouri would soon be as crowded as a big city, with Mormons elbow to elbow and no space left for a man to hunt and fish. If the Mormons voted away the slaves, there wouldn't be much time for hunting and fishing anyway, some moaned.

"During the summer and fall of 1832, there was a growing feeling among the Missourians of Jackson County that the Mormons must go. That's how the anti-Mormon feeling began.

"Rockwell was more aware of this feeling than most Mormons, being in constant contact with the old citizens as he ferried them across the river. He could sense the unrest, the distrust, even the growing hate for his people. But the young ferryman naively thought that if he charged fair prices and was friendly and helpful, he would help win over the old citizens to the Mormon cause. At least they would leave him alone.

"Cyrus Ward, the prominent horse breeder from Independence, brought horses to Rockwell on a regular basis for training. He said no one else in the state could start a green horse as well as the young ferryman. Rockwell would work with the horses during the lulls when no one was wanting to cross the river.

"When not ferrying or working with horses, he was usually with Luana in their increasingly comfortable cabin. By fall she was heavy with child.

"In addition to sensing the pulse of the Missourians, Porter's ferry also became a focal point for the Mormons, a place to meet, to gossip, to take a natural break on their journeys. Sometimes, in good weather, meetings were held on the ferry; in less desirable weather, they were held in Port's cabin. Everyone in the vicinity, Mormons and non-Mormons, not only knew the Rockwells, but spent time at the ferry landing on the Big Blue."

"They held church meetings on the ferry?" I asked.

"Especially in the summer months," Polly responded. "The railing around the edges made comfortable seating. Being on the water and in the shade of the big cottonwood trees, the ferry was a cool, comfortable place when the weather was hot.

"There was one testimony meeting I'll never forget. It was the fall of 1832, on a warm Sunday afternoon. A gentle breeze was blowing upstream. About twenty of us gathered at the ferry to end a fast and bear testimony. Porter and Luana were there, as usual, but Porter never spoke or prayed in meetings or bore testimony. Never.

"Four or five testimonies had been given when a fourteen-year-old girl stood to speak. Children usually didn't participate in testimony meetings, so I think most were surprised when a child stood. Most were listening closely to hear what she had to say and didn't notice an approaching rider—at least no one said anything about the well-dressed man on a black horse.

"The girl was saying some of the usual things, about being thankful for the restored gospel, how she loved and appreciated her parents, and things like that—when she suddenly began to speak in a language no one could understand."

"Was she a foreign convert to the Church, speaking her native language, perhaps German or Danish?" I asked.

"No. She was born in America and knew only English. She was speaking in tongues."

"The gift of tongues?" I asked.

"Yes. But no one could interpret. She just kept talking, saying the strange words no one could understand. One man said he thought she might be speaking Cherokee. Another said it was the pure Adamic language that everyone spoke before the Tower of Babel. No one could understand a word she said. One woman said she thought the girl was faking the strange tongue."

"Was she?" I asked.

"No. She really was speaking in a strange tongue."

"How do you know she wasn't faking it?"

"I was that girl."

I looked at her in surprise and then asked what it was like.

"The words just started coming into my mind," she said. "It seemed only natural to speak them. It wasn't like they were strange or new words, but old familiar ones that I had forgotten. I couldn't remember the meanings, though. At first I didn't want to speak the words because I didn't know what they meant. But I felt compelled to speak, so I did."

"And no one offered to interpret?" I asked.

"No. But I think someone would have, with time, perhaps when I finished, but I didn't finish."

"Why not?"

"Suddenly, everyone noticed the stranger. While I was talking, he had ridden his horse right up to the edge of the ferry. I remember looking at him while I spoke in the strange language. At first he appeared to be curious, then afraid."

"Afraid of a fourteen-year-old girl?" I asked.

"Yes. It was strange. The words seemed to give me power over him."

"Like God was on your side, but not his?"

"Something like that, but stronger. I felt physical power over him. He felt it too. I know he did. He became afraid, then angry."

"Did he say anything?"

"No. He just jerked his horse's head around and galloped away."

"Did you know who he was?"

"I didn't while I was speaking. But Porter told me after the man was gone that he was the lieutenant governor, Lilburn Boggs."

# Chapter 7

It was the following July when Port emerged from his cabin late one night after hearing voices across the river. Men were calling for him to bring the ferry over. Rubbing the sleep from his eyes, Rockwell hung his glowing lantern on a tree limb. Then he harnessed the mare and hitched her to the ferry rope. After loosening the ferry from its moorings, he led the mare up the trail as the ferry began moving to the far side of the river.

One hand held the mare's lead rope. The other rested on the butt of a Colt Navy revolver tucked snugly down the front of his trousers. Since April he had been carrying the pistol with increasing frequency, especially at night and when he traveled alone.

In April a large group of old citizens had met in Independence, deciding the Mormons must leave Jackson County. Lieutenant Governor Boggs had been among them, issuing the official ultimatum to the Mormons that they must leave the county before January 1, 1834.

The Mormons held a meeting of their own, deciding they would not obey the unjust ultimatum. They would fight back in the courts and in the press. Many guessed, however, that the battle would spread beyond the courts and newspapers, especially after another of W. W. Phelps's blistering editorials against slavery, inviting free blacks to join the Mormons in Missouri. That's why Port was carrying a gun.

When the mare stopped at the end of the path, Port could hear the clatter of shod hooves on wood as horses scrambled onto his boat. He had ferried a group of mounted Missourians across the river earlier in the afternoon and guessed the same men were returning. Earlier, the Missourians had been sullen and angry. One had told Rockwell they were on their way to the *Evening and Morning Star* headquarters in Independence to have a little talk with "nigger-lover Phelps."

Upon receiving the signal that the craft was loaded, Port led the mare toward the landing as the ferry began moving back across the river. Port was relieved to hear a generous amount of laughter and good-natured swearing coming from his craft. He figured the men on the boat wouldn't be acting that way had they had any intention of doing harm to Port or his property. He couldn't help but wonder why they were so jovial. Perhaps they were drunk.

When the ferry bumped against its moorings, Port was there to secure it snugly against the dock. The men were silent now as they began to remove their horses.

"How was your little talk with Elder Phelps?" Port asked as he helped unload the first horse. He was eager to know what had happened, thinking they might just tell him if he asked.

"Wonderful," responded one of the men, a note of sarcasm in his voice that Porter didn't trust.

"Blackest white man I ever seen," another said.

"Especially after we dabbed him with hot tar," the first man added.

"But he wasn't black long, 'cause we sprinkled him with white feathers," the second man responded.

"Smashed the press."

"Cracked the type with a hammer."

"Tarred and feathered some of his Mormon cronies."

The comments continued as Port helped unload the horses. He wondered why he was helping the men who had just tarred and feathered some of his friends. But there were nine of them. What else could he do? He certainly couldn't fight them.

Port felt the warm steel of the pistol against his stomach, but it gave him little comfort. The thought of having to use the pistol made him sick.

For a moment Port felt like he should say something to the men about what they had done to Phelps. That it was wrong, a terrible thing to do, and that they would be sorry. But he said nothing. He told himself there were no words that could change or undo what these men had done.

After the last horse stepped from the ferry Porter asked for his fare.

"Already paid," one of the men said.

"No, you haven't," Port responded, thinking the comment might be an honest mistake.

"Yes, we did," the man said, "by not tar and feathering you too. We done you a real favor, worth a lot more than a ferry ride."

"Each of you owes me a nickel," Port said, feeling a wave of warmth in his hands and neck, hoping the men couldn't see his left knee quiver.

"We don't pay hard-earned cash to Mormons," said the man who appeared to be the leader of the group. He stepped forward, facing Rockwell. "Now what are you going to do about that?"

The thought of reaching for the gun in his belt made Rockwell so sick he thought he was going to throw up.

"What are you going to do about it?" the man repeated, the tone of his voice more threatening than before. Though the man could see the gun in Rockwell's belt, the stranger's hands remained on his hips. "What are you going to do about it?" he repeated.

"Nothing," Rockwell said, looking down at his feet. The men began to laugh as they climbed onto their horses and galloped into the night.

After turning the mare loose in the corral and fetching his lantern from the tree, Port returned to his cabin. He hoped Luana was sleeping. He didn't want to discuss his humiliation with anyone.

He blew out the lantern. Quietly, he opened the door and entered the cabin. He could hear the deep breathing of six-month-old Emily as he tiptoed past her crib. Sitting on the edge of the bed, he quietly removed his boots and trousers. Luana didn't stir, not even when he laid back and rested his head on the pillow. There were no covers on the bed, it being a warm July night.

"How much fare?" Luana asked, her voice heavy with sleep.

Port didn't answer, hoping she would resume her sleep. She didn't.

"How much fare?" she repeated.

"None," he said, knowing it would do no good to lie. Luana kept close count on the fares he collected.

"Old man Bennett wanting another free ride?" she asked.

"No, nine Missourians. Just tarred and feathered Elder Phelps. Wouldn't pay."

"Did you tell them you would turn them in to the sheriff?" she demanded.

"No."

"Did you demand their names so you could take them to court?"

"No."

"Did you have your gun?" She was sitting up now, fully awake.

"Yes."

"And you didn't use it?" She was beginning to shout. The baby was waking up.

"No."

Luana started to ask about Phelps, but her husband wasn't listening. He quickly slipped into his trousers and boots and headed for the barn. This wasn't the first time he had gone to the barn in the middle of the night. Port was getting used to it. But what had happened at the ferry was something he would never get used to. He was confused, frightened, and in no mood to argue with Luana. And that sick feeling in his stomach persisted.

# Chapter 8

Mob action against the Mormons in Jackson County increased throughout the summer and fall. On September 28, Porter, along with nearly all his Mormon neighbors, signed a petition to the governor demanding that depredations against the Mormons be stopped.

While the burnings and beatings were not sufficient to stir the Mormons to arms, the actions of a judge in Independence were. A Missourian by the name of Richard McCarty was caught pillaging a Mormon store. When he was brought before Judge Weston, there were seven Mormons present to testify against the man. The seven witnesses had seen McCarty removing stolen goods from the store or had seen the goods in his possession.

After listening to the testimony, the judge acquitted McCarty, who promptly filed a complaint against the three Mormons who had captured him—John Corrill, Isaac Morley, and Sidney Gilbert. Judge Weston threw the three Mormons in the Independence jail.

It was now clear to the Mormons they were not going to get any protection, or justice, from the Missouri legal system. If there was going to be any safety for the Mormons, they would have to provide it themselves.

The mob got its first surprise when a raid on the Mormon meeting house at Colesville was repelled by an unknown number of armed Mormons. A few days later, a band of seventeen Mormons scattered a mob of nearly fifty Missourians, killing two. One Mormon died in the skirmish.

Flush with confidence following the two victories, two hundred Mormons gathered at the Rockwell ferry. Their mission was to ride into Independence in broad daylight and free Corrill, Morley, and Gilbert. The militia leader was Lyman Wight.

"Coming with us?" George Beebe asked as Port ferried him and several others across the river to join the Mormon army, already two hundred strong. George was Port's brother-in-law, Luana's brother.

"Don't know," Port said. "Hate to leave Dad and the women alone. Too many pukes looking for something to burn."

"We'll be making history," George persisted. "Hundreds of Mormons marching on Independence. The Army of Zion putting the fear of the Almighty into the hearts of every puke. With God on our side, how can we fail?"

"I'll ask Luana if I can join you," Port said.

An hour later, Port was riding with George and the rest of the Mormon army to Independence. Port was on his tall gelding, Bill. The horse's neck was arched more than usual as he cantered beside the other horses, sensing the excitement of the maneuver.

The fear Port had felt initially upon joining the company was gone. Riding beside his comrades, mounted on the fastest horse in Missouri, armed with his revolver and rifle, he began to feel invincible, that God really was on their side, especially when Wight led the men in singing all six verses of "Onward, Christian Soldiers." All the men sang, some louder than others, some more on tune, but all sang as they hurried along the dusty road to Independence.

As the enthusiastic Mormons galloped around the bend, emerging from an oak forest onto an open prairie, the singing suddenly stopped. Blocking their path, in a straight line across the golden sod, was an equal number of mounted Missourians, rifles and pistols drawn.

With nothing more than a wave from Wight, the Mormons drew and cocked their weapons as they spread out, forming a straight line facing the enemy. Port and George Beebe ended up in the middle of the line, directly behind Wight, who pushed his horse forward to meet Colonel Pitcher, the leader of the Missouri militia. To the surprise of the Mormons, Pitcher rode right up to Wight and offered his hand.

The conversation between the two leaders lasted what seemed a long time. The excitement and confidence Port had felt while singing "Onward, Christian Soldiers" had vanished. The men facing him had loaded guns and would use them, if necessary. If a battle erupted with so many men in the open field at such close quarters, some would die. Many would be wounded. Port guessed the Missourians probably outnumbered the Mormons. He felt the same sick feeling he had experienced the night at the ferry when the mob refused to pay. He hoped he would have courage to fight, if a battle began. The sick feeling became more intense.

Finally, Wight turned to face his men.

"They want peace, if we will surrender our arms," he shouted.

There was grumbling among the Mormons, who didn't trust Pitcher.

"In good faith, they have already released Morley, Corrill, and Gilbert from jail," Wight added.

Some of the grumbling stopped. Releasing the three Mormons was indeed an act of good faith, though some doubted the three men had actually been let go.

"Where are they?" shouted a man near Rockwell.

"Should be here any minute," Wight answered.

"Let's wait and see," the soldier responded.

Wight turned his horse and rode back to Pitcher. They resumed their private conversation. Most of the men put their rifles and pistols away, while still keeping a close eye on the enemy.

By the time Corrill, Morley, and Gilbert rode into view, the enthusiasm to fight had all but vanished on both sides of the line.

Rockwell felt not relief but reluctance when he was asked to surrender his weapons, but following his comrades, he obliged. He handed his pistol and rifle to an old acquaintance, Willard Sweeney.

"How's Luana?" Sweeney asked as Port handed him the weapons.

"Fine," was all Port managed to say. Sweeney wanted to continue the conversation but was ordered over to Pitcher, who handed the young man a dispatch to take to Lieutenant Governor Boggs as quickly as possible. Wight explained to his men that the dispatch contained news of the treaty. As soon as Boggs received it, the conflict would end. Sweeney spun his horse around and spurred it toward Independence.

As the Mormons rode home that night, they felt relief. Peace, at last, had been achieved. From now on the rights of the Mormons would be respected.

Sweeney found Boggs at the courthouse in Independence, enjoying a late supper with Judge Weston. After delivering the dispatch, Sweeney answered some questions before being dismissed to return home.

Pushing his food aside, Boggs placed a piece of white paper before him, dipped his pen in the ink bottle, and began to write his report to the governor. The judge waited patiently, finishing up the last of the roast chicken on his plate.

When Boggs was finished, he looked up grinning, obviously pleased with what he had written. He read a few passages to the judge.

"Not only was a force of two hundred armed Mormons seen approaching Independence today," he read, "but there are reports the Mormons have aligned themselves with the Indian tribes to the west, and that the combined force is at this very minute planning a complete massacre of the entire state of Missouri."

Boggs concluded his letter by asking the governor for authorization to double the size of the state militia in Independence to remove the Mormons once and for all from Jackson County. The message was sent by night courier to St. Louis.

# Chapter 9

—————

"Where's your gun?" Luana asked as Port entered the cabin.

"Surrendered to Pitcher."

"Was there a fight?"

"No, just talk."

"They talked all two hundred of you out of your guns?" Luana bellowed in an angry voice.

"We decided to have peace instead of war," he said, determined not to get angry too, trying to explain what had happened. "We gave up our weapons as a sign of goodwill."

"I just can't believe you did it!" Luana exclaimed.

Port wondered why women had such a difficult time understanding the things men did. He wondered how she could sit here in the cabin and disagree with Wight and the two hundred men who had decided to give up their arms. Figuring he would never fully understand Luana, he headed back out the door. Time for his evening visit to the outhouse. It was almost dark.

Port had covered about half the distance to the new two-seater when he heard indistinct shouting from across the river. A group of men wanted to cross. Looking closer, they appeared to be Indians— bare-chested, paint on their faces, wearing headbands.

It was unusual for red men to want to cross the river on the ferry. Seldom was an Indian willing to spend hard cash on a river crossing. Their ponies were accustomed to swimming the rivers.

Port didn't notice that all the ponies carried saddles. He just figured that with a cold October night coming on, the Indians didn't want to get wet. He could understand that.

He led the mare up the trail as the ferry moved slowly across the river to the men. He hoped they had money. It wasn't uncommon, on the rare occasion that an Indian did decide to use the ferry, to find out after the crossing that the man had no money to pay the fare.

It wasn't until the first man led his horse ashore, uttering the word *How* with a distinct Missouri accent, that Port suspected the men were not Indians.

"Got to borrow your boat tonight," the man continued in excellent Missouri English. "More of us coming shortly."

"Isn't for rent," Port responded, angry with himself that his voice was high and broken, that it gave away the growing surge of fear welling up inside.

"Didn't say we wanted to rent it," the counterfeit Indian said, "just borrow it."

Port looked at the men more closely. They were white men with paint and grease rubbed over their faces and chests. One was carrying a red flag. There were six of them. He could smell whiskey. All of them carried guns.

"That'll be five cents each," Port said, unable to think of anything else to say. His voice was higher now, almost a screech. The men began to laugh, just one or two of them at first, then all six.

Port couldn't figure out why they were laughing so loud, until he noticed them looking down at his legs. He felt the wet warmth. His embarrassment was overwhelming.

"Better git over to the two-seater," said the first stranger. Port didn't move. The man pulled a pistol from his belt and cocked back the hammer. Port turned and walked slowly toward the outhouse, his eyes on the ground. The six men followed him, laughing all the way. They were leading their horses.

Port paused at the door, not wanting to go in.

"Inside, Mormon," ordered the man with the drawn pistol. "And don't come out unless you want a final resting place in the basement."

It was dark inside. Port could hear the men circling the outhouse. There was a scratching sound, the unmistakable sound of rope against wood. They were tying a rope around the little building to prevent Port's escape. He reached for his knife. It was not in his belt. He had left it in the cabin. Without a knife it would be hard to get out.

"If we see the door moving, Mormon, or you trying to git out, we'll shoot this little house so full of holes you'll have to dive down the hole if you don't want to get shot." The men were still laughing as they galloped back to the ferry.

Port decided to wait until dark to make his escape. No one would see him then. It wouldn't be long. He was angry with himself for not having his knife, and he vowed never to be outdoors without it again. There were tears in his eyes at the shame of having lost control of his bladder before a group of men. He wondered what was wrong with him, why he was not brave like other men. He wondered why his voice became high and broken, giving away his fear. He hated his voice. He hated the outhouse. He hated the men who put him there. He hated himself for allowing them to do it.

The darkness didn't come, at least not at the usual time. Port could hear shouting, hoof beats, screaming, and some shooting. The approaching darkness was held back by the blaze of yellow-orange flames. Port guessed from the direction of the firelight that old David Bennett's cabin was burning.

Port decided he couldn't remain in the outhouse while people's homes were burning. Maybe his would be next. Luana and Emily were without protection. So were his mother and sister.

He began kicking furiously at the door, but before any of the boards began to give way, three or four bullets sliced through the soft pine wood. Port dropped to the floor, hearing approaching hoof beats.

"Rockwell," a familiar voice shouted, "try to git out again and forty men will open fire on this little house. Think about it, Mormon." Port could hear the horse galloping away. Cautiously, he got to his feet and began pushing at the boards on the side away from the firelight, hoping he might find a loose one. The outhouse was new and sturdy. None of the boards were loose.

As he continued his search, Port tried to put a face to the voice that had threatened him. He kept thinking it belonged to Lieutenant Governor Lilburn Boggs, but it was hard for him to believe that Boggs, a high public official, would be riding with a gang of mobbers dressed like Indians. But Port couldn't put any other face with the voice. It had to be Boggs.

During the next half-hour, Port heard sounds of splintering wood, the bleating of sheep, the mooing of cattle, the screaming of people, more gunshots. When he heard what sounded like a crying baby, he began to cry too. His Emily wasn't even a year old, and he was helpless to defend her.

Then all was quiet. The mobbers were gone, though the fire at Bennett's cabin continued to spread a flickering yellow light. Port kicked off the bottom door hinges and wiggled outside. He ran frantically toward his cabin.

The first thing he noticed was that the roof was gone, ripped off log by log by riders with long ropes. The door had been jerked from its hinges. As he reached the open doorway, he saw the white floor, thick and fluffy like it was covered with newfallen snow.

The white was not snow, but millions of feathers, everywhere. The down of a thousand doves. The feather quilt he had given Luana before their marriage had been ripped to pieces. Port waded inside the cabin, feeling immediate relief upon finding Luana and Emily, apparently unhurt but badly frightened, huddling in the corner.

"Where were you?" Luana sobbed as she recognized her husband. Port couldn't tell her. He wished he were dead.

# Chapter 10

By the time the night passed, twelve Mormon homes had been unroofed, including both Rockwell cabins. David Bennett was left for dead with a bullet in his head. He miraculously survived. Luana's brother, George Beebe, and Hyrum Page were flogged. The feathers from Luana's quilt were spread all over the Big Blue settlement. When someone commented that the mobbers had even kicked the door off the outhouse, Rockwell said nothing.

After leaving the Big Blue, the mobbers headed for the Colesville Branch, where they continued their spree of beating, burning, and ripping roofs from homes. The only damage to the mob was that one man was shot in the leg. Without arms, the Mormon resistance crumbled.

Then came the rains, an incessant, torrential downpour. Tiny rivulets became raging torrents. The rivers were impossible to cross, often swelling far beyond their banks.

The worst storm of the decade continued day after day as the reluctant Mormons packed what belongings and food they could gather into wagons and began congregating on the swollen banks of the Missouri River. The Mormon camp contained over a thousand people.

As the downpour persisted day after day, the refugees waited to cross into Clay County, where sympathetic citizens offered refuge. But the Mormons had to wait until the raging waters of the swollen Missouri subsided. While the rain made crossing the river impossible, it also kept the mobbers at home, leaving the Saints to themselves in their soggy encampment.

Through it all Rockwell remained silent, speaking only when spoken to and sometimes not even then. While his body was busy preparing his boat for the crossing, his mind was elsewhere.

Luana did not try to console her husband. At first she nagged, wanting to know where he was when their home was destroyed, why he hadn't stood up to the mob, why he hadn't arrived sooner. Her questions remained unanswered and unexplained. When presented with the inquiries, Port only turned away. His shame was too deep for probing, even by a wife.

Few neighbors and friends noticed the change in young Rockwell, so engrossed were they with their own problems. Port wasn't so much thinking or plotting as just hurting, bearing his pain in silence.

When the Saints gathered for prayer, a frequent occurrence during desperate times, Port was there too, but he was never the one to say the words. He remained silent.

Finally, the rain stopped. The sky cleared. The nights became cold. Gradually, the raging waters subsided.

On a clear, frosty November night, when it was almost time for the crossing, the skies were suddenly full of meteors, thousands of them streaking in every direction. The heavenly display of fireworks continued for hours, and the Saints began to comment among themselves that God was giving them a sign that all would be well, that their prayers had been heard, that they would find new homes, and that God—after all the agony—was still on their side.

Spirits brightened. Prayers of gratitude were offered. Plans began to form for a new settlement in Clay County. Many of the refugees began to smile.

But not Port. His shame was too deep and dark even for a heavenly shower of shooting stars to throw light on.

The crossing was uneventful. The old citizens of Clay County welcomed the Mormon castaways. Crude shelters were improvised. Firewood was gathered. Men found jobs clearing land and building fences, receiving corn and pork in return. New farms were arranged for in anticipation of spring.

When spring finally arrived, the Mormons went to work building a new community. The mobs from across the river hadn't bothered them during the winter and left them alone in the spring. But one day in mid-June as the Mormons gathered on the grassy banks of the wide Missouri for outdoor worship meetings, word was received that a delegation of twelve men from Jackson County was crossing the river in an effort to purchase Mormon lands left behind in Jackson County.

Not daring to get their hopes up that they might receive payment for their abandoned farms, the Mormons agreed to meet with their former enemies.

It was not easy for the twelve men to cross the wide Missouri, swollen far beyond its natural bounds with melted snow water from the distant Rockies. When the men from Jackson County finally arrived and stepped out of their boat onto the grassy shore, it appeared they had come with serious intent. They carried a large box containing deeds and surveys.

The Mormons gathered around, hopes and speculation soaring in anticipation of receiving at least partial payment for the property they had left behind.

While Port had been at the gathering with his family earlier in the day, he was not with those crowding around the table. A man saw him carrying a long rope over his shoulder, headed for the river. A boy saw him seated at a rocky portion of the shore, tying rocks to the rope at regularly spaced intervals, like a fisherman would tie stones to weight down the bottom of his gill net.

Another child saw Port wade into the river, dragging the weighted rope behind him. Someone thought they saw him, up to his waist in water, near the rear of the boat belonging to the men from Jackson County. Soaked to the shoulders, Port was next seen sitting on a grassy knoll above the boat, by himself.

Any hopes the Mormons had of being compensated for their lands quickly vanished. The men from Jackson County simply laid the documents out on the table and asked the Mormons to sign them, thereby relinquishing, without compensation, all claim to Jackson County lands. Something was said about the Mormons not having to reimburse the county for maintaining the militia the previous fall if they would sign the documents.

The Mormons howled in protest. If the men from Jackson County wanted the Mormon farms, they would have to steal them outright. The Mormons were not about to sign papers that would make the wholesale theft look legal. The clash of angry voices became louder and louder. Red-faced men shook fists at each other.

The twelve men from Jackson County decided they had best be going. Without bothering to assemble all their unsigned papers, they tumbled into the boat and pushed off. Port was still on the grassy knoll, watching silently.

The twelve men paddled strongly toward mid-stream and were making good progress when the boat stopped abruptly. Some of the men put up their oars and began frantically bailing water out of the boat.

A Mormon with a telescope said it looked like one of the sideboards was removed from the boat, allowing the cold river water to gush in. In a few minutes the boat disappeared from sight, and the fully clad men could be seen swimming frantically toward the far shore as the raging torrent carried them downstream, around a bend, and out of sight.

Newspaper reports later claimed that seven of the twelve men drowned.

Just before dark, long after the Mormons had gone home, Port could be seen walking downstream from the gathering place, slowly coiling a wet rope as he pulled it from the river, removing rocks at regular intervals. There was a long board attached to the end of the rope, like the kind used in boat building. After removing the rope, Port threw the board out into the current.

He watched the piece of wood float out of sight. He adjusted the heavy rope coiled over his shoulder and then turned silently toward the grassy bank.

# Chapter 11

After picking up the package at the counter of the Davies Mercantile in Gallatin, Missouri, Port hurried outside and sat down on the edge of the wooden porch.

It was late summer, 1835. Luana and Emily were living with Luana's parents in Independence, leaving Port mostly to himself to wander from farm to farm looking for work. He chopped wood, followed plows behind mules and horses, built fences, and rode the buck out of green colts. He had strict instructions from Luana to send her every penny he earned until they had enough to make a down payment on a good piece of land. Port had sent her most of his money but not all—not the sixteen dollars he had paid for the package just received.

Pulling his knife from his belt, Port cut the white string and removed the brown paper. Inside was a wooden box, made of new, rough-sawed pine. Carefully, using the back edge of his knife, he pried off the wooden lid. Underneath a layer of wood shavings was the object of his search—a Colt Dragoon pistol. The blue-black steel was smooth and clean, except for a skiff of sawdust. The walnut handle was still unfinished, the wood looking as new as the day it was screwed into place.

Slowly, Port reached into the box and removed the pistol. It was heavy and solid in his hand. The cold steel and hard wood warmed quickly to his touch. He felt like he had a new friend. Port thought back on the humiliation he had suffered in Jackson County. With the help of this new Colt, that would never happen again, he hoped.

"That's some toy," offered a familiar voice, not very far away. Port looked up into the grinning face of Willard Sweeney. The young Missourian was mounted on the sorrel mare. "Know how to use it?"

Port remained silent. He couldn't comprehend how Willard could be so friendly, not after riding with the Jackson County mobs. Sweeney was the enemy and might someday be a target for the new Colt.

"Look, I'm sorry about what happened on the Big Blue," Willard offered, dismounting and extending his hand. Port didn't loosen his grip on the pistol handle. He remembered being so afraid that he'd lost control of his bladder. The memories of being locked in the outhouse flooded back, especially the sounds—the screaming, the shooting, the splintering wood, the burning. An apology and a handshake could not erase all that, ever.

"How's Luana?" Willard asked.

*So that's it*, Port thought. *Willard's still interested in Luana.* He wasn't about to tell Willard anything about Luana, certainly not that she was in Jackson County with the Beebes. He definitely wasn't going to tell Willard how cold she had been since the Jackson County conflicts.

"She's pregnant again and hidden away where folks like you can't find her," Port said, wondering why he was bothering to say anything.

"Can I look at your new gun?" Willard asked, changing the subject and reaching out his hand. Port handed over the pistol, wondering how Willard could forget the hostilities and conflicts so easily. The weapon was not loaded.

"Ever hear of Sylvester Pussy?" Willard asked as he eyed the pistol, cocked back the hammer, and removed the cylinder.

Port nodded. Everyone had heard of Sylvester Pussy. Before the Mormons had come to Missouri, the state had hired Pussy as a guard during a bank panic. He had killed eight men in two weeks, all in fair fights. Port had never seen the man.

"Pussy could teach you how to use this," Willard said. "He lives straight north of here, up near Iowa Territory, off by himself in the woods somewhere, with a squaw."

"You rode with the Jackson County mob," Port said soberly, reaching out and taking his pistol back. "How can you just ride up to me and start talking as if nothing happened? You're the enemy."

"You take things too personal," Willard said. "My father and brothers and cousins tell me to get on my horse and ride with them against the Mormons. So I go."

"Just like that?"

"Look, I was as embarrassed as you were when you peed down your leg and got roped in the outhouse," Willard explained. "It was like they were doing it to an old friend. We had raced; we had courted the same woman."

"Why didn't you do anything to help?" Port asked.

"Can't just go against family and neighbors."

"They were tearing down houses and hurting people."

"When my cousin wanted to return for some unfinished business with Luana, I talked him out of it."

"I suppose you want me to thank you."

"Do whatever you want," Willard responded, taking a step back and swinging into the saddle. His horse started to lunge forward, but he jerked it back.

"Don't know if you can see it, Rockwell," Willard warned. "But Jackson County is happening all over again, right here. Hope you're ready this time. Don't forget what I said about Sylvester Pussy."

Willard leaned forward, loosening the reins. The horse lunged forward, carrying the young Missourian out of view. Port got to his feet, pushing the new pistol into his belt.

# Chapter 12

Sylvester Pussy was an unlikely name for a gun-fighter. Still, Port couldn't get the name out of his mind. Owning a pistol was one thing, but knowing how to use it was another. And being able to use it, instead of wetting one's trousers, was still another. Port headed north, in search of Sylvester Pussy.

Two days later, after getting directions from a farmer with a load of hay, Port approached the Pussy cabin. It was all by itself in a clearing by a spring. It was a small cabin, and old, except for a new layer of irregular, hand-split oak wedges covering the roof. Sheets of oilskin hung over the two windows. The door was open.

Nearby was a patch of corn and pumpkins, a plentiful supply of weeds competing for the same space. In a meadow beyond the corn, three horses lifted their heads to watch the approaching bay. One whinnied a greeting. There were no fences to contain the animals, which were picketed Indian style. A long rope secured to the front foot of each animal was attached to a two-foot picket pin.

Behind the cabin was a log shed with an open front. Inside, Port could see two saddles, garden tools, some barrels, and a partially consumed deer carcass hanging from one of the rafters.

There was no outhouse. Though Port had never met the man, it was obvious that Sylvester Pussy, like many of the old citizens, was not an ambitious farmer and builder. He did what was necessary to get by, nothing more.

"Sylvester Pussy," Port called out, reining Bill to a halt about thirty feet in front of the open door. There was no response for what seemed a long time. It being midday and too late for anyone to be in bed, Port wondered if perhaps Pussy was off in the woods somewhere.

Port was about to call out a second time when a black-bearded man appeared in the doorway. He had no boots on and was buttoning up his gray home-spun trousers. His upper body was covered with long-sleeved, red flannel long johns with buttons down the front. He didn't seem to be in any hurry, either, to finish buttoning his trousers or to speak to Port. If anything, he seemed annoyed that Port would bother him.

"Are you Sylvester Pussy?" Port asked.

"Why do you want to know?" Pussy replied, his voice gruff and unfriendly.

"Folks say Sylvester Pussy is the best gunfighter west of the Mississippi," said Port, hoping flattery might warm things up a bit.

"You come to find out if you're better?" Pussy snarled.

"No!" Port exclaimed, his voice suddenly high and tense. "No," he said a second time, alarmed that Pussy was thinking the visit a challenge.

"Then what's your business?" Pussy demanded.

"Came to learn. Want you to be my teacher."

"Don't read and write, so how can I teach you?"

"I'm not talking about reading and writing. Teach me to fight with a gun."

Pussy began to laugh, a harsh belly laugh.

"What's funny?" Port asked, seeing no humor in his request.

Gradually, the laughter turned to anger. Pussy took a big step forward onto the porch. With hands on hips, he yelled at Port.

"You stupid idiot. Lessons from Sylvester Pussy won't give you backbone to stand up to a man who's trying to kill you. I can't teach you to spit in a man's face, curse him to hell, and then kill him before he kills you. That's not something you learn from a teacher, you stupid idiot. Some men have what it takes. Most don't. That's all."

"Teach me. I'll pay you."

"I'm not for sale. Now get out of here."

Port started to turn away, but then he stopped, his mouth twisted with emotion. When he spoke, his voice was high and broken, like he was about to cry.

"I wet my pants when they took away my gun." He could hardly get the words out. Tears were streaming down his cheeks, dripping onto the front of the saddle. He was looking down at his horse's neck. "They roped me in the outhouse," he said. "They ripped the roof off my cabin. Scared my wife and baby half to death. I was too afraid to . . ."

He swallowed hard, overwhelmed with shame for showing so much emotion. But he had to continue. He looked up into Pussy's face.

"Never again. Now I want to fight. Teach me."

"You a Mormon?" Pussy asked. Port nodded.

"I figured as much. What's your name?"

"Orrin Porter Rockwell. Folks call me Port."

"Nice to meet you, Port. Sorry about what happened in Jackson County. Now, please go."

"You won't teach me?" Port asked.

"As I said, some things can't be taught. Now go."

"I don't know where else to go."

"That's your problem."

"Teach me."

"No. Now git before I get mad." Port didn't move.

"Teach me," he repeated.

Without another word, Pussy reached inside the door. A second later he was aiming a large German holster pistol at Port's chest.

"If you value your life you'll leave," Pussy warned.

Port made no effort to turn his horse away.

"My life has no value without the knowledge of gunfighting," he said. "Please tell me what you know."

"I'm not bluffing," Pussy warned, cocking back the big hammer.

"Neither am I," Port whined, still making no effort to leave.

Without any movement or warning, not even a blink, Pussy

pulled the trigger. There was a loud bang and a burst of smoke. The large ball knocked Port out of the saddle. Bill galloped off to join the three horses in the meadow.

His eyes fixed firmly on Pussy, Port got to his feet, his right hand pushing against his left shoulder, blood oozing between his fingers.

"Teach me," Port said, his voice more calm and not so high. Pussy had replaced the smoking pistol with another.

"Git your horse and go," he ordered. "The next ball will be closer to your heart." Port stood his ground.

"Teach me."

Pussy cocked the hammer back and pulled the trigger.

As the smoke cleared, Port was on the ground, holding his thigh.

"I've got lots more ammunition," Pussy said. "Now get out of here."

"How can I, with a ball in my leg?" Port groaned.

By now his leg was covered with blood. He began to feel dizzy and nauseated.

"Git on your feet," Pussy snarled.

Port tried to get up but couldn't.

Suddenly, an Indian woman appeared in the doorway behind Pussy. She was young, wearing a white woman's dress, but her hair was braided as was customary with natives of the area. She pushed past Pussy and hurried to Rockwell.

"Mormon," Pussy said, the edge gone from his voice, "meet Mary Blackfeather, my squaw. Aims to patch you up, I suppose."

As Rockwell looked up into Mary Blackfeather's face, he thought she was the most beautiful woman he had ever seen. Then he passed out.

"First thing he's got to learn is more respect for loaded guns," Pussy said as he stepped forward to help Mary carry the unconscious Rockwell into the cabin. "But I suppose he learned that today."

# Chapter 13

Within three days, Port was well enough to get up and move about with the help of a willow crutch, though he was still weak from loss of blood. Each morning Mary Blackfeather applied clean dressings, sprinkled generously with smashed yarrow plants.

In addition to tending Port's wounds, Mary kept the little iron stove fired up, cooked the meals, cleaned up the cabin, and washed clothes. She seemed content, even happy, with her chores. She spoke only when it was necessary, never just to pass the time.

While Port was mending, Sylvester Pussy was outdoors most of the time. Though he chopped some wood for the stove, mostly he was gone, hunting deer and turkeys. When he brought home more than they could eat in a day or two, Mary would tear or cut the meat in strips to dry on green willow rods lashed horizontally to a tripod standing in a sunny spot beside the cabin. Below the tripod, she maintained a smoking bed of half-burned hickory and cottonwood chips. The heat from the chips helped dry the meat faster. The smoke, in addition to flavoring the meat, kept the flies away.

On the evening of the third day, as the three seated themselves around a small plank table to enjoy an evening meal of roasted venison ribs and corn bread, Port asked Sylvester how he had become a gunfighter.

"All began the day I was born" was the quick reply. "My pa named me Sylvester Pussy. Soon as I began running around with other kids I learned I either had to fight or get teased. I chose to fight. First with fists and sticks, later with guns."

"Did someone teach you how to fight with a gun?" Port asked.

"Yep. Had eleven teachers," Sylvester replied.

"Eleven teachers!" Port exclaimed. "I didn't know there were that many men in the whole country who could teach gunfighting. Who are they? Why haven't I heard of them?"

"They're all dead."

"They are?"

"Killed them myself."

"You killed your teachers?" Port was puzzled.

Pussy explained himself. "Their intentions were not to teach me. They were the men who tried to kill me. One at a time I killed them. And each time I came away a little smarter. My teachers were the men I killed."

"I hope you can teach me without dying," Port responded. Both men laughed.

After supper Sylvester retrieved a ball mold from a wooden box and placed a small pan full of lead on the hot stove.

"Port, tomorrow you're going to learn how to shoot."

"I'm already a pretty good shot."

"Then why did you come to see me?"

"Figured there was more to gunfighting than hitting a target."

"The key to gunfighting is shooting your target before it shoots you," Sylvester said with authority. "Show me how you shoot."

Port loaded his Dragoon and stepped out onto the porch. Sylvester and Mary followed. The sun was just going down. There was still plenty of light to see a target.

Port picked a small block of wood from the woodpile and threw it out into the yard, where it rolled to a stop about forty feet from the porch. Holding his Dragoon steady with both hands, Port aimed carefully down the barrel and fired. The ball hit one corner of the block, causing it to spin like a top. Port was proud of his shot. He looked over at Sylvester, who had already turned to go back into the house to get his gun.

"In a gunfight you can't take a lot of time to aim, like you did with that piece of wood," Sylvester said when he returned to the porch. "You got a silver dollar?"

Port nodded, reaching into his pocket and retrieving one of his last three dollars.

"Flip it into the air," Sylvester ordered.

"Straight up?" Port asked, knowing there would be less chance of losing it if he threw it straight up.

"That's fine," Sylvester said.

With an upward jerk of his good arm, Port flipped the coin as high as he could, then looked over at Sylvester, whose pistol was already pointing at the coin. The report of the gun was followed by a zinging sound. The coin didn't return to the ground. The force of the bullet had sent it spinning off in the meadow somewhere. Instead of going to look for his dollar, Port just stared at Pussy in amazement.

"Tomorrow I'll teach you to shoot like that," Pussy said as he shoved the pistol barrel under his belt.

After dark, under the light of an oil-burning lantern, Port and Sylvester made lead balls one at a time in the mold. Holding the handle of the pot with a glove, Sylvester poured the molten lead into the mold, which he then dipped into a bucket of cold water. The water cooled the lead sufficiently for it to become hard again. Sylvester then opened the mold and rolled the shiny new ball across the table to Port, who rubbed off the unwanted edges with a rough rock.

They had produced enough balls to cover the bottom of a frying pan before Sylvester finally removed the hot lead from the stove and put the ball mold back in the box. Port thought they were finished, but Sylvester returned to the table with a small jar of white powder. He mixed in a little water and began to stir with a twig.

"What's that?" Port asked.

"Paint," Sylvester said as he poured a little pool onto the table and began pushing the new lead balls through it, coating each one thoroughly with the white paint.

"Why are you doing that?" Port asked.

"So you can learn to shoot better."

"Don't josh me," Port said. "I don't care much for teasing."

"You'll see in the morning," Sylvester said, suddenly turning his attention to Mary Blackfeather, who had been sitting on the bed, her knees drawn to her chest, watching the two men.

Leaving the freshly painted balls to dry, Port hobbled over to his cot to try and get a little sleep. Sylvester blew out the light.

# Chapter 14

"Are we going to start shooting now?" Port asked when they had finished breakfast the next morning.

"Follow me," Sylvester said as he stepped out the door onto the wooden porch. He picked up a garden hoe and a shovel, handing the hoe to Port.

"I thought we were going to start shooting," Port said.

"We are."

"With a hoe and a shovel?"

"Want to be able to hit a silver dollar in the air?"

"Sure."

"Then follow me." Port followed, having no idea what Sylvester intended to do.

The two men walked across the meadow to a small draw. They followed the bottom of the draw about fifty feet until it made a sharp curve. Sylvester stopped, instructing Port to clear all the grass and brush from the top of the outside bank down to the bottom of the draw.

"I don't want to see anything but clean, black loam," Sylvester explained. "Clean off every blade and twig. I want it smooth and black."

"Mind telling me why?" Port asked.

"You'll find out soon enough. Start digging." Sylvester climbed out of the draw and headed back to the cabin while Port began hacking away at the grass and brush. The work increased the pain in his wounds, but he persisted, wondering why Sylvester wanted the ground cleared, hoping the gunfighter knew what he was doing.

By the time Port finished, Sylvester had returned, carrying Port's gun, a small keg of powder, an old shirt, and a pouch containing the freshly painted lead balls. He placed everything on the ground about thirty feet from where Port had finished clearing the bank. Port put down the tools and joined Sylvester, who was wrapping the old shirt around the barrel of Port's pistol. When Sylvester loaded the weapon, Port was surprised at how little powder he used. When the white ball was driven home, Sylvester turned to Port.

"Forget everything you ever learned about shooting a pistol," he said. "Pretend your gun is a long fishing pole, that instead of shooting you are just reaching out and touching your target."

"I don't understand," Port said.

"Shoot toward the bank."

"But you've wrapped a shirt around the barrel. I can't see the sights."

"That's because I want you to ignore the barrel and sight. Focus your eyes and all your attention on the black dirt. Try to see the white bullet approaching the target."

"You can't see a bullet in flight," Port objected.

"You can if the bullet is white, the target area is black, and the powder load is small enough," Sylvester insisted. "Try it."

Port pointed the pistol at the black dirt and fired.

"Did you see the white ball?" Sylvester asked.

"Yes."

"Where did it hit?"

"A couple of feet left of center."

"Good. Now do it fifty times. Use just a little powder, so you can see the bullet every time. Remember, the path of the bullet is a long fishing pole. You are just reaching out and touching the target. Don't worry about accuracy. Watch the path of the white ball with both eyes, seeing where it hits every time. Ignore the sights and gun barrel."

Sylvester headed back to the cabin. Port began shooting. Except for several times when he used too much powder, he could see the white ball before it hit the bank.

It was midday when Port fired the fiftieth round. Tucking the pistol in his belt, he walked back to the cabin. After a brief lunch of salt pork and boiled eggs, Sylvester ordered Port to return to the draw and fire another fifty rounds.

"Are you sure it's necessary?" Port challenged.

"Do you want to hit a silver dollar in the air?"

"I want to be able to shoot an opponent before he shoots me, Port said. "I'm not sure hitting a silver dollar has much value."

"Has more than you will ever realize," Sylvester said with finality. He invited Port to sit beside him on the edge of the porch.

"The first two gunfights were the hardest," he began. "Those men were not afraid of me. Each thought he would win and fought accordingly. I was fortunate enough to survive, but the outcome could easily have gone the other way. It got easier with each additional fight because my opponents knew about the earlier gunfights and were afraid. The fear made their hands sweat and their knees shake. One forgot to cock back the hammer on his gun. One man even wet his pants while trying to raise his pistol to take aim. The undertaker got to clean him up."

"And what does all this have to do with hitting silver dollars in the air?" Port asked.

"Hitting a silver dollar in the air is impossible for almost all men," Sylvester said. "If you can do it, they will think you are better than they are. They will be afraid of you. This is especially important in your first fights when you don't have a reputation like I have. If you can shoot a silver dollar, most men will avoid you. Those that don't will have sweaty palms and shaking knees. You will have the advantage."

Port returned to the draw and fired fifty more white bullets.

For three days Port did nothing but shoot white balls into the black dirt. When he became restless, Sylvester reminded him that the path of the white bullet was like a long finger with which he could just reach out and touch whatever he wanted to shoot, even silver dollars. But thousands of practice shots were necessary for that to happen.

Several times Port wanted to set up bottles or pieces of wood in the black dirt, so he could have something to shoot at. Sylvester didn't allow this. On the morning of the third day he explained why.

"Before you came here, you shot with your hand and your eye. I am teaching you to shoot with your heart. Every time you shoot, your hand tells your heart how it held the gun, and your eyes tell your heart where the white ball went. Your heart doesn't forget, and with time, if you let it, it will guide your hand when you shoot, aiming for you. Just aiming down the barrel of a pistol, the way you used to shoot, will never enable you to hit silver dollars in the air. Once you learn to let your heart do the aiming, you can hit them nearly every time."

Sylvester paused to let Port think about what he had said. Then he continued.

"For three days you have been teaching your heart where the bullet goes when the gun feels a certain way in your hand. Now you need to teach your heart that it's supposed to guide your hand so you can hit the target every time. It's a faith thing; like it says in the Bible, 'If you believe you can do it, you can do it.' "

"The Bible says that?" Port asked.

"Maybe not in those exact words, but the meaning is the same. Whenever you miss a target, your faith is weakened. Whenever you hit a target, your faith is strengthened. That's why I haven't let you shoot at targets yet. I don't want a lot of misses recorded in your heart."

"When will I start shooting at targets?" Port asked.

"In a few days, but only when I say, not before. In the meantime, I want you to start dry firing at everything you can see."

"What's dry firing?" Port asked.

"That's when you don't have any powder in the gun," Sylvester said. "You aren't really shooting, just pretending, like when you were a child. I want you to dry fire at every squirrel, bird, tree knot, dirt clod, anything you want. I want you to do it all the time."

"Are you sure this is necessary?" Port asked.

"Absolutely, and every time you do it, imagine in your mind that you are actually hitting the target. I want you to send a thousand messages to your heart, messages that you always hit your target, no matter how small or far away. The result will be faith. And only with faith can you hit silver dollars in the air."

Port strapped on a holster and began carrying his pistol everywhere he went. He dry fired at everything that moved, and at hundreds of objects that remained still. He tried his hardest to imagine hitting the target every time. At the same time, he continued shooting hundreds of white balls into the black dirt. Though Sylvester wouldn't let him set up specific targets, Port got so he knew exactly where the white ball was going to strike the black dirt.

After about a week, Sylvester introduced Port to targets. The first day it was a large basket, which was not only easy to hit on the ground, but also when Sylvester heaved it into the air. The next day Sylvester used a smaller basket. Again, Port had no trouble hitting it. After several more days, Sylvester was throwing chunks of wood about the size of large apples into the air and Port was hitting them every time. Between shooting sessions, he continued dry firing at everything in sight.

"I can't afford to have you shoot up my silver dollars," Sylvester announced one morning, "so these will have to do." Earlier that morning, Sylvester had taken a green pine limb, about as thick as a woman's wrist, and sawed off a pile of half inch–thick wafers, about the size of silver dollars.

Sylvester handed some of the wafers to Mary, offering her the opportunity to give Port the silver dollar test. She hurried outside. The two men followed, Port carefully checking his pistol.

When Port nodded that he was ready, Mary flung the first wooden wafer high above her head. It was flipping end over end and had just reached the top of the arc when Port fired. The wafer shattered into five or six pieces. She threw a second, third, and fourth wafer. Each time the result was the same. Port didn't miss.

"How much do I owe you?" Port asked as they walked back into the cabin.

"We'll discuss that when the lessons are over."

"We're not finished?"

"You've learned how to shoot a pistol. That's the first lesson. There are two more lessons yet to be learned."

"What are they?" Port asked.

"Both are more important than learning how to shoot. We'll do the first in the morning. You'd better get a good night's sleep. Tomorrow will not be easy."

# Chapter 15

"You're not going to throw them up in the air?" Port asked the next morning when Sylvester set up a plank with five bottles on it.

"Nope. They'll be hard enough to hit on the plank," Sylvester responded.

"At a hundred yards," Port said.

"At twenty yards," Sylvester replied. He paced off twenty yards, and then drew a six-foot circle in the dirt, using the toe of his boot. "Want you to break all five bottles without stepping outside the circle."

"Too easy," Port said. "What am I missing?"

"I'll be shooting at you from beside that tree over there."

"Wait a minute . . ."

"It's one thing to hit a target on the practice range," Sylvester explained, "but quite another to hit your target when someone is shooting at you. If you can't do that, you'd better hang your gun up and forget the whole thing."

"I'm not sure I want to do this," Port said.

"Won't teach you as much as a real shootout, but it'll be as close as you're going to get."

"Where will you aim?" Port asked. "I won't be much good to anyone if you kill me or blow my arm off."

"Oh, I won't kill you. Might take a heel off your boot, a little finish off your belt buckle, or even draw a little blood on the side of your neck. Don't make any sudden movements." Sylvester turned and started walking toward the pine tree he had referred to earlier, about fifteen feet left of the plank with the bottles.

"I need some time to think about this," Port said. Sylvester ignored the comment, continuing toward the tree. He had a pistol tucked in each side of his belt and one in his hand.

"If you leave the circle, I'll put a bullet in your leg," Sylvester warned as he reached the tree and turned around. "If you shoot at me, I'll kill you. I'll stop when you've broken the five bottles. Enough said."

"Let's talk about . . ." Port was beginning to say, his voice high and squealing, when Sylvester fired his first shot. The ball hit the ground, spraying dirt on Port's legs. Port raised his pistol and fired at the first bottle. He missed.

With Sylvester's bullets hissing past his ears and between his legs, Port missed his first four shots. Not only was it difficult to concentrate on the bottles, but his hand was shaking so badly it would have been difficult to hit a wine barrel at ten paces.

"If you don't start hitting them bottles, I'm going to start drawing blood," Sylvester warned. Taking a deep breath and concentrating on the bottles with all his might, Port finally hit one on the fifth try. He hit the next four in a row, finally silencing Sylvester's smoking pistols. When the dust settled, Port noticed a bloodstained crease across his left thigh and a piece missing from the outside edge of his right ear. The rest of the bullets had missed, but not by very far.

"You said there were two more lessons," Port said as they were walking back to the cabin. "What's the second?"

"The last lesson is the hardest and most dangerous," Sylvester replied. "Not sure how I'm going to do it."

"What is it?"

"You'll find out when the time is right, but not before."

When they reached the cabin, Mary cleaned up Port's new wounds. She seemed neither surprised nor shocked that Sylvester had been shooting at Port again. White men had strange ways, and it was like she wasn't about to start trying to figure them out.

Port liked Mary Blackfeather. Her easy-going manner gave him a relaxed, comfortable feeling. He liked the way she lived one day at a time without complaint, without worry. He sometimes wished she would talk more, but was grateful she didn't talk too much like some women he knew. When he was around her, he thought a lot about Luana, sometimes wishing Luana could be more like Mary, just content to be his wife, do his cooking and cleaning, and not be worried about everything going on in the neighborhood.

Port wondered if things would change between him and Luana, now that he knew how to use a gun. The mobs would never shame him again. But could Luana forgive and forget? Would things get better or worse when they tried living together again? He needed to see her. He hoped Sylvester's last and final lesson would come soon, whatever it was.

That evening, as Mary was putting the final touches on a roasting turkey with nut dressing, a voice called from the yard. Port was sitting at the table, watching Mary and thinking about Luana. Sylvester was lounging on the bed, reading the Bible. It was still light outside.

"Anybody home?" a strong male voice shouted a second time.

Port went to the door and exchanged greetings with a young, blue-eyed stranger who asked if he could water his horse at the spring before continuing his journey into Iowa Territory. Port told him to go ahead and returned to the table. Sylvester had scooted across the bed and was looking at the stranger through the window.

"Ready for the final lesson?" Sylvester asked.

"Sure," Port said, with enthusiasm.

"Grab your gun and kill that drifter."

"He asked for a drink of water, and you want me to kill him?" Port asked.

"When you're in a gunfight, you don't have time to think over all the reasons the man across from you doesn't deserve to die," Sylvester said. "Maybe he has a pretty wife and a bunch of little kids. Maybe his life savings is in the bank you're hired to stop a run on. Maybe he's an elder in the local church. It doesn't matter. When it's time to kill, you kill. That's all. I want to see if you can do it, if you have the stomach for killing. Better to find out now than when your life is in the balance. Do it."

Drawing his gun from the holster, Port looked through the open door toward the young man, who was just beginning to water his horse. The boy was shabbily dressed in a soiled gray coat that was threadbare at the elbows and torn under both arms. The boy's uncombed, wind-tossed hair was soiled and badly in need of a trim.

"You're asking me to murder a man," Port said.

"We'll bury him in the woods," Sylvester said. "No one will ever know. You can have his horse."

Port returned his gun to the holster and turned toward Sylvester. "The boy has done nothing to deserve killing. I won't do it."

"If you don't try you'll never know whether you can or can't do it."

"I guess that's one lesson I'll just have to learn the hard way. I won't gun down the boy without good reason."

"Are you sure?" Sylvester asked, staring intently into Port's eyes.

"I'm sure," Port answered, returning the stare.

Sylvester turned to Mary. "Guess Port passed the final test."

"What are you talking about?" Port asked.

"You passed. Now I won't have to kill you."

"What are you saying?" Port demanded.

"If you had raised your pistol to kill that kid, I'd have killed you."

"But you told me to do it."

"As I said, I was testing you, but not the way you thought," Sylvester continued. "You're good with that gun, almost too good. Didn't want to send a cold-blooded killer away from here, not with my stamp on him. The world doesn't need another cold-blooded killer. Didn't think you were that kind of man, but I had to make sure. You passed." Sylvester smiled and then offered his hand. The two men shook. Mary Blackfeather smiled.

The next day Port headed south, having decided it was time to see Luana again.

# Chapter 16

Port and Luana finally found a place of their own, eighty acres in west Caldwell County near Shoal Creek. By the spring of 1838, about 150 other Mormon families had settled in the same area. The town was called Far West.

It was a peaceful time for the Mormons and Port and Luana. The long days of hard work establishing a new farm left little energy for the bickering that had burdened their marriage earlier. By now they had two little girls, Emily and Caroline. Port's parents joined the young family in Far West, while Luana's mother and father remained in Independence.

The most serious area of contention between Port and Luana was the money he spent on lead and powder for his frequent trips into the woods to practice shooting. She couldn't understand how Port could spend so much on ammunition when they needed a butter urn, glass for the windows, more dishes, a new garden, and farm tools. Though Port listened politely to her objections, he continued spending the money on ammunition, and Luana usually spent her frustration by taking a hoe to the weeds in the pumpkin patch.

In the spring of 1838, Far West underwent a sudden transformation. The peaceful little town of displaced Mormons working hard to reestablish farms and businesses suddenly became the world headquarters of the Mormon Church. Joseph Smith arrived in May to become the town's most prominent resident.

Joseph's bank in Ohio, the Kirtland Safety Society, had failed, leaving the young prophet with over one hundred thousand dollars in personal debts and a hornet's nest of disgruntled stockholders and investors who wanted their money or blood. Foremost in this group were former stalwarts Oliver Cowdery, David and John Whitmer, W. W. Phelps, and Lyman Johnson, all of whom followed Joseph to Far West.

Petitions and letters with multiple signatures circulated about, signed by the faithful, demanding that the unfaithful leave. When some refused, Jared Carter and Sampson Avard formed a secret band of enforcers called the Danites. The dissenters finally departed, but not before stirring up considerable fuss.

Port's reaction to the new wave of excitement was to spend more time in the woods practicing his shooting. And Luana was driving the weeds in the pumpkin patch toward extinction.

Undaunted by the departing gripers, Joseph began a religious revival. He founded a new town to the north, Adam-ondi-Ahman, on the exact spot where he learned by revelation that the father of the human race, Adam, had once built an altar and offered sacrifice. Joseph introduced the law of consecration, a modern brand of New Testament socialism wherein the faithful turned over all their material possessions to the Church. There was a flurry of ordinances and baptisms. Port was ordained to the office of deacon in the Aaronic Priesthood.

The time had come to join hands and build the kingdom of God. Unfortunately, some of the faithful became too zealous, fanning into flames the smoldering resentment and differences existing between the Mormons and their Missouri neighbors.

Probably the single most inflammatory event was Sidney Rigdon's Fourth of July speech that same year. The Saints were gathered at Far West to celebrate Independence Day. Highlights of the day included stick wrestling, fried chicken, homemade ice cream, horse racing, and a patriotic speech by Sidney Rigdon, who wasn't about to put anyone to sleep.

His text was the prophet Daniel's interpretation of King Nebuchadnezzar's dream in the second chapter of Daniel in the

Old Testament. In vivid detail, Rigdon described the terrible and bright image or personage that stood before the king in his dream. Sometimes Rigdon's voice was almost a whisper. Then he was shouting as loud as he could. He never took his blazing eyes off his captive audience.

Rigdon described the image as a great warrior with a head of gold, breast and arms of silver, belly and thighs of brass, legs of iron, and feet part iron and part clay, representing the many kingdoms that would rule the world in the last days.

Then, with a freshness of intensity that surprised all but those who knew him, Rigdon described the stone that was cut out of the mountain without hands to roll forth and break to pieces the iron and clay feet, or the kingdoms of the last days.

"And what is that stone?" he demanded. Before anyone could answer, he began reading from Daniel 2:44, " 'The God of heaven [shall] set up a kingdom, which shall never be destroyed . . . but it shall break in pieces and consume all these kingdoms, and it shall stand forever.' "

Rigdon went on to explain that the rock that crushed the kingdoms of the earth was the restored Church established by God in the last days, the same church that was restored through Joseph Smith. The kingdom of God would prevail over the kingdoms of the earth. The Mormon people were the salt of the earth.

As Rigdon wound down, he was out of breath. A thousand tear-filled eyes were glued on him, almost mesmerized by the power of his message. Yes, the listeners believed they were God's chosen people, the salt of the earth.

No one was thinking about fried chicken, ice cream, stick pulling, or the upcoming events—except Port. He was about the only Mormon around who never got very excited about anything Rigdon said. Port had something else on his mind—the upcoming horse race to determine the fastest animal in Caldwell County. Rumors were circulating that the black stallion that Joseph had brought from Kirtland could beat any horse west of the Mississippi, even Rockwell's big bay, Bill. Following a lot of talk and speculation, the time of reckoning was less than an hour away.

After Rigdon's sermon, the festive mood quickly returned, and soon a large crowd was gathering on both sides of the finish line at the end of a half-mile straightaway. Early in the day five horses had been scheduled to run in what was happily being called the Moroni Sweepstakes. Someone had suggested the name after surmising that Moroni, the Book of Mormon's last Nephite survivor, probably had a very fast horse when he escaped the Lamanite armies. The name stuck.

By race time, three of the five animals had been withdrawn. No one from Kirtland wanted to run against Joseph. None of the Missouri Mormons thought they had a chance against Bill. And since the entry fee was a whole dollar, with all the money going to the winner, only two animals were left to compete.

The differences between the two horses were substantial, not only in appearance but in disposition too. Joseph's tall black was prancing sideways in anticipation of the race, already in a sweat, its head high, tail outstretched. The reins were tight, requiring almost all the strength in Joseph's strong arms to hold the black at a walk.

On the other hand, the shorter, stockier Bill was walking calmly down the road, plenty of slack in the reins, his neck relaxed, ears forward, almost like he was enjoying the scenery. Port had never had a horse that remained so calm before a race, but he was sure Bill knew a race was about to begin. Though Port thought the horse's calm manner odd, the young Mormon was not worried. Bill was a seasoned performer. When they turned to begin the race, Bill would be ready. He would give the race everything he had.

"What do you call the big black?" Port asked as he and Joseph approached the starting line.

"Boggs," Joseph said, grinning.

"After the governor?"

"Of course," Joseph responded. "My horse has a hard mouth. When I jerk on the reins I always wish I could do the same thing to Boggs." Both men laughed.

Joseph was dressed like a president, in a long black coat and top hat. Port wore homespun trousers and a clean wool shirt.

Upon turning to face the finish line, Joseph and Port nodded simultaneously at each other, and the race was on, eight steel-shod hooves thundering powerfully toward the finish line, churning up a billowing cloud of brown July dust.

Port was aware he was in no ordinary horse race. He was racing against the prophet of God in front of all the prophet's followers. Perhaps he should let Joseph win.

But Port was also aware of Bill, the formerly quiet gelding now gone mad, streaking toward the finish line, every muscle exploding and contracting in perfect harmony—nose outstretched, ears flat against his head, hooves pounding solidly in perfect rhythm. Bill didn't know who Joseph Smith was, nor did he care. God Himself could have been on the rangy black, and Bill wouldn't have cared. Winning the race was the only thing that mattered, nothing else. Port made no attempt to hold his horse back.

Bill won, but only by half a length.

"Is the bay for sale?" Joseph asked as he and Port slowed their horses to a walk, turning back toward the cheering crowd at the finish line.

"No," Port said, out of breath. "But if you want him, he's yours."

"You keep him," Joseph grinned, suddenly galloping ahead to greet his friends.

After cooling Bill off and staking him out to graze, Port approached a group of men and boys who were shooting rifles and pistols at bottles swinging on strings. As Port watched, he noticed that none of the shooters could hit the bottles with any degree of consistency. He felt the urge to show off his newly learned skills with a pistol, but he held back.

None of the Mormons had any idea what Port had learned from Sylvester Pussy, and Port wasn't sure he wanted them to know, not yet. He wasn't sure why he felt this way, only that the feeling was more than his normal shyness before groups and gatherings.

To the Mormons around him, he was a displaced ferryman who was trying to start a farm. He was pretty much ignored, left alone. He wasn't sure he wanted to give up his anonymity, at least not yet.

If the Mormons knew how well he could shoot, he might be called upon to do things he was not yet ready to do.

Port knew he must wait for the right time to put a gun in his hand. When that would be, he didn't know, only that it was not now. He also knew that if and when he engaged in a confrontation, he would have a definite advantage if his opponent perceived him as a displaced ferryman instead of a polished gun hand. There was no sense throwing away such an advantage in a bottle-shooting contest.

When one of the men invited Port to join in the fun, he politely refused.

As the weary Mormons returned to their homes that night, groups of furious Missourians were already gathering to discuss Rigdon's suddenly famous Salt Sermon. The Missourians who discussed the sermon all came to the same conclusion: If the Mormons were going to rule the world, they sure as hell were not going to do it from Missouri. It was time for the Mormons to be driven from their promised land.

# Chapter 17

One month later on August 6, Port was absent when a mob of drunken Missourians tried to prevent Mormons from voting at Gallatin. Otherwise timid John Butler picked up an oak stick and began swatting heads like they were flies until the Mormons followed him up the steps and into the tavern to vote. When the furious Missourians returned with their guns, the Mormons were gone.

Two days later Port joined 150 armed Mormons who surrounded justice of the peace Adam Black, demanding that he sign a statement not to take sides against the Mormons in the conflict. As a result, charges were filed against the Mormons who presented the demands. Missourians from eleven counties gathered to help arrest the Mormons.

A few days later a band of armed Mormons intercepted a wagonload of arms being shipped to the mob in Daviess County. In early September Governor Boggs responded by declaring a state of insurrection in Daviess and Caldwell Counties, ordering the state militia to march on the Mormons and crush the rebellion.

On October 2 the Mormon community of DeWitt was under siege. On October 12 the Saints retreated to Far West while Joseph and his men frantically tried to establish a defense at Adam-ondi-Ahman. But they were too late. The militia burned homes and stampeded livestock, leaving a trail of flogged Mormons lashed to trees. Two Mormons were ridden out of town on a cannon. The mob boasted they would drive the Mormons from Caldwell County to hell.

The Mormons struck back at Gallatin, Millport, and Grindstone Fork. When Lyman Wight, David Patton, and Seymour Brunson rode into Far West with several wagonloads of plunder they had obtained before setting Gallatin on fire, most Saints cheered the victory. Others, including Thomas Marsh and Orson Hyde of the Council of the Twelve Apostles, felt plundering was not consistent with the gospel of Jesus Christ. These men took their families and belongings and left Far West.

Two Methodist ministers, Samuel Bogart and Cornelius Gilliam, began gathering the mob at Crooked River for an assault on Far West. It was reported that the preachers had Mormon hostages in their camp. Mormon volunteers followed David Patton to Crooked River to rescue the prisoners and stop the mob. It was reported that John D. Lee, Parley P. Pratt, and Porter Rockwell were riding with Patton. The Mormons routed the enemy into a full retreat, killing one Missourian. However, three Mormons were killed in the skirmish, including David Patton, who received a bullet through the hip, penetrating the bladder. Though victorious, the Mormons were discouraged. They were not as invincible as they had thought they would be.

The exaggerated report reaching Governor Boggs indicated that the entire mob had been wiped out by the Mormons. The governor ordered an additional two thousand militiamen sent against the Mormons, who found themselves gathering at Far West for a last stand.

So there wouldn't be any doubt on the part of the Missouri militia as to what they should do, Boggs issued his famous extermination order. Mormons who would not surrender their arms, sign over their real estate, and leave the state by the end of 1838 would be killed.

On October 30 about thirty Mormon men and boys were slaughtered at Haun's Mill by a militia force over two hundred strong. On October 31 the Mormons were under siege at Far West, their fighting men outnumbered four to one by what appeared to be half the state of Missouri.

The Mormon Alamo had arrived. Port was carrying a Bowie knife, named after the famous Alamo hero. It appeared the time had finally come when he would be able to use the skills learned from Sylvester Pussy. The Mormons were wearing white headbands to distinguish themselves from the enemy in the event the two armies became engaged in hand-to-hand combat.

Some Mormons welcomed the prospect of all-out war with the Missourians. The hit-and-run skirmishes and guerilla tactics of the previous few months had been both frustrating and largely unproductive. Now, the uncertainty was gone. It was time to kill or be killed, to stand toe to toe with the enemy and conquer or be conquered. And since God would determine the winner, the Mormons would be victorious.

Joseph wasn't so sure. The big problem, in addition to being greatly outnumbered, was that the Mormons were more than just a fighting force. Women, children, babies, and old people were there too. When the battle began, innocent people would be hurt, perhaps slaughtered.

To the disappointment of some but the relief of many, Joseph approached the enemy under a white flag to negotiate a peace. No such negotiations took place. Joseph was taken prisoner and orders were issued by General Lucas to execute the Mormon prophet on the morning of November 2.

On November 1 Lucas's troops marched into Far West, disarmed the Saints, and under the pretense of searching for arms, tore up floors, upset haystacks, plundered anything of value, wantonly destroyed a great amount of property, and ravished women, one to death. While all this was going on, the Mormons were signing deeds of trust, giving up their property to pay the cost of the mob action.

One of the militia generals, Alexander Doniphan, who had been an attorney for the Saints in Jackson County, objected so strongly to the order to kill Joseph that the order was finally withdrawn. Joseph Smith and about eighty others were herded to Independence, then Richmond, to appear before Judge Austin King. The charges against the Mormons included high treason against the state, murder, burglary, arson, robbery, and larceny.

All were released except Joseph and Hyrum Smith, Lyman Wight, Caleb Baldwin, Alexander McRae, and Sidney Rigdon, who were sent to jail in Liberty, Missouri, pending further legal action.

Port signed over his new farm to help cover the state's cost to quell the Mormon insurrection. He signed a statement that he would leave the state before the end of the year. But Port did not surrender all his guns, just one. The other two, along with his Bowie knife, he wrapped up in an oilcloth and buried.

Luana didn't object when Port announced he was taking her and the two little girls home to Luana's parents in Independence. Instead of joining the Saints at Far West, Isaac Beebe had remained in Independence, where he got along sufficiently well with his non-Mormon neighbors that they determined Boggs's extermination order did not apply to Beebe.

Port returned to Far West, where Brigham Young was organizing the Saints for the winter trek eastward to Quincy, Illinois. Port helped his parents load what few belongings they had into a wagon. His father was short of breath and constantly coughing, not in any condition for a three hundred–mile journey through the snow and cold. With most of the summer crops not harvested, food supplies were critically short. Besides parched corn, there was little to eat.

Under cover of darkness, Port dug up his guns and knife. He breathed a sigh of relief when he felt the stiff oilcloth. His weapons were still there. He stashed the guns and knife under his coat, the cold steel feeling good against his warm skin. With the guns under his belt, he felt comfortable and secure for the first time in weeks.

Port thought it odd that his newfound skills with his weapons had not been tested during the Far West skirmishes and conflicts. He had ridden with the Mormon troops on several occasions, but always seemed to be in the wrong place at the wrong time when hostilities erupted. His skills with a gun still remained mostly untested. It was one thing to shoot chips of wood and silver dollars, but another to stand toe to toe with an enemy and start shooting.

Port was still haunted by memories of the Big Blue and being roped in the outhouse. He had to keep reminding himself that he had changed, that the boy who had been roped in the outhouse had been left behind in Jackson County, that the lessons learned at the feet of Sylvester Pussy had somehow changed him. The Missourians ought to be shaking in their boots upon hearing his name, he thought. They just didn't know it yet. But they would. For Port the fighting was not over. His friend Joseph was in jail at Liberty, and Port intended to do something about it. As the discouraged Saints began their eastward journey to Illinois, a heavily armed Porter Rockwell headed south toward Liberty Jail.

# Chapter 18

———➤◆◀———

It was snowing when Port arrived at Liberty. It was late afternoon—a gray, dark December day. He had cold corn dodgers and strips of dried beef in his saddle bags, and a well-worn buffalo robe draped across the front of his saddle. What little money he had he did not intend to spend on room and board. His first priority was to see Joseph. He could make camp later, after dark.

The Liberty jail was a rock and log fortress standing alone in an open field. The twenty-foot outer walls were made of stone, the inner walls of logs. The jailers had their office on the main floor, which contained two small windows. The six prisoners were in the basement dungeon without the benefit of windows for fresh air or light.

A thin wisp of black smoke was trailing from the stone chimney as Port approached the jail. The single door was closed against the winter storm as Port dismounted and tied Bill to a post. He had hidden his guns in the woods about a mile out of town. He knew the jailers would want to search him before allowing him to visit the prisoners, and he couldn't take the chance of losing his weapons.

After riding through a storm all afternoon, the inside of the jail was a welcome sight. A black, potbellied stove in the far corner was rattling with warmth.

There was a continuous row of wooden pegs along all four walls. Every peg was being used—holding up coats, bridles, ropes, chains, hats, pails, and burlap bags. There was a pile of saddles and saddle blankets in one of the near corners.

Port was ushered through the door by a burly man with a black mustache. The man was wearing a white sheepskin vest. Without any kind greeting or questions about what Port wanted, the jailer quickly rejoined two companions on a bench against the far wall. They were engrossed in a competition of tossing playing cards into a pail in the center of the room. They seemed determined to finish their game before finding out who Port was or what he wanted.

On a plank table against the left wall were three tin plates stacked high with boiled beef, thick slices of heavy brown bread, and slices of raw onions. As Port seated himself at the table, the jailer with the sheepskin vest said, "Have some food. I'll be with you in a minute."

Filling his mouth with bread and beef, Port continued to look around until his eyes rested on an iron grate covering a hole in the floor just a few feet beyond the table. He guessed this was the door to the basement dungeon where his friend and prophet was held prisoner.

"What can I do for you?" the man in the sheepskin vest asked in a friendly voice, when their game was finished. He got up from the bench and walked toward Port.

"I'd like to visit your prisoners," Port said, nodding toward the grate.

"You a Mormon?"

"Yes."

Without the jailer saying another word, Port noticed a sudden chilling in the room, as if someone had thrown open the door and let in the cold December wind. Upon reaching the table, the jailer pushed the plate of food away from Port.

"Had me fooled," the jailer said. "You look more like a muskrat hunter than a Mormon fanatic. What's your business?"

"I'm Joseph's cousin. Just want to visit."

"Sorry. Visiting hours were over at three. You'll have to come back tomorrow."

Port made no effort to leave. He figured the jailer was probably lying about the visiting hours just to be ornery. The other two men had retrieved the cards and were urging the jailer to join them in another game of throwing cards in the hat.

"Please let me see him, just for a few minutes," Port said.

"If you don't get out of here," the jailer said, "I'll throw you in the dungeon with the prisoners."

"A lot warmer down there than in the woods where I'm going to camp," Port said, remaining in his seat.

"Five minutes, on one condition," the jailer said.

"What's that?"

"You empty the swill bucket." Port nodded his willingness to do it.

Removing a large key from his vest pocket, the jailer bent over and unlocked the grate. Lifting it open, he motioned for Port to descend the ladder into the black hole.

"Visitor coming down," the jailer shouted into the hole. As Port stepped onto the ladder, the overwhelming stench of human urine and feces made him nauseated until his nostrils began to deaden to the smell.

"It's me, Orrin Porter Rockwell," Port responded to anxious queries as he descended into darkness. The jailer slammed the iron grate over his head.

"How are you, Port?" asked one of the voices.

Port thought it curious that the man wanted to know how he was. They were the ones in jail, not Port.

"Someone light a candle," Port requested. He could hear the jingle of chains as the prisoners surrounded him, all talking at once.

"We don't have any candles," someone answered. "Bring us some."

"Don't forget matches."

"And paper, pens, and ink."

"The swill bucket has been full for two days. It's running over."

"Through the grate we hear them reading our mail before they burn it."

"Food's full of maggots and rat dirt. Bring us something decent, if you can."

"What's become of our families?"

Port pulled a wooden match out of his pocket and struck it on the nearest log. Joseph stood directly in front of him, tall and erect, even with chains on his wrists and ankles. His hair was matted and dirty, his clothes soiled and torn, but his alert blue eyes were clear and intense. The prophet was smiling. Beyond Joseph, on a bed of dirty straw, was Sidney Rigdon, looking very ill.

"Sidney will die if we don't get him out of here," Hyrum said.

"We'll all die if Judge King gets his way," Caleb Baldwin added.

"Help us escape," Joseph whispered. "In the meantime, bring us what you can to make our stay more comfortable."

The match went out, but rather than strike another, Port handed the last of his matches to Joseph, plus some dried meat that was in his pocket.

"They let me in on the condition I would empty the swill bucket," Port explained. One of the men carefully handed the bucket to Port. It was too full for the wooden lid to fit tightly.

"One swill bucket coming up," Port shouted toward the grate. As he began to climb the ladder the grate was lifted open. The jailer stepped back as Port climbed onto the floor. The bucket was too full for him to prevent it from dripping.

"If you spill that in here I'll rub your nose in it," the jailer snarled. Port resisted the urge to return the insult. After dumping the contents of the pail into the outhouse, he returned it to the jail. He then leaped upon Bill and galloped off toward the woods, where he intended to make his camp.

# Chapter 19

As Port removed his guns from their hiding place, he wondered what chance he would have in a shootout with the three jailers. He imagined what it would be like to just walk through the front door of the Liberty jail, whip out two guns from under his coat, and start to shoot. His guns would be fast and accurate. Two jailers would go down immediately. The third might be more difficult, but probably not.

On the surface, it seemed an easy task. Just step through the door and start shooting. The prophet had asked for help, and eliminating the three jailers would be the fastest way to open up the jail.

Moving deeper into the woods until he found a clearing with plenty of grass beneath the snow, Port began fashioning a shelter, similar in size and appearance to an Indian wickiup. He figured he was probably going to spend a number of nights in Liberty, and, it being winter, he wanted to be comfortable.

He set up a tripod near the edge of the clearing. Then he began to lay dead trees, brush, and strips of bark up against the tripod, leaving a smoke hole in the top and an opening in the front just large enough to crawl through. After the brush and bark were in place, he scooped up armfuls of damp leaves from beneath the snow with which he covered the shelter, except for the two openings. Last, he covered the entire shelter with loose snow, which he would later soak with water so it would become hard and crusty in the cold

December wind. A half moon reflecting off the newfallen snow gave Port plenty of light to see what he was doing.

As he worked, he continued to wonder about possible consequences if he were to shoot the three jailers. Townspeople undoubtedly would hear the shooting, and armed men would race toward the jail. Some of them would have to be shot too.

The prisoners were in chains. It would take time to remove the shackles, every second increasing the chances of one or more of the prisoners getting shot as they tried to leave the jail. Then there would be the problems of getting horses, coats, food, and weapons for each of the prisoners. Certainly they would be chased across the frozen land and half-frozen rivers. It was three hundred miles to Illinois. The cold would take its toll.

A shootout would probably stir up the mobs to renewed violence against the now unarmed Mormons, most of whom were still in Caldwell and Daviess Counties. Reluctantly, Port concluded that charging into the jail, guns blazing, was not the right way to handle this situation. Though he was eager to test his new skills with a gun, now was probably not a good time to do it. He would have to think of another way to help the prisoners escape.

After heaping plenty of snow on his wickiup, Port dug out a small fire pit just inside the door. After building a fire, he prepared his bed against the back side of the wickiup, just beyond the fire. With a saddle blanket for a mat, and his saddle for a pillow, Port rolled up in the warm buffalo robe, chewing on a big chunk of dried beef. Bill was picketed in the center of the clearing, a long rope tied to one of his front feet.

As Port chewed on his beef, he could hear Bill pawing down through the new snow to the rich Missouri prairie grass. By morning Port had an escape plan figured out.

It was two days later when Port brought candles, matches, writing materials, and a handful of rock candy to the prisoners. The jailer in the sheepskin vest allowed Port to deliver everything except the candy, which he divided with his two companions, telling Port it was against the law in Missouri to give candy to prisoners. Port offered no objection as he waited for the jailer to unlock and lift up the heavy iron grate.

"Can I empty the swill bucket for you again today?" Port asked before descending into the dungeon.

"Would be much obliged," the grateful jailer responded.

The prisoners were delighted with the candles and writing materials, especially Joseph, who dropped to the floor and began writing furiously—first to his wife Emma, then to Brigham Young and Heber Kimball. The others began to write too as Port watched, impressed by the miracle of writing, thinking that perhaps he should have allowed Luana to teach him to read and write. Maybe someday, when things settled down.

"We can't trust our correspondence to the mails," Joseph said as he stood up, handing the carefully folded letters to Port. "Take these to Far West for me. Bring the responses back yourself. Trust them with no one else."

"I'll do it," Port said, pushing Joseph's letters deep in his pocket. The other men handed him their letters.

"The Lord will bless you, Orrin," Joseph said.

"Thank you," Port responded, feeling emotion well up in his heart. He wondered how Joseph's words always seemed so much more forceful and important than words coming from the mouths of other men.

After shaking hands with all six prisoners, including Sidney Rigdon, who did not get up from his bed, Port turned toward the ladder, picking up the swill bucket on the way. This time the wooden lid was secured snugly.

"When I bring this back, be sure to look inside," Port whispered to Joseph as he started to climb the ladder.

The jailers held their hands over their noses as Port hurried toward the door. After emptying the swill bucket in the outhouse, he walked over to a nearby ditch that was not frozen over and washed out the bucket. No one noticed that he slipped in two augers with steel bits and wooden handles before replacing the lid.

Earlier, he had dropped the augers into the snow beside the ditch while Bill was drinking. The augers would enable the prisoners to cut through the log walls and begin tunneling to freedom. After returning the bucket to the dungeon, Port headed for Far West to deliver Joseph's mail.

Because of the winter weather, there were few travelers on the road. On the second day, as Port was entering Caldwell County, he was approached by two riders from the rear, who ordered him to halt. Port reined Bill in and turned the tall bay to face the approaching strangers, two bearded men in buffalo hide coats and wide-brimmed hats. One had a rifle in a scabbard attached to the side of his saddle; the other was balancing a rifle across the front of his saddle.

"What's your business?" the smaller of the two asked as he and his partner pulled their horses up in front of Port.

"Delivering mail," Port responded, seeing no need to deceive.

"To the Mormons at Far West?"

"Yes."

"Get off your horse and take your coat off."

"Why?"

"We're going to search you for guns and knives. Got to make sure the Mormons are not rearming theirselves."

Port started to feel the same helpless feeling of panic and fear that had overwhelmed him on the Big Blue. He looked down at the saddle horn and began to lean forward in preparation for dismounting.

He noticed something different. This time his hands were not shaking. Maybe he had changed. But he would never know if he gave up his guns. He began to feel angry.

"No," Port said firmly, his voice shrill but under control. "No," he said a second time, looking both men square in the eye. His gaze was steady, almost calm, but both men could sense the fire beneath.

"Get off the horse," the smaller man repeated.

Port put his hands in his big coat pockets, grasping a pistol in each, slowly cocking back the hammers without removing the weapons from his pockets and without looking away from the faces of the two men threatening him.

"I've got a pistol aimed at each of your hearts," Port growled. "If one of you reaches for a gun, I'll kill you both."

"You're bluffing," the small man replied.

"Then call me," Port said, surprised at his boldness. Though his voice was still shrill, he felt a calmness and confidence he had never felt before. He was actually wishing the man would reach for a gun.

"Look," the larger man began, speaking for the first time. "We're just following orders. Governor Boggs says only state soldiers can bring arms into the county."

"You're not going to search me," Port hissed.

"Let's kill him," the smaller man said.

Port thought about removing the pistols from his coat, but decided to leave them where they were. The men were only about ten feet away. He wouldn't miss, not even if the bullets had to pass through pockets to reach their targets.

"Are you ready to die?" asked the smaller man.

"I'm ready to see if you are man enough to search me, if that's what you mean," Port answered. "The big question is if you pukes are willing to risk your lives to make that search." Port was surprised at his eloquence in the face of danger. He realized he was actually enjoying the confrontation.

"I think I have some business in Lawson," the bigger man said, beginning to back his horse away from Port. Now that he was isolated, the smaller man lost courage too, allowing his horse to follow the one ridden by the large man.

"Tell Boggs that if he wants to search Orrin Porter Rockwell, he'd better do it himself," Port shouted after the two retreating Missourians.

Port had never felt better in his entire life than he did that day as he resumed his journey to Far West. As he rode along, he thought it interesting that the memories of the outhouse incident on the Big Blue had lost much of their pain.

When Port returned to Liberty a week later, carrying a vest full of letters for the prisoners, he was disappointed with their progress in drilling through the log wall. In their eagerness to cut through the wood and stone, they had pushed too hard on the augers and shattered both wooden handles.

"I'll get you some new handles," Port promised.

"But for heaven's sake, don't put them in the swill bucket," Sidney Rigdon groaned from his sickbed. "You might try baking them into a chocolate cake." Everyone laughed.

As Port turned to leave, Joseph handed him more letters and a revelation he had received and written down. He instructed Port to deliver the letters and revelation to Emma and the Twelve in Far West as soon as Port had obtained the new handles for the augers.

"Stay by me, Porter. The Lord has a mission for you" were Joseph's last words as Port hurried up the ladder.

As Port entered the jail the next day with the empty swill bucket that he was returning to the dungeon, the jailer in the sheepskin vest—called Clancy by his companions—hesitated in unlocking the grate.

"Ever wonder why a man would be so eager to empty someone else's swill bucket?" he asked his two companions, who were seated at the table and enjoying a supper of fried salt pork and potatoes.

"Maybe the dung of a prophet has a sweet smell," one of the jailers responded, his mouth full of food.

"Just want to make things more comfortable for my friends," Port said.

"Take the lid off. Give us a little sniff," Clancy ordered.

"While you're eating your supper?" Port inquired.

The jailer drew his pistol and pointed it at Port's chest.

"Just a little peek will do."

Slowly, Port removed the lid and then stepped back.

Swearing, Clancy picked up the bucket and dumped the auger handles into the top of the wood stove. Then, shaking his finger at Port, he shouted, "Get the hell out of here. I never want to see your face in this jail again. Understand?"

Port turned and headed out the door. From the porch he could hear some of the shouting inside.

"They're probably cutting our jail apart with augers. Better get down there and see what we can find."

"If they got enough energy to drill holes in the logs. We better cut their food in half."

"And feed it to them in the swill bucket. That'll learn 'em."

Not knowing what else to do, Port decided to deliver the letters and the revelation as Joseph had requested. Wearily, he climbed into the saddle and turned Bill toward Far West.

As he trotted down the road, Port joined company with Steven Winchester, one of the Mormons who had been acquitted at Richmond and was returning to Far West after conducting some business in Independence. Port told Winchester about the revelation he was carrying.

"What does it say?" Winchester asked.

"Don't know."

"Do you think Joseph would mind if we read it?" Winchester asked.

"Don't think so," Port said thoughtfully, "since revelations are usually published for all to read anyway."

He slowed Bill to a walk, removed his glove with his teeth, and retrieved the piece of white paper from his pocket.

"I don't read," Port said, handing the paper to Winchester, who unfolded it and began to read.

" 'And if thou shouldst be cast into the pit, or into the hands of murderers, and the sentence of death passed upon thee; if thou be cast into the deep; if the billowing surge conspire against thee; if fierce winds become thine enemy; if the heavens gather blackness, and all the elements combine to hedge up the way; and above all, if the very jaws of hell shall gape open the mouth wide after thee, know thou, my son, that all these things shall give thee experience, and shall be for thy good. The Son of Man hath descended below them all. Art thou greater than he?

" 'Therefore, hold on thy way, and the priesthood shall remain with thee; for their bounds are set, they cannot pass. Thy days are known, and thy years shall not be numbered less; therefore, fear not what man can do, for God shall be with you forever and ever.' "

# Chapter 20

Port spent a good part of the winter in his wickiup in the woods near the Liberty jail. Much of his time was spent traveling back and forth between the jail and Far West carrying mail. There was a steady stream of visitors at the jail who were more than happy to carry the mail to the prisoners and bring out messages for Port to take to Far West.

The visitors also brought out reports of increasingly severe conditions in the jail. Not only was the food unfit to eat, but it was sometimes served in the swill bucket. The prisoners did not receive new food until the old food was consumed. Were it not for bits of concealed bread and meat brought in by visitors, some felt the prisoners would not have survived the winter.

The lice-covered inmates had recurring bouts of dysentery. Sidney Rigdon, whose health continued to deteriorate, was released early in 1839. The shackles on the prisoners' hands and feet were tightened on a regular basis as the captives lost weight. Through it all, Joseph and his fellow prisoners maintained a healthy correspondence with friends and loved ones, with Rockwell always on hand to make prompt and safe deliveries. Joseph received numerous revelations while confined in Liberty Jail, and carrying those gave an added sense of importance to Port's work.

On Saturday, April 6, ten armed men arrived at the jail to join one of Clancy's companions, deputy jailer Samuel Tillery, in transporting the prisoners to Gallatin in Daviess County for another hearing.

Port watched closely from the safety of the woods as Joseph and his companions climbed onto their horses. The journey would take several days, perhaps providing an opportunity for the prisoners to escape, but first Port had some unfinished business at Liberty Jail.

When the prisoners were well out of sight, a good mile or two down the road, Port leaped upon Bill and galloped up to the front of the jail. It being a comfortable spring day, the front door was open as Port marched up the steps.

Clancy and his two companions were seated at the plank table, just beginning a huge breakfast of eggs, potatoes, bacon, toast with jam, coffee, and whiskey—apparently celebrating the departure of the prisoners. They were surprised to see Port.

"You got a lot of nerve coming here," Clancy growled, his mouth full of eggs. He didn't get up.

"One of the prisoners left a bundle of letters behind," Port said. "Can I get them?"

"Go ahead, but make it fast," Clancy said, turning back to his breakfast.

The grate was unlocked and open, so Port didn't need any assistance as he climbed down the ladder into the smelly dungeon. As expected, the swill bucket was full. Grabbing the handle, Port hurried back up the ladder.

"Thought I'd empty the swill pail one last time for you," Port said as he climbed out of the hole.

"Thanks," Clancy said, without thinking.

Before any of the jailers realized what was happening, Port had glided across the floor and was dumping the contents of the bucket onto their breakfast table. By the time the cursing jailers thought about reaching for their guns, Port had raced out the door, leaped upon Bill's back, and was galloping into the woods.

Figuring the angry jailers would try to catch him and not wanting to cause any additional trouble for the prisoners, Port headed in the opposite direction, southwest toward Independence. When it appeared he was not being followed, he continued into

Independence, where he visited with Luana and the children for several days. Then he proceeded back toward Gallatin, making a wide circle around Liberty and the furious jailers.

In Gallatin the prisoners appeared before a drunken grand jury, which brought in a bill for murder, treason, burglary, arson, larceny, theft, and stealing against Lyman Wight, Alexander McRae, Caleb Baldwin, Hyrum Smith, and Joseph Smith.

Fortunately, Judge Morin from Mill Port was able to help the prisoners receive a change of venue to Boone County, about eighty miles to the east. On Monday morning, April 15, Sheriff William Morgan and several deputies began escorting the prisoners to Boone County, against the furious protesting of local citizens who feared an impartial jury might acquit Joseph and his friends.

No objections were offered when Port joined the guards and prisoners a few miles outside Gallatin. Word had been received that many of the old citizens were fed up with the slow legal proceedings and that the mob intended to take the prisoners from the law officers by force. Port was welcomed as an additional guard.

That night after camp was made, while the supper dishes were being cleaned up, Port pulled a bottle of Missouri white lightning out of his saddlebags. After taking a deep drink himself, he passed the open bottle to the nearest guard. The bottle kept moving among the grateful guards until it was empty. To everyone's delight, Port retrieved a second bottle from his saddlebags. After removing the cork and taking the first drink, Port passed the bottle to the guards.

Two hours later, four empty bottles and six guards were resting peacefully on the ground. The prisoners, whose chains had been removed upon leaving the jail, began to quietly saddle their horses.

Port had a problem though. He had participated too freely in the drinking spree with the guards. He managed to stay on his feet, but he simply could not get the saddle on Bill. Before any of the prisoners realized what was happening, Port had splashed a panful of ice water on the face of the nearest sleeping guard, ordering the startled drunk to help put the saddle on Bill.

Worried the guard might see them and awaken his sleeping companions, the prisoners quietly positioned themselves out of sight behind bushes, trees, and horses. Port and the guard wrestled the big leather saddle onto Bill's back.

"Where're ya going this time of night?" the guard mumbled, his words badly slurred from too much alcohol.

"Gallatin, for more white lightning," Rockwell responded, his words slurred too.

Satisfied with the answer, the guard dropped back onto his bed and closed his eyes. He didn't notice that the prisoners were not in their beds and their horses were saddled.

After helping Port into the saddle, the prisoners turned their horses toward Quincy, Illinois, where the Saints had gathered during the winter. They arrived safely in Quincy on April 22.

When Sheriff William Morgan rode back to Gallatin the day after the escape and announced that his prisoners had gotten away from him, angry locals ran the poor sheriff out of town on a rail.

# Chapter 21

Port didn't hear his sister Electa whisper that a stranger was approaching. He was too angry to hear anything. He was standing up to his neck in a freshly dug grave. His three brothers were handing him the frail, emaciated body of his father, who had passed away two days earlier. The body was wrapped in a blue blanket.

It was a windy September afternoon in 1839. Port's father had never fully recovered from the exposure he had suffered the previous winter while leaving Missouri. The nagging cough never went away, nor did the temperature. The weight loss was gradual yet persistent, finally resulting in death.

Port was angry because the death was senseless. His father was only a farmer, a simple man who wanted nothing more out of life than a quiet little farm where he could raise enough food for his wife and the three of his nine children who were still at home.

Thanks to the extermination order issued by Governor Lilburn Boggs, Port's father—along with the rest of the Mormons in Missouri—was forced to abandon his farm in the middle of the winter. To force Mormon families to sign away their farms and leave the state was bad enough, but to do it at the coldest time of year added a touch of cruelty that the Saints would never forget.

At the funeral speech earlier in the day, Sidney Rigdon had promised that Boggs would pay a hundredfold for the cruelties he caused to come upon the Mormons.

Port was also angry because there was no coffin for his father, not even a pine box, only a blue wool blanket, and that had been donated by a friend of the family. If all nine brothers and sisters reached at the same time into their pockets and purses, they would be hard pressed to find enough pennies, nickels, and dimes to make up a single dollar. Having left everything behind in Missouri, the family was now scattered, living here and there in borrowed quarters with equally destitute friends and neighbors. And if there was any one individual who could receive the blame for the senseless poverty of the Rockwell family and the death of this hard-working farmer, it was Lilburn Boggs.

Port and Luana were living out of their wagon on a thousand-acre tract overlooking the Mississippi River. Joseph had made a down payment on it at Commerce. Joseph said he was going to call the new community Nauvoo. Port purchased a piece of the land, nothing down, and was frantically trying to erect a cabin before winter set in. It was too late in the season to plant crops, and with no money to buy food, Port fed his family and others by hunting and fishing. Luana's being eight months pregnant gave an added sense of urgency to their impoverished situation. And Port believed it was all Boggs's fault.

Port was also angry that Joseph, a close family friend, had not attended the last rites of Orin Rockwell. No, it was not Joseph's fault. The previous week word had arrived from across the river that Boggs had authorized a five hundred–dollar reward to anyone who could bring Joseph back to Missouri to face the charges that had been pending against him since his imprisonment in Liberty Jail. In 1839, five hundred dollars, invested wisely, could set a man up for life. Fortune hunters from near and far were scrambling toward Nauvoo to get their hands on the prophet. Joseph had prudently disappeared until the latest form of persecution passed. Again, as far as Port was concerned, the blame for this senseless inconvenience rested squarely on the shoulders of Lilburn Boggs.

After gently placing the frail, cold body in its final resting place, Port crawled out of the grave, grabbed a shovel, and joined his three brothers in throwing moist Illinois soil on top of the blanketed body of their father.

Electa repeated what she had said earlier about an approaching stranger. This time Port heard her. While his brothers continued to cover their father, Port looked up.

The first thing he noticed was the horse, a tall, fleshy roan stallion, eager and strong, cantering across the open fields toward the tiny cemetery. The rider, a broad bear of a man with a barrel chest and full brown beard, was as impressive as the stallion. He could have passed for a burly deck hand on a river boat, except that he wore a black broadcloth coat, like those worn by ministers. The stranger's head was bare, allowing his long brown hair to toss loosely in the cold fall wind.

Port stepped forward to meet the stranger. The roan stallion churned to a halt. The two men looked into each other's faces. The stranger was first to speak.

"Looking for Joe Smith," he said in a pleasant voice.

"Won't find him here," Port responded.

"Maybe I'll just look around a bit. Could be old Holy Joe is hiding behind one of them headstones."

"Could be you won't be snooping around here," Port responded, his voice high but firm. "We've got a funeral. Won't have a puke getting in the way of things."

"I've got a paper that offers five hundred dollars to the man who can fetch Holy Joe back to Missouri," the stranger said. "Out of the way, plow boy."

The stranger urged his horse forward. Port stood his ground.

"Out of the way, farmer," the stranger repeated. Port's only response was to push the front of his coat aside and pull out the Colt Dragoon, allowing it to hang loosely in his hand, pointing at the ground.

"I hope you know how to use that," the stranger snarled, finally getting angry.

"I hope you die with dignity like a man ought to," Port said, his voice almost a whisper, but the stranger hearing every word. "And not like a stuck pig, kicking and squealing."

"You got a lot of mouth for a plow boy," the stranger said. Port didn't respond. The hand holding the gun was calm and still.

"I didn't notice anyone who looked like Holy Joe as I rode up. If he was hiding, I'd probably have seen him by now," the stranger rambled on, his confidence shaken. He was looking past Port, toward the small group of mourners, as if he still hoped to see Joseph. Port remained still.

Looking down at his horse's neck, the stranger suddenly pulled the horse's head around and began his retreat. It wasn't until he was several hundred yards away that Port finally returned the gun to his belt and walked over to his father's grave.

Port's mother was the first to speak. "You should know better than to bluff an armed man."

"Mother, I wasn't bluffing."

"But he might have drawn his gun."

"Then I would have killed him," Port said with such finality that there were no further questions. He picked up the shovel and resumed filling the half-empty hole.

When word reached Joseph of Port's courage in standing up to the big stranger, the prophet asked Port to accompany him and Rigdon to Washington to seek government compensation for church members who lost property when fleeing Missouri. Port agreed to go, as soon as Luana had her child.

A healthy son, Orrin DeWitt Rockwell, was born October 27. Two days later Port joined Joseph on the trip to Washington, where they presented claims totaling $1,381,044 from 491 displaced Mormons to President Martin Van Buren, who responded, "Gentlemen, your cause is just, but I can do nothing for you . . ." The federal government wasn't about to interfere in Governor Boggs's crackdown on Mormons.

The following summer the Mormons built 250 block and hewn log homes on the thousand-acre tract now known by all as Nauvoo. In spite of continued harassment from across the river, the Mormons wanted only to be left alone to build their kingdom of God on Earth.

Requests presented to the state legislature for a city charter so the Mormons could govern themselves were repeatedly turned down. Then one day a small Napoleon of a man who called himself

Dr. John C. Bennett arrived on the steamer from St. Louis. He had a quick tongue and a disarming smile. More than that, he was a gifted salesman. He announced that after reading the Book of Mormon and finding it to be true, he had come to serve God with the Saints at Nauvoo. The new convert quickly convinced Joseph he was the man to get a city charter out of the Illinois legislature, and he did just that in a matter of weeks.

Not only did Nauvoo have official permission to establish its own court system, complete with the power of issuing writs of habeas corpus to determine the validity of warrants coming from Missouri, but the city now had legal power to muster its own army, the Nauvoo Legion, for which the state happily provided two hundred rifles. Joseph was so delighted with Bennett that he allowed the new hero to become Nauvoo's first mayor and second in command of the Nauvoo Legion, soon to become the largest military force in what was then the western United States. Nauvoo began to prosper as thousands of new converts poured in from England and Europe, where the Twelve Apostles were converting entire congregations.

And for a time, the Mormons got along with their neighbors, except those to the southwest in Missouri, where Boggs had lost his re-election campaign for governor. Voters were furious over construction overruns on the new state capitol building. There were accusations of kickbacks and payoffs by subcontractors to the governor. But through it all, an endless stream of warrants was issued in an effort to bring Joseph Smith back to Missouri to stand trial. Joseph and his Nauvoo Legion were constantly on the lookout for Missouri law officers attempting to serve questionable papers.

After one particularly close call in 1841 involving a rescue by the Nauvoo Legion in the nick of time, Joseph prophesied that within a year Lilburn Boggs would die by violent hands.

All of Nauvoo celebrated as both Mormon and non-Mormon newspapers published the prophecy to the world. Probably the only Mormon who didn't cheer the prophecy was Orrin Porter Rockwell. Port disliked Boggs as much as anyone, perhaps more than most. Still, there was something about the prophecy that made him very uncomfortable, and he couldn't put his finger on it, at least not at first.

He knew one thing, that Mormonism was not a passive religion, but a very active one in which individuals set out to fulfill prophecy. In fulfillment of biblical prophecy, Orson Pratt was being sent to Palestine to dedicate that land for the return of the Jews. After the Saints had been driven from Far West, Brigham Young and the Twelve returned under cover of darkness the following May so they could leave for their missions from Far West as Joseph prophesied they would.

Now Joseph had prophesied that Boggs would die a violent death. Did he expect his followers to make sure it was fulfilled? Who would the responsibility fall on? Certainly not Sidney Rigdon or any of the Twelve. A job like that would take a man's man, someone like Stephen Markham or the newly arrived Bill Hickman. But Port was the bodyguard, the one the prophet had trusted to protect him on the way to Washington. Did Joseph expect Port to carry out the latest prophecy? Port decided to ask.

"What about the Boggs prophecy?" Port asked one day when he and the prophet were riding alone on the prairie. "Do you expect me to carry it out?"

Joseph stopped his horse. Port did the same. The two men looked at each other. Joseph made it clear he was not ordering Port to do anything, particularly not to kill a man. Joseph said he had prophesied as moved by the spirit, that was all. The only order he had for Port was to follow the spirit of the Lord and his own conscience, that between the two he would be guided right. With that comment, Joseph changed the subject. Port was as confused as ever. There was nothing else to do but wait and see what happened.

Something did happen, but not what Port expected. The following February, Luana, who was pregnant with their fourth child, announced she was going to her parents' home in Independence to have the new baby. She was due in a month and wanted Port to accompany her.

In a strained, weak voice, Port said he would. His face was pale. Luana couldn't understand her husband's strange behavior. She couldn't help but wonder if it had something to do with her or the new baby. Port said nothing to clear up the matter.

Port had a feeling that events seemingly out of his control were leading him to Independence, the home of Lilburn Boggs. He also knew there were less than six months remaining in the year in which Joseph had prophesied the Mormon-hater would die. If Joseph was a true prophet, Port would be in Independence when prophecy was fulfilled. Would he be the one to fulfill it? That he didn't know. He only knew that if someone else did it, Port would be close enough to catch the blame.

Port felt a strange, even grotesque, destiny drawing him to Independence. It didn't occur to him to tell Luana that he would not go with her. He trusted her intuition to want to have this baby at home. As her husband, he would take her. He would not go against the tide. If fate put him in a position to prove Joseph Smith a true prophet, so be it. He looked down at his thin, strong hands, wondering if they were the ones Joseph had prophesied would end the life of Lilburn Boggs.

# Chapter 22

After leaving Luana and the children at her parents' home, Port started looking for work. With so many unemployed Mormons in the Nauvoo area, jobs that paid cash were almost impossible to find. On the other hand, jobs were plentiful in Independence. It would be good to have some money again.

Port found work with Cyrus Ward, the man who had sold him Bill. Ward had a three-year-old sorrel stallion that needed breaking and was delighted to hire Rockwell.

Port, however, had a favor to ask of Ward. He didn't want the jailers in nearby Liberty to find out he was in town. Just the fact that a Mormon had returned to Jackson County could arouse some ire. Port asked Ward to call him Brown, James Brown. The farmer readily agreed.

Port rode over to Ward's place every morning, saddled the big stallion, and began his ride. The first few days he confined his activities to the high-fenced corrals near Ward's barn. But as the beautiful animal began to get accustomed to its new rider, Port began venturing beyond the corrals.

After a few days, his travels led him to a red brick house on South Spring Street. It was one of the finer homes in Independence and was surrounded by others of similar construction and value. The well-kept yards and cobblestone walkways were evidence of wealth. It was the kind of neighborhood where cows and pigs could not be found in front yards.

Port didn't stop at the house, but as he rode by he tried to memorize every detail. The year in which Joseph prophesied Boggs would die by violent means was rapidly coming to a close.

Boggs had been governor for less than two years, having lost his re-election campaign in 1840. He had been in the mercantile business with one of his older sons, but now he was getting back into politics, seeking a senate seat in the Missouri legislature. The Mormons believed that if the man was elected, there would be renewed efforts to bring Joseph back to Missouri to stand trial.

Port didn't have a plan, nor had he made up his mind to do anything, that first time he rode by the Boggs home. He just wanted to see the house of the man who had done more than anyone else to hurt the Mormons. Port believed Joseph's prophecy predicting a violent death for Boggs would come true, but he didn't know if he would be involved. There was no sign of Boggs that first time Port rode by the home.

A few days later, Port rode out to the Big Blue settlement. To get to the cabin he had to swim the big stallion across the river. The ferry he and his father had built was no longer there. Nearly ten years had passed since the roof had been ripped from the cabin and the outhouse shot full of holes. Other than looking older and more weathered, the place was pretty much the way he had left it.

Port tied the stallion to a tree, entered the outhouse, and sat down. After glancing at the bullet holes, he closed his eyes and tried to bring back the horrible memories of that unforgettable night when he had been roped in the outhouse, listening to the screams of his wife and baby.

Port tried to think of all the Mormons he knew who had been beaten, whipped, shot, or raped. There had been many, and Boggs, as lieutenant governor of the state, had encouraged the mob, then made sure afterwards that none of the mob faced criminal charges for what happened to the Mormons. For that alone, Boggs deserved a violent death. Port stepped out of the outhouse, mounted the big stallion, and returned to Independence.

A few days later, he rode up to Liberty, being careful to avoid the jailers, who he was sure would seek revenge if they knew he was in the area. He rode to the meadow where his old wickiup was still standing, though clogged with brush.

Dismounting, Port walked to the middle of the meadow, dropped to his knees, and began to pray. Joseph said God answered prayers. This was a secluded place like the sacred grove where Joseph, following an earnest prayer, had seen God. Port felt that if the Lord wanted him to help fulfill Joseph's prophecy concerning Boggs, the Lord ought to give him a confirmation.

Port prayed out loud for a long time. But there was no answer, no voice from heaven telling him to kill Boggs. Eventually, Port got to his feet, mounted the horse, and began his roundabout journey back to Independence. He was still confused as he thought about the persecution the Saints had received in being forcibly driven from Far West while Joseph was being held in Liberty Jail.

Thanks to Boggs, the Saints had been forced at bayonet point to sign legal deeds of trust, turning their property over to the state. No one had been compensated for this property. Even a formal petition to the president of the United States, Martin Van Buren, had failed to get the Saints any compensation for the land and buildings they had been forced to vacate under the Boggs extermination order.

As governor, Boggs had caused more damage to the Mormons than he had as lieutenant governor. Now Boggs was running for the senate. What damage would he do to the Mormons there? None, if Joseph's prophecy came to pass. Port wasn't concerned about breaking laws to protect his people from the mob. As far as he was concerned, laws that didn't apply equally to Mormons and non-Mormons were unjust and didn't deserve respect. If he felt it was right to kill Boggs, he'd do it, regardless of the law.

And Port felt like he could really do it. Not only had he learned how to use his weapons, but even more important, he had found a vein of courage in himself that had not been there earlier.

Port continued to ride by the Boggs home several times a week. Though he never saw Boggs during the day, occasionally he would see the ex-governor reading in the parlor in the early evening, either before or after supper. Boggs read a paper every night, and he did it near a front window. Shooting the man would be easy. Port began to get the feeling that perhaps the Lord was delivering the old enemy into his hands.

Though he still wasn't sure he would kill Boggs, Port began the necessary preparations. First, he thought that shooting through glass might cause deflection of the bullet, perhaps enough to miss, perhaps not. With buckshot there would be less chance of missing. On the other hand, he wouldn't want to be seen carrying a shotgun through town. He needed a pistol large enough to handle a large load of buckshot and deliver it with enough force to take a man's head off.

Port didn't own such a gun, so he began visiting several gun shops in town, being careful to introduce himself as Brown whenever someone wanted to know his name.

Finally, in a little gun shop in the older part of town, Port discovered the right weapon. It was a heavy German holster pistol, one of the new repeating pistols that held four rounds. If he missed the first time, the pistol would provide three additional opportunities to kill the ex-governor.

Port knew better than to buy the pistol. That could cast suspicion his way after the shooting. Noticing a broken lock over one of the windows, Port broke into the shop late one night and stole the German pistol. The following week, the newspapers mentioned the missing pistol, placing the blame on a Negro slave that had been seen in town that night. Port hid the gun deep in a grain barrel at Ward's barn.

Weeks passed. Luana had her baby, another little girl. But Port wasn't around much. Luana was glad her man was hard at work earning money. It didn't occur to her that something else was on his mind.

Winter gave way to spring, and spring edged into summer. It was time to return to Nauvoo. If crops weren't planted soon, there would be no hope of a fall harvest. Luana was eager to return. And the year in which Joseph had prophesied Boggs would experience a violent death had nearly passed.

Port was getting more anxious every day. Joseph had not told him to kill Boggs. Neither had the Lord answered his prayers. Yet,

Boggs deserved to die as much as any man living, thought Port. And if someone else wasn't going to do it, then maybe he should. An opportunity like this would never present itself again. He knew he could count on Boggs reading in front of the parlor window nearly every night. The German pistol was the perfect weapon. Was the Lord delivering the ex-governor into Port's hands? Did Port not have enough faith to see it?

Had Port been in Nauvoo and able to discuss the matter with a friend, perhaps Joseph, the outcome might have been different, but by himself, not willing to confide in Luana or anyone else, the same subject going over and over in his mind, Port finally came to the conclusion that he should kill Boggs.

It was a rainy evening in early April when Port turned onto South Spring Street just a block from the Boggs residence. His horse was tied to a hitching post in front of a tavern several blocks away. Earlier in the afternoon he had told Luana he was returning to Nauvoo on some urgent business for Joseph, that she could follow at her own convenience and meet him there. He was done with the job at Ward's.

The German pistol, all four cylinders loaded with buckshot, was tucked down the front of Port's pants. His raincoat was wrapped tightly around his body, partly to keep off the rain, but mostly to keep the gun dry. The sky was already dark. Because of the rain, there were few people in the streets. Conditions were perfect. Again Port had the feeling the Lord was delivering the archenemy into his hands.

Boggs was seated in the parlor, facing away from the window. Without hesitation, Port left the street and walked up to the window. The killing almost seemed too easy, too certain. All he had to do was raise the pistol and pull the trigger. With Boggs only five or six feet from the window, it would be impossible to miss.

Port stopped just short of the window, knowing he could not be seen in the blackness of the pouring rain. There was no reason to wait. He reached through the front of his raincoat and grasped the handle of the gun.

As he began to pull out the gun, his eye caught movement in front of Boggs on the floor. It was a little girl, maybe nine or ten years old, playing with a doll. He couldn't chance hitting her.

Beyond Boggs, in the dining room, Port caught a glimpse of Mrs. Boggs preparing the dinner table. A boy about twelve years old was pushing wood into the stove. It was a warm scene of domestic tranquility, like something an artist would draw to be used in an advertisement for family Bibles.

For the first time, Port realized that Boggs had a family too. If Port succeeded, the woman would become a widow, and the children would lose their father.

Port wasn't so sure now. If Boggs had been riding with a mob destroying Mormon property, pulling the trigger would have been easy. But with Boggs's back turned, harmlessly reading the paper, surrounded by family, Port didn't want to shoot. He started to back away.

But he remembered Joseph's prophecy. He forced himself to remember the beatings, burnings, rapes, even murders that Boggs had encouraged. He forced himself to remember Boggs's continuing efforts to bring Joseph back to Missouri. Boggs deserved to die, but Port doubted his own ability to shatter a warm, domestic scene with a fatal gun shot.

Then it occurred to Port that if the Lord wanted Boggs dead, perhaps there was a way to let the Lord do it. Port pulled the pistol from under his raincoat and held it sideways in front of him, letting the heavy rain splash over the barrel, cylinder, cocked hammer, and handle. He held the gun in front of him for several long minutes as he continued to watch Boggs through the window.

Wet powder would not fire. Damp powder would not fire. If the gun was held in the rain long enough, water would seep in around the buckshot and dampen the powder.

Port's strategy was simple. If the Lord wanted Boggs dead, he would keep the powder dry. If the Lord wanted Boggs alive, he would allow the powder to become wet.

Port held the pistol in the rain until he figured the powder was wet and ineffective. He held the pistol out in the pouring rain for another minute just to make sure. There was no way it would fire now, unless God wanted it to. He aimed the pistol at Boggs' head and pulled the trigger.

There was a loud explosion. The window shattered. Boggs lurched forward and then fell back limply in his chair, blood gushing from his mouth. The little girl screamed. She appeared to be unhurt, but there was so much smoke that it was difficult to tell. The boy raced into the room to see what had happened. Port suddenly felt sick to his stomach. The woman began to scream.

Port could feel warm tears mixing with the cold raindrops on his cheeks. What had he done? He looked at the huge pistol in his hand. Repulsed by the weapon, he threw it down in the mud, never wanting to touch it again.

"Oh, God," he prayed. "Please don't let him die."

As the boy approached the window to see where the bullet had come from, Port backed reluctantly into the wet blackness, finally turning and running to his waiting horse.

# Chapter 23

Port stepped off the steamboat onto the Nauvoo dock in mid-May. He hurried straight to Joseph. Word of the Boggs shooting had not yet arrived in Nauvoo. Port was the first to tell Joseph. They were walking, just the two of them, along the edge of a freshly plowed field at the edge of the new town.

Joseph's first response was to say that it was a relief to know Boggs wouldn't be bothering the Saints anymore. He supposed some people would view the shooting as fulfillment of prophecy.

Port told Joseph how he had found the Boggs home and then ridden by on a frequent basis, discovering that Boggs read his newspaper every night in front of an uncurtained window facing the street. He described finding the German pistol in the little gun shop and then stealing it. Joseph listened intently.

Port described the night of the shooting, the pouring rain, the little girl playing with her doll, the son filling the stove, the wife setting the dinner table. He described in detail how he felt, his reluctance to shoot a man, even Boggs, in the back of the head. Port described his load, buckshot backed by a double portion of powder.

Port told Joseph of his growing reluctance to follow through with the killing, how he had turned the decision over to the Lord by holding the pistol in the rain, allowing plenty of time for the powder to become wet and ineffective. If God had wanted the shooting to take place, he would have kept the powder dry, reasoned Port. Then he described the shooting, the explosion, the shattering of glass, Boggs lurching forward in his chair with blood gushing from his mouth, the room filling with smoke, the woman and children screaming. Joseph said nothing.

"Then I prayed that he wouldn't die," Port whispered.

"Was it an earnest prayer?" Joseph asked.

"As earnest as I've ever offered in my life," Port responded. "Tears were rushing down my cheeks."

"Are you sure Boggs is dead?" Joseph asked.

"Of course. I was only six feet away. At least three or four balls entered his head. I saw him lurch forward. I saw blood gushing from his mouth. No man could survive that."

"But you prayed that he would live. Don't underestimate the power of God to answer prayers."

"He's dead," Port insisted, his voice becoming high and forced. "I shot him in the back of the head. Gunned him down in front of his wife and little ones."

Before Joseph could respond, they became aware of two approaching horses. There was only one rider, Stephen Markham. He was leading the second horse. As he pulled the horses up, he said Joseph was urgently needed at the temple site. Two of the brethren were fighting. Joseph leaped upon the spare horse and the two galloped across the plowed field toward the hill where the Nauvoo temple would someday stand.

Port walked back to town, entering the tavern belonging to Amos Davis, a colonel in the Nauvoo Legion. Using the last of his wages from Cyrus Ward, Port rented a room and purchased two bottles of Missouri white lightning. He was waited on by Davis's friendly wife, one of the more attractive women in Nauvoo. Ordinarily, Port would have stayed and talked with her for awhile, but not today. He hurried to his room, locked the door, ripped the cork out of the first bottle, and began gulping down the numbing firewater.

The next thing he remembered was a gentle touch on his shoulder.

"Wake up," urged a pleasant female voice.

Port opened his eyes and looked up into the smiling face of Mrs. Davis. It was an easy face to look into, with a smooth olive complexion, dark hair and eyes, and a warm smile. Port could feel her thigh against his arm as she sat on the edge of the bed.

"Are you all right?" she asked.

"No. I murdered a man."

"Boggs had it coming," she said. "You shouldn't feel bad about shooting that rat."

"I shot him in the back, in front of his wife and children. I feel so ashamed, so dirty, like I'll never get clean again." Port stopped, wondering why he was saying so much to a stranger. He realized he must have been drunk a long time, at least several days. That would explain why she was in his room.

"You may have shot him," she said, "but you didn't kill him. Reports from Independence say Boggs is alive."

"He couldn't be alive," Port said, suddenly sitting up. "I shot him in the head."

"He's alive, all right, and getting stronger every day. He's sworn out a complaint against you. There's a $1,300 reward on your head."

"That's wonderful," Port cried, jumping to his feet.

"What's so wonderful about having a reward on your head?"

"I don't mean the reward," Port explained, slipping into his trousers. "Boggs is alive. I didn't murder him. That's wonderful. God heard my prayer."

"You prayed to save the man you shot?" the woman asked.

"Yes, afterwards, but with all those balls in his head I didn't think it could be done. Isn't it wonderful?"

"If you say so," she said as Port pulled on his boots.

"Where are you going now?" she asked.

"I need a shave, a bath, and a beef steak. Then I'm going to see Joseph."

"Sure you feel all right?"

"Never felt better in my life."

"It will be different for you when you leave this room," she warned.

"I don't understand."

"For three days everyone has been talking about the shooting. You're a hero. People will slap you on the back, congratulate you."

"I don't want to be congratulated for shooting a man in the back of the head at six feet," Port said.

"I'm just warning you so you'll be ready for it."

"Thanks," Port said as he hurried out the door and down the stairs.

"Don't forget the reward. Be careful," the woman called after him.

Mrs. Davis was right. As Port bathed, shaved, and fed himself, he was surrounded by men who slapped him on the back and congratulated him. Port held his tongue. He had said too much to the woman. With a reward on his head, he wasn't about to say any more.

It was early afternoon when he found Joseph at the partially completed Mansion House, the prophet's future home.

"What are you going to do now?" Joseph asked, when they were alone.

"Plan to get some crops in," Port answered. "Got to eat this winter. Luana and the kids will be coming along soon."

"Would you consider being my personal bodyguard?" Joseph asked.

"With Boggs in his place, are you sure that's necessary?"

Joseph began to explain a new problem that was surfacing in Nauvoo. Dr. John Bennett, mayor of Nauvoo and second in command of the legion, had been excommunicated. Not only had the self-proclaimed doctor been performing abortions, he had also been engaged in illicit sexual activity.

"Sounds like he deserved to be excommunicated," Port said.

"He knew about celestial marriage."

"What?" Port asked.

Joseph explained carefully how he had gone in prayer to the Lord several years back asking why David and Solomon in Biblical times had plural wives with the apparent sanction of the Lord. Joseph said his prayer was answered, that it was revealed to him that plural marriage had a place in God's eternal plan. Furthermore, he said he and some of the brethren were commanded to take plural wives.

Port had heard rumors that such practices were going on but was never sure if the rumors were true. He had known Joseph since childhood, and he just assumed that Joseph would never do such a thing. Now he knew differently.

Joseph said Bennett knew too much. Now that he was on the outside, it was certain the little man would not remain quiet, and with Bennett stirring things up, Joseph sensed he needed a bodyguard. Port said he would fill the position.

"But I have no money to pay you," Joseph said.

"Then how will I live, and what about my family?" Port asked. As always, Joseph had a solution to the problem. He would see that Port was given a carriage and two good horses. The new bodyguard could ferry people from the landing to various points in Nauvoo. The fares would provide sufficient income to support the Rockwell family, and Port would always be nearby if the prophet needed him. Port agreed to do it.

Joseph was right about Bennett. A month later all the newspapers in Illinois and Missouri were carrying stories about Joseph's "spiritual wifery" and about Porter Rockwell, Joseph's Destroying Angel who received fifty dollars and a carriage for shooting Lilburn Boggs. The reward on Rockwell's head was raised to three thousand dollars.

To the Mormons, however, Rockwell was a newfound hero. His carriage was filled day after day, not just with people wanting to go somewhere, but with many who just wanted to be near the Mormon gunfighter who shot Lilburn Boggs.

When visiting reporters asked Rockwell about the shooting, he vehemently denied having been ordered by Joseph to shoot Boggs. When asked the same question, Joseph also denied having given the order, saying that if he had told Rockwell to do it, the job would not have been botched, implying that Boggs would not have survived being shot by Rockwell.

One afternoon in early August, Port allowed two strangers into his carriage. They had just gotten off the steamboat from St. Louis and wanted to be taken to the Mansion House. No sooner were they seated than both drew pistols and pointed them at Port, saying they were arresting him for the attempted murder of Lilburn Boggs.

Fortunately for Port, the steamboat was not scheduled to depart for several more hours. While they were waiting to board the boat, Stephen Markham arrived with a writ of habeas corpus in which the Nauvoo municipal court assumed jurisdiction in the case. Against the protestations of the two deputies, Markham and a dozen Nauvoo legionnaires escorted Port to Judge Elias Higbee, who promptly released Port on his own recognizance. The angry deputies headed for the state capital to report the matter directly to Governor Carlin. Rockwell saddled Bill and headed east. He wasn't about to be taken back to Independence to stand trial for the attempted murder of Lilburn Boggs.

# Chapter 24

Port wandered eastward, limiting his travels to back roads and small towns. He had no idea how far the wanted posters would circulate, so he passed through the less populated areas, figuring there would be less chance of being recognized.

His first goal was to put a lot of miles between him and the Missouri authorities. He wandered across Illinois, Indiana, Ohio, and much of Pennsylvania before finally thinking about his second goal, which was to find work so he could have extra money to send home, both to his mother and to Luana, whom he thought would probably be in Nauvoo by this time.

Work was difficult if not impossible to find, even during harvest time. While most farmers would let a man work for his food, Port could not find a single farm where cash wages were paid.

After passing through the Amish farming communities near Lancaster, he finally ended up in Philadelphia, where on the second day he found a job that paid cash and all the food he wanted.

And so Port began a short but exciting career as a dishwasher at the London Flame Restaurant on F Street. Port responded to a sign in the window and was promptly hired after introducing himself as James Brown from Illinois. His wages were four dollars a week, with two dollars being taken out to cover the cost of his sleeping room and a place for his horse in the barn. The fee included a forkful of hay for Bill every day, and Port was entitled to any leftover food returned on restaurant patrons' plates. He was assured the pickings would be good because many rich women ate at the restaurant but did little more than pick at their food, returning most to the kitchen. Of course, Port had to share the leftovers with two waitresses, a busboy, and a cook. He was to be on hand seven days a week to keep dishes washed from the beginning of breakfast at seven o'clock until dinner was over at nine o'clock.

Port was hired by the owner, a tall, thin man with receding black hair combed straight back with lots of grease and a bad habit of biting his fingernails when someone was talking to him.

Port tried to appear attentive as the restaurant owner showed him how to wash dishes, how to make a swirling clockwise motion across the front of the plate with a soapy dish rag, how to always check the bottom of the plates and glasses for bits of food, and, most important of all, how to clean between the tines on a fork.

The owner made it clear that Port was to do whatever the cook said. He was also to take orders from the two middle-aged women who waited on the tables. Last, he was to do whatever the twelve-year-old boy said. The gunfighter from Illinois was at the bottom of the pecking order.

Port could hardly believe he had agreed to do all this for only two dollars a week, but until something better came along, at least he would be able to send some money home to his family.

It seemed odd to him that the man who had learned gunfighting from Sylvester Pussy was now taking orders from a boy. It seemed strange that the man who had shot the former governor of Missouri was now being bossed around by two women who waited on tables, a cook, and a cleanup boy.

As Port went to work, the owner explained that the cost of broken plates and glasses would be deducted from Port's weekly pay.

The first night began as a busy one, with a delegation of state senators and representatives and their wives due any minute. Port rolled up his sleeves, put on an apron, and went to work cleaning up a few dishes left over from lunch.

He soon learned why his job was so important to the restaurant. There were not very many plates and glasses. The boy brought the dirty dishes into the kitchen, Port washed them, and then one of the women would return them immediately to the dining room.

No one seemed particularly interested in conversing with the new dishwasher, and that was all right with Port. The less anyone knew about him, the better.

Everything was fine until about halfway through the evening. Port spilled some mint jelly from one of the plates onto the floor. Fortunately, he caught the largest glob square on the toe of his left boot. He was so busy sloshing the plates clean that he decided to wait until later to clean the jelly off his boot.

The next time he looked down at his foot, just to make sure the jelly was still there, he jumped back with a start, breaking one of the plates on the edge of the sink.

The largest gray rat Port had ever seen was licking at the green jelly while looking fearlessly up into Port's face with shiny black eyes. Port kicked at the rat but missed. The rodent disappeared beneath the sink.

The next time the owner passed through the kitchen, he noticed the broken plate and coldly reminded Port that a dollar would be deducted out of his first week's pay. Port wanted to protest about losing half his pay over one lousy plate, but he said nothing. He determined to be more careful.

A minute later the boy told Port to get the lead out of his pants, that he was not washing fast enough. Port felt like tossing the little runt through the door, but he didn't. He just tried to work faster, until he accidentally rolled two glasses against each other, breaking both of them. Now he figured he would be working the first week for nothing.

As he was fishing the broken glass out of the sink, Port happened to look down. The huge rat was cautiously licking the last of the mint jelly off his boot. Carefully, Port reached for a meat cleaver that was hanging on a peg near the back of the sink.

The cleaver felt more comfortable in his hand than a dishrag. With a flick of his wrist, the cleaver flashed downward. There was a loud thunk as the blade sunk into the soft pine floor about an inch in front of Port's boot. The poor rat hadn't seen it coming, and suddenly his head was separated from the rest of his body by the thick, heavy blade.

"The new dishwasher killed Rudolph!" the cook shouted to the women, who rushed into the kitchen to see. "Wow," said the boy when he arrived.

The only one not impressed with Port's quickness was the owner. All he saw were the two broken glasses, a cleaver buried into his expensive floor, and Port using a new dishrag to wipe up a pool of red rat blood.

"Stupid farmer," the owner yelled. "One more stunt like this and you're through! Understand?" Port nodded that he did.

"In fact," the owner continued to yell, "one more broken dish and you're through."

Port had never been yelled at like that before. He felt like punching the man in the nose. Instead he asked a question.

"How much will be taken out of my pay for the glasses?"

"Twenty-five cents for each glass," the owner snapped back.

Port returned the cleaver to its peg and resumed washing dishes, realizing he had already used up three-fourths of his weekly take-home pay, and it was only the first night. By the end of the week, he'd probably owe the man so much money that he couldn't afford to quit.

Between the cook and Port, there was a table where the cook placed the plates of food when they were ready for the women to take into the dining room. The next time the cook had his back turned, Port reached over and placed the rat's head on top of a generous portion of mashed potatoes and gravy. With his forefinger he pushed the head downward, just far enough so the little black eyes could not be easily seen staring upwards from the pool of gravy.

A short minute later, one of the women carried the plate into the dining room. Port continued to wash dishes, patiently waiting for the disturbance that was sure to come.

He didn't have to wait long. There was a loud scream, followed by the sound of crashing furniture and breaking dishes. As the cook and boy rushed to the dining room to see what had happened, Port ducked out the back door and hurried to the stable, where he gathered up his things, threw the saddle on his horse, and disappeared into the night.

Port continued his journey eastward into New Jersey, searching for work that paid money but not finding any. Fall turned to winter.

He didn't so much mind the cold because he could always burrow inside a haystack for a warm night's sleep. He didn't terribly mind the lack of jobs because he could always find a farmer who would give him a square meal for a couple hours' work. He didn't mind being among new faces in new towns and not being recognized.

What he did mind was the loneliness. He missed his little girls and his son. He missed Luana, even the frequent arguments they never seemed to be able to avoid. He even missed the pretty Mrs. Davis at the tavern.

As much as anything, Port missed Nauvoo and Joseph. The young prophet was making history. The kingdom of God was being established. The city of Zion was being built in the wilderness with a new temple on a hill. Hundreds of foreign converts were arriving every month. A new law of marriage that included polygamy was being established. All of hell, including the entire state of Missouri, was combining forces to stop the Mormons—while Port was in New Jersey looking for a two-bit job, missing possibly the greatest series of events of the nineteenth century. He longed to go home.

By the time February and its hint of spring arrived, Port could stand it no longer. Ignoring the reward posters, he headed for the Erie Canal and home, deciding he would just have to take his chances with the Missouri law. He figured that even jail couldn't be any worse than the lonely wanderings of the past few months. How wrong he was.

# Chapter 25

"Hands up," said a gruff male voice. Port knew he was in trouble. He was on the last leg of his journey home, riding a Mississippi steamboat from Cairo to Nauvoo. Feeling bold, he had decided to go ashore during a stopover at St. Louis. He had a Bowie knife in his belt and a pistol in each pocket. Slowly, he raised his hands over his head.

"That's him. That's him," said a second voice, belonging to a man named Elias Parker. He was a saddle and tack salesman who had seen Port at Cyrus Ward's place in Independence.

"My name is Fox," said the first man, who had moved up close to disarm Port. "Aim to collect a big reward and don't much care if you are dead or alive." Port didn't move while Fox removed both pistols and the Bowie knife.

"That's him. That's him all right," the second man repeated.

As they started across the dock toward the city, Fox walking behind Port with a loaded pistol, Port stopped a black deck hand he recognized. He handed the barefoot youth a fifty-cent piece, telling him to make sure Port's horse, the tall bay, got off the boat at Nauvoo and was delivered to Joseph Smith. "Tell him Rockwell was arrested at St. Louis," Port said.

"Yassir, yassir," shouted the barefoot boy as he ran toward the waiting boat.

"What about the reward?" Parker asked Fox as they resumed their short walk to the county jail.

"Aim to collect every penny," Fox said.

"And split it with me?"

"If and when I collect the reward, I'll send you ten dollars."

"But the reward is three thousand dollars," Parker protested. "If I hadn't seen him, we wouldn't have caught him."

"We didn't catch him," Fox said, an annoyed tone to his voice. "I caught him. I disarmed him. And I am taking him to Independence. I'll be paying his stage fare and buying his meals. I am risking my time, my money, and perhaps my life. You saw a face and reported it. That's all. I'll have earned every penny of that reward by the time I get this man to Independence. Still, I'll send you the ten dollars. Give me your address."

To Port's amazement, Parker bought the argument, pulling a piece of paper from his pocket and writing down his address for Fox. Parker then disappeared down a side street. Port never saw him again.

"I hope I remember to send him the ten dollars," Fox laughed. They resumed their walk to the jail. There was enough contempt in Fox's voice that Port doubted Parker would ever see the ten dollars.

"When this is all over, I think I'll become a bounty hunter," Port said. "A man could live pretty decent on one or two catches every ten years or so."

"When this is all over, I think you'll be hanging at the end of a rope and won't need any bounty," Fox responded.

Port spent the rest of the day in the St. Louis county jail, stretched out on a straw mat, contemplating what he guessed might be a miserable future. He decided he would be a cooperative prisoner, always kind and helpful but continuously on the lookout for avenues of escape. If an opportunity presented itself on the way to Independence, he intended to take full advantage.

No sooner had Port gone to sleep for the night than he was awakened by Fox, who had purchased two stage tickets to Independence. The coach was scheduled to leave within the hour. The night jailer helped Fox secure iron shackles to Port's ankles.

An hour later Port was shoved into a big overland stage coach with seven other passengers, including two women. Before the coach began its journey, Port had an escape plan. During the all-night ride everyone would certainly go to sleep. When they did, he would quietly open the door and jump out. Perhaps no one would notice.

It was as if Fox had read his mind. As soon as the coach began its journey, Fox made a speech. He introduced his prisoner to the curious passengers, who had noticed the shackles. "This is Joe Smith's Destroying Angel, the man who shot the former governor of Missouri in the back of the head. He'll slit a baby's throat or rape an old woman without blinking. Just thought you folks ought to know who is traveling with you."

Port wanted to object to the lies about him but didn't figure he would be believed, so he remained silent.

"One more thing," Fox added. "I need some shut-eye, so I would appreciate it very much if some of you could keep an eye on this killer while I sleep. In fact, if you'd like to keep him awake for me I'd be grateful. Like to keep my prisoners too tired to escape."

Fox pulled his hat over his face and went to sleep while the other seven passengers stared coldly at Port, who realized there was no longer any chance of jumping out the door unnoticed. Every time he tried to close his eyes, the man behind him jabbed Port in the back with a fist in an effort to keep him awake.

After several hours the stage stopped unexpectedly. The driver yelled down that he would be right back, that he needed something to cut the dust. There was a tavern beside the road. When the driver returned he had a bottle in his hand. The coach resumed its journey.

Less than a mile down the road, the now drunk driver guided the lead span of horses into a big oak tree, the force of the collision jerking three of the horses off their feet and overturning the stage.

Finding himself in a tangle of shouting, squirming people and total darkness, Port began to feel about, hoping to get his hand on a gun or knife. When one of the women screamed, he tried to be more careful.

Eventually everyone scrambled out of the coach. Port helped untangle the horses while Fox kept a close watch on him. While the male passengers were debating what to do about a sheared kingpin, Port climbed into the boot and found a spare. Working together, the men pushed the stage back on its wheels. The unconcerned driver climbed back upon his seat, and the stage was again on its way, until the driver guided it into an embankment. The driver was thrown to the ground, unconscious, and several of the horses were momentarily stunned. This time the coach remained upright.

The passengers readily accepted Port's offer to drive on the condition his shackles would be removed, but Fox flatly refused to do it. With his shackles still on, Port climbed into the box and drove the stage to Jefferson City on the Osage River, where he was promptly thrown in jail until a new driver could be found. Port was rapidly losing any hope that there might be a chance to get away from Fox.

When the stage arrived in Independence the next day, it was apparent that news of Port's pending arrival had preceded it. An angry mob of several hundred citizens was gathered at the depot to greet Port.

Some carried ropes. Others held hickory sticks.

Sheriff Reynolds was waiting when the stage door opened. He had a shotgun in one hand and a pair of irons in the other. As soon as the shackles were secured to Port's wrists, the sheriff turned to the crowd, cocked back the hammer on his shotgun, and demanded a passage be opened through which his prisoner could pass. Reluctantly, the mob responded.

As Port hurried toward the jail, hundreds of people were shouting at and cursing him. Some were crying to "lynch the murderer." He was grateful for the protection of Reynolds and Fox.

What surprised Port most of all was the presence of children in the mob, scampering here and there among the safety of the adults, cursing, spitting, and throwing rocks.

Shooting Boggs had made him a hero and defender of the faith in Nauvoo and a despicable villain in Independence. One thing he knew for sure was that his life as a quiet, unnoticed person was over.

The Boggs shooting had changed the way people looked at him, both in Nauvoo and Independence. The privacy and anonymity he had once enjoyed were gone forever.

With Reynolds in front and Fox in the rear, Port was dragged and shoved through the heart of the angry mob. He wished Joseph could see him now and know the price he was paying for defending the kingdom.

Once inside the jail, the door shut safely against the mob, Reynolds led Port to a second-story cell. Without removing the shackles, he shoved Port inside and locked the door. The only furniture in the cell was a pile of urine-soaked straw in one corner. Port walked over to the single window with bars and cautiously looked out. The grumbling mob was beginning to scatter. He wondered how long it would take for news of his capture to reach Nauvoo. He also wondered how long it would take for him to return to Nauvoo, if at all.

Two days later Port was brought before a justice of the peace who ordered that he be held without bail. As Port and the guard hurried back to the jail, they saw the mob out in force again, some of the men carrying hickory sticks. One had a rope. The cry was unanimous, "Lynch Rockwell."

# Chapter 26

The first few weeks in jail, Port had the distinct feeling that the main purpose of the bars and locked doors was to protect him from the mob rather than confine him, and that Sheriff Reynolds was his protector more than his keeper. Every day groups of men of varying sizes would gather in front of the jail. They would stand around talking and looking up at Port's window. Some of the men carried hickory sticks. Once in a while one had a rope.

While these men never got beyond the talking stage, it was perfectly clear what they wanted to do—get Rockwell. Whenever the sheriff or one of the deputies would leave the jail, the men would make their demands, always the same, that Rockwell be delivered to them so they could administer true Missouri justice. Port watched it all from his second-story window.

But with time, the groups grew smaller and smaller, and life in the jail became more routine, less interesting. Port had a lot of time to reflect. He thought back on Joseph's confinement in Liberty Jail, seeing many similarities but one big difference. Whereas Joseph had been confined with half a dozen friends, Port was alone and had no one to confide in.

Other prisoners were ushered into the cell from time to time. Port would sometimes ask those who knew how to read to read to him from old newspapers. But he didn't have anyone to confide in. He became more lonely every day.

Port thought a lot about the shooting. He was sorry he had done it. He still thought Boggs had deserved killing. He just didn't like the way the shooting had happened—in the back of Boggs's head with his family nearby. Port wished he could tell someone how he had felt sorry the moment he had done it. He wished he could tell the judge how he had held the gun in the rain until there was no way it should have fired, but it did.

But he knew better than to say anything. The only evidence they had against him was circumstantial. He had been seen in a gun shop from which the weapon that shot Boggs was stolen. They didn't have anything else, and Port was determined not to help them find any new evidence.

The food in the Independence jail was no better than that at Liberty. Port received his meals twice a day, the fare usually consisting of cold corn dodgers sprinkled with leftovers from the jailers' plates—never very much. He was always hungry.

He was cold most of the time too, at least the first few weeks until spring began to give way to summer. There was no source of heat in the basement dungeon or in the second-story cell. Sometimes the only way to keep warm was to pace back and forth in his cell for hours at a time, and that only made him more hungry.

One afternoon Port was sitting by the barred window overlooking the alley between the jail and the neighboring house when he noticed a black servant girl walking up the alley. He guessed her to be about twelve years old. She was a thin girl, still at the awkward age but healthy. She wore her hair in two long, black braids. She was wearing a clean homespun dress.

The girl had a handful of rock candy and was picking out the larger pieces and popping them in her mouth. Looking down at her open hand as she walked, she was unaware that Port was watching her.

"That candy looks mighty good," Port said when she was directly below his window.

She looked up in surprise, quickly closing her hand and hiding the candy behind her back. She had a guilty look, like she wasn't supposed to have the candy.

"Don't worry. I won't tell," Port said, grinning at the girl.

"You won't?" she asked, obviously not trusting the man behind the bars.

"Nope, I won't. And you don't even have to give me some of the candy either."

"I don't?" she responded. "What's an ol' jailbird like yoself want with candy anyways?"

"Oh, I'd enjoy it more than you could ever know."

"Why's dat?"

"Because all they feed me everyday is cold corn dodgers. I'd let 'em cut off a finger for a handful of candy."

"You would?"

"A man gets powerful hungry for something good when all he gets is cold corn dodgers every day."

"You wanna piece of my candy?" she asked. Port tried not to sound too eager.

"If you can spare a piece, sure."

"Sho you won tell de missus?"

"Cross my heart, hope to die."

Slowly, the girl removed her closed hand from behind her back. Opening her palm, she looked down at the candy. Carefully picking out one of the larger pieces, she tossed it up to Port, who was reaching through the bars with both hands. He caught the candy and popped it into his mouth. He closed his eyes in delicious ecstasy, totally enjoying his first sweets since entering the jail.

When he opened his eyes, the girl was looking up at him, a happy grin on her face.

"I'd forgotten how good candy could be," he said. "Thank you very much."

"Yer welcome," she said, tossing up a second piece, which Port promptly popped in his mouth. "Umm, umm," he mumbled. She put another piece in her mouth, and they dined together.

"What's your name?" Port asked, when they were finished.

"Violet," she said.

"That's a very pretty name, Violet. You're as pretty as you are kind."

She looked down, embarrassed but obviously pleased at having received such a nice compliment from a white man.

"Giving me that candy was the nicest thing anyone has done for me since I returned to Missouri," Port continued. "Violet, I thank you from the bottom of my heart." Port could feel a tear beginning to form in the corner of his right eye. He had never felt such feelings of gratitude toward anyone in his life. Violet turned and ran back to her house.

She was back the next day, tossing up a small ball of yarn and a thin willow stick from which Port fashioned a crude fishing pole. From that moment on, his diet improved substantially. Every day and sometimes twice a day, Violet appeared beneath his window. When he lowered the string, she would tie on an apple, a piece of fried chicken, a cold pork chop, or a freshly baked biscuit with honey inside. Sometimes her little brother, Bo, came with her. He was six, stocky and strong, with short kinky hair. He loved to watch his sister feed the prisoner.

One day in June, Violet arrived with her apron pockets full of fresh corn dodgers filled with butter and currant jelly. Port had just finished gulping down the first one and was watching Violet carefully wrap the string around the second when he was suddenly aware that he was not alone in the cell.

"What in hell is going on here?" Reynolds demanded. The sheriff was standing a few feet behind Port, whose first concern was not to get Violet in trouble. He had to think of something fast.

"What's going on here?" Reynolds shouted.

"Those cold corn dodgers you feed me are not fit for human consumption," Port growled, turning slowly to look at the sheriff. The willow fishing pole was still in Port's hand.

"But they make excellent bait. I'm fishing for pukes. Haven't caught any yet. Just the niggers are nibbling."

Reynolds walked over to the window, looking down just in time to see Violet running down the alley. He pulled the string up far enough to see the corn dodger tied on the end. He turned and walked toward the far side of the room. Port pulled up the string and removed the corn dodger, which he placed on the window ledge. Then he tossed the stick and string onto his bed of straw. He was amazed the sheriff was letting him keep the pole and line. Apparently Reynolds had other things on his mind.

"How would you like to make a pile of money?" Reynolds asked.

"Sure," Port said, cautiously, having no idea what Reynolds had in mind.

"How would you like to get out of here and go home?"

"I would like that a lot."

"Get Joseph to meet you out on the prairie. That's all I ask. Do that and you can name your pile."

Port now understood what Reynolds wanted. The sheriff was offering him freedom and money to betray the best friend he'd ever had. Port felt like kicking Reynolds.

"You could write him a letter," Reynolds continued. "Tell him you are free and have to see him. Tell him a place, anywhere between here and the Mississippi River. That's all. We'll take care of the rest."

"A letter from me would raise suspicion," Port said. "Joseph knows I can't write."

"Someone else could write it for you."

"What makes you think I would betray the best friend I ever had?" Port snarled, his voice getting high and out of control.

"I figured anyone who could shoot a man in the back in front of his wife and kids wouldn't find it very hard to pull a fast one on a friend, if the price was right," Reynolds said. "I'm offering you freedom, and you can name your pile."

Port turned away. The sheriff's words had hurt. He realized the Boggs shooting would probably haunt him for the rest of his life. He turned back to Reynolds, his voice normal again.

"I will not help you trap Joseph," he said.

"Then I'll just have to do it myself," Reynolds said. "But if you change your mind, let me know." He turned and walked out of the cell, slamming the door firmly behind him. Port yearned to be free, to be in Nauvoo protecting his best friend.

# Chapter 27

A few days later, the heavy oak door to the cell swung open and Port was introduced to a new cellmate, a young, chubby fellow. He was dressed well, in a dark suit. There were no shackles on his hands or feet. Port was still wearing the same ankle shackles he had worn during his trip from St. Louis to Independence.

The young stranger carried a pair of saddlebags over his shoulder. To Port's surprise, the jailer didn't take them before leaving and locking the door behind him.

"The name's Watson," the young stranger said, reaching out to shake Port's hand.

"They didn't take your saddle bags," Port said when introductions were finished.

"I'm not dangerous," Watson said. "Just circulated a few fake treasury notes. But I've heard of you. They call you the Destroying Angel."

"What's in the saddle bags?" Port asked.

"Personal belongings."

"Like what?" Port demanded.

"See for yourself," Watson responded, dropping the saddlebags to the floor. "I could use a little shut-eye. Think I'll rustle me up a bed." He dropped to his knees and, using only his hands, began scraping together a pile of straw upon which he intended to take an afternoon nap. Port picked up the saddlebags and spilled the contents on the floor in front of him.

Port could hardly believe his good luck. There were two fire steels and a gunflint. "Can I have these steels?" he asked, picking them up.

"As long as you don't set the straw on fire," Watson answered as he settled down for his nap.

"Don't aim to start any fires," Port said, dropping to the floor and striking one of the steels against his irons. "Just aim to get out of here. Thank you for bringing the key."

"Don't cut through those irons too quickly," Watson yawned. "The deputy kept me awake all night bringing me here, and before I get involved in any escape attempt, I'm going to get some sleep." He laid his head back on the straw, and a short minute later was snoring, apparently not disturbed by the steady clicking of the flint striking against Port's ankle bracelet.

By the next morning, Port's fingers were bloody and blistered, but the incessant clicking continued. The link connecting one of the bracelets to the chain was cut nearly all the way through, and Port had a good start on the other. When the jailer brought breakfast, there was plenty of straw about the shackles, so the damage wouldn't be noticed.

Watson had finally awakened after about a thirteen-hour sleep. He was impressed with the progress Port had made on the shackles. But he wasn't impressed with the cold corn dodgers they had been served for breakfast.

"After seeing the breakfast they serve here, I think your desire to escape is well founded," Watson said after they started gnawing on the hard corn dodgers. "If you succeed, where will you go?"

"Back to Nauvoo," Port said.

"That's not very far from here," Watson said. "Wouldn't they come after you?"

"Arrest papers from Missouri don't have much success in Nauvoo," Port explained. "Mormon judges may be a little flagrant in their use of habeas corpus, but no one is ever brought back to Missouri legally."

"Will you take me with you?"

"Sure will," Port said, "and maybe I'll make a Mormon out of you too. Do you know much about the Mormons?"

"Only that they don't get along with their neighbors."

"Believe me, that isn't all the Mormons' fault."

"What do you believe?"

"I'm no preacher, but when we get to Nauvoo, I'll take you to Joseph. He'll tell you the whole story, how he saw an angel who showed him the gold plates."

There was a tapping sound coming from outside. Port got up and sauntered over to the window, motioning for Watson to follow.

"Looks like the real breakfast has arrived," Port said. "Want you to meet a friend of mine." He introduced Watson to Violet, who had brought a basket of fresh biscuits.

As Port was raising the biscuits to the window with his fishing pole, he told Violet he needed a knife.

"No," she said. "The missus will miss it."

"Got to have a knife," Port persisted.

"I can't," Violet said.

"You've got to," Port said as he removed the last biscuit from the basket.

"Perhaps this will change the young lady's mind," Watson said. He tossed a hundred dollar bill into the basket. Port stared in amazement.

"You can't give a hundred dollars to a slave girl," Port said.

"Thought you wanted a knife. With that she can buy several dozen or more."

"But a hundred dollars? I've never seen so much money at one time in my whole life."

"Don't worry," Watson said. "There's plenty more where that came from. I can make one in a couple of hours."

"It's counterfeit?"

"Don't be so surprised. Why do you suppose I was selected to share this suite with you?"

"But it looks real," Port said.

"You can flatter me all you want, but I'm still going to give it to Violet."

"Don't want to get the girl in trouble."

"The people who make the bills go to jail," Watson explained, "never the people that accept them as legal tender. I'm living proof of that." Port lowered the basket.

"Never had a dollar before," Violet said when she removed the bill from the basket.

"It's a hundred dollars," Port explained. "Don't let the missus get it from you." Violet shoved the bill in her apron and turned to leave.

"Don't forget the knife," Port whispered through the bars.

The next morning as the guard entered the cell with the usual breakfast of cold corn dodgers and water, he noticed that the shackles were no longer on Port's feet. He started to say something, but it was too late. Port kicked the guard's heels out from under him, pouncing on top as the man went down. When the jailer started to resist, he found a knife at his throat. He decided to hold still. Port tied the man's hands behind his back and shoved a cold corn dodger in his mouth to stop him, at least temporarily, from shouting.

Port and Watson charged through the open door. Port slammed it shut and shoved the bolt home by turning the key in the lock. He removed the key and tossed it out the hallway window. As they raced down the stairs, they suddenly found their way blocked by the jailer's overweight wife. She was as surprised as they were and a lot more frightened.

Port shoved his hand over her mouth as she opened it to scream.

"Your husband is all right," Port explained. "I locked him in the cell and tossed the key out the little window by the door. You don't need to scream. Find the key and let him out."

The woman expressed her willingness to do as Port said by nodding her puffy face up and down. Port let go of her. He and Watson squeezed past, resuming their race toward the back door. The woman began screaming.

Neither Port nor Watson had ever seen beyond the back door of the jail. If they had, their plan of escape would have been different. They suddenly found themselves in a back yard enclosed on three sides by a twelve-foot board fence with a locked gate.

With the jailer's wife screaming that they had escaped, there was no turning back. Port jumped on a barrel, which enabled him to reach the top of the fence. Using all his strength he pulled himself up and over, urging Watson to follow.

Port dropped to the ground on the outside and was racing for the woods when he realized that Watson had not yet reached the top of the fence. Port hurried back, calling through the fence to Watson, urging the young man to hurry.

"I can't pull myself up," Watson replied, sounding like he was nearly in tears.

"Try again," Port urged.

"I have, but I can't do it" was the desperate reply.

Port looked toward the woods less than a hundred yards away. There was no time to lose. He could hear the woman's screams inside the jail. He could hear excited shouts in the street from people who realized something was wrong in jail. Should he leave, or should he help Watson over the fence? He must decide quickly.

Port scampered up a small tree that enabled him to get on top of the fence. Hanging on with his leg and one hand, he reached down to take Watson by the hand. It took all the strength of both men to finally wrestle Watson to the top of the fence. Then they both tumbled to the ground outside the yard. Scrambling to their feet, they began running to the woods.

But it was too late. People were hurrying toward the jail from every direction to see what was the matter. Someone saw Port and Watson and sounded the alarm. Reynolds raced around the corner of the jail and up the alley toward his two prisoners.

Watson could not keep up with Port and soon stopped. Port realized he had grown soft from the confinement. His lungs were on fire. His legs were turning to rubber. His old strength was not there. He could hear Reynolds rapidly gaining, but he could do nothing to go faster.

When Port felt Reynolds's hand on his shoulder, he collapsed in the dirt. Fighting for air, he didn't have the strength to resist the firm hand. Reynolds pulled Port to his feet and shoved him toward the jail. Somehow Port managed to keep his feet under him.

The sheriff was rough and impatient, pushing Port ahead whenever he thought the prisoner was going too slow. They marched past Watson, who was on the ground still catching his breath.

When they reached the front of the jail, a sizeable crowd had gathered. Some had already begun a chant to lynch the Destroying Angel. The angry sheriff dragged Port through the crowd, giving a hard shove to anyone who got in his way. Port braced himself against the insults.

They were stumbling up the front steps of the jail when the sheriff suddenly stopped, turning to face the mob.

"So you want to lynch him," Reynolds said. There was a loud cheer.

"Here he is. God damn him. Do what you please with him," shouted Reynolds, shoving Port down the steps into the waiting mob.

Port suddenly found his second wind. Clawing, kicking, and slugging like a desperate animal, he somehow managed to work his way free, to earn a little space and inch his way toward the jail wall until his back was against it. He was facing the enemy, his rear secured.

"I'll kill the next man that touches me," he snarled.

The half-circle of cursing mobbers stayed out of reach, not wanting to incur Port's wrath. With nothing more than sheer ferocity, he had gained some breathing room. But what should he do now?

A Mexican wormed his way through the close bodies to where he was facing Port. There was a coiled lariat in the Mexican's hand. Slowly, he began uncoiling it. The two men's eyes were locked on each other.

"Just try it," Port snarled. "I'll rip off your testicles and shove them down your throat. Then I'll mash your damn face in."

The Mexican stopped but did not back away. Port, with his back against the wall and the mob in front of him, simply didn't know what to do. He only knew that he would not go willingly to the gallows. Someone called for someone else to get a gun.

Finally, it was Reynolds who came to the rescue. Pushing roughly through the mob, the big sheriff grabbed his prisoner by the collar and started toward the front door. Reluctantly, the mob made room for the sheriff and his prisoner to pass.

With the door shut safely against the mob, Reynolds went to his desk, where he retrieved a pair of brand new iron shackles out of a bottom drawer.

Without a word, he slapped them on Port's ankles and then pushed Port down the ladder into the basement dungeon.

A few minutes later, Watson followed but without shackles. The two were no longer allowed into the upper cell, which meant no view of the outside and no treats from Violet.

A few days later, the jailer allowed Watson to come out of the dungeon. Port never saw the young man again. Without companionship, the dark dungeon was doubly oppressive.

In addition to being dark, it was a cool place, too cool. Port was always cold, except when he paced the floor, not an easy task with shackles on his ankles.

Port studied every inch of his cell. Stone by stone, he studied the floor and walls. He moved his hands over every inch of the huge logs that made up the ceiling. He was looking for something loose, something that could be moved or cut. He became consumed with the need to escape. There was nothing else.

In one corner there was an old stovepipe extending upward through the ceiling. Apparently, at one time prisoners had been allowed to burn charcoal in a can beneath the stovepipe.

Though the hole itself was too small for a man to squeeze through, Port discovered—mostly by feel because the light was so poor—the original hole that had been cut through the logs was quite a bit larger. It had been cut larger purposely so the heated pipe would not catch the logs on fire. The pipe was surrounded by several inches of clay, which had become dry and brittle and with a little effort could be cracked away.

Port went to work chipping the clay, using his spoon as a tool. As the pieces of clay fell to the floor, he trampled them with his feet until there was nothing but fine powder, which he spread across the floor. If the guards looked, they would see nothing. To avoid being heard, Port did most of his work at night, when the guards were gone. Sometimes guards slept in the jail, but usually they all went home for the night, making it possible for Port to make all the noise he wanted, as long as he couldn't be heard outside the jail.

Finally, Port was ready to escape. He waited one night until he figured the guards and Reynolds were all safely asleep in their beds. Carefully, he worked the stove pipe loose, lowering it to his cell. After chipping away the last few pieces of clay, he tried to worm his way up into the hole.

Progress was difficult. Not only was he working against gravity, but the hole, even with the clay out of the way, was still too small for most men. He couldn't quite squeeze through, no matter how hard he tried. Had he not been on a diet of corn dodgers and water, he wouldn't have had a chance. But along with the pounds, he had also lost much of his strength.

Dropping back to his cell after three or four tries, Port started running around the cell as fast as he could go. He ran until he began to sweat. Then, suddenly stopping, he ripped off his shirt. Once more he wormed his way up into the hole, hoping the sweaty bare skin would allow him to slip through more easily. It worked, and in a few minutes he crawled onto the floor of the jail office where the guards bided their time during the day.

The doors to the front street and rear yard were locked. Port hurriedly searched through drawers, boxes, and coat pockets. He could not find a key anywhere. Apparently the jailers took them all home.

He did, however, find a piece of wire, and he proceeded to fashion a key of his own to pick the lock to the front door. He fiddled for several hours with the wire in the keyhole. It was beginning to get light outside. He was running out of time.

Finally, he knew that if he was not going to get caught, he'd better return to his cell. With the help of gravity, it was easy dropping back down through the hole to his cell. Carefully, he put the stovepipe back in place, hoping the guards would not notice the missing clay. When the guards entered the jail that morning, Port was lying exhausted on his pile of dirty straw, determined to try again the coming night.

Getting through the hole the second night was more difficult. Port just didn't quite have the strength to push himself all the way through. The heavy shackles on his ankles didn't help any. He tried again and again, feeling his arms get weaker each time he failed. His naked body was black from the soot of the chimney and streaked with the red of his own blood from cuts caused by the jagged edges of the logs.

He didn't know where the strength came from, but finally, using every last ounce of energy, he wiggled once more into the jail office. Getting his wire, he resumed picking at the front door lock. He had picked locks before, but this one must have had some different workings, because he simply could not get the bolt to move.

This time he didn't notice the first light of morning, so determined was he to conquer the lock. It didn't help that his hands were shaking. He could hardly keep his knees from buckling. He began to feel dizzy. The room began to spin.

When the jailers entered the jail that morning, they found their prisoner unconscious on the floor—naked, black, and streaked with blood.

By the time Reynolds arrived, Rockwell had been revived with a bucket of cold water. Without a word, the sheriff walked over to the drawer and pulled out a second pair of shackles. When he was through, Port had one shackle connecting his left wrist to his right ankle, and the other connecting his right wrist to his left ankle. The chains connecting the bracelets were not sufficiently long to allow Port to stand up straight.

"Let's see you crawl through the hole now," Reynolds growled.

Crouched over like an ape, Port shuffled toward his basement cell. Behind him he could hear Reynolds ordering the guards to cut his rations in half.

In the weeks to come, Port crouched in the corner of his cell mustering all his strength just to hang on and fight the cold, which never seemed to go away now. He no longer disliked cold corn dodgers, devouring them like a starving wolf. With shackles on both wrists, the only way he could reach his mouth to feed himself was to sit against the wall and curl into a tight ball.

Port could no longer reach his hair at all. Without care, it soon became a matted wad of greasy filth. Sometimes he spent hours trying to follow the travels of lice in their search for food across his scalp—a task that became impossible as the number of lice increased.

With the shackles on his hands and feet, the sanitary handling of his bathroom functions became impossible. While his own smelling senses were deadened, he knew anyone coming to his cell from the outside would be sickened by the stench.

Port knew he was losing weight because the shackle bracelets that had once been too tight on his wrists could now slide to his elbows. The once powerful muscles in his arms and shoulders were gone, replaced by white skin stretched tight over sinew and bone. He could feel gaping crevices between his ribs.

His body was shriveling up, wasting away, except for his hair. It seemed to thrive in the jail cell, growing longer and longer. His beard now reached below his bottom rib when he tried to sit up straight. The matted, filthy wad on his head extended to the middle of his back.

Port longed for blazing sunshine, a cozy fire, a hot bath, and a warm woman. He started to cry one afternoon when he realized he couldn't remember what a steak tasted like.

He wondered why there had been no trial. He had been arrested for shooting a man. They should find him guilty or innocent. Why did nothing happen, week after week? Where was Luana? Why didn't she visit him or write? Why wasn't Joseph trying to get him out? Had something happened to the prophet?

Port wondered how he would survive come winter. He was cold all the time, even when he tried to exercise. Could he live if the cell became any colder? Would he ever be allowed to talk to anyone again? Was God punishing him for shooting Boggs in the back of the head?

He lost track of time. He didn't know what day or week it was, not even which month. He only knew that winter would be coming soon, and the cold would get him if something didn't change.

One day the door flew open, the sudden burst of light forcing Port to close his eyes.

"The nigger girl brought you a present," the guard said, tossing a brown bundle toward Port and quickly slamming the door before anymore of the wretched smell escaped.

Carefully, Port unwrapped the bundle. It was a coat, a cougar-skin coat, worn and ragged, but still a coat, and a warm one at that. The shackles prevented him from putting it on, so he stretched it over his shoulders. The warmth was wonderful. Then he noticed a lump in the right pocket. He felt inside and found a big, red apple.

Pushing it to his mouth with both hands he began biting and chewing like a wild man. He devoured the apple, the core, the seeds, and the stem. Then he licked the juice off his hands and wrists.

Port discovered a second apple in the left pocket.

This one he took more time with, savoring every bite. He thought he could feel the strength from the apple surging into his bloodstream and flowing to his arms and legs. He was filled with a tingling sensation. Suddenly, he felt stronger, more alert, and certainly more happy. He was forever in debt to Violet, the slave girl.

Two days later, one of the guards removed his shackles, telling Port to go up the ladder to receive a visitor. As Port crawled into the upper room, he looked up into the alarmed face of his mother, who began to cry when she saw her son.

"Mother, I'm all right," Port lied. He was fighting desperately to control the emotion surging in his chest. "I've lost a little weight, and I need a bath and a shave, but I'm fine. It's good to see you. If you can stand the smell, I would like a kiss."

She flew into her son's arms, the two hugging each other for a long minute. Then, sitting beside one another on a bench, she explained that Joseph had raised two hundred dollars for Port's defense. Not daring to come to Missouri himself, the prophet had sent the money with her. She had given it to General Doniphan, who agreed to take the case. She was planning to stay in Independence until the matter was resolved. She handed Port a bag of oatmeal cookies to take back to the dungeon.

Suddenly, life had become very good. As Port returned to his cell, for the first time in weeks he dared hope that soon he might be free.

# Chapter 28

Port's next visitor was Alexander Doniphan, who had provided legal services for many of the Saints who were driven from Jackson County in 1833. Doniphan had also been an officer in the state militia that marched on Far West to drive out the Mormons in 1838, but he had redeemed himself in the eyes of the Saints when he successfully put a stop to an order by another officer to have Joseph executed by firing squad. Doniphan had been a hero to the Mormons ever since.

Doniphan was a tall, good-looking man, well dressed and well schooled. Rather than enter the smelly dungeon, he arranged to have the prisoner brought to him in the upstairs cell.

Port was grateful for any excuse to get out of the dungeon. With his chains clanking along the floor, he shuffled to the upstairs room. He noticed, through the window by the stairwell, that the leaves that were only buds when he entered the jail were turning colors and beginning to fall. He had spent an entire season in the jail.

Doniphan explained that a special term of court had been arranged, and it would convene in several days. To Port's surprise, the charges against him had been changed from attempted murder to attempted jailbreak.

"There was simply nothing in the Boggs shooting upon which they could build a case," Doniphan explained. "But they don't want to let you go, so they have invented this thing on attempted escape."

"Why have I been in jail all this time if they don't have anything against me?" Port whined, his fists clenched in anger at the injustice that had been heaped upon him.

"They think you shot Boggs, so they keep you in jail, hoping something will turn up so they can press charges," Doniphan explained. "But nothing has turned up."

"How long can they keep me on the attempted escape charge?" Port asked.

"I don't know how they can keep you beyond the end of the trial, not with me representing your interests. Legally, they can't keep you any longer." Then Doniphan looked Port square in the face and asked, "Did you shoot Boggs?"

"The question people usually ask is if Joseph ordered me to do it," Port responded, without looking away. "Joseph is the one they really want, not me. My answer to that question is no, he did not order me to do it. Enough said."

"Don't give up hope," Doniphan said in parting. "Soon you'll be a free man."

It didn't happen as quickly as Doniphan said it would, but in time Port, in chains and rags, was taken to the courthouse. With Austin King presiding, he was found guilty of attempted jailbreak and sentenced to five minutes in the county jail.

On the morning of December 13, 1843, Port walked out of Independence Jail a free man. He was greeted by his mother and Alexander Doniphan. The lawyer offered Port his hand and a warning.

"There are some old citizens who don't intend to let you leave the state alive," he said. "They figure to finish what the law didn't. If I were you, I'd get out of Independence in a hurry. I wouldn't let anybody know which road I was taking. I'd travel at night and hide out during the day."

Port thanked Doniphan for the warning. Then he let his mother take him to the home of a widow who was preparing his first real meal in nine months—fried chicken, mashed potatoes, gravy, stuffing, and green beans. Port ate until he thought his insides would burst, thanking the woman every few bites.

He asked his mother how Luana and the kids were getting along. She said they were fine and then changed the subject. He didn't guess until later that something might be wrong.

Getting up from the table, Port changed into some clean clothes his mother had brought for him, including a pair of boots. It felt good to discard the filthy rags that had not been washed or changed in nine months. The only thing he didn't discard was the cougar-skin coat Violet had given him.

The widow offered to prepare a hot bath for Port, but he declined. Being free felt awfully good, but with it came the concern for safety. He believed what Doniphan had told him. His life was in danger. He had no time for luxuries like baths. Nor did he have the time to visit Violet and thank her for the kindnesses she had shown him. He asked his mother to do that.

After borrowing four dollars from the widow and stuffing his pockets with fried chicken and biscuits, Port headed north toward the river. His mother would follow a few days later. No one would bother her. Port's intention was to cross north over the Missouri River and put as many miles as possible between him and Independence before dark.

He was following a lane northward through a grove, just after crossing the river, when he heard two horses approaching at a fast trot. Quickly, he concealed himself behind a tree.

"He hasn't been gone many minutes," one of the men said to the other as they approached the tree where Port was hiding. "We'll soon overtake him."

When they were out of sight, Port headed into the trees in search of a more secluded route.

After nine months in a jail cell, Port found walking difficult, and he tired quickly. Frequent rests would have been nice, but he couldn't afford such luxury, at least not until he had put many miles between him and Independence. Soon there were blisters on his feet. He continued walking. The blisters popped. He continued walking. His feet became raw. He continued to place one hurting foot in front of the other, mile after mile, long into the night.

Sometime in the middle of the night, he buried himself in a haystack. The total exhaustion from the miles of walking overshadowed the pulsating pain in his feet, and he fell into a deep sleep, the thick, dry hay keeping him warm against the December night.

The next morning the muscles in Port's back and legs were so sore he didn't know if he could stand up straight, and when he finally did, the pain in his raw feet shot through his legs with such force he doubted if he would be able to take a step.

But Port was too close to Independence, even closer to Liberty. If he were discovered, his enemies would flock to him like buzzards to a carcass. He had to keep moving, and he had to keep off the main roads. With nothing more than sheer force of will, he forced himself forward, trying desperately to ignore the pain. Still, he was happy. The freedom to move, to breathe fresh air, to feel the sun and wind again, even in December, were supreme blessings. To drink out of a spring, to look at the trees, the sky, the birds, even to feel his muscles working hard, were blessings he had nearly forgotten.

"Feet must be pretty sore," a strange male voice said. Port looked to his right. A large man in a buckskin jacket was walking toward him through the woods. Port could hardly believe he hadn't seen the man sooner. He told himself he must have lost some of his alertness during the long months in jail. His first thought was to run, but as sore and worn out as he was, he didn't figure he could outdistance the man, who strode through the woods with the ease and strength of one who could travel many miles without stopping.

The stranger was grinning and didn't appear to have a gun. Port sat down on a fallen log, nodding for the stranger to join him. "The name's James Brown," Port said, offering his hand to the man, who appeared much larger up close than he had at a distance.

"My name's Frank. Going over to Crooked River to help my sister put in a store of firewood for the winter," the stranger said, his speech slow and his words slightly slurred. He had not been drinking.

"Got any money?" Port asked, suddenly getting an idea. The stranger seemed extremely strong, and from his slow speech, not very smart.

"Nope."

"Want to earn fifty cents?"

"Would like to," Frank replied, "but got to be to my sister's by nightfall."

"You can earn the money while walking to your sister's."

"You're joshing," Frank laughed. "How could I earn money walking to my sister's house?"

"Carry me on your back. I'll pay you fifty cents to take me to Crooked River."

"Why would you do that?" Frank asked, a smile on his face. It was obvious the big man was not taking the offer seriously. Clenching his jaw against the pain, Port carefully removed one of his boots, showing Frank the bloodstained sole of his foot.

"Got me a job starting in Montrose next week," Port explained. "Can't get there on these bloody feet. Until I can rent a horse, I'd be more than happy to rent a big strong feller like you."

"Crooked River is only a dozen miles or so," Frank said thoughtfully. "Be glad to oblige. Hop on." He stood up and turned his back to Port, who quickly pulled his boot on and climbed on Frank's back, much like a child climbing on his father for a piggyback ride.

Port had lost a lot of weight in jail. Frank marched along with such ease that Port guessed the big stranger had the strength of a mule.

"How come you were over here in the woods and not traveling the main road to Crooked River?" Port asked.

"Ma tole me to stay off the roads. The Destroying Angel is on the loose."

"The Destroying Angel?"

"The Mormon that shot Mr. Boggs."

"You mean Porter Rockwell."

"That's him. A mean son-uv-a-bitch."

"Do you know what he looks like?" Port asked.

"Never seen him. But they say he has eyes like the devil and is muscled up like a bull. Carries two pistols and a Bowie knife. Rides a big stallion."

"Good thing the two of us are together," Port said, totally enjoying the conversation. "Better chance he'd leave us alone if he saw us."

"As long as we stay off the main road, don't think we'll run into him," Frank said.

"Good."

Port kept waiting for Frank to stop and rest, but the big fellow kept trudging along, effortlessly taking big strides. Frank was a happy man, simple but happy. Port was thoroughly enjoying the trip, though his legs were beginning to go to sleep. Compared to the lonely confinement of jail, this was paradise.

Frank's pace didn't slow until they came to a long hill. Port could feel the big muscles straining. Frank's shirt was getting wet with sweat.

"If you want to stop and let me cut a willow, I could use it to help you along," Port said, wondering if Frank would be quick enough to pick up on the attempt at humor. Frank began to laugh.

"Or even better," Port continued. "Stop at the next cabin and I'll borrow a pair of spurs." Frank laughed harder.

"Maybe a saddle too," Port continued. "Hell, with a man like you, who needs a horse?" By now Frank was laughing so hard he had to stop and catch his breath.

When they sat down on a log to rest, Frank pulled a large wad of oilcloth from his pocket. Inside were four boiled eggs and a huge chunk of salt pork between two thick slices of bread. Enjoying the cool but comfortable December sunshine, the two men shared the lunch.

"Could I suggest something?" Frank asked when they were finished.

"Sure," Port said.

"You ever thought about taking a bath?"

"Soon as I get to Nauvoo—I mean, Montrose," Port said. Both men began to laugh again as Port climbed onto Frank's back for the final leg of the journey.

Port spent the night at Frank's sister's place, sleeping in a bed for the first time in nearly nine months. He paid Frank seventy-five cents, and the sister fifty. After breakfast, as Frank and his sister's husband disappeared into the woods to gather wood, the nine-year-old son saddled the family's only horse and carried Port ten or twelve miles farther east.

And so the journey continued, Port renting rides when he could and walking the rest of the time. For fifty cents, most nights he could get two meals, a bed to sleep in, and a ten-mile ride the next morning.

When Christmas Eve arrived, Port was still about twenty miles from Montrose, where he hoped to catch a ferry across the Mississippi River to Nauvoo. He had only fifty cents left, just enough to get him on the ferry. Unable to afford another night's lodging, he continued on through the night, thankful his feet, except for a few lingering sores, had healed. While the night was clear, he guessed the cold wind from the west was blowing in a storm.

He arrived in Montrose on Christmas morning. The wind was blowing harder now, and the sky was covered with thick, black clouds. Port was weary from the all-night march, but more than rest, he needed food. He hadn't eaten since the previous morning. He was tempted to spend his last fifty cents on a hot breakfast. He pushed the thought away, saving the last of his money to board the waiting ferry. There would be food in Nauvoo.

After a wait that seemed like hours, the ferry finally pushed from shore into the heart of the river, now raging with white-capped waves. Port leaned on the railing, looking down into the black water, knowing that if the boat capsized, he would not have the strength to swim to shore. He decided that in the event the boat did sink, he would not fight. He would just relax, sink to the bottom, and provide a happy meal for the catfish.

In the meantime, he needed something to feed himself before he fainted from lack of nourishment. Entering the ferry's cabin, Port spotted a man sleeping on one of the benches. On the floor in front of the man was an apple core, apparently fallen from the man's hand while he was sleeping. When no one was looking, Port snapped up the core and popped it in his mouth.

The boat didn't capsize, and as Port walked down the plank onto the Nauvoo dock, he felt like dropping to his knees and kissing the ground. He hoped someone would be there to meet him, perhaps Joseph or Luana and his children. But there was no way they could have known he was coming. He didn't see anyone he recognized.

With the wind continuing to blow and the snow beginning to fall, the streets of Nauvoo were deserted. With Christmas day coming to an end, there was no reason for people to be out.

Pulling the cougar-skin coat tight around his shoulders, Port headed for the Mansion House. He knew Joseph would want to see him, even on Christmas. Joseph would give him food, perhaps even a bed.

The storm became a blizzard, with the snow so thick in the air that one could hardly see the houses along the streets. Still, Port didn't have any trouble finding the Mansion House, painted white with green shutters, with lamps on the gateposts. Light was coming from every window. A dozen or more carriages were parked in front, the horses already white from the raging storm. Port could hear music. It appeared the prophet was having a party.

Walking up the steps, Port remembered that he hadn't had a bath in nine months, and even though he had changed into fresh clothes only twelve days earlier, the shirt was torn and the trousers soiled from the long journey across Missouri.

But he had come too far to turn away. It was too far to his own partially finished cabin. And he didn't know if Luana would be there. Without knocking, he opened the front door of the Mansion House and stepped inside.

Port recognized most of the faces—Brigham Young, Thomas Marsh, Sidney Rigdon and his daughter Nancy, Wilford Woodruff, Emma Smith, Agnes Smith, Amos Davis, and finally Joseph, on the far side of the room. The prophet looked well and strong, laughing as he conversed with Stephen Markham. Port started toward Joseph.

"What do you want?" demanded a stranger, suddenly stepping in front of Port.

"Came from Missouri to see Joseph," Port answered coolly.

"He's busy, so you can leave now."

"I'll see Joseph first."

Port felt a surge of pride—and he didn't know why—that prevented him from identifying himself. He felt offended, that in spite of his long hair and lost pounds, his friends did not recognize him. Without another word, he pushed forward toward the prophet.

"Get that filthy puke out of here," someone shouted. Men were grabbing at Port from every direction. A woman screamed. Twisting and turning to avoid being grabbed, Port continued to work his way toward the prophet.

But there were too many people trying to stop him. Port found himself stretched out between two men, one holding each arm. A third man, Brigham Young, was about to punch him in the stomach when the unmistakable sound of Joseph's voice filled the room.

"Stop," the prophet shouted. "I'll throw this rascal out myself." Joseph approached quickly, his stride firm and confident. He was grinning in eager anticipation of the approaching scuffle. Without breaking stride, Joseph removed his coat, and by the time he reached Port, he had rolled up both sleeves.

"Let him go," Joseph ordered, still not recognizing his friend. Port felt his arms drop to his sides. He looked the prophet square in the face, still not saying anything.

"No," the prophet said, his voice suddenly growing faint. "It couldn't be. It is. Orrin Porter Rockwell."

The two men embraced each other. Port felt wonderful. His best friend, the prophet, recognized him after all.

"But you have so much hair," Joseph said, holding Port at arm's length to get a good look. "Such a long beard. You could use a good meal or two. And my, how you smell. It's good to see you again, friend."

Joseph and Port seated themselves on a bench, and others gathered around as Port quickly related the events of the last year—his arrest, his confinement, his release, and the journey back to Illinois. Joseph commented several times on Port's long beard. Emma brought Port a cup of apple cider and two cakes, which he gulped down.

"I'm going to give you a blessing," Joseph said when Port had finished his story. Joseph turned sideways on the bench and, without standing up, placed both hands on Port's head.

"I prophesy in the name of the Lord," he began, his voice firm and clear, "that you, Orrin Porter Rockwell—so long as you shall remain loyal and true to thy faith—need fear no enemy. Cut not thy hair and no bullet or blade can harm thee!"

Joseph said "amen" and removed his hands from Port's head. Someone whispered something about Sampson, the Old Testament prophet who received a similar blessing.

"Does this mean I shouldn't shave either?" Port asked, not intending to make light of what the prophet had said. On the contrary, he was deeply moved by the blessing and was fighting to hold back the emotion that was welling up inside.

"I prophesied in the name of the Lord as moved by the spirit," Joseph responded. "You interpret it the best you can."

"Thank you," Port said.

"What now?" Joseph asked.

"Food, sleep, and a bath. Thought I'd go home to Luana."

"She's in Independence," someone said. Port was confused. How could Luana be in Independence? He had come from there. She had not visited him in jail. Surely she would have done that. Then he remembered the dinner at the widow's house in Independence and how his mother hadn't wanted to talk about Luana. He had thought nothing at the time. Now he knew something was wrong.

"We have an extra room over at the tavern," a strange voice offered. It was Amos Davis, owner of the inn where Port had stayed after shooting Boggs.

"Mrs. Davis will fix you up," Amos continued. "She hadn't finished the cleaning, so I left her home tonight." Several of the women gave Amos strange looks, but neither Joseph nor Port noticed.

After shaking hands with some of the people and answering a few more questions, Port headed out the door. He was desperately in need of food and rest. Nine days of constant travel, nearly two days without a meal, and one night without sleep had finally caught up with him. With the storm blowing in his face, and his knees beginning to shake, he didn't know if he could make it to the inn.

He noticed the increasing cold and didn't have the strength left to shiver. It occurred to him that he should return to the Mansion House. If he collapsed in the street, he would not be found until morning. By then he would be cold and dead.

But Mrs. Davis would be at the tavern. He would rather be with her than back at the party. He remembered her pretty face, her warm conversation and friendly smile. He didn't even know her first name, but suddenly he wanted to be with her.

Port forced one foot in front of the other. He could feel his leg muscles beginning to cramp from weariness and cold, but he refused to lose control. He willed his feet to keep moving, one in front of the other, over the snow-covered ground. He didn't have far to go. He just had to keep walking for a few more minutes. Then he could collapse, and Mrs. Davis would take care of him.

The ground began to reel. Port's stride became unsteady, like that of a drunken man. More muscles were trying to cramp. It was as if his muscles were begging him to stop, to quit, to relax and give up. There had been too much suffering, too much pushing. There was nothing left to push. His whole life was boiled down into one thought, one effort: that of making one foot place itself in front of the other. Nothing else mattered.

The storm was a hungry monster, licking away his warmth faster then he could produce more. The cramping worsened until he finally collapsed, his legs in knots, just a few feet from the front door of the tavern.

The fall jarred him to his senses enough to know that if he didn't get inside he would die. His legs were useless now. Ignoring the pain from the cramping muscles, he pushed forward with his arms, inching his way through the soft powder snow until he could reach out and touch the door.

Again, his life boiled down to two simple alternatives. Knock or die. He reached out with his bare fist and thumped the base of the door. It was all so simple. Just keep knocking until someone opened the door or until the cold killed him. All of his remaining strength focused on one hand motion—thump, thump, thump.

# Chapter 29

The next thing Port remembered was the pretty face of Mrs. Davis looking down at him as she dragged him over the threshold into the tavern, firmly slamming the door against the storm.

"Thank goodness you're alive," she said, noticing that his eyes had opened. Her voice was calm and soothing. "Can you get up?"

"Cramps," Port muttered. "Cold." She knelt beside him, feeling his hands and neck with her warm, firm hands. She began kneading the muscles in his legs until he could straighten them out. She helped him to his feet. With his arm over her shoulder for support, she guided him into the kitchen.

"If I could just get into a warm bed," Port began to say, but she had ideas of her own. After seating Port on a chair by a red-hot rattling cook stove, Mrs. Davis pulled a copper bathing tub into the center of the room and proceeded to dump four buckets of hot water into it.

"Lucky for you I was getting ready to take a bath myself," she said. "The water is already hot."

When the bath was ready, she walked over to Port, removed his coat, then began unbuttoning his shirt. He tried to push her hands away.

"Look here," she said. "Another minute on the porch and you'd have been a dead man. Right now, getting warm and clean is more important than preserving your delicate modesty." She proceeded to unbutton and remove his shirt, then his boots and socks, then his trousers and underwear. Ported wished she were fat or old. He hated for a young, beautiful woman to see him like this, so filthy and skinny. But she wouldn't be denied.

"Now that you have my underwear off, could I ask you a question?" Port asked.

"Of course," she said, standing close to him, looking into his eyes.

"What's your name?"

"It's Sarah, but people call me Cora," she said with a smile, guiding him over to the tub and helping him step inside and sit down. At first the water burned. Then it felt deliciously warm. Port leaned back and closed his eyes.

Cora handed him a glass of whiskey and then began pouring hot water over his head and shoulders. She rubbed soap in his hair and beard, then over his back and shoulders. Her hands were firm yet gentle. Port hoped she would never stop.

Cora ran over to the stove to drop a big red steak into an already hot frying pan. She returned to rinse Port's hair with fresh water. She continued rubbing more suds over his back.

There were warm, tingling sensations in Port's arms and legs as the feeling returned. The warm water was reviving his body quickly. He felt good.

"My first bath in ten months," Port said between sips of whiskey.

"I believe you," she said, continuing to rub his back, gentler and slower now. The aroma of frying steak was filling the room.

"Joseph talks about how wonderful the celestial kingdom is," Port said, the whiskey beginning to loosen his tongue. "I don't know how it could be any better than this."

"I could get in with you," she said matter-of-factly. Port began to flush. Then she blushed too. "I shouldn't have said that," she said. "Sometimes I speak before I think. I'm sorry."

"If you did, Luana would probably walk through the door," he said. They both began to laugh. Port was trying to think of something to say to change the subject. He didn't want to think about her last comment. Sensing his uneasiness, Cora hurried to the stove to get the steak.

She pulled the chair over to the tub, seated herself, and began cutting off pieces of pink juicy meat sprinkled with plenty of salt and pepper, feeding Port while he relaxed in the hot water.

"Want me to give you a shave?" she asked.

"I'm never going to shave again," he said, telling her about Joseph's blessing and prophecy.

"Do you believe him?" she asked when he had finished. Port thought a minute before answering.

"Yes," he said. "Joseph is a prophet."

"Even when he talks about polygamy?" she asked, feeding Port the last piece of steak.

"Why do you say that?" he asked.

"Because Amos wants to take a plural wife," she said, "and he says it's all right with Joseph. I don't like it." She stood up and threw the plate into the dishpan. The plate broke.

"Is that why you didn't go to the party tonight?" Port asked.

"Yes. Agnes was going to be there. She's the one he wants to marry."

"Agnes Smith, Don Carlos's widow?" Port asked.

"That's the one. Poor, pretty Agnes. I used to love her. Now I hate her. Maybe that's why I was so forward with you tonight. I wanted to hurt Amos. I'm sorry."

"The only thing that happened tonight is that I was dead and now I'm alive. And you're the one who saved me. Thank you, Cora."

"Do you feel strong enough to dry off and dress?" she asked.

"You don't want to do it for me?" he asked. She threw a towel at him.

"There's clean underwear and pajamas on the table by the door," she said. "I'm going upstairs to prepare your bed. The first room on the left at the top of the stairs is yours. I'll get a down quilt for you." She turned and left the kitchen, closing the door behind her.

Port climbed out of the tub, rubbing his pink, warm skin with the soft towel. Slipping into the underwear and pajamas, he allowed himself to yawn deeply. He hurried out the door and up the stairs. Nodding his gratitude to Cora, he slipped beneath the down quilt, buried his head in the big, soft pillow, and closed his eyes. By the time Cora blew out the lamp and closed the door he was sound asleep.

# Chapter 30

"Your enemies are my enemies," Port responded when Joseph asked him to become his bodyguard. They were seated at a table in an upstairs room of the Mansion House. Emma, who was preparing to depart for St. Louis on a furniture-buying expedition, entered the room briefly from time to time, asking Joseph about her trip or telling him something about the care of the children while she was gone.

Joseph told Port why he needed a bodyguard. First, Nauvoo, now a frontier river town, had attracted a lawless element—counterfeiters, murderers, and thieves who brought others with them, including prostitutes and gamblers. Joseph had plans to clean up the city by reorganizing the police force and hiring forty new policemen, a number unheard of in frontier towns at that time. He knew there would be resistance to his efforts to clean up the town and that there might be attempts to harm him.

Second, Joseph was getting ready to announce his candidacy for the presidency of the United States. "But why?" Port asked. "You can't win."

Joseph explained that his purpose in running was to earn more political respect for the Mormons. He said the Illinois legislature was considering withdrawing the Nauvoo charter, an act that would dissolve the Nauvoo Legion and remove all political and judicial power now enjoyed by the Saints in Nauvoo. In running for president, Joseph would be in the news throughout the United States.

With increased public attention, he hoped the Illinois legislature would feel more reluctant to withdraw the Nauvoo charter. Joseph also felt that the increased attention would infuriate some of his old enemies, especially those in Missouri, which was another reason for Rockwell's protection.

Joseph was more cautious in explaining the third reason. He watched the door closely, changing the subject whenever Emma entered the room. The young prophet said he had received a revelation and written it down. It concerned the new and everlasting covenant of marriage and included the plurality of wives. Joseph explained that some of the church leaders had already taken plural wives, while others had rebelled against the new commandment. Some of the women who were asked to become plural wives had accepted, while others were openly offended and were now talking about it all over Nauvoo.

While the women were discussing plural marriage over back fences and quilting frames, the men had a different reaction upon discovering that there was substance to the rumors of plural marriage. They either went to Joseph asking to be included, or they joined the rapidly growing opposition force of formerly devout members. The opposition, which included several former members of the Quorum of the Twelve Apostles, was sufficiently strong that Joseph feared for his life. He felt much more threatened by his former friends and followers now organizing against him than he felt threatened by his old gentile enemies outside Nauvoo.

"Your enemies are my enemies," Port said again.

"But I don't know how I'm going to pay your salary," Joseph said, explaining that building a new city demanded all available cash.

"I've got an idea," Port offered. "How about me opening a barber shop across the street? I could earn my money cutting hair, I could keep up on the local gossip, and would be close at hand if you needed my protection."

Joseph began to laugh.

"What's funny?" Port demanded. He had given the barber shop idea a lot of thought. It was a good idea, certainly not a funny one.

Joseph apologized for laughing, explaining that it just struck him funny that the only man in Nauvoo who did not shave or cut his hair now wanted to offer those services to others. Still, he thought it was a great idea.

The two men got up from the table, went downstairs, and put on their coats. Joseph called to Emma that she wouldn't have to cut his hair anymore, that Port was going to build a new barbershop across the street. Walking across the muddy road, Joseph and Port began marking the corners of the new building in the crusty snow.

"If something's afoot I might get wind of it early," Port said. "There's a lot of talk in a barber shop."

"You'd hear more of what was going on if you were selling whiskey," Joseph added.

"Why not make it a barber shop–bar combination?" Port asked, getting more excited about the venture all the time. "It would be the busiest place in town, and if you ever needed protection, I'd have a ready-made posse. I'd just have everybody turn in their glasses for guns."

"Great idea," Joseph said. They made new corner markings, doubling the size of Port's new business establishment.

"Won't be able to build until spring," Port said as they walked back to the Mansion House. "What'll I do in the meantime? I don't have a nickel to my name. I'm staying at Davis's on credit."

"By the way, how is Cora?" Joseph asked.

"As beautiful as ever. A little upset with Amos though."

"Why's that?"

"He wants to take a plural wife."

"Do you know who?"

"Yes. Agnes, your brother's widow."

"He and about twenty more of the brethren have the same idea. Want to be let in on a little secret?"

"Sure," Port said, not sure he really did.

"Agnes is already someone else's plural wife."

"Are you sure?"

"Yes. But don't tell."

"I won't."

"Do you want to know who?"

"Not particularly."

"Good. You're catching on," Joseph said. "When we get out west all by ourselves, everyone will know who is married to whom. In the meantime, I suppose the great Nauvoo guessing game will continue. Now we've got to figure out how you can support yourself until your new building is finished."

As they entered the front door of the Mansion House, Joseph suddenly stopped, looking about the entry hall like he'd just had a brilliant idea.

"We'll do it here," he said. "The bar, the barbershop—you can do it all right here until the new building is finished. Lots of people come to see me. You can sell them a drink and a trim while they wait."

"The glory of God is intelligence," Joseph began, and Port wondered why the subject had been changed. "Or light and truth," Joseph continued. Emma had entered the room. Apparently Joseph didn't want her to know what the two men were discussing.

"There's no way she'd go for it now," Joseph said when she was gone. "But when she gets back from St. Louis and can see how it's all working, with everything in place, she'll agree that it is a good idea."

Joseph instructed Port to go down to the general store and charge all the supplies he'd need, including spirits, glasses, scissors, aprons, dishpans, and brooms. But he cautioned Port not to bring anything back to the Mansion House until the steamer had departed, with Emma aboard.

Joseph and Port's business venture was profitable from the start. While there weren't many requests for trims, Port kept very busy filling glasses. Word spread quickly through Nauvoo, and by the end of the first day, Port had a steady clientele. Business was so good he hired the Smith children to keep the glasses washed and the floor swept for a nickel a day.

By the end of the first week, Port had paid the bill on the start-up materials he had charged, caught up his bill at the inn where he was staying, paid the Smith children, and still had over five dollars in clear profit.

Ten days later, when Emma returned from St. Louis, she wasn't as receptive to having a tavern in her front room as Joseph had anticipated. She only needed one look at the crowd of men drinking and her children off in one corner washing glasses. She marched Joseph into the kitchen, slamming the door behind her.

Even with the door closed, Port could hear pieces of her excited monologue. "This is our home," she said. "We raise our children here. I'll not live in a tavern."

Port knew enough about Emma to know that once she had her mind set on something and had taken a stand, there was not much even the prophet could do to turn her around. Port announced the bar was closed and began packing his things.

# Chapter 31

In December Joseph reorganized the Nauvoo Police Department with forty new officers. Nauvoo had become the most lawless city on the frontier, and he was determined to put a stop to it.

In January Joseph announced his candidacy for president of the United States. In running, he hoped to draw nationwide attention and sympathy to Mormon problems in Nauvoo.

In February Joseph uncovered a plot for his own assassination by insiders. He believed those involved included William and Wilson Law, Chauncy and Francis Higbee, Joseph Jackson, and Dr. Robert Foster. Port was by Joseph's side continually.

In March Joseph unleashed scathing indictments against the conspirators, hoping to frighten them off. Those conspirators who had membership in the Church were excommunicated.

In April Nauvoo had its first public performance, a play called "Pizarro." Port played the part of Davina, a Spanish soldier holding a spear—a real one. In the event anyone tried to bother Joseph, who was seated in the front row, Port was ready to run them through.

In May Dr. Robert Foster received shipment of a new printing press. Not only did those opposing Joseph refuse to leave, but they were now preparing to publish their own newspaper. The Mormons had been the subject of much critical press over the years, but the attacks had always come from the outside. Now, those who had been on the inside, in positions of authority and responsibility, were going to start publishing.

The feeling of anticipation was intense among both the faithful and the apostates. The presidential campaign, at least in Nauvoo, was nearly forgotten in anticipation of the new anti-Mormon newspaper getting ready to go to press. Joseph spent more and more time out on the prairie, riding Joe Duncan, his big black stallion, usually accompanied by Port. Joseph needed time to think, to weigh alternatives, to sort things out—time to prepare his mind and heart for the tragic, history-making events he knew were about to transpire but didn't know how to avoid.

One afternoon, after leaving Joseph at the Mansion House following a long ride on the prairie, Port was walking down to the general store when he ran into Chauncy Higbee, one of the editors of the new paper. Higbee was a large, husky man, too large about the middle from too much time behind a desk and too little exercise. His hair was mostly gone and his cheeks were pink and smooth like the hindquarter of a pig. He wore a new white shirt.

"Rockwell, I would like to speak to you for a moment," Higbee said.

"Only if you have something kind to say about the prophet," Port responded, not in the mood to give ear to the heaps of criticism men like Higbee were piling on Joseph.

"Your prophet is a kind and gentle man," Higbee began, "and I believe he received the gold plates from a heavenly messenger."

"Then why do you persecute him?" Port asked.

"Because he can't distinguish feelings of sexuality from the spirit of the Lord," Higbee said. "He's allowing both kinds of promptings to chart his course, and he's not able to tell the difference."

Port turned to leave.

"Wait," Higbee said. "Why do you think I stay here? Do you think I would remain if I didn't love the gospel, its mission, and its members?"

"You can't love the gospel and hate the messenger that brings it," Port said, stopping and turning to face Higbee a second time.

"Can't you see it?" Higbee asked. "The man who spoke face to face with God, who translated the Book of Mormon, who restored the true gospel—the man that did all that can't keep his trousers buttoned up!"

Port wasn't aware of making a conscious decision to act. He only knew that someone he loved was threatened, and he reacted instinctively. His left hand shot forward, grabbing the collar of Higbee's clean white shirt before the stubby man could step back.

Now that the subject of his wrath was held firmly in place, Port felt his right fist closing and the muscles in his right arm and shoulder stiffening. The fist shot forward, crunching against the apostate's side, then his face. The man fell like a stunned ox in a semi-conscious heap upon the ground. Port turned and walked away. He didn't understand the polygamy issue. He only knew that Joseph was his friend and that his mission in life was to defend and protect him.

On Friday, June 7, the first issue of the *Nauvoo Expositor* rolled off Foster's new printing press. The carefully worded editorial called for separation of church and state, rejection of political revelations, repeal of the Nauvoo city charter, freedom of speech and worship, and an end to the gross moral imperfections of the spiritual wife system.

Any hopes Joseph had of winning friends and support though his presidential campaign were shattered by the *Expositor*. The former claims of John C. Bennett about the Nauvoo spiritual wife system had been suspect because of Bennett and his background. The new accusations, by former leaders of the Church who still believed the Mormon Church to be true, were accepted as truth. At last, the world knew beyond any reasonable doubt that the Mormons led by Joseph Smith really were practicing polygamy or something like it.

Anti-Mormons began to assemble in Carthage, where most members of the Law, Higbee, and Foster families had taken up residence in recent days. The subject of discussion was how to get rid of "Holy Joe." The anti-Joseph rallies resulted in petitions to the president and governor and legal charges that never survived the habeas corpus veto of the Nauvoo municipal courts.

The Nauvoo city council met Monday, June 10, and passed an anti-libel ordinance carrying a penalty of six months in jail and a five hundred–dollar fine. The council remained in session, finding the *Expositor* publishers guilty of abusing the poor, printing bogus money, and having illicit sexual relations. The council declared the *Expositor* and its publishers a public nuisance and finally ended the day's business by ordering Marshall Greene to destroy the press and arrest anyone who resisted his efforts.

It was eight o'clock, already dark, when Port and Joseph followed Greene and seven deputies down Main Street to the Expositor office.

Higbee and Foster met the delegation at the door, the two publishers quickly stepping outside and locking the door behind them.

"Give me the key," Greene demanded.

"No," Foster said. He asked to see a search warrant, which Greene did not have.

An argument ensued, with Greene insisting he be given the key and Higbee and Foster refusing to turn it over.

"Let them keep the key," Port said, when it appeared the argument was not nearing an immediate conclusion. Greene and the deputies looked at Port, obviously surprised at what they interpreted to be lack of backbone or persistence on the part of Joseph's bodyguard.

Port surprised them all by stepping up to the door, raising his right leg high, bending the knee until the heavy leather boot was close to his body, then striking forward with all his might. The pine door was no match for Port's boot. It was ripped from its hinges and crashed heavily to the floor.

"See, gentlemen, there is no need for a key," Port said.

The seven deputies entered the building and began wrestling the heavy press into the street. Once outside, a safe distance from the building, several men began beating the press with hammers, while others went back into the building, bringing out armfuls of copies of the *Expositor* that had not yet been distributed and trays of type, which were dumped upon the ground around the damaged press.

Finally, the type and equipment were soaked with three or four gallons of coal oil. Port struck a wooden match on the heel of his boot and tossed it into the nearest puddle of fuel oil. As the Expositor press blazed its way into history books, Higbee and Foster were marched off to jail to answer charges of violating Nauvoo's new anti-libel ordinance.

The commotion created by the publishing of the *Expositor* was nothing compared to the uproar caused by the destruction of the *Expositor*. The people of Illinois had been embarrassed in 1837 when an abolitionist press belonging to Reverend Elijah Lovejoy was destroyed in Alton, Illinois. Lovejoy was killed in the attack. Afterwards, as people had time to think, there was a general feeling of regret statewide and a new determination that nothing like that would ever happen again in Illinois.

The Mormons had destroyed the *Expositor*, and the gathering mob in Carthage now turned its attention from petitions and legal proceedings to lynch justice. The mad prophet had to be stopped without delay.

A message was sent to Governor Ford, demanding executive powers be invoked to halt Joseph's legal powers in Nauvoo. At the same time, Joseph sent a letter to the governor explaining why the *Expositor* had been a public nuisance that needed to be stopped. The governor decided to visit Hancock County to see what measures might be taken to settle the conflict.

In the meantime, Joseph mustered the Nauvoo Legion and, so there would be no question about who was in charge, declared martial law in Nauvoo. Well trained and well armed, the Legion was the largest military force in Illinois.

Calling the Legion together at the Mansion House, Joseph walked across the street and climbed upon the just-completed plank floor of Port's new tavern–barber shop.

"Will you all stand by me to the death?" the young prophet shouted. "And sustain me at the peril of your lives, the laws of our country, and the liberties and privileges which our fathers have transmitted unto us, sealed with their sacred blood?"

"Aye," responded the troops in unison, the roar of their voices echoing through the City of Joseph.

"It is well," Joseph responded. "If you had not done it, I would have gone out there and would have raised up a mightier people." He was gesturing to the West.

"I call God and angels to witness," he continued, thrusting his sword to the sky, "that I have unsheathed my sword with a firm and unalterable determination that this people shall have their legal rights and be protected from mob violence, or my blood shall be spilt upon the ground like water, and my body consigned to the silent tomb."

Governor Ford arrived in Carthage on June 21, and after meeting with delegations representing both sides, demanded that Joseph come to Carthage at once to prove "the Mormons wished to be governed by law."

Joseph believed that going to Carthage would cost him his life, so he announced he was fleeing to the Rocky Mountains. The Saints could follow the next spring.

On Joseph's orders, Port located a small boat. Shortly after midnight on June 22, Joseph, his brother Hyrum, and Willard Richards crawled into Port's boat, which immediately began to leak. With three passengers to bail out the excess water, the boat remained afloat as Port rowed his friends across the wide Mississippi.

The next morning, while Joseph and Hyrum were busy planning their journey west, Port returned in the leaky boat to get horses and supplies.

As he stopped by the Mansion House to get some of Joseph's belongings, Emma made him wait while she penned a note to her husband. As she wrote, she made it clear to Port that she had changed her mind about her Joseph's decision to go west. She now thought it was a big mistake to desert his family and friends who so desperately needed him. She asked Port to please persuade Joseph to return.

The small boat could not ferry the supplies and horses across the river, so Port persuaded Amos Davis and Reynolds Cahoon to ferry him across in a large boat. Both men agreed with Emma, that Joseph should return.

Upon reaching the Iowa shore, Davis stayed with the boat and horses while Port and Cahoon approached the prophet. Cahoon promptly accused Joseph of cowardice, at which Port stepped forward to silence the man, but Joseph intervened.

"If my life is of no value to my friends," the prophet said, after reading Emma's letter, "it is of none to myself."

"What shall I do?" Joseph asked Port.

"You are the oldest and ought to know best. And as you make your bed, I will lie with you," Port responded, his jaw firm. Joseph then turned to Hyrum and asked the same question.

"Let's go back, give ourselves up, and see the thing through," Hyrum responded.

Joseph pondered what had been said for about an hour, the rest of the men just sitting around and watching him.

"If you go back, I will go with you," he finally said to Hyrum. "But we shall be butchered."

"The Lord is in it," Hyrum responded. "Whether we live or die, we must be reconciled to our fate."

"All right, Brother Cahoon," Joseph said. "If you'll tell Captain Davis to have the boat made ready, we will return to Nauvoo."

While walking down to the river, Joseph and Port lagged behind. Ignoring shouts from the rest of the party to hurry up, Joseph muttered, "It is of no use to hurry, for we are going back to be slaughtered. If only I could speak to the Saints one more time."

"If that is what you wish, I will get them together," Port said. "You can speak tonight by starlight." As they entered the boat, the others thought the speaking idea was a foolish whim, that it was best to get on with the business of settling the conflict.

After spending the night in Nauvoo, Joseph departed for Carthage. He was accompanied by his brother Hyrum, Willard Richards, John Taylor, and others. Joseph ordered Port to remain in Nauvoo in the event it became necessary for the Nauvoo Legion to march on Carthage to rescue him. Reluctantly, Port obeyed, though he rode the first mile or so with his friend before turning back.

Port knew that if he accompanied the prophet to Carthage he would be arrested and thrown in jail too. At least this way he was free to ride with the Legion, if rescue of the prophet became necessary.

Port heard Joseph remarking to those who were riding with him, "I am going like a lamb to the slaughter, but I am calm as a summer's morning. I have a conscience void of offense toward God and toward all men. If they take my life I shall die an innocent man, and my blood shall cry from the ground for vengeance, and it shall be said of me, 'He was murdered in cold blood.'"

Port returned to the tavern, where Cora joined him for breakfast. Amos was riding with Joseph to Carthage.

"What are you going to do now?" she asked.

"Wait, maybe get a little sleep. If Joseph changes his mind and wants us to get him out of there, I'll be riding with the Legion to rescue him."

"Do you think they'll try to kill him?"

"The mob will, but the state militia that came with the governor ought to protect him."

"How do you think it will all end?" she asked.

"We'll go west to the Rocky Mountains."

"Will Joseph be with us?"

"I wish I knew," Port said, excusing himself, getting up from the table, and heading for his room. He didn't feel like talking to anyone. He was worried about Joseph. Everyone was saying Joseph would be fine, that it probably would not be necessary for the Legion to intervene. What bothered Port the most was that Joseph had predicted his own slaughter. If the man was a prophet, why, then, was everyone so calm? Wasn't what he said supposed to come to pass? Port regretted that he had not insisted on riding with Joseph.

Port tried to sleep but couldn't. Finally, he got up and wandered down Main Street toward the Mansion, hoping to hear some news from Carthage.

"Rockwell," someone called from the shadows between two buildings as he passed the Expositor office. Port turned toward the sound of the voice, unable to recognize the man he could see standing there.

Stepping closer, Port rested his right palm on the butt of one of his pistols, just in case the stranger turned out to be enemy instead of friend.

It was an enemy, Francis Higbee, the brother of the man Port had knocked down a month earlier. Higbee was beginning to say something about Port having to buy a new press for the *Expositor.* Port continued to walk toward the man.

"After he's dead you'll know we were right," Higbee said.

"You seem fairly certain he'll be killed," Port responded.

"I know some things you don't know."

Without warning, Port's fist shot forward like a pile driver, striking Higbee square on the jaw. Higbee collapsed in a heap.

Port was about to turn to leave when he noticed Higbee's bowler hat rolling to a rest against the nearest building. Something white was flapping around inside. Port picked up the hat and looked in it. There was a piece of white paper, folded twice in half. Port opened it, regretting once more he had never allowed Luana to teach him to read. All he knew was that there was blue writing on the paper, some kind of message perhaps.

"Give me that," Higbee bellowed, suddenly coming to his senses. He began an awkward charge, not waiting for Port to answer his challenge.

Stepping back, Port braced himself against the charge. Cocking his right arm back he let it fly in a wide swinging arc, the timing just right to catch Higbee in the ear. This time Higbee didn't get up. Port hurried toward the Mansion to find someone who could read the note.

The council was meeting in the library when Port entered to give them the letter. After removing his hat and placing it on a table near the wall, Port handed the note to William Stout. The letter said seventy men were waiting on the Iowa side of the river for a signal to come across and attack Nauvoo. Immediate orders were given to send a detachment of one hundred legionnaires down to the shore, hoping the display of strength would discourage the Iowa mob. Forgetting to pick up his hat, Port began a slow, sauntering journey back to the tavern.

When the inn was in sight, he heard shouting from the east. Looking up the Nauvoo road, he saw several dozen approaching riders.

It appeared Joseph was coming home. Port wanted to shout with joy, but as the horses came closer, he couldn't see anyone who looked like Joseph. He soon recognized Governor Ford at the head of the group.

Upon entering town, the governor announced his intention to give a speech at the grove as soon as the Mormons could assemble. An hour later, the governor was speaking to several thousand concerned Mormons.

"A great crime has been done by destroying the Expositor press and placing the city under martial law," Ford said. "A severe atonement must be made, so prepare your minds for the emergency." A murmur ran through the crowd. What was he talking about? He should make himself more clear.

"Depend upon it," Ford continued. "A little more misbehavior from the citizens, and the torch, which is already lit, will be applied. The city may be reduced to ashes, and extermination would inevitably follow. It gives me great pain to think that there is danger of so many innocent women and children being exterminated."

The crowd was very sober now. It was as if their lives were in the balance. Ford's frequent use of the word *extermination* brought back familiar memories of Lilburn Boggs and the fall of Far West.

"If anything of a serious character," Ford concluded, "should befall the lives or property of the persons who are prosecuting your leaders, you will be held responsible."

There was a feeling of quiet desperation hanging over the crowd when Ford finally stepped down. Port wandered up Water Street, wishing Joseph hadn't ordered him to stay away from Carthage, wondering if he should ignore the order and follow Joseph.

He stopped by the Mansion House, remembering he had left his hat on the table in the room where the council had discussed the Higbee letter. The prophet's home was enough of a public place that he did not knock before entering.

"The deed is done before this time," someone was saying as Port stepped into the room, but the subject was quickly changed when they saw Rockwell. To Port's surprise, the governor and several associates occupied the room. Port apologized for disturbing them, picked up his hat, and departed. Haunted by what he had heard, he returned to the tavern. Before going inside, he went to the stable and saddled his horse, anticipating that at any moment word could arrive from Carthage for the Legion to ride to Joseph's rescue.

What he didn't know was that hours earlier the Nauvoo Legion commander, Major General Jonathan Dunham, had received a message from Carthage requesting he bring the Legion, but for an unknown reason Dunham had done nothing. Nor did he tell anyone else about the message, perhaps a result of Ford's speech.

Port paced the floor until long after dark, growing increasingly restless. He checked and re-checked the loads in his pistols. He sharpened his Bowie knife. Several times he went outside to check the saddle on his horse.

It was late into the night when Port finally decided he could wait no longer. Running from the tavern, he leaped upon his horse and galloped up the road toward Carthage. He had been on the road several hours, pushing his horse hard, when he heard a rider approaching from the direction of Carthage. Whether or not the man was friend or enemy wasn't so much a concern as whether or not the rider had news concerning Joseph.

"Who are you?" Port shouted, slowing his winded horse to a walk.

"George Grant," the approaching rider responded. Grant was a Mormon.

"Porter Rockwell here," Port responded.

"They have killed him," Grant shouted. "Joseph is dead."

"What happened?" Port demanded as the two men jumped off their weary horses.

"Just before sunset," Grant explained breathlessly, "Frank Worrell led the Carthage Grays on the jail. The guards just stepped aside. Joseph tried to fight them off, but there were too many. I think he was trying to escape by jumping out the window when he was shot in the back and chest at the same time. He fell from the second story window to the ground, where they sat him up against a wall and shot him again and again. He's dead. So is Hyrum. Taylor is badly wounded. Richards appears to be all right."

Port turned away, unable to think, unable to feel. "My horse can't go much further," Grant said. "There's nothing you can do in Carthage. You must take the news to Nauvoo. The Saints have to know."

Without another word, Port jerked his horse's head around and began the long journey back to Nauvoo.

It was just getting light when he spurred his jaded horse onto Main Street. "Joseph is killed," he shouted. "They have killed him! God damn them! They have killed him!"

It was June 28, 1844.

# Chapter 32

That same night ten thousand people lined the streets of Nauvoo as Willard Richards returned from Carthage. He was driving a wagon carrying the bodies of Joseph and Hyrum. Weeping men and women crowded close about the wagons, sobs mingled with cries for revenge. Alan Stout was heard swearing he would teach his children to the fourth generation to seek revenge for the murders of Joseph and Hyrum.

Port had already thought long and hard on that subject, deciding he would not wait even one generation. Frank Worrell, the man who had led the attack on the jail, would pay dearly. How and when Port did not know, only that Worrell's days were numbered. The man more responsible than anyone else must pay for what he had done, if not legally and lawfully, then by a more informal form of justice.

The next day the bodies were on display for viewing at the Mansion House. Bitter herbs were boiled in pans on the stove to cover the growing stench of the bodies now in their second day of exposure to the summer heat. Pink fluid drained from the open wounds onto the plank floor as thousands of sobbing Mormons crowded by to get a last look at the prophet and his brother.

At dusk two caskets carrying sandbags were buried in the cemetery in a mock ceremony. Later that night, near midnight, Port stood guard as the real bodies were buried in the basement of the partially completed Nauvoo House. There was concern that Joseph's enemies would not leave him alone, even in death, and every precaution was made to make sure the bodies would not be desecrated. Even as the burial was taking place, Willard Richards was busy compiling a list of all those who had participated in the mob action at Carthage. Frank Worrell led the list, which also included Chauncy and Francis Higbee, William and Wilson Law, the Fosters, and Joseph Jackson.

In the next five weeks, Mormons witnessed a mad scramble for the reins of leadership over them. Everyone who had ever had anything to do with leading the Mormons seemed to pop up in Nauvoo with a persuasive pitch and possibly a revelation from God, explaining why they should be selected prophet. Even apostates John C. Bennett and James Strang gave it a try.

The Mormons, after having moved so much, were not a wealthy people. Money was not the lure. Perhaps the attraction was power, with the prophet having nearly absolute control over twenty thousand people. Perhaps the attraction was polygamy at a time Church leaders were assembling followings of plural wives. At any rate, the leadership of the Mormon Church was a coveted prize for which there was no lack of striving candidates.

With most of the Twelve Apostles across the ocean on foreign missions, the reins of leadership seemed, at least to some, an easy grab. The gentile press was wondering if anyone would get control, or if the Mormons, now that Joseph was dead, would scatter to the four winds.

Sidney Rigdon was the first serious contender, arriving from Philadelphia in July. He had been a counselor to Joseph for many years and, next to Joseph, was the most popular speaker in the Church. To strengthen his position, Rigdon struck a deal with Joseph's widow, Emma, promising that when her son became of age, young Joseph could replace Rigdon at the helm. Not a fan of the forceful Brigham Young, Emma went along with Rigdon.

But the Saints were reluctant to sustain anyone until the Quorum of the Twelve Apostles returned. Joseph's disaffection with Rigdon in recent years was common knowledge around Nauvoo. In fact,

Port reminded all he came in contact with that Joseph had wanted to release Rigdon from Church leadership, but that the council had voted him down.

The Saints waited until Brigham Young returned before making their decision. Marching up the hill from the dock, Young didn't waste any time trying to make it absolutely clear that with the prophet gone, the authority now rested on the Twelve Apostles over which he was president.

A few days later Brigham Young and Sidney Rigdon addressed the assembled Saints. While Rigdon's remarks were persuasive and eloquent, Brigham Young spoke with such force that he could not be denied. Some present thought a transformation had taken place, that they saw and heard Joseph, not Brigham, speaking. When it was over, the Saints unanimously sustained Brigham Young and the Twelve Apostles as the controlling body of the Church. They also voted to continue tithing until the Nauvoo temple was completed. A few weeks later, Sidney Rigdon was excommunicated.

The Mormons tried to get back to normal living, not an easy task with Joseph gone. Luana and the children returned from Independence. Port moved them into the partially finished cabin. Luana was critical of Port for not planting crops and finishing the cabin. She told him to put away his guns and get to work. But Port wasn't about to do that. He still had unfinished business with the Carthage mob.

Every day Port checked and double-checked the loads in his pistols and rifles. He practiced shooting, against the protests of Luana, who knew the cost of powder and lead. Luana got after Port for not spending more time at home getting ready for winter.

One day Port received a message that Brigham Young wanted to see him. Brigham was strong and forceful, like a young bull, and full of energy and vigor, like Joseph, but that's where the similarity ended. Whereas Joseph had been a visionary man, a dreamer of what could be, Brigham was a well-organized pragmatist determined to turn the Church and city into a well-oiled machine. The most noticeable manifestation of Brigham's ability was a marked increase in construction activities on the temple.

Brigham's first word to Port was one of caution. The Church was initiating legal proceedings against Frank Worrell and others who had participated in the Carthage mob action. It was important to the Church that Port not interfere by taking the law into his own hands. Justice would be served through due process of law. Reluctantly, Port promised not to interfere.

Port wondered if Luana had put Brigham up to this in her efforts to get him to put the guns away. While Port sustained Brigham and the Twelve in leading the Church, he was not prepared to offer the same blind obedience he had given Joseph. In fact, he often wondered if he had disobeyed orders and followed Joseph to Carthage, the outcome might have been different.

Brigham explained that it was becoming more and more apparent that the mob was not satisfied with Joseph's death. The Mormons were still the largest voting block in Illinois. Nauvoo was rapidly becoming a major economic center along the Mississippi River. It was becoming increasingly clear that the mob would not be satisfied until the Saints scattered or moved.

To make matters worse, there seemed to be an increase in crimes against prominent gentiles and mob leaders, possibly a result of an unquenchable thirst for revenge on the part of many Mormons who refused to forget the murder of their beloved prophet.

The situation was going to get worse before it got better, Brigham believed. That's why he wanted Port to move into town and provide him with the same protective services Port had given Joseph. But, unlike Joseph, Brigham offered a salary. After the men shook hands, Port headed home.

"Cora ought to be happy with that," Luana said, when Port told her he was moving back into town. The comment caught him by surprise. He had never discussed Cora with Luana. Apparently the local gossip network had put more into his friendship with Cora than was really there. Port decided his future conversations with Cora would have to be more discreet. But he conveyed none of these thoughts to Luana. He responded to her comment by changing the subject, telling her how the new job would provide enough money to keep her and the children in food and clothing through the winter.

Brigham Young was persistent in his efforts to bring Joseph's killers to justice. Detailed legal proceedings were initiated against Frank Worrell and other mob leaders. When the state legislature repealed the Nauvoo charter that winter following Brigham Young's announcement that he was raising a five hundred–man police force, Young made the necessary adjustments in the proceedings against Worrell, allowing the slow wheels of justice to grind forward.

In May of 1845, Worrell was finally brought to trial in Warsaw. The proceedings lasted twelve days. Port was on hand most of the time, assigned by Young to carry news of what was happening back to Nauvoo on a daily basis, sharing the duty with Stephen Markham and others.

The Mormons produced dozens of witnesses, some of whom had seen Worrell leading the mob on Carthage Jail, though none could be produced who had actually seen Worrell shooting Joseph or Hyrum. Whenever an attempt was made to question Worrell, his answer was always the same, "I refuse to testify on the grounds I might incriminate myself."

At the end of the twelfth day, Worrell was acquitted. All charges were dropped. He received not so much as a hand slap.

The Mormons were outraged. They felt cheated. There was talk in Nauvoo of forming a Mormon mob to take care of Worrell. Brigham calmly reminded Port that if anything happened to Worrell, no matter how carefully planned and executed, the blame would fall upon the Saints and would result in a host of problems, including vicious retaliation.

Brigham's attempts at reconciliation with the mob were too little too late. The repeal of the Nauvoo charter had removed the last line of restraint, turning the beautiful City of Joseph into the most lawless town on the western frontier. With the charter went Brigham's power to run a police force and hold court on criminals. Word spread quickly up and down the river. Thieves, counterfeiters, and criminals of every sort hurried to Nauvoo, where they would be unhampered in their illegal activities. An increasing number of Mormons found "righteous retaliation" against the gentile community could be a profitable business, much more so than clearing swampland and planting crops that might be destroyed by mobs.

The mobbers increased their activities too, with plenty of help from their friends across the river in Missouri. An activity known as the wolf hunt became commonplace. At dusk a group of Missourians would gather at the river, dress up like Indians, pass around a jug of white lightning, and then cross the river to see how many Mormon homes could be burned to the ground before morning. Some of the groups carried red flags to distinguish themselves from Mormon raiders. The most notorious of the wolf hunters was Levi Williams, who swore he would leave a trail of burned Mormon homes all the way to Nauvoo and then set a match to the city too.

Forty-four Mormon homes were destroyed during the first two weeks in September. Hancock County sheriff Jacob Backenstos announced he was going to raise a posse to put a stop to the wolf hunts.

Backenstos was not a Mormon, but he had taken an oath to uphold the peace, and the Mormons had helped vote him into office. During his campaign he had promised fairness in enforcing the law. The Mormons had believed him. Now he intended to keep that promise.

His request for posse members was posted in Warsaw, the county seat. But there were no volunteers, even when he offered to pay wages. On the evening of September 15, the sheriff announced he was going to Nauvoo the next morning. Brigham Young would give him a posse to help stop the looting and burning.

It was mid-morning by the time Backenstos reached the corner where the Nauvoo road met the Carthage road. He was riding alone in a one-horse buggy and was just turning onto the Nauvoo road when he saw three riders and two wagons approaching from Carthage.

"It's that damn Backenstos," the middle rider shouted. The sheriff recognized the stern voice. It belonged to Frank Worrell, whom he suspected might try to stop him from going to Nauvoo to get a Mormon posse. As the sheriff turned onto the Nauvoo road, Worrell and his companions whipped their horses into full gallops to cut off the sheriff, who by now had whipped his buggy horse into a dead run. Backenstos had a good lead on his followers—over a hundred yards—but he knew his one-horse buggy could not stay ahead of mounted riders for long. Still, he had to try. He was in no mood to be intimidated and harassed by Frank Worrell.

Backenstos had just reached the top of the first hill when he saw several wagons and saddle horses at a watering hole in a little valley just ahead. A number of men were standing around talking.

Port had arrived at the water hole a short while earlier. He and Return Redden had been helping burned-out Mormons move to Nauvoo. While watering their horses, they had recognized another Mormon, Peter Conover. They were discussing the recent burnings when they noticed the sheriff's buggy streaking toward them. As Backenstos pulled his puffing horse to a halt, there was still no sign of Frank Worrell.

"Rockwell, if you don't mind," Backenstos shouted excitedly after recognizing Port, "I'd like to deputize you to protect me from Frank Worrell and the mob."

"Seeing as we have two rifles in addition to our pistols," Port responded, "I suppose we could lend a hand. Where's . . ." Before Port could ask, Frank Worrell and one of his companions came racing over the hill. Backenstos got out of the buggy, raised his hand high in the air, and shouted for Worrell to halt.

Worrell's reaction was to reach for his pistol. He made no effort to slow his galloping horse.

"Shoot the son–uv–a–bitch," Conover shouted.

Worrell was still out of pistol range, so Port raised his rifle to his shoulder. His eye caught the glimmer of a large metal belt buckle. The Carthage Gray lieutenant was not wearing a coat.

Port closed his eyes for a brief instant, offering a silent prayer. He was not praying for accuracy—this was an easy shot. Nor was he praying for protection—he had Joseph's promise that he could not be harmed by bullet or blade if he did not cut his hair. He was merely offering thanks that the leader of the Carthage mob was now in his sights.

Taking careful aim at the belt buckle, Port fired.

"You got him," Conover shouted. "You got him."

"I think I missed the buckle," Port responded, "but only by an inch or so."

Worrell tumbled from his horse, then lay still on the ground while the horse continued ahead to join the others at the water hole. Worrell's companions stopped at the top of the hill. Several crept cautiously ahead to retrieve their fallen leader. He was still alive but died minutes later on the way to Warsaw.

"Did you see the way he jumped when the bullet hit him?" Conover asked Redden.

"Like a jackrabbit catching a double load of buckshot," Redden responded.

"That was a nice shot," Backenstos said.

Port accompanied Backenstos to Nauvoo. After giving Brigham the details of the Worrell shooting, Backenstos asked for a posse to help him put a stop to the wolf hunts. Brigham Young promised him two thousand men in the morning.

# Chapter 33

While Backenstos was discussing posse maneuvers with Brigham Young, Port headed over to the Davis tavern for a bite to eat. It was early evening, and he and Cora were the only ones in the restaurant. She fried him a thick steak with mashed potatoes, cornbread, and honey. She sat down across the table from Port while he was eating.

"How do you feel?" she asked.

"Huh?" he asked, a big piece of meat in his mouth.

"I mean, after you shot Boggs you felt terrible. You went on a two-day drunk. Was shooting Worrell easier? Boggs lived. Worrell is dead."

Port swallowed his meat and looked into Cora's beautiful eyes.

"The man who led the mob on Carthage Jail was galloping toward me," he explained. "He had a gun in his hand and was probably going to shoot me or Backenstos. I raised my rifle to my shoulder, aimed at his belt buckle—not an easy target that far away on a galloping horse—and pulled the trigger. The man needed killing, and I thank the Lord I got to do it. I feel great!" Without taking his eyes off Cora, he cut another piece of rare steak and shoved it in his mouth.

"How's Luana getting along?" Cora asked, changing the subject.

"Glad to get the money I bring her, but she doesn't seem to mind me being away," Port said.

"I can't understand that," she said.

"While everybody else in Nauvoo is getting a plural wife, I can't seem to hang onto my first one," Port said.

"I think I can understand how you feel."

"You and Amos have problems?"

"I'm not so sure he does, but I do."

"Tell me about it."

"I work around the clock keeping this place going, cleaning rooms, washing dishes, cooking meals, and earning all the money— while he's off courting a second wife and playing soldier. He's a slave driver, and I'm sick and tired of being the slave."

While Port was glad to listen, he wasn't sure if he should say anything because he strongly suspected he wasn't any better of a husband than Amos.

"Just the other day he told me to polish his boots before he went to call on Agnes Smith," Cora continued, an unmistakable note of anger in her voice. "Can you imagine that?"

Port couldn't see anything terribly wrong with a man asking his woman to shine his boots. "Did you do it?" he asked.

"Yes," she admitted. "But never again, not as long as I live."

"What'll you do if he brings home a second wife?"

"I've thought a lot about that," she said, suddenly thoughtful, looking down at her hands. "They say the first wife is the boss. If that's true, and if I can make the new wife do most of the work around here, I might stay around."

"A minute ago you complained about Amos being a slave driver," Port said. "Sounds like you want to be one too."

"It's not the same."

"Isn't it?"

"Then maybe I'll just leave."

"Where would you go?" he asked.

"I don't know," she said, looking into his face again.

"Maybe the two of us could pair up," Port said, looking down at his half-eaten steak, feeling embarrassed at having said something so personal.

"Porter Rockwell," Cora said, her voice suddenly loud again, a note of anger returning, "you had better not be fooling with me. I won't have that. If you are not totally serious about what you just said, you shut your mouth right now. I have tender feelings for you and won't be trifled with."

Port stared at her in amazement, wondering why she was angry with him. His comment about teaming up with her had been a serious one. Still, he was not ready to propose marriage or anything else to another man's wife. He wasn't sure what he should say to her.

Suddenly, the door crashed open, and Jacob Backenstos marched into the room. He was a large, brash man with piercing blue eyes, pink cheeks, and wind-tossed hair, a handsome man. He and Port had become fast friends as a result of the morning's conflict with Frank Worrell. The sheriff felt that Port had saved his life, and his gratitude was deep and sincere. On the other hand, Port was grateful to Backenstos for providing him with an opportunity to partially avenge the murder of his best friend, Joseph Smith.

Neither man had had any love for Worrell, and both felt very satisfied at the way things had turned out. Now they were going to go out together and put the fear of heaven and hell in those who had been burning Mormon homes.

"I'm so hungry I could eat a boiled rat," Backenstos roared. Cora headed for the kitchen to throw another steak on the stove, while the sheriff crashed into the chair opposite Port, who promptly poured the big man a glass of white lightning.

"I propose a toast," Backenstos said as he raised the glass high in the air. "To Frank Worrell. May his balls toast in hell for a thousand years, and his old lady become a plural wife to Brigham Young."

After laughing heartily at his own toast, Backenstos lowered the glass to his lips and consumed its entire contents in three or four swallows.

A few minutes later, Cora returned, placing a huge plate of meat and potatoes in front of the sheriff, who thanked her warmly.

"The hard thing about stopping the wolf hunts," the sheriff began to explain, more serious now, "is that you never know where they are going to strike. Even with the two thousand men Brigham promised, I can't guard every Mormon home in the entire county every night."

"Sometimes the best defense is an aggressive offense," Port suggested.

"The problem with that is that you never know for sure who is doing the wolf hunting and who isn't. Burn down the home of an innocent farmer and you're as bad as the mobbers themselves," Backenstos responded, referring to the retaliatory burnings and lootings some Mormons were carrying out.

"I agree about not wanting to burn out an innocent farmer," Port said. "But it's easy to tell who's innocent and who's not."

"How's that?"

"Knock on the door first," Port explained. "If the man's home, you know he isn't out wolf hunting. But if he's gone, you have a pretty good idea where he is, especially if the woman says she doesn't know where he is. You invite her and the kids outside, pour on the coal oil, and strike the match. It's that simple."

"Sounds like you've done it," the sheriff said.

"I'll admit there are a few pukes I'd like to try it on," Port said.

"Like who?"

"Levi Williams, for one. Bet he won't be home tonight."

"Want to ride with me to pay him a visit?" Backenstos asked. "If he's not home there'd be grounds for some serious questioning tomorrow. Like to drop in on some of his neighbors too. If they're not home, we might have a case on a whole band of wolf hunters."

"I'll go," Port said. "Do you know where Levi lives?"

"Somewhere along the road to Carthage, I've heard," the sheriff said. "Not exactly sure where it is."

"I'll draw you a map," Cora said, suddenly entering the conversation. She pulled a piece of brown paper from her apron pocket and began to draw directions.

"We'd better take along some coal oil and matches," Port said. "Nothing like a bonfire to warm a man's bones."

"If an occasional wolf hunter came home to a pile of ashes," Cora added, "others might think twice before going out into the night."

"That's the idea," Port said. "Sometimes the best way to stop a fight is by giving the enemy a heavy dose of his own medicine."

The two men wolfed down the rest of their food and then got up from the table. Cora would not let them pay.

"One more toast," Port said, picking up his glass. "To Levi Williams. May his house soon be as warm as those he has torched." Both men drank to the toast.

"When will you return?" Cora asked.

"Tomorrow."

"We can talk some more then," she said to Port.

"All right," he answered as he turned toward the door.

"Do you and that woman have something going?" Backenstos asked when he and Port were outside.

"Just good friends," Port said. Backenstos was grinning.

# Chapter 34

The non-Mormons at Carthage and Warsaw were enraged over the shooting of Frank Worrell. They were even more enraged over Sheriff Backenstos's police actions against suspect non-Mormons. Articles in the *Warsaw Signal* began referring to the sheriff as Napoleon Backenstos. Like when Joseph had been killed, anti-Mormons from near and far began to gather at Carthage and Warsaw.

While the police action by Backenstos had brought about a temporary lull in the burning of Mormon homes, everyone could see that the conflict was going to get worse.

On October 1 Brigham Young made an announcement he hoped would bring peace. He said that in the spring, "when the streams were flowing and the grass was green," the Saints would abandon Illinois to the devil and move west to the Rocky Mountains.

Young had sent a scouting party to the Great Basin area surrounding the Great Salt Lake in early September, but the increasing conflict between his people and their neighbors made it impossible for him to wait for the report before making a decision. Without the report, Brigham still wasn't sure where the Saints would end up. If the Great Basin wasn't suitable, Oregon or Vancouver Island appeared to be attractive alternatives.

Brigham saw two main purposes in making the premature announcement. One, he hoped the non-Mormons would back off in their persecutions, knowing that in the spring the Mormons were leaving. Two, he hoped the announcement would cause his people to focus their attention on something besides getting revenge on their neighbors. To a large degree, the announcement accomplished both objectives.

Almost overnight, Nauvoo was turned into a wagon factory. The basement of the still-unfinished temple became an assembly area for wheels, double trees, and wagon boxes for ten thousand wagons. Cash became critically short as purchasing parties hurried to St. Louis to buy horseshoes, grease, harness buckles, rope, canvas, and a hundred other items needed to outfit the wagons.

At the same time, Nauvoo became a speculator's paradise. Virtually everything that couldn't be moved or was too large to be placed in a wagon was for sale. Pianos could be purchased for five dollars.

The biggest economic tragedy was the inability of the Saints to get fair prices for their well-cared-for farms and homes. John D. Lee was offered eight hundred dollars for a house that only a year earlier had cost eight thousand to build. He refused the offer. The Church committee later sold the house for $12.50.

Most of the Mormons were city people—from the east coast of America and the large cities of Europe. For most of the adults, the thought of embarking into the vast American wilderness was a frightening one. Some of the men, and a good portion of the children, however, looked forward to the journey as a fantastic adventure.

Apparently, federal officials were having trouble figuring out where Brigham Young was getting the money to outfit ten thousand wagons. They knew counterfeiting was going on in Nauvoo, and they just couldn't believe Brigham Young was not involved. In early December Young received a letter from Samuel Brannan, who had learned in Washington, D.C. that the secretary of war and other members of the cabinet were laying plans to prevent the Saints from moving west. The men were alleging that it was against the law for an armed body of men to go from the United States to any other government. To make matters worse, counterfeiting charges were filed and warrants issued for the arrest of Brigham Young, Amasa Lyman, and others of the Twelve Apostles.

After what had happened to Joseph and Hyrum, Brigham wasn't about to turn himself over to the law. He ignored the warrants, figuring if he could avoid contact with the authorities until spring, they would not attempt to catch up with him once he left the United States.

On December 23 Port and William Miller were delivering wagon parts in the basement of the temple. Miller was well-liked in Nauvoo. He was president of the high priests. Some thought he looked like Brigham Young. In fact, strangers visiting Nauvoo for the first time sometimes mistook Miller for Young.

Rockwell and Miller were about ready to leave when someone shouted from the top of the stairs, "State troops and federal marshals have surrounded the temple. They have a warrant for President Young's arrest."

"Tell them he's not here," someone else shouted.

"I did, but they don't believe me. His carriage is out front."

Rockwell and Miller raced to the top of the stairs. While running, Port was checking his pistols to make sure they were fully loaded and ready to fire.

Fifteen or twenty armed men, including Port, lined up opposite the door to resist the marshals.

"I don't want a gun battle in the house of the Lord," Brigham said as he glided down the stairs, dressed in a white robe and green apron.

"Almon Babbitt is outside trying to stall," someone explained, "but the troops are determined to serve their papers."

"Let them in," Port growled, sensing a weakening resistance on the part of the others. "I've got forty-seven rounds. We can stack their bodies like cord wood to block the door." He had a pistol in each hand. "Let them in," he repeated.

"I'm still in charge here," Brigham said. "And I said I do not want a gunfight in the house of the Lord. Does anyone else have any ideas?"

There was silence, except for the muffled sound of angry voices outside the door on the front porch.

"I'll stand by Brother Rockwell when they come through that door," William Miller said. "But I've got an idea that might prevent shooting."

"What is it, Brother Miller?" Brigham asked.

"Since they are charging you with passing bogus money, why don't we give them a bogus Brigham?"

Most of the men present didn't know what Miller was talking about until he walked over to the coat rack and removed Brother Kimball's cloak and Brother Young's hat. "Sir," he said, addressing President Young, "it's a little chilly outside. May I wear your hat and drive your carriage home tonight?"

"Brother Miller," Brigham responded, "you may take my hat and keep it along with my eternal gratitude."

"Only wish I could have done the same for Joseph or Hyrum," Miller said. He and Brigham embraced. Then, as Brigham ducked out of sight, Miller marched over to the door and opened it wide. After nodding a friendly greeting to the marshals and Almon Babbitt, he started walking toward Brigham's carriage, which was waiting just outside the door. The startled officers finally caught up with him and made their arrest.

"There must be some mistake" was Miller's only comment before they pushed him into the carriage. Miller demanded to be taken before a judge who could determine if the papers against him were legal. His captors honored the request by taking him to the Mansion House, where Judge Edmonds, after careful examination, announced the papers were in order. The judge knew the marshals had the wrong man but wasn't about to interfere in what he thought to be an excellent practical joke.

Miller asked for permission to summon witnesses who could prove his innocence, but the marshals—already too wary of Nauvoo legal processes—hurried their prisoner off to Carthage, an eighteen-mile journey that lasted about two hours.

It was the middle of the night when the carriage and accompanying troops arrived in Carthage. There was plenty of whooping and hollering to let everyone know that the biggest catch of all, Brigham Young, was being brought to jail.

The marshal locked Miller in a room at Hamilton's Tavern and tried to get a little sleep, still not suspecting that he had the wrong man.

"I am informed you are not Mr. Young" were the marshal's first words when he entered Miller's room the next morning.

"I never told you my name was Young, did I?" Miller responded happily.

"No," the marshal said sheepishly, "but one of my men professed to be acquainted with Mr. Young and pointed you out to me."

"I said you were making a big mistake," Miller said, shrugging his shoulder.

The marshal left, returning a few minutes later with Sheriff Jacob Backenstos, who happened to be in town.

"Do you recognize this man?" the marshal asked.

"Of course," Backenstos said. "It's William Miller. A lot of people think he looks like Brigham Young." Backenstos was laughing heartily as he left the room.

"I have no reason to hold you any longer," the marshal said, stepping to one side. Miller was surprised, after the trick he had pulled, that the marshals and deputies didn't at least try to give him a whipping. After stopping to chat with Backenstos for a minute, he climbed onto the driver's seat of Young's carriage and headed for Nauvoo. He didn't look back, or he would have noticed five men following him.

It was Christmas Eve, and Port was heading home to spend the evening with Luana and the children when he saw Brigham's carriage, with Miller on the seat, approaching the tavern. News of Miller's release had already reached town, but Port wanted to hear Miller's version of what had happened.

Port expected Miller to be in a cheerful mood after having pulled such a glorious trick on the enemy. Instead, Miller was hunched over in the seat like a man about to die. His face was gray-white like the inside of an oyster shell, and his jaw was set against some horrible pain.

"Help me down," Miller said to Port as he pulled the horses to a halt. Port stepped toward the carriage. As he reached up, Miller tumbled into his arms. There were blood stains on the front and rear of Miller's trousers.

"What happened?" Port asked.

"The guards," Miller moaned. "They caught up with me. They castrated me. Won't be having any more children."

Port helped Miller through the door and up to his room. While passing through the busy front room, he asked Cora to bring up a pan of hot water and some clean bandages. He ignored questions as he and Miller pushed through the Christmas Eve crowd.

Port itched to put on his guns, sharpen his Bowie knife, and head for Carthage. But he knew the guilty men would have scattered by now. They would be impossible to find. Later, perhaps, he could get the names of some of the guards, certainly the names of the marshals in charge of the previous night's work.

After cleaning up Miller and making sure the man was comfortably settled, Port tied his horse to the back of the carriage and drove over to Brigham's home. He knew President Young would want to know, even on Christmas Eve.

"The sooner we leave these United States the better" was Brigham's tearful reply. While Port headed for the cabin to spend Christmas Eve with Luana and the children, Brigham hurried over to the tavern to see Miller.

Port wasn't in much of a mood to celebrate Christmas, but for the children's sake he tried to be cheerful. As the little ones were decorating a small fir tree, he explained to Luana what had happened to Miller.

"The poor fellow won't be having any more children," he said, concluding his narrative.

"Neither will you," she responded matter-of-factly. "At least not with me."

"What?" he asked, feeling like he was suddenly out of breath.

"It's over, Porter. I'm going to be sealed to Alpheus Cutler. I hope you will let me keep the children." Port knew Cutler well. He was in charge of finishing the temple. He was a strong, steady man, already married. Luana would become a plural wife.

"Does this mean we're getting divorced?" he asked.

"Since we're leaving the United States, I don't think that's necessary," Luana said. "The temple sealing to Alpheus will be the ceremony that counts." It was apparent by her calm, cool manner that she had been preparing for this conversation for a long time.

"Do I get an explanation?" he asked, fighting hard to accept the rejection without getting angry, without trying to strike back or hurt her.

"You haven't planted a crop in six years, and this cabin is still not finished," she said, unloading for the first time the things that had been bothering her for years. "You don't like to tinker and fix things. You don't like to farm. You are gone too much. You swear too much. You drink too much. And you kill people." She paused for breath.

"Is that all?" he asked.

"No," she said, her voice growing softer, more kind. "You don't read. You don't write. You don't bathe often enough. And you don't shave. Kissing you is like trying to bite into a piece of raw venison through a hole in a shaggy horse blanket. And you know how I hate the smell of horses."

"I guess this means you prefer I not spend the night," he said, wanting to change the direction of the conversation. He'd had about all the criticism a man could take for one evening. He gave each of the children a hug and a Merry Christmas wish and headed for the door. Luana blocked his way.

"Can we still be friends?" she asked, extending her hand.

"Why would you want to be friends with a beast you obviously think is less than human?"

"Porter," she said, still holding her hand out, "there are a lot of sisters who would give anything to be the woman of the man who killed Frank Worrell. I'm just not one of them."

"Then don't ask to be my friend," he said, stepping past her outstretched hand and out the door. He hurried back to the tavern.

When he opened the front door, the front dining-drinking room was empty. He was glad he didn't have to do any explaining or answer any questions. After grabbing a bottle of white lightning, he ran up the stairs to his room. He figured Miller would still be in his bed, but that didn't matter. There'd soon be enough white lightning in his belly to remove any noticeable difference between a straw mattress and a plank floor.

To his surprise, when he opened the door Miller was gone. He found himself standing there unable to think. Too many things had happened too fast. The Miller tragedy, compounded by Luana's surprise announcement, was too much for a man to handle all at once. Now this. Where was Miller? He just stood there, staring at the bed.

"His family took him home," said a familiar female voice. It was Cora. He turned and looked at her. She was carrying a bundle of bedding under her arm.

"He won't be back?" he asked numbly.

"No. Is something wrong?"

"Luana is marrying Alpheus Cutler."

"I wondered why you came back tonight, it being Christmas and all. There's some blood on the bedding. I'll change it. Would have done it earlier, but I didn't think you'd be back tonight."

"Thank you," Port said, stepping aside to let her enter.

Cora worked quickly, removing the soiled blankets and putting on clean ones. He didn't offer to help but was content just to watch.

"Could I ask you a very personal question?" he asked when she was finished with the bed. She turned to face him, smiling.

"Ask anything you like," she said. "But I may not give you an answer, if it's too personal."

"Would it repulse you to bite into a piece of raw venison through a hole in a shaggy horse blanket?" he asked.

"Are you sure you are all right?" she asked.

"Just answer the question."

"Everybody knows I prefer my meat rare," she said thoughtfully. "And I love the smell of horses. No, it would not repulse me to do that. Who knows, perhaps I would enjoy eating deer meat that way. Why do you ask?"

"Let's talk about it tomorrow," he said, suddenly feeling very tired. "If you'll excuse me, I've got some urgent business with this here bottle."

"Merry Christmas," she said, retreating into the hall and closing his door behind her.

# Chapter 35

"Why do you think she left you?" Cora asked. She and Port were walking along Main Street. It was Christmas night. Except for Port and Cora, the street was deserted.

"Said I didn't like to bathe, farm, or fix things, and that I swore too much, drank too much, and killed people," he said.

"I would have to agree with all that," Cora said.

"Do you think there was anything else, perhaps something she didn't tell me?" he asked.

"I'm sure losing the baby had something to do with it," she said. Port stopped.

"Losing what baby?" he asked.

"You know, the miscarriage."

"What miscarriage?"

"The one last fall, of course. You knew about it, didn't you?" she asked, turning to face him.

"I didn't even know she was expecting," he said, his voice faint. "It must have happened while I was out riding with Backenstos. Why didn't she tell me?"

"You could probably answer that question better than I could," she said. "All I know is that you and Luana didn't talk to each other nearly as much as a man and wife should."

"Like you and I talk?"

"I suppose," she said as they resumed their walk down the street.

199

"Cora?" Port asked. "Is Amos still planning on taking another wife?"

"I think he's asked Agnes Smith, but I don't know if she's agreed to do it yet."

"She's a very beautiful woman," Port said. "At one time Joseph gave me the impression she was already a plural wife to someone. I guess I misunderstood him."

"Maybe she was at one time," Cora said, "but Amos has his heart set on her now. I'd rather he marry a homely woman with rough hands and a strong back, a woman who could take over a lot of my work."

"You don't think Agnes will help?"

"Sure, but she's so pretty. I have nightmares of her and Amos having an endless honeymoon while I'm cleaning, cooking, and managing the business. She's too pretty." Cora's voice was breaking with emotion, like she was about to cry. Port put his arm around her shoulders and drew her close as they continued to walk.

"They can talk about sisterhood, love, and sharing all they want," she continued. "But Amos is my husband and I don't feel like sharing him with anybody, least of all with a pretty woman like Agnes. It makes me angry. I feel like taking a butcher knife to Amos and doing a job on him so poor Brother Miller won't be all alone in his suffering. When I see Agnes I feel like digging my fingernails into her pretty face and slopping mud on her fancy dress."

"What are you going to do when they marry?" Port asked.

"I don't know," she said. "Do you have any suggestions?"

"Yes, I do."

"What?"

"Leave Amos and marry me."

"But you don't shave." She laughed nervously, caught off guard and attempting to buy time to think by bringing humor into the situation. "You drink too much, and you kill people."

"I promise to cut back on the white lightning and not to kill anybody you like, but the shaving I can't do anything about. Joseph's promise, you know."

"Porter, are you serious?" she asked, stopping and turning to face him.

"I have never been more serious in my life."

"Don't you think we should give this more time?"

"There is no time. In three or four months we're heading west into the wilderness. There's a million things to do. I want you to come with me, help me settle a wild land. We'll build a cabin in a beautiful mountain valley surrounded by snow-capped peaks. There'll be a stream winding through our valley, crystal clear and full of fat trout begging to be caught. From our front porch we'll look out across our land, as far as the eye can see, grazing herds of cattle and horses, all ours. Up close there will be a half-dozen of our children playing in the sun—and no mobs for a thousand miles."

"Is that what you really want, Porter?" she asked.

"Yes, and I want you to share it with me. There is so little time to get ready. Will you marry me?"

"Will you take me to town once in a while to see a play or buy a new dress?"

"At least once a month, and we'll go to church every Sunday."

"Yes, I'll marry you."

"Let's go see President Young right now," Port said, pulling her close, giving her a strong hug.

"I think we'd better see Amos first," she answered. "He's still my husband."

A few minutes later they entered the tavern. Amos was seated alone near the fire, cleaning a rifle. No one else was in the room.

"Do you want to tell him, or should I?" Cora whispered to Port.

"You do it," Port said. He leaned back against the inside of the door as Cora marched over to Amos, who was now looking into the barrel of the rifle.

"Amos," she began, "I've been thinking about what you said about wanting to marry Agnes."

"You have?" Amos said in a startled tone, looking up at her.

"I think it's a wonderful idea. I want you to do it."

"You do?" he shouted, standing up and throwing his arms around her. "Oh, thank you, thank you. You'll never regret it."

"You're welcome," she said coolly.

"It'll be wonderful," he said.

"I'm sure it will," she responded.

"I mean, the three of us working and living together," he said.

"Actually," she said cautiously, "it'll just be the two of you because I'm going to marry Porter. Now, if you'll excuse me, I've got to run upstairs and pack a few things." She turned and ran up the stairs, Amos too startled to respond.

"You can't do this!" Amos shouted, after he had a few seconds to recover. "You're my legal wife! You can't just run off with another man!" Cora didn't respond. She apparently didn't hear him. "I won't let you!" he bellowed.

"I'm afraid, friend," Port said, his voice quiet and firm, "there's not a thing you can do to stop her."

Amos looked over at Port, who was playing with the cylinder on one of his pistols.

"You can't just muscle your way in here and steal my wife!" Amos screamed. "There are laws against that." Port didn't respond. He continued to play with the pistol.

In a few minutes, Cora glided down the stairs, a canvas bag in her hand.

"I hope you and Agnes have a wonderful life together," she said, approaching Amos carefully. She leaned forward and kissed him on the cheek. He was as still as a statue. "I hope we can still be friends," she said, stepping back, wanting to offer her hand but hesitating. Port began to laugh. He opened the door and, taking Cora by the hand, led her outside, leaving a stunned Amos Davis all by himself, still holding his rifle.

Port and Cora walked hand in hand for several blocks, neither saying anything, both deep in thought. Cora was the first to speak.

"What did you mean last night when you asked if I would be repulsed trying to eat a piece of raw venison through a hole in a shaggy horse blanket?"

"See if you can figure it out," Port said, taking her in his arms and kissing her.

# Chapter 36

The non-Mormon population of Nauvoo and the neighboring communities stood back in awe as twenty thousand Mormons rolled up their sleeves to build a thousand wagons. The town was an anthill of activity with everything for sale, except items needed for the journey west.

What the non-Mormons didn't understand was why throngs of Mormons were entering the partially finished temple every day. When the first Mormon temple had been built in Kirtland, Ohio, Joseph had introduced the endowment ceremony, similar in purpose to baptism but a much more detailed ceremony, similar in appearance and content to some of the Masonic rituals dating back to King Solomon's Temple in the Old Testament. And like Solomon's rituals, the Mormon endowment was only to be performed in temples.

Since there were no temples where the Mormons were going, thousands of Mormons were anxious to receive the endowment ordinance prior to the westward departure. To facilitate matters, President Young had dedicated the temple for this sacred work before the temple was completed.

On January 5, 1846, Port participated in the endowment ceremony for the first time. He then became a regular participant, playing the serpent, or Satan, as the ceremony was performed for others.

On January 14, Luana received her endowments and was sealed to Alpheus Cutler, who in addition to being president of the high council was in charge of completing the temple. The Rockwell children were sealed to Cutler too. Port was not present at the ceremony.

Except for a critical shortage of cash to buy needed supplies, the Saints were making good progress in getting ready for a May departure. The worry of leaving civilization without sufficient supplies was offset by the excitement of embarking on a new adventure in a wild land. It gave the Saints additional hope to know they would be leaving the Missouri, Carthage, and Warsaw mobs far behind.

On February 2 Brigham shifted migration preparations into an even higher level of activity. He announced that instead of waiting until May, the migration would begin immediately.

Some resisted the announcement. Not only were the Saints not yet ready to depart, but it was winter. It was pure nonsense, even suicide, to send twenty thousand unprepared people into the wilderness in the middle of the winter.

"I've thought about all that," Brigham replied. "Still, we must begin the migration now." He explained that the decision to leave immediately had been prompted by a communication from Sam Brannan, who handled Church affairs in New York. The former postmaster general of the United States, a Mr. A. G. Benson, and others told Brannan that unless the Church leaders signed an agreement with them, to which the president of the United States was a silent party, the government would not permit the Mormons to proceed on their journey westward. The agreement required that the Saints sign over to A. G. Benson and Company the odd number of all land and town lots in the new land where they settled. If Church leaders refused to sign the agreement, the president would issue a proclamation that it was the intention of the Saints to take sides with other nations against the United States, and he would order the Mormons to be disarmed and dispersed.

Young told his people that the council considered the offer and concluded that "as our trust was in God . . . we would not sign any such unjust and oppressive agreement." Brigham wanted his people to be as far west as possible when the crooked politicians realized the Mormons would not be blackmailed.

Port was asked to be guide and hunter for the lead party, which meant he had to be on his way by mid-February. The plan was simple. Cora would drive the wagon with the lead party while Port hunted and scouted in advance of the party.

Having already lined up a wagon and team, Port and Cora began final preparations for an immediate departure.

There was a feeling of panic in Nauvoo as Saints scurried about making final preparations. To the surprise of many, the work at the temple did not slow down. In fact, there was a dramatic increase in the number of Mormons receiving endowments. Four days after Young's announcement of the early departure, a record 512 persons received their first endowment ordinance. The next day the record was broken again, with nearly six hundred receiving ordinances. Since no one knew what was going to happen out in the wilderness, everyone wanted to be sure the ordinances of salvation were performed before their departure into the unknown.

Port had his wagon loaded and was making final adjustments on his harnesses when Cora returned from a visit down the street.

"Everything's ready," he said cheerily.

"Amos hasn't begun to pack yet," she responded.

"He'd better get Agnes to lend a hand."

"Agnes isn't there."

"Where is she?"

"I don't know, only that she is not going to marry Amos."

Port began to laugh.

"What's funny?" Cora asked.

"A man isn't content with one beautiful woman," he tried to explain, "so he tries to marry another, and ends up with none. That's funny."

"I don't see the humor," she said. Port shrugged his shoulders and went back to work.

"Porter, he needs me," she said. Port stopped what he was doing and turned to face her.

"So do I," he said.

"I'm not so sure about that," she said. "You'll be off scouting and hunting. I'll be an unnecessary worry for you and the other men in the company who will have to help me with the team."

"Cora, what are you trying to say?" he asked.

"I want to go back to Amos." Port couldn't believe what he was hearing. The last month with Cora had been wonderful. They had gotten along so well. He thought she had been happy too.

"You don't love me?" he asked.

"Of course I do," she said.

"Then why do you want to leave?"

"Amos needs me. As your wife I'm an unnecessary burden."

"But you don't love Amos."

"I thought I didn't a month ago. But I miss him. It seems you are always gone. Though he didn't do much, he was always around, sometimes bossing me, but he was there. I miss him."

"Are you sure about this?" Port asked.

"I think so," she said, beginning to cry. "Those years Amos and I spent together . . . I thought I could just walk away from them. I was angry because he wanted another wife. I was hurt. But now that he hasn't taken a second wife, I feel bad about leaving him. Can you understand that?"

Port didn't answer. Taking a deep breath, he walked to the rear of the wagon, removed a bag of personal belongings, and tied it to the back of Bill's saddle. He untied Bill from the back of the wagon and swung into the saddle.

"What are you doing?" she asked.

"I'm giving the team, the wagon, and everything in it to you and Amos," he said. "Consider it a wedding gift."

"Oh, I couldn't accept all this," she protested.

"Then tell Amos I'm giving him all this stuff for letting you live with me for a month."

"I like the wedding present idea better," she said.

"Fine. It's settled," he said. "But can I ask one last question?"

"Sure."

"Can we still be friends?" Before she could answer, Port began to laugh. He pulled Bill around and began galloping toward the river.

Port found a place for him and Bill on one of the departing flatboats. Two hours later, he and the horse were alone on top of a hill on the Iowa side of the river, taking a long last look at Nauvoo.

The gray river was over a mile wide, clogged with chunks of floating ice. Four or five empty flatboats were working their way back to Nauvoo so they would be ready to bring more emigrants over to Iowa Territory the next morning. It would soon be dark, and Port thought he could see lights in the upper windows of the temple.

Port looked toward the unfinished Nauvoo House where his best friend, Joseph Smith, was buried with his brother Hyrum. He looked at the Mansion where Joseph's widow, Emma, lived with her children. She had said she would not come west with Brigham Young. Port wondered if she would change her mind.

The city looked gray and cold. Soon it would be empty, a graveyard for the shattered dreams of a people who had worked hard to make it the city of God.

"So long, Nauvoo," Port shouted, removing his hat. "Can't say I will miss you. But I can promise you one thing: the Mormons will never forget you."

Port placed his hat back on his head. He was glad to shove Nauvoo and its many memories into the back of his mind. He was ready to begin a new life. He had the fastest horse in the territory beneath him, the best guns money could buy in his belt, and he knew how to use them. He was free.

Port pulled Bill around and let the horse reach out into a full gallop down the west side of the hill. If he hurried, he could cover the twelve miles to Sugar Creek before dark.

# Chapter 37

The first casualty of the Mormons' westward migration occurred the next morning. Port, having spent the night in Sugar Creek, was not present. Some brethren were crossing the river at Nauvoo in a flatboat, when to their rear they saw a man and two boys in a skiff that was sinking from too large a load and a lack of skill at the helm. The brethren turned the flatboat around, offering assistance to the man and boys, helping them board the already too full flatboat.

Soon they were headed for shore again, the skiff in tow, when one of the men spit a mouthful of tobacco juice into the eye of an ox yoked to Thomas Grover's wagon. The startled animal jerked itself free of the wagon and plunged into the river, dragging its yoke mate with it. As the two oxen went overboard, they tore off one of the sideboards, which allowed water to flow into the flatboat just as it touched shore. The boat sank to the bottom before all the men could leap off. Several nearly drowned before they could be picked up by another boat. Two oxen drowned, and a few things floated away and were lost. Grover's wagon was dragged out of the river with its contents damaged.

Hosea Stout, who was in charge of the crossing, threatened to have the man who had spit in the ox's eye excommunicated if he ever did anything like that again.

At Sugar Creek, Port built himself a little brush shelter much like the one he had spent the winter in at Liberty when Joseph was in jail. Everyone seemed to be waiting for Bishop Whitney, Heber Kimball, and William Clayton to come forward with supplies. It appeared it would be at least several days before the lead company was ready to move ahead, so Port spent his time building a shelter. He noticed most of the other men just stood around campfires, swapping stories.

The camp consisted of nearly four hundred wagons, all very heavily loaded and with not even half the teams needed to make a rapid journey. Most of the families had enough provisions for several months. A considerable number, against counsel, had started in a destitute condition, and some with only enough provisions for a few days. In the fear of being left behind, many were willing to enter the wilderness unprepared, placing unnecessary burdens on those who were prepared.

On the second day, President Young called everyone together to hear what he had to say. He guessed Kimball and Clayton would be along shortly so the company could begin its journey, but in the meantime he had instructions for the men.

"I wish you brethren would stop running to Nauvoo," he began. "Stop hunting and fishing and roasting your shins. Fix the nose baskets for your horses so we don't waste corn. Fix comfortable places for your wives and children to ride. And never borrow without asking leave, and be sure and return what was borrowed.

"All dogs in camp will be killed if the owners will not tie them up, and any man who keeps a horse in camp that has distemper ought to forfeit all his horses. We want every man to quit the camp who cannot quit swearing. You had better go now. If you do not, the law will be put in force by and by. We will have order in the camp. If any want to live in peace when we have left this place, they must toe the mark . . ."

President Young then asked all who wanted to go with the camp to raise their right hands. All hands went up. He ordered the brethren to build a pen for corn and hay. He appointed George Harris head of the commissary. He said all spare men were to be guards and watchmen, and that all men with families must organize into companies of tens, fifties, and hundreds. William Clayton was appointed general clerk of the camp, and Willard Richards, historian.

On February 24 the thermometer dropped to twelve degrees below zero. The cold weather continued, freezing over the river all the way to Montrose and Nauvoo. While it was too cold for the companies to break camp and move ahead, the ice made the river crossing easy. For several days, all who were ready just got in their wagons and drove across on the ice.

When the thermometer climbed back into the twenties, at least in the daytime, the companies began forging west. One of the biggest problems was the lack of food, but with corn available from local farmers for eighteen cents a bushel, the food shortage was not critical. Those who didn't have money to buy grain could chop wood or build fences for enough corn to feed their families.

Plenty of firewood was available along the way. One could keep warm by walking instead of riding. There were no bugs—no flies and mosquitoes to pester people and livestock. Following cold nights, rivers and streams could be crossed on the ice. Frozen mud was bumpy, but easy to drive on. While uncomfortable, the cold weather was bearable. One could always look forward to the spring temperatures just around the corner.

Once the cold weather passed, by far the worst enemy of the pioneers was the mud—black, brown, and gray. Wet, cold, and slippery, it was on everything—boots, hands, faces, jackets, bedding, even the food. One couldn't get away from it. The oxen and horses always matched in color the most recent mud hole.

Earlier, mobbers had been a threat, burning homes and beating people. Later, Indians would be a threat, shooting occasional arrows, stealing food, and sometimes horses. But in Iowa the only important threat was mud—the endless Iowa mud that swallowed up hopes and dreams.

A group of wagons would start out in the morning with the intention of covering twelve or fifteen miles. An hour later, not one, but eight or ten wagons, would be buried to the axles in an unexpected mud hole. Up to their bellies, the oxen would be practically helpless. Nevertheless, sometimes as many as a dozen teams had to be unhitched from their wagons and coaxed forward to help pull the first wagon free, then the second, until all were through. Sometimes wagons had to be emptied of everything, including heavy iron stoves and plows, which were then carried on weary shoulders to high ground.

When the oxen were in place, men and boys would gather around the wagon, lifting and pushing, sometimes up to their waists in muck. It wasn't uncommon for the mud to suck off a boot, sometimes two. If the wagon was almost free and the bootless man continued to push, sometimes he couldn't find his boot afterwards.

In addition to boots, the mud swallowed up countless tools, utensils, even baby dolls. But most of all it swallowed up wagon wheels, dashing all hopes and plans for forward progress. Sometimes it took days to get through less than a mile of mud.

Port was with the scouting parties in front, selecting roads and campsites, building bridges, and killing game. Sometimes the mud was so deep that ten-foot poles could be pushed out of sight, straight down.

Never was sunshine so welcome, or rain so disheartening. Rain made mud, and it rained every day during March and most of April. The Iowa mud sucked the Mormon people to their knees, made boys into men, turned back the less dedicated, hardened muscles, welded lifetime friendships and loyalties, and demanded patience as endless as the mud itself. In February thousands of frightened city dwellers entered the mud. In May a nation of hardened pioneers emerged from the mud.

The favorite story around the thousands of smoky Iowa campfires that spring was the one about the man who was discovered up to his armpits in a very ugly mud hole.

He was rocking back and forth, making a clucking sound with his tongue. When asked if he needed help getting out, he said, "Yes, but first help me get my horse out."

In addition to helping with the scouting duties, Port was frequently called upon to carry messages back and forth between Brigham's lead company and Nauvoo, where the Church committee was launching a steady flow of westward-bound Saints and trying to dispose of real estate. For a while the Catholic Church was considering buying the temple.

In mid-March, while bringing messages from Nauvoo to the lead company, Port ran into a group of Mormons at Indian Creek. William Hall had been to the Des Moines River to pick up a load of grain for Allen Stout. One of the horses had sickened with bloating and colic and laid down. The men tried to give the animal medicine but did not succeed. The horse lay on its side, with its forefoot over its ear. A group of Mormons traveling in the same direction had gathered around.

Reuben Strong said he believed there was breath in the horse yet, and he proposed to lay hands upon it and give it a blessing, the same kind of blessing Mormons administered to their sick brothers and sisters. Some present doubted whether it was right to lay hands on a horse. A discussion followed, until one of the men pulled out his Bible and read a scripture that said in the last days the Lord would pour out his spirit on all flesh.

Thus satisfied, Elders William Hall, Reuben Strong, Lluellen Mantle, Joseph Champlin, Martin Potter, and Porter Rockwell laid hands on the horse and commanded the unclean and foul spirits of every name and nature to depart and go to the gentiles at Warsaw and trouble the Saints no more.

The horse suddenly rolled over twice in great distress, sprang to its feet, neighed, vomited, emptied its bowels, and the next morning was harnessed to a load of about 1,200 pounds and performed its part as usual.

Because of shortages of supplies, it became apparent the Saints would not go much beyond Iowa Territory this first season. There was increasing talk of spending the coming winter near Miller's Hollow, at the western edge of the Iowa Territory.

As the wet spring began turning to summer, Brigham organized the men into groups of farmers for the purpose of clearing and planting large tracts of land along the route so there would be food to harvest by those coming along in the fall. Wheat, corn, and barley were the main crops.

Port was helping fence one of the large fields of wheat near Garden Grove on May 7 when he spotted a familiar non-Mormon approaching him. Port would have recognized that smile anywhere. It was Jacob Backenstos, sheriff of Hancock County, Illinois, the man Port had saved from Frank Worrell.

Port wiped his hands on the grass and reached out to shake hands with his old friend.

"Never thought I'd see you working like a farmer," the sheriff said as he dismounted.

"Brother Brigham says the ones that don't work don't eat," Port said. "And seeing as I like to eat, I work with the rest of them. What brings the likes of you clear out here?"

"Got a proposition for you, Brother Rockwell," the sheriff said. "A way to get out of all this farm work and make a thousand dollars at the same time."

"Want me to rob a bank with you?" Port asked.

"Easier than that," Backenstos responded, motioning for Port to follow him into the woods where they could talk undisturbed.

"My term as sheriff will be up this fall," Backenstos began, after they had seated themselves on a fallen tree. "Last fall when I took sides with the Mormons I figured my re-election was ensured. But then old Brigham moved all the Mormon votes out of the county. Without the Mormons, there's not a chance in hell I'll ever win another election in that county."

"You came half-way across Iowa to tell me that?" Port asked, wishing Backenstos would get to the point.

"I have a warrant for your arrest," he said.

"I'm in no mood for jokes," Port responded.

"For the murder of Frank Worrell. That's no joke."

Port jumped to his feet, reaching for the pistol in his belt.

"Hold on, damn it," Backenstos roared. "I'm not fool enough to try to take you in by force. You know me better than that. Do you think I'm stupid enough to come clear out here for that?"

"Then why did you come?" Port asked, easing his hand away from his gun.

"Just making some plans for my retirement, and I thought you'd like to get in on it."

"Get in on what?"

"There's a two thousand dollar reward on your head," Backenstos explained. "You come back to Carthage with me so I can collect the reward. I told the judge I could probably find you and bring you in if he would agree to give you a change of venue to Galena, about 150 miles upriver. There's a fair judge there. You would have to agree to stand trial for first-degree murder."

"Wonderful," Port said. "But I think I'd just as soon stay . . ."

"Hear me out," Backenstos insisted. "After you get to Galena, I'll waltz in and tell the judge that you were my deputy and I ordered you to shoot Worrell. If that doesn't get you acquitted, we'll bring Redden and Conover up there to testify they heard me swear you in and order you to shoot Worrell. They'll have to let you go. They'll have no case."

"I'm missing something," Port said. "Why should I do this?"

"Because I'd split the reward with you. Your share would be a thousand dollars!"

"What if the Carthage mob comes after me like they did Joseph?"

"I wouldn't leave Carthage the entire time you were there. The mob wouldn't come through me, the elected sheriff. I'd ensure your safety."

"Seems Governor Ford said the same thing to Joseph and Hyrum when they went to Carthage."

"It would be different this time. Everybody that hates the Mormons is in Nauvoo trying to steal a farm or house or something. We'll be in and out of Carthage before anybody knows what's happened."

"Are you sure it'll work?" Port asked.

"Sure as a man can be. The pieces are in place. Still, you might slip on a banana peel and break your neck. But if nothing goes very far wrong, we'll both come out of it a thousand dollars richer. Either way, it'll be a hell of a lot more exciting than digging post holes."

"That's for sure," Port said, offering his hand. "We've got a deal. When do we leave?"

"Where's your horse?"

"Over in those trees."

"Get him. We'll split a bottle of white lightning on the way."

Eight days later Port and Backenstos arrived in Carthage. Three days later the Warsaw Signal reported how Sheriff Jacob Backenstos had single-handedly penetrated the "heavily armed" Mormon camp at Garden Grove and arrested the dangerous killer, Rockwell, who at the time of his arrest was carrying seventy-one rounds of ammunition in his pockets, two Bowie knives, two pistols, and a shotgun. The article said Backenstos had gone beyond the call of duty in traveling half-way across Iowa to make one of the most daring arrests of all time.

"Where did they get this story?" Port asked, after Backenstos had read the article to him.

"From me, who else?" Backenstos responded.

"Why did you lie?"

"Wanted folks to think I'm the toughest, bravest gunfighter in these parts."

"So you can get re-elected?"

"No. So if they see me guarding you, they'll be afraid to try anything."

It took longer to get the change of venue than Backenstos had thought, but eventually it came and Port was escorted north to Galena, where the judge was on vacation for a few weeks. But eventually the judge returned.

Backenstos told him under oath that he had deputized Rockwell before ordering him to shoot Worrell. The judge did as Backenstos had predicted. He acquitted Port, saying there was insufficient evidence to hold trial. Port was free and a thousand dollars richer. He and Backenstos rode back to Nauvoo together. After one last ride through the City of Joseph, Port crossed the Mississippi River one more time and headed west to join Brigham Young on the Missouri River, a place the Mormons now called Winter Quarters.

# Chapter 38

With new babies being born every day and others being buried, no one knew exactly how many people were at Winter Quarters, spread out in tents and cabins on the bluffs overlooking the Missouri River. But President Young had William Clayton count the wagons. There were 1,805.

On his way across Iowa, Port learned that five hundred Mormon men had enlisted in the U.S. Army to march to California along the southern route, participants in what so far was a non-shooting war with Mexico. Port found it hard to believe there were five hundred Mormons willing to enlist in the army of a country that had allowed their people to be treated so badly in Missouri and Illinois.

Upon arrival at Winter Quarters, Port asked Brigham about the enlistment. The Church's president said the mustering of five hundred men into the Mormon Battalion was the first decent thing the United States had ever done for the Mormons. In fact, he thought the arrival of Captain James Allen to seek volunteers had been a direct answer to prayers. Unwittingly, the Mormons had established Winter Quarters on the Potawatomi Indian Reservation in violation of federal law. They had insufficient resources to move ahead to the Rocky Mountains. The mobs were behind them, and it was illegal to stay where they were.

Brigham explained that the clothing allowance for the volunteers alone—$3.50 per month per soldier—provided enough cash to feed the entire camp at Winter Quarters through the winter. Add to that the wages the soldiers received every two months and the Saints would be able to buy the additional supplies needed to push on to the Rocky Mountains in the spring. The enlistment agreement allowed the Mormons to remain on the reservation until spring. There was no doubt in President Young's mind that the Mormon Battalion was a heaven-sent opportunity for the U.S. Government to finance the Mormon migration.

Leaving President Young's cabin, Port set out looking for a place to spend the winter. Most of the Saints had built crude cabins, mostly from cottonwood and pine logs. With the trees in close proximity already cut down, other Saints seemed content to spend the approaching winter in wagons and tents.

Others were more creative. John Wright, concerned with keeping his young wife and four small children warm, climbed down the steep bank to the Missouri River and dug a hole back in the bank. He crammed his crude furniture inside and covered the opening with a sheet of canvas. The family seemed comfortable living like muskrats in the mud hole, until one day President Young asked John to take a second wife, a young woman whose husband had left her. Being a faithful Latter-day Saint, Wright dutifully agreed to do it, and the wedding was performed on the spot in President Young's cabin.

Needless to say, there were no squeals of delight, from the new wife or the first wife, when John brought the new addition home to the mud cave. Two weeks later, when the new wife announced she was going to St. Louis with no intention of ever returning, no one tried very hard to stop her. Nor did anyone judge her harshly.

Port didn't want to spend the winter in a mud hole, even if it might be warmer. Nor did he want to be in the main camp, crowded with barking dogs and squealing pigs. A lot of horses were still suffering from distemper, so in an effort to keep Bill healthy, Port located his camp in a wooded draw several miles from the main camp, against counsel of some of the brethren.

The elders said one should not camp alone with so many Indians in the area. In addition to the Potawatomis, there were Omahas,

Otoes, Poncas, and an occasional band of wandering Sioux. While there had been no direct confrontations with the red men, an occasional cow or horse turned up missing.

Port constructed a wickiup similar to the one he had stayed in at Liberty Jail, with the opening facing south to catch the winter sun whenever it was shining. The south-facing slope above the camp would provide plenty of feed for Bill when the snow wasn't too deep.

Port didn't anticipate spending a lot of time in his new camp because he would be carrying the mail back along the trail to Mormon camps at Mt. Pisgah and Garden Grove. He would even be going to Nauvoo occasionally, carrying messages to those who had not yet crossed the river.

At the end of the second day, Port had his camp ready for winter. His wickiup was large enough to stand up in. There was plenty of brush and bark around the sides to keep out the wind, rain, and snow. There was a canvas across the doorway and a stone fireplace just inside the doorway.

Port was preparing his first supper in the new home when he heard an approaching horse. It was still light, and he could see a lone Indian walking down the hillside toward him. The Indian had a wrinkled face, and a shaggy buffalo robe was wrapped around his shoulders against the cold. He was riding a skinny dun horse that looked like it had traveled too many miles that season. Its head hung too low, and its ears flopped too far sideways as it picked its way down the hill, stumbling frequently on the rocks. The old horse had seen better days. The coming winter would be cruel to such a horse.

"Howdy," Port called out in greeting. The Indian was armed only with a bow and several arrows.

"Ugh," the Indian grunted as he slid from his horse. After tying the animal to the nearest tree, he walked up to the wickiup.

"Nice night," Port said.

"Ugh," the Indian responded, beginning to rub his stomach.

"Like to stay for supper?" Port asked.

"Ugh," the Indian said, beginning to smile. It was apparent the red man did not speak English.

Port led the Indian into the wickiup, where a pan of beef chunks and turnips was simmering over the new stone fireplace. The two men sat facing each other, the pan of food between them. Using their knives they began spearing chunks of food and popping them in their mouths. Though the Indian didn't speak, he offered frequent smiles of gratitude. Port was happy to share his meal.

When the food was finished, the two men stepped outside. It was still light enough for the Indian to offer an admiring glance at Bill, who was tethered nearby in knee-deep grass. Offering a final smile of gratitude, the old Indian climbed onto his weary horse. The animal was in no mood to continue the journey, but when the Indian applied a vigorous slap with a leather quirt across its rump, it reluctantly broke into a trot up the draw, eventually disappearing into the trees. Port retired to his wickiup, pulling down the canvas door cover against the cold fall air.

The next morning Bill was gone. Hoping the horse might have pulled his picket pin free and strayed a short distance, Port raced to where the horse had been. The pin was still in place. A close examination of the end of the picket rope realized Port's worst fears. The rope had been cut with a knife. There were frost-covered tracks leading north to the top of the hill, indicating the horse had been taken early the previous evening before the ground had frozen, and before the frost had covered the ground.

Port raced to the top of the hill, following the tracks. There had been so many horses in the area he couldn't be sure the tracks belonged to Bill, or even that they were fresh. But all doubt was removed when he reached the top of the hill and saw the jaded dun horse. It was grazing in the tall grass less than a hundred yards away. There were no ropes attached to the horse, indicating it had been abandoned. Port knew no Indian in his right mind would abandon a horse, not even a jaded one, unless he had acquired something better to ride. Port was angry enough to kill. The man he had invited into his new home and shared his dinner with had stolen his horse. Port raced toward Winter Quarters, where he intended to borrow a fast horse. He intended to get Bill back and, in the process, decrease the number of horse thieves in the world by one.

As soon as he had borrowed a horse, Port hurried back to camp, grabbed some food and ammunition, and then headed north, following Bill's trail. It was easy at first because the tracks had been made before the ground froze, but as the Indian had ridden into the night, the ground becoming harder and harder against the freezing air, the tracks had become fainter and fainter until they were almost impossible to follow. But Port persisted, frequently dismounting and dropping to his hands and knees to analyze every pebble, blade of grass, and twig at a particular spot where he suspected the horse had passed.

Port continued following the trail all day, not stopping until the sun went down and it was too dark to see signs. The next morning at first light he was on his way again. He was not traveling very fast, but he hoped his persistence would pay off. Eventually, the Indian would feel safe and slow down.

About noon of the second day, the horse Port was riding went lame. In Port's hurry to get on the trail of the Indian, he had not been patient enough to borrow a horse with shoes. He would have liked to have continued on foot, but he didn't want to abandon a borrowed horse. The supply of horses at Winter Quarters was critically short. He couldn't risk losing two. Discouraged and frustrated, Port led the limping horse back to Winter Quarters. It took him two and a half days to make the journey.

During the long walk, he had a lot of time to think about Bill, the best horse he had ever owned. Bill was a strong runner, a good companion, obedient and willing. Not easily rattle but not lazy either. Port doubted he could ever find another horse as good as Bill. What bothered him as much as anything was the rough treatment he was sure Bill would receive at the hands of his new owner. The Indian probably wouldn't treat Bill any better than he had the dun. The red man probably wouldn't care for the horse's feet. He probably wouldn't make sure Bill had plenty of feed. And he would certainly ride him too long and hard. In a few months Bill would probably be skin and bones, with drooping head and ears like the dun.

Upon returning to camp, Port paid eighty dollars for a roan stallion, the best horse in camp, according to some. The stallion was a strong, aggressive animal, always eager to get moving. Port named him Boggs, in memory of the former governor of Missouri.

At the same time, he paid a dollar for a dog, or at least it was half dog. The mother had been bred by a wolf. The shaggy white pup had long hair and bright green eyes. The pup looked alert, and like it could get mean if the need presented itself.

The dog was not yet a year old. With a half wolf tied in his camp, Port figured there would be less chance of someone sneaking up on him or his horse in the middle of the night.

When Port returned to camp that night there was a hind quarter of beef and a sack of grain tied on the new horse's back. Port intended to fatten up his two new companions in preparation for winter. He named the dog Joseph, after the best friend he had ever had.

The next morning, Port was considering resuming his search for Bill when a courier arrived from President Young with a packet of letters to be delivered to Nauvoo. After stashing the supplies he didn't need for the trip in some brush, Port headed for the trail leading to Mt. Pisgah. Boggs was eager to get along, and Joseph, free at last from the leash, was bounding happily back and forth through the brush.

It was in the middle of the second night that Port was awakened by Joseph's barking. Port reached for his gun and waited. He couldn't hear anything. The dog barked a few more times, then was quiet. Port was awake the rest of the night, wondering what had startled the dog.

The next morning he scouted in the direction the dog had been barking, half expecting to find moccasin tracks. Instead, he found boot tracks. He followed them into the woods, where the man that made them had gotten on a mule and ridden north. If the man had been friendly, why had he left when the dog started barking? If the man had had evil intentions, what were they, and why had he been so easily discouraged?

Port thought a lot that day about the boot tracks, finally concluding that he had to teach Joseph not to bark. To warn Port, yes, but not by sounding an alarm for the enemy to hear too. The dog had served a useful purpose in sounding the alarm, but now Port would never know who the intruder was or what he had wanted. If the man was trying to kill Port, he was still alive, free to try again at a time of his own choosing. It would have been better if Port had been silently warned of the approaching stranger, allowing Port to sneak into the night and hunt the unsuspecting hunter.

By nightfall, Port had a training plan all figured out for Joseph. He stopped just outside Mt. Pisgah. As soon as camp was set up, he hurried to the nearest Mormon cabin, where he gave a boy fifty cents to visit his camp an hour after dark and again an hour before daylight the next morning. He explained to the boy that he was training his dog how to respond to approaching strangers, and he assured the boy he would not be bitten. Port told the boy to make plenty of noise as he approached. Port then returned to his camp.

It was about an hour after dark when Joseph began to bark, having heard the approaching boy long before Port could hear anything. Port scolded the dog for barking, but at the same time he showed interest in the approaching stranger. When Joseph tried to bark again, Port slapped him with a stick. The dog was tied with a short rope to the saddle. Port was seated on the ground beside the saddle. He scolded the dog for whining and repeatedly slapped him with the stick when he tried to bark. Joseph was beside himself wanting to bark, but Port made it very clear that he wanted silence. He continued to show as much interest in the approaching stranger as the dog did.

Port didn't let the boy stay in camp long enough to get familiar with the dog. He just reminded the boy to be sure and return an hour before daybreak.

The next morning, Port was awake and ready when Joseph heard the approaching boy. The dog was just starting to bark when Port slapped him with the stick, following up with a firm no whenever the dog tried to whine or growl. At the same time, Port looked toward the approaching boy, asking the dog who was there. He wanted the dog to know he was very interested in knowing what was out there. He just didn't want any noise.

That day Port continued on to Garden Grove, where he hired another boy to do the same thing. He no longer needed to hit Joseph to keep him from barking.

The second morning at Garden Grove, Port pretended to be sleeping when he knew the boy would be approaching. Joseph jumped up when he heard the boy, but he didn't bark, whine, or growl. He paced back and forth at the end of his rope, looking in the direction of the sounds, and then back at Port, who appeared to be sound asleep.

The dog turned in circles, frustrated, wanting to sound a warning but knowing he would be scolded for making any noise. Suddenly he had an idea. He trotted up to his master and began licking his face.

"What is it, boy?" Port whispered, sitting up, pushing the wet nose away. The dog returned to the end of his rope, looking in the direction of the approaching boy.

"Good boy, good boy," Port whispered, crawling over to the dog, scratching his ears, giving him a piece of meat.

Port hired another boy that night, and a man the next, just to make sure Joseph had learned his lesson well. Joseph would bark occasionally, but with time he learned that a few quick licks across his master's face was the preferred way to sound the alarm. From that time on, Port slept a lot better on the trail, at least when Joseph was with him. Never again would he have a horse stolen from under his nose while he was sleeping.

Port looked forward to the night when Joseph would awaken him with a lick. Whoever was lurking nearby would be in for a big surprise.

# Chapter 39

On December 29, 1846, the first pioneer company was organized. It consisted of 143 men, three women, and two children. Its leader was Brigham Young, and his purpose was to find a place to settle and to blaze a trail for others to follow. The plan was to follow the Platte River west and then head over South Pass to the Great Basin. If that was not a suitable place to settle, then the company would move on to Oregon and possibly Vancouver Island. The company was to leave Winter Quarters as soon as the weather would permit.

On Tuesday, February 23, Port delivered a packet of letters from Mt. Pisgah to the historian's office. Brigham Young, who had been sick for some time, had just arrived to address the Twelve Apostles, most of whom were present. Port was invited to stay.

"I just want you brethren to know there has been a change in plans," President Young began. "We're leaving in February instead of April." His comment was followed by laughter and knee slapping. They certainly hoped he was joking. The early departure the previous year from Nauvoo had resulted in so much hardship that no one wanted to repeat that.

After assuring his audience that his first comment was nothing more than an attempt at humor, Young then talked about his sickness, and how for a while he thought he might be like Moses and not be permitted to enter the promised land. If death were his fate, however, he could think of no better company than those six hundred already buried on the hill above Winter Quarters. He expressed concern over the great mixing up of families that was occurring as a result of the migration.

There were many organizational details to be worked out in preparation for the coming migration, but Brigham chose to address a different subject. He related a dream.

"While sick and asleep about noonday on the seventeenth," he began, "I dreamed that I went to see Joseph. He looked perfectly natural, sitting with his feet on the lower round of his chair. I took hold of his right hand and kissed him many times and said to him, 'Why is it we cannot be together as we used to be? You have been from us a long time, and we want your society, and I do not like to be separated from you.'

"Joseph, rising from his chair and looking at me with his usual earnest, expressive, and pleasing countenance, replied, 'It is all right.'

"I said, 'I do not like to be away from you.'

"Joseph said, 'It is all right. We cannot be together yet. We shall be by and by, but you will have to do without me a while, and then we shall be together again.'

"I then discovered there was a hand rail between us. Joseph stood by a window and to the southwest of him it was very light. I was in the twilight and to the north of me it was very dark. I said, 'Brother Joseph, the brethren you know well, better than I do, you raised them up and brought the priesthood to us. The brethren have a great anxiety to understand the law of adoption or sealing principles, and if you have a word of counsel for me I should be glad to receive it.'

"Joseph stepped toward me and, looking very earnestly yet pleasantly, said, 'Tell the people to be humble and faithful, and be sure to keep the spirit of the Lord, and it will lead them right. Be careful and not turn away the small still voice; it will teach you what to do and where to go; it will yield the fruits of the kingdom. Tell the brethren to keep their hearts open to conviction, so that when the Holy Ghost comes to them, their hearts will be ready to receive it. They can tell the spirit of the Lord from all other spirits; it will whisper peace and joy to their souls; it will take malice, hatred, strife, and all evil from their hearts, and their whole desire will be to do good, to bring forth righteousness, and to build up the kingdom of God. Tell the brethren if they will follow the spirit of the Lord, they will go right. Be sure to tell the people to keep the spirit of the Lord, and if they will, they will find themselves just as they were organized by our Father in Heaven before they came into the world. Our Father in Heaven organized the human family, but they are all disorganized and in great confusion.'

"Joseph then showed me the pattern, how they were in the beginning. This I cannot describe, but I saw it and saw where the priesthood had been taken from the earth and how it must be joined together, so that there would be a perfect chain from Father Adam to his latest posterity. Joseph again said, 'Tell the people to be sure to keep the spirit of the Lord and follow it, and it will lead them just right.' "

On April 14 the lead company that had been organized in December headed west with Port as scout and chief hunter. About thirty miles west, at the Elk Horn River, the company divided into two groups, one under Stephen Markham, the other under A.P. Rockwood. The purpose of the division was two-fold. Smaller groups seemed to travel faster, and at night, with fewer animals to compete for the grazing, it would be easier to keep their animals close to camp.

The breakfast bugle sounded at five o'clock every morning, with the company's goal to be on the trail by seven. The wagons formed a half-circle at night, with the horses and oxen secured in the middle.

Twelve days after departure, Port was awakened one morning at three thirty by one of the guards, who was so excited he could hardly talk. There was a full moon, and he claimed he had seen five or six Indians crawling in the tall grass just north of camp.

Port slipped on his boots, tucked both pistols in his belt, picked up his rifle, and asked the guard to show him where the Indians were. They climbed onto a wagon box, the guard pointing excitedly toward some bushes to the north. Port didn't see five or six Indians, but he saw two, and that was enough.

"What should we do?" the guard asked. "Should we wake up President Young?"

"I don't think that will be necessary," Port whispered, setting down his rifle and drawing both pistols. "Get ready to fire with me. Let's make a lot of noise." He pointed both pistols toward the Indians and was about to fire when the guard said, "Maybe they're friendly Indians. Shouldn't we find out first?"

"Sneaking through the grass at three in the morning is not exactly a token of friendship," Port responded as he opened fire with both pistols, firing eight times as fast as he could pull the triggers. Six Indians exploded from the grass, scrambling to put as much distance as possible between them and Port's blazing pistols. Port didn't hit any of them.

The camp came alive, sleepy men in long underwear rolling out from under wagons, grabbing rifles. But the Indians were gone, and all was safe. Nevertheless, the guard was doubled from then on. The company was more careful, knowing it was in hostile Indian country.

A few days later, Port and a group of men were riding back along the trail toward the Elk Horn River, looking for a mare that had strayed from Willard Richards, when one of the men spotted something that looked like a wolf. When Port raised his rifle to fire a warning shot, fifteen Pawnees in breechclouts charged from the brush. They were all on foot, each brave carrying a bow and arrows. Several had rifles.

Port's men held their fire while Port waved for the Indians to halt, which they eventually did. Putting their arrows back in the quivers, the Indians walked up to the white men.

" 'Bacco, 'bacco," one of the braves begged, wanting tobacco. The Mormons indicated they didn't have any.

"Want squaw?" another whined, pointing to the thick brush along the river. Smiling, he motioned for the white men to follow him to the river. Port remembered a similar smile back at Winter Quarters, on the face of the Indian who had stolen his horse.

Port and his men refused to follow the Indians to the river. Instead, they continued their journey along the wagon trail. When they were about fifty yards from the Indians, the braves with rifles opened fire on Port and his men.

As the men dove for cover, Port held back. Ever since that Indian had stolen his horse, he had felt a growing desire to tangle with an Indian deserving his wrath. Now there were fifteen of them less than a hundred yards away.

Port spun the big roan around and dug his spurs into its sides. Two or three lunges and Boggs was at full gallop, headed straight for the startled Indians. Port drew his pistols and began firing. The red men scattered like hens before a fox, diving into the thick brush along the edge of the river. Port wounded several, but couldn't find any bodies to indicate a kill. He received an awestruck greeting when he returned to his men.

"Need to let 'em know right off the Mormons are fearless fighters and deserve plenty of traveling room," Port explained. After finding the stray mare, the men returned unharmed to camp.

A few days later everyone was standing high in the wagon boxes, looking over the first large herd of buffalo. They had just crossed Wood River. Some guessed the number of buffalo in view to be ten thousand. William Clayton said he had heard that one couldn't kill a bull buffalo by shooting it in the head.

"Let's find out," Port said, jumping down from the wagon box onto the back of the roan stallion. "Fresh meat tonight," he shouted, galloping off toward the herd.

Members of the company watched from their wagon boxes as Port and several of the hunters galloped among the stampeding buffalo, shooting several fat cows and bulls for an evening feast. Port finally reined the stallion in front of a huge galloping bull. With his rifle in one hand, he reached back, pointed the barrel at the bull's broad forehead, and pulled the trigger.

Instead of going down, the huge bull bellowed in rage, increasing its speed in an effort to catch and destroy Port and his horse. It was all Port and the big roan could do to keep out of reach until one of the other hunters shot the bull through the lungs.

When the hunt was over and the dust had settled, Port dismounted next to the big bull, determined to assay the damage to its forehead. While the ball had penetrated the skin, it had not gone through the thick skull.

Finding a bawling bull calf near one of the fallen cows, Port threw a rope around its neck and led it back to camp where he presented it to Brigham Young, who promptly named it Governor Ford.

# Chapter 40

One night in mid-May, after a particularly hard and dusty day, some of the men gathered around a fire after supper. It was announced a mock trial would be held, one of the favorite nighttime activities. Orson Pratt got things started by handing a summons to Port. Pratt read it out loud to the group, as follows:

"To Marshal O.P. Rockwell: Sir, you are hereby commanded to bring, wherever found, the body of Stephen Markham before the right reverend Bishop Whipple, at his quarters, there to answer to the following charge—that of emitting in meeting on Sunday last a sound a posteriori from the seat of honor somewhat resembling the rumble of distant thunder or the heavy discharge of artillery, thereby endangering the steadiness of the olfactory nerves of those present, as well as diverting their minds from the discourse of the speaker."

The completion of the reading was greeted with loud laughter. Upon hearing the laughter, others joined the group, eager to share the fun. Port handed the paper to a sheepish Markham, motioning for him to move front and center to answer the charges. The old scout refused, shaking his head, while those about him continued to laugh. Others urged him forward. He just shook his head. He was the only one not laughing.

"I wish you boys would forget what happened in church last week," Markham said. "It was too embarrassing to be funny. Just leave me alone."

"I had something more embarrassing than that happen to me once," Port offered, loud enough for all to hear, suddenly taking the attention away from a grateful Markham. Port paused.

"Tell us about it, Port," a voice called out.

"It's too embarrassing to talk about," Port teased, his voice high with excitement.

"Tell us," another shouted. Everyone cheered.

Port had never much cared for speaking in front of groups, particularly in church or at political gatherings. But this was different. These men were his friends, eager to have their legs pulled. They were having a good time together. He was getting Markham off the hot seat.

"It all started with a horse I bought down in Pennsylvania," he began. "Was raised in Middlesex, a town. His name was Sex, after the town, I suppose."

"You're joking," someone challenged.

"No," Port said. "But his name didn't get me into trouble until last year, when Luana and I decided to see the judge about a divorce. We had pretty much agreed on how to divide things up, except for Sex, the horse." Some of the men were beginning to laugh. "Luana wanted to have Sex, but so did I. We agreed to let the judge decide.

"After the judge looked over the divorce papers Luana had filled out, Luana up and said, 'Porter won't give me Sex.'

"The judge put on his specs and took a closer look at Luana." The men roared.

"Then the judge says, 'I suppose that's grounds for divorce.'

" 'But, your honor, you don't understand,' I said. 'I had Sex before we were married.'

"The judge said, 'So did I.'

"About that time I heard a ruckus outside the courtroom and what sounded like a horse galloping down the street. Thinking someone might have stolen my horse, I ran over to the window. The judge asked what I was doing. 'Looking for Sex,' I said.

" 'Divorce granted,' said the judge."

By this time every man in the circle was roaring with laughter, some slapping their thighs, other with tears running down their cheeks, including Stephen Markham.

After a hard, dusty day on the trail, it felt good to let go and laugh unreservedly, at least until Brigham Young stepped front and center. The laughter quickly subsided as he reminded the men there had been altogether too much cursing, bickering, light-mindedness, and loud laughter. He reminded the men they were not any ordinary group of pioneers, but God's chosen people seeking the promised land—and they needed to act accordingly, so the spirit of the Lord could abide with them.

The men dispersed to complete their evening chores and check their animals. But the weariness of an hour earlier was gone. The laughter had given the men needed relief from their labors and, with that relief, new strength to continue.

# Chapter 41

The novelty of seeing buffalo wore off. The shaggy beasts were almost always in sight. Sometimes a huge herd traveling north or south would block the path of the wagons, making forward progress impossible for hours. The single biggest problem, however, was keeping the wild bison from mingling with the herd of oxen and horses following the wagon train. Once an ox was mixed in with the buffalo it was hard to get it back out again. The herders had to keep the trailing herd bunched up close whenever large numbers of buffalo were near. Sometimes the grass was grazed so close by the bison herds that there wasn't enough feed for oxen and horses for miles. And sometimes water holes were so polluted with buffalo manure and urine that the settlers were forced to drink from the muddy Platte.

While the bison didn't mind or feel threatened by the cattle and horses, they became very excited at the sight of a dog. Sometimes they would charge. When buffalo were near, settlers put their dogs in their wagons, tying them up if necessary. Port, having no wagon, solved the problem by placing Joseph behind him on the horse's back. The dog didn't like to be that high off the ground, but with coaxing and practice he soon learned to ride in relative comfort. With time, Joseph learned to stand on his hind legs, his front paws on Port's shoulders. He could ride like that even at a full gallop.

Both night and morning the Saints ate fresh roasted buffalo meat, cooked over smoldering buffalo chips. On the open plains there was no wood to burn, so dry buffalo droppings, which were in abundant supply, were used. The only problem was finding chips dry enough to burn, particularly after a rain.

One morning, while the wagons were pushing through a particularly large buffalo herd, Port spotted a lone horse, a paint, moving along with the buffalo. The paint was carrying a crude rawhide saddle but it was not wearing a bridle. Apparently an Indian had lost his seat while chasing buffalo, and his pony had run off with the buffalo.

Port had no trouble getting close to the mare and putting a lead rope on her. She was a beautiful animal, well fed, and appeared to be well broke. As soon as he arrived back at the wagons with his new catch, Port bridled the mare and leaped upon her back. Instead of offering to buck, she responded to every command. It was apparent someone had spend a lot of time training this horse.

On May 31 the company arrived at Fort Laramie, a trading post surrounded by a wall of vertical poles with pointed ends. Outside the wall were a dozen or more tepees. Naked children and yapping dogs ran forward to greet the first immigrant company of the season.

Port accompanied Brigham Young to meet the owner of the fort, James Bordeaux, a French trapper turned trader. Except for a long black beard, Bordeaux would have been difficult to distinguish from his Indian friends. His clothing was identical to theirs.

Bordeaux regretfully informed the Mormons that because his spring shipment of supplies from the east had not yet arrived he had very little in the way of trade goods. While he had no sugar, coffee, salt, or pepper, he did have some whiskey and tobacco, though it cost thirty-two dollars a gallon for the whiskey and one dollar a pound for the tobacco.

The Frenchman informed the Mormons that Lilburn Boggs, former governor of Missouri, had stopped at the fort on his way to California the previous summer. Boggs had warned the trader to watch his cattle and stock when the Mormons were around. Brigham was about to tell Bordeaux he wouldn't have to worry about the Mormons, at least not the ones in this company, when the trader explained that while Boggs was telling him how bad the Mormons were, Boggs' companions were stealing everything they could get their hands on.

Bordeaux explained that since it was necessary to cross the Platte just upstream from the fort, the Mormons might want to buy his two-wagon flatboat for fifteen dollars. The Platte, swollen with spring runoff water, was a hundred yards wide and about ten feet deep. The trader said if they didn't want to buy the flatboat, he would ferry the entire Mormon outfit across for eighteen dollars. The Mormons decided to save three dollars and buy the boat, knowing full well they would have to leave it behind for Bordeaux to sell to the next company.

While most everyone in the company moved down to the river to make preparations for the crossing, Port lingered behind to let Bordeaux try to buy the pretty little paint mare he had found among the buffalo. With immigrant companies coming through, Port guessed there would be a strong demand for fresh horse flesh.

Bordeaux wanted the mare, all right, and after an hour of haggling, in which Port announced at least three different times he had changed his mind about selling the animal, a trade agreement was finally reached. For the mare, Port received two cows with calves, a heifer, two pair of moccasin shoes, and two rawhide lariats.

The company traveled about a week on the south side of the Platte before it became necessary to cross over to the north side again. This time there was no raft to buy, so the Mormons went to work building a cottonwood ferry from a scarce supply of logs scattered along the edge of the stream. The livestock welcomed the chance to rest and recuperate. There was plenty of grass, there being few buffalo in the area.

The Mormons finished the raft and were ferrying their wagons across the river when a company of emigrants from Missouri caught up with them. While Brigham Young wasn't about to give his old enemies a raft that had taken his men three days to build, neither was he inclined to initiate new hostilities by burning it.

Brigham came up with a better alternative. He agreed to ferry the Missouri company across the river at a rate of $1.50 a load, payable in flour valued at $2.50 a hundredweight. By the time the last Missouri wagon had crossed the river, the Mormons had earned thirty-four dollars in provisions. Seeing a good business, Brigham left nine men behind to operate the ferry for the remainder of the summer.

When the Mormon company reached Pacific Springs at the head of the Sweetwater Valley, just two miles east of South Pass, they saw a lone rider coming from the west. The man was dressed in buckskins and a fox fur hat and was riding an Indian saddle.

What distinguished the rider from other mountain men was the fact that he was black. He introduced himself as Moses Harris, a former slave turned mountain man. He had come from California and was headed east to St. Louis. He had newspapers from California. He showed them to the Mormons.

To everyone's surprise, one of the newspapers, the *California Star*, was published by Sam Brannan, the Mormon from New York who had filled a ship with Saints and sailed around the horn to California. The newspaper was published in Yerba Buena, later called San Francisco.

Harris spent the night with the Mormons, telling one yarn after another—about a different time, a better time, when beaver pelts brought five dollars each, and a man could make a fortune following the cold, unexplored streams of the Rocky Mountains, provided he could avoid the Blackfoot and other hostile Indians.

"Those were shining times," Harris said, "when everyone got together at the summer rendezvous for a drunk that lasted weeks, and every year or two you got yourself a new squaw. Those were shining times."

When asked about the valley of the Great Salt Lake as a suitable place to settle, Harris said the land was "about as barren as the back of your hand and just as fertile." He said a much better place to settle was Cache Valley to the north, where the mountain men held several of their rendezvous.

Moses Harris was the first of a series of visitors to run into the Mormons the next ten days. The next morning Harris continued his leisurely journey eastward while the Mormons crossed the Continental Divide.

The second visitor was Jim Bridger, probably the first white man to see the Great Salt Lake. "Old Gabe," as his two companions called him, was headed east to Fort Laramie. He reluctantly agreed to spend the night with the Mormons and tell them what he knew of the area surrounding the Great Salt Lake.

He said that while the soil appeared fertile, the nights were probably too cold to grow corn. South of Utah Lake, however, he said the Indians grew as good a crop of corn, pumpkins, and wheat as white men grew in Kentucky. He said the Indians around Utah Lake were a mean bunch and to be avoided. The Shoshones that lived in the Salt Lake basin and the country to the north had the prettiest squaws.

The next morning Bridger continued his journey east, while the Mormons continued on to the Green River, which was still too swollen with spring runoff to cross on foot. Those not ill with mountain fever began to gather logs to construct what hopefully would be the last raft.

In the past week many of the Mormons had come down with a fever fondly called Rocky Mountain Quickstep because those with the sickness often moved very quickly to private places to relieve themselves.

It was Port who first saw the next group of visitors, three white men riding hard from the west. When they reached the far side of the river, someone recognized the leader as Sam Brannan. Now, the Mormons thought, they would receive a reliable report from one of their own of what lay ahead.

Sam Brannan, however, did not want to talk about the Great Basin, though he had just been there. The articulate young Mormon wanted only to talk about California, a place he called the richest land on the face of the earth. He told how several Mormons had already made fortunes filling ships with redwood headed for Europe and Asia. He described a land that would grow anything, including oranges and lemons. He described endless rolling hills of wild oats crowded with vast herds of fat cattle, horses, deer, and elk. One never got hungry in California, he said. It was a big land with enough room for fifty million Mormons, in addition to everyone else who wanted to live there. In a decade the Mormons would become the richest people on the face of the earth.

By the time Brannan finished his description of California, Port and about a hundred other people were ready to go back with him. But President Young had a different idea. He seemed indifferent to Brannan's lavish description of the land beyond the Sierra Nevada Mountains. He didn't disagree with anything Brannan had said about California, except when Brannan said it was the best place for the Mormons to settle. Without giving any reasons, Young made it clear he didn't want the Saints going to California. Port thought that perhaps Young didn't feel well. Maybe he was coming down with the mountain fever. Offended by the cool reception, Brannan and his two companions swam their horses back across the river, beginning their return trip to California without waiting for the Mormon pioneer company to accompany them. Later, they came back to accompany Brigham's company to the valley of the Great Salt Lake.

Soon after crossing the Green River, the company could see the Bear River Mountains (later called the Uinta Mountains) off to the south. They followed Black's Fork past Ham's Fork, arriving at Fort Bridger on July 7.

After leaving Fort Laramie, everyone had talked about Port's trade involving the paint mare. At Ft. Bridger it was Howard Eagan who made the trade everyone talked about. He gave an Indian two well-used rifles for nineteen scraped and tanned deerskins, three elk hides, and moccasin-making materials.

On July 10 the company met Miles Goodyear, its fourth visitor since South Pass. Goodyear owned a ranch near the north end of the Great Salt Lake. He said the best way to enter the valley was down the canyon leading to his ranch. Port was sent ahead to check the route. The earlier plan had been to follow the trail left by the Donner-Reed party two years earlier, dropping down to the valley at the south end of the lake.

When Port returned to make his report he said the canyons leading to Goodyear's ranch were rough, wooded, and nearly impassable. He guessed Goodyear had made the proposal because he wanted the Mormons to build a road for him. Brigham decided to remain on the trail of the Donner-Reed party.

Two days later Brigham Young came down with a bad case of mountain fever. While he lay sick in his wagon, Parley Pratt led twenty-three wagons to the head of Echo Canyon, the men hacking their way into the valley with axes and shovels as they attempted to make the Donner trail more passable.

On July 21 Orson Pratt and Erastus Snow rode down what later became known as Emigration Canyon and entered the Salt Lake Valley. The next morning, Porter Rockwell, George Albert Smith, John Pack, Joseph Mathews, J.C. Little, and John Brown accompanied Pratt to plant seeds and test the soil.

On July 23 Pack and Mathews returned to Brigham Young to announce their findings. Young, still fighting the fever, entered the valley on the afternoon of July 24, making the announcement that shaped the destiny of his people. "This is the place," he said.

# Chapter 42

Some were disappointed with Young's announcement to settle in the Great Basin. The Salt Lake Valley was a dry, desolate land with barren stretches of salt flats and alkali marshes to the west. The desert mountains, where not barren and rocky, grew endless sagebrush and stubby junipers. The rugged granite mountains to the east had sparse stands of fir, aspen, maple, and oak.

To a people used to the lush green forests and valleys of the Mississippi River Valley, the Salt Lake Valley was a vast wasteland. To many, Sam Brannan's invitation to keep moving to California made a lot more sense.

Sam Brannan had rejoined the pioneer company on the last leg of its journey into the valley, hoping that once the Saints saw the barren salt flats and endless sagebrush, his invitation to come to California would be more appealing. But Brigham Young was firm in his conviction to remain in the Great Basin.

"California is the promised land, not this forsaken place" were Sam Brannan's last words when he took his leave to return to California.

Brigham Young didn't see a barren wasteland. He saw a rugged, magnificent land bordered by inspiring snow-capped peaks. To the west, he saw a lake so blue that sometimes one could not tell where the lake ended and the sky began—until sunset, when the light reflecting off the water turned the sky a dozen different shades of red, resulting in some of the most beautiful sunsets on the face of the earth.

Brigham Young saw a rich land that would not surrender its abundance easily—the rocks and sagebrush would have to be cleared and the streams dammed. He saw rich mountain forests that would not surrender their wealth of timber willingly—roads and trails would have to be forged up steep inclines through cities of house-sized boulders. He saw rushing mountain streams that would not be dammed and diverted easily, especially during the spring runoff.

He saw a land where only those willing to work long and hard would survive. Any lesser efforts would result in failure and starvation. He saw a hard land that would not attract the gentile masses seeking easy living, a land where the Mormons would be left alone to build churches, temples, a righteous people, and the kingdom of God on earth. As far as Brigham Young was concerned, the journey was over. The Mormons had come home to their promised land.

By the end of the first week in the Salt Lake Valley the Mormons had raised crude shelters, begun a city survey, dammed up several streams, and broken the first plow in the hard soil.

Port spent the first week exploring with his horse and dog. He found deer and elk in the foothills, fish in the streams, and ducks and geese in the marshes. He found tall grasses, reeds, and willows that could be used in weaving baskets and mats. He found clay, both red and gray, for making pottery. He saw wolves, coyotes, mountain lions, badgers, beavers, skunks, ground squirrels, meadowlarks, seagulls, blackbirds, bald and golden eagles, crows, mice, gophers, and all the usual insects.

Port visited two Indian villages, making an important discovery. The Salt Lake Valley was a middle ground, a no-man's-land between the Ute stronghold to the south and the Shoshone lands to the north. While both tribes camped in the Salt Lake Valley from time to time, neither tribe made territorial claims to the valley. The Mormons, in settling here, had displaced no one. An army of interpreters and Indian agents couldn't have picked a better place to settle for a people wanting to avoid conflict with the natives.

The river connecting a large freshwater lake to the south with the Great Salt Lake was called the Jordan River, after a stream serving a similar function in the Holy Land. The two most magnificent peaks to the east were promptly christened Ensign and Olympus. The first canyon explored by Parley Pratt was named Parley's Canyon. The stream running past the new city lots was named City Creek. The land to the north with the richest, blackest soil was called Bountiful, after a prosperous community in the Book of Mormon.

On August 2, nine days after Brigham Young's arrival, the Council of Fifty met and decided to send Port, along with three other men, back along the trail to find out how two other Mormon companies, led by Ezra T. Benson and Charles C. Rich, were doing.

Port left immediately, grateful he had a tireless horse. The stallion, Boggs, was never lazy, no matter how long the day or steep the hill. He plunged ahead eagerly, relentlessly. The dog, Joseph, was trail-hardened too. Skinny in appearance, he trotted tirelessly beside the big horse, never lagging far behind, unless he was on the trail of a rabbit. Between rabbits and squirrels, Joseph provided most of his own food, seldom needing to be fed by his master.

Port and his companions pushed hard, catching both emigrant trains before August 20. They found the Benson Company at Deer Creek in Wyoming and the Rich Company on the Platte.

After delivering the messages, along with as much detail as possible on the new Mormon homeland, Port turned around and headed back, soon leaving the two companies of emigrants far behind.

He had only been on the trail five days when he met Brigham Young coming east with a herd of about a hundred fresh horses. Brigham was on his way to Winter Quarters to help organize the rest of the Saints for the trip to the Great Basin. Port joined up with the group as hunter since Young hadn't brought food with him, knowing the Saints in the valley would be critically short on food supplies until next year's crops were harvested. The challenge for Port now was to find enough deer and elk to feed Brigham and his men until they reached the open plains, where buffalo were abundant.

Everyone was so concerned about finding enough to eat that not enough attention was paid to a band of Crow Indians that passed the Mormons on the trail one afternoon. That night, the camp was awakened by the whooping and hollering of half a dozen Indians as they drove off fifty of the Mormon's horses. They didn't get Boggs, however, because Port always kept the big stallion close to where he slept, staked out with a long lariat tied to one of his front feet. Port quickly saddled the horse, grabbed his guns, and headed into the night after the Indians. Boggs was eager to engage in the chase after the departing horses.

There was no moon, so Port held the stallion back. He knew the Indians wouldn't be able to travel at top speed either. He let Boggs choose the direction, trusting the horse's ability to know which way the horses had gone.

They were headed in a northerly direction. In his hurry to get after the Indians, Port had not waited for any of the other men to join him.

Just before dawn, Port heard the clanking of shod hooves on rocks ahead of him. He slowed down, knowing he was nearly close enough to shoot but waiting for the light.

When daylight finally came, no horses or Indians were in sight. There was a single draw ahead of Port, veering off at an angle. Port guessed that was where the Indians and horses had to be.

Port hurried to the edge of the draw and looked over. He saw eight horses, grazing peacefully in a sagebrush flat, and two Indians. Apparently the horse thieves had divided the herd during the night, a common practice by marauding Indians when stealing horses. Small groups of horses could be driven faster, and by scattering in different directions, pursuit became more difficult.

The two Indians had dismounted from their horses and were eating something, perhaps jerky. One of the Indians was a large, muscular man; the other appeared to be a boy, perhaps twelve or thirteen years old. Both were dressed in buckskin leggings and shirts. The big Indian was carrying a rifle.

Port reached for his rifle and took careful aim on the big Indian, about three hundred yards off, and fired. The man dropped in a heap, without even looking in Port's direction. The smaller Indian raced for the nearest horse, leaving the rifle where it had fallen. Port leaped upon his horse, galloping down the steep hill into the draw.

By the time the boy was on his horse, Port was only a short distance away and closing the remaining distance between them at a full gallop. Port was close enough for an easy pistol shot, but it appeared the young Indian was unarmed. As angry as Port was at having lost the horses, he was in no mood to shoot a child.

Galloping alongside, Port reached over and pushed the boy from the horse. The child tumbled through the brush to an abrupt halt. Port pulled his horse around and rode up to the young dust-covered Indian, who was sitting up now, holding his left wrist, glaring defiantly at Port.

"Only want my horses back," Port said, soothingly. "Don't intend to do you any harm. Let me take a look at that wrist." Port dismounted. He was amazed at the child's good looks—fine facial features, clear black eyes. Someday the boy would grow into a handsome brave.

Port knelt down, reaching out to touch the wrist. The child pulled it away.

"I'll push you down and sit on you if that's what it takes," Port said sternly. While the child didn't understand the words, he did understand the intent, and he reluctantly offered his injured wrist.

The forearm didn't appear broken, just sprained. Port removed his bandanna and wrapped it tightly around the wrist. Then he got up and walked over to the Indian he had shot. The big brave was dead. Port picked up the rifle and headed back to the child. "Want to come with me?" he asked. There was no answer. Port nodded for the boy to follow him back to his horse.

As the boy got to his feet, there was something in the way he moved that caused Port to start laughing. As he looked closer at the confused child, he laughed harder. He was not looking at a boy, but a girl, a young squaw, and a very pretty one but still a child.

He had intended to leave the child to find its own way back to its people, but there was no way he could leave a girl alone in this wild land.

Getting on his horse, Port reached down, taking the child by her good wrist and pulling her up behind him. She offered no protest, nor did she take a second look at the dead brave on the ground. Port was puzzled by her apparent lack of concern for her companion.

It wasn't until about a week later, after Port had left Brigham Young in buffalo country to hunt his own meat and was returning to Salt Lake, that Port learned the reason for the girl's indifference to her dead companion.

Port crossed paths with an old trapper named Johnson who could speak the girl's language. To Port's surprise, she spoke Shoshone, not Crow. She told the trapper the Crows had kidnapped her from her village on the Snake River a month earlier. They were taking her to their home village when they saw the Mormon horses being driven east by Brigham Young and decided to make the raid.

The trapper said the girl's name was Boiling Dog. Port didn't much care for that, so he called her Emma. His plan was to leave her with a Mormon family in Salt Lake for the winter and then return her to her people in the spring, if he could find them.

Once Emma realized Port had no intention of harming her, she seemed happy to travel with him. She especially liked the company of Joseph. At night she would get the dog to curl up next to her for warmth.

With Shoshones being the major tribe north of Salt Lake, Port was constantly badgering Emma to teach him the language. At the same time, he taught her to say English words, mostly nouns. He would point up and say, "Sky." She would say, "Sky," and then the Shoshone translation, which Port would try to repeat. All the way from Ft. Laramie to Salt Lake they taught each other words.

Upon arrival in the valley in early October, Port visited his friend John Neff, who agreed to take in Emma for the winter. Neff's pretty nineteen-year-old daughter, Mary Ann, was eager to befriend the Indian girl.

# Chapter 43

On November 18 Port departed for California, the land Sam Brannan had praised so lavishly. Port was guide and hunter for a group of men headed to San Diego to collect Mormon Battalion wages, buy cattle, and guide men recently released from the Mormon Battalion back to the Great Basin.

Former battalion captain Jefferson Hunt was in charge of the expedition, with Asahel Lathrop the religious leader. There were eleven others in the party.

Port thought it amusing that once again he was assigned as guide to a place he had never been, over a trail he had never traveled. When given the assignment, he shrugged his shoulders, thinking that if these assignments continued, soon he would have gone everywhere and would be deserving of the title of guide. As for now, he supposed he was selected simply because there was no one else and because his skills in the wild, mainly his ability to handle guns and horses, were respected. No wagons slowed the party down. Each man had a saddle horse, and there were twenty pack animals, mostly mules.

The party made excellent time traveling south through what later became Utah, finally stopping to rest a day at Mountain Meadow, a last chance to fill the horses with good grass and water before heading out onto the vast desert.

Jefferson was the only one who had been to California before, but in getting there with the battalion he had traveled farther south along the Mexican border. His trip back to the Great Salt Lake had been along the northerly route from Sacramento through the Humboldt River Valley. He was not familiar with the landmarks or terrain of the southern route, and neither was Port.

Once they got out in the desert, Port was uncertain whether to head due west, southwest, or south. They were supposed to follow an old Spanish trail but couldn't seem to find it. Port just forged ahead, hoping they would eventually see the southern end of the Sierra Nevada Mountains in the distance, the point where they wanted to pass into California. All Port knew for sure was they needed to stay on the north side of the Colorado River and pass south of the Sierra Nevada Mountains. With those two guidelines, it would be impossible to get lost, he thought, even though there was no easy-to-follow wagon trail.

"I don't like taking orders from a blind man," Hunt announced one morning, when Port suggested a more southerly direction of travel that day. "Since I'm the only one to have passed through this country, I'm taking over the guiding responsibilities."

For the next week the group headed northwest. Though Port had a feeling they should be going in a southwesterly direction, he offered no objection, figuring that since Hunt had been in the area, the captain might know better. But as the days passed, Port noticed that the group was zigzagging.

It wasn't until they saw the snow-capped Sierra Nevada Mountains directly ahead of them that everyone knew the group had strayed far to the north. Port tried to suggest to Hunt that since the journey was now going to take much longer than originally expected, it might be wise to cut the men's food ration.

"Nonsense," Hunt said. "Without enough food, the men will not have strength to travel."

By the time they reached Mountain Spring near what later became Las Vegas, they were out of food. They at least knew where they were now. They also knew it was two hundred miles to the first California settlements.

That night, as the men chewed slowly on the last of the flour-water ash cakes, Lathrop began to describe some tasty dog recipes he had heard were enjoyed by the Chinese in New York. William Cornogg joined in, describing a dog soup he had shared with some Cherokee Indians at one time, and how easy it was to prepare. He said juniper berries added much to the flavor. Port didn't like the direction of the conversation. Joseph was the only dog in camp.

"I propose we cook up a mess of dog meat," Cornogg finally said. Lathrop offered his hearty approval. The rest of the men looked at Port.

"It's either the dog or one of the horses," Cornogg explained. "And since we need every horse to bring men and supplies back from California, the sensible choice is to begin with the dog. Not only does he serve no useful purpose for the expedition, but he eats food too. By eating the dog we'll have one less mouth to feed in the future."

"Joseph catches most of his own food," Port challenged, "mostly rabbits and snakes." Port wished he were better with words, that he could use words with the same skill he could use a gun. But words didn't come easy, so there was little use trying to argue. He simply said, "You are not going to eat my dog."

Joseph was sitting alertly at Port's side, unaware of the subject of discussion. Port placed his hand on the dog's head and scratched Joseph's ears.

"Let's be democratic about this," Hunt said, entering the conversation for the first time. "All in favor of eating the dog raise their right hand." Nine hands went up.

"Do I have a volunteer to shoot and dress our supper?" Hunt continued. Things were happening too fast for Port. More discussion was needed, yet the way things were going, in a matter of seconds someone was going to pull out a gun and shoot Joseph.

"Since Joseph is my dog, I guess I ought to be the one to do it," Port said, surprising everyone. He drew a pistol from his belt and checked the load. Standing up, he disappeared into the darkness, the dog following. The men were quiet, waiting, listening.

When the shot finally rang out, Hunt gave a satisfying grunt, as if the shot was a confirmation that he was still in charge.

"I would have done that for you," John Greene offered when Port returned a minute later, the pistol still in his hand.

"It takes character for a man to kill his own . . ." Hunt began, but stopped when he saw Joseph, alive and well, following Port.

"Missed and hit Cornogg's horse," Port explained. "And since the old cayuse will start rotting tomorrow, I guess we'll have horse instead of dog for supper.

"I just want to make one thing clear," Port continued, his voice getting high and tense. "I killed a man once to avenge the death of a good friend named Joseph. I'll do it again."

"Rockwell, you have no respect for authority," Hunt roared.

"Not your kind, anyway," Port shot back, pushing his coat aside so Hunt could see his pistols.

"Insubordination is grounds for excommunication," Lathrop yelled. Rockwell ignored the warning, keeping his eyes on Hunt, wondering if the man had the courage to handle a challenge to his authority.

"You men can fight if you want," John Greene said. "As for me, I'm hungry for a thick horse steak. He drew his knife and started walking toward the dead horse. The rest of the men followed, including a reluctant and angry Hunt.

A second horse was killed at Amargose Springs, and a third near the Mojave River. After finding the trail through the Cajon Pass, the group arrived at Rancho Santa Anna del Chino near San Bernadino on Christmas Eve, after forty-five days on the trail.

The ranch was its own community, a dozen or so families, mostly Mexican, working a vast kingdom of cattle, horses, and mules. No one knew exactly how many acres the spread contained, only that it was many thousands.

The ranch was owned by a white man, Isaac Williams, who warmly welcomed the party of trail-weary Mormons. He turned his sprawling adobe house over to them for as long as they wished to stay, with all the flour, beef, and milk they could eat. The Spanish dons were blessed in an abundant land, and they shared freely with visitors and strangers. It was not uncommon for a traveler, in addition to receiving all the food he could eat and a soft bed, to find a plate of money beside his bed, in the event he needed cash to complete his journey. Isaac Williams was eager to continue the Spanish tradition of hospitality.

But Port was tired of the company of Hunt and Lathrop, and after a couple of days he began making preparations to move on to San Diego and Los Angeles. Several of the men agreed to go with him. They received orders from Hunt to return within thirty days.

Hunt and Lathrop had negotiated with Williams the purchase of two hundred cows at six dollars each, forty bulls, and some mules and horses. Williams, in typical California generosity, said there would be no charge for all the bulls they could round up—and there were enough bulls on the spread to keep the entire Mormon population in beef for a year. Lathrop and Hunt saw a chance to become heroes by bringing home the beef. But Port had other ideas.

In Los Angeles he approached the United States military outpost, offering to deliver a dispatch of mail to the United States. The matter was discussed by military officials for some weeks, and they eventually decided not to trust their dispatches to a Mormon.

In early February, Hunt and Lathrop were getting ready to push the huge herd they had assembled back to the Great Basin when Port announced he was not going with them.

"As your military commander I can have you shot," Hunt threatened. Port didn't like being treated like a private in Hunt's personal army. He didn't like being bossed around by a man who took so much pleasure in giving orders, at least that was the way Port saw it.

"We are on a mission for the Lord," Lathrop said in an effort to change Port's mind. "By refusing to accompany us, you are hindering the work. President Young will be very disappointed. Men have been excommunicated for a lot less than this."

"I joined this expedition as guide and hunter," Port explained. "Having just come over the trail, you do not need a guide. And with all the cattle you'll be driving, you do not need a hunter." Having finished his speech, Port climbed on his horse and headed for San Diego. Several of the men accompanied him, leaving Hunt shouting for them to return.

In San Diego, Port found twenty-five Mormon Battalion recruits who wanted to return to Utah. Port agreed to be their guide.

In preparing for departure, Port purchased a wagon and 135 mules. One of the reasons for the delay in coming to California was the time consumed every morning loading the twenty pack animals—and keeping them loaded throughout the day. Carrying the supplies in a wagon would save countless hours. And once the wagon was nursed over the Cajon Pass, travel would be easy. Faster travel would reduce the risk of losing animals to thirst between water holes in the desert. By moving quickly, there would also be fewer opportunities for Indians to plan and execute raids.

Port knew Hunt and Lathrop would report his insubordination to Brigham Young. He also knew the Saints were in desperate need of draft animals for the migration. The 135 mules he would be driving home would be considered a blessing from heaven and would probably outweigh any concern over his friction with Hunt and Lathrop. Plus, he had a recent news item that he knew would interest Young. Some Mormon Battalion boys had discovered gold near the Sacramento River.

In late May, after nearly a hundred days on the trail, Hunt and Lathrop arrived in Salt Lake with sober reports of the long and difficult trail to San Bernardino. They reported how the trail had been so hard it had taken all but one of their bulls and half their cows. Most had died of thirst, some had been stolen by Indians, and some had simply been lost. One of the things that made the trail so difficult, they reported, was the fact that it was too rough for wagons.

A week later Porter Rockwell drove his wagon into the city, accompanied by twenty-five young men singing the favorite Mormon marching song, "Come, Come, Ye Saints." They were driving 135 mules and had made the journey in half the time, without losing a single animal.

That same day, Port was asked to report to the council, where he was presented with accusations of insubordination and apostasy presented by Hunt and Lathrop. Port explained that since he had joined the expedition as guide and hunter, services not needed for the return journey, he had thought it would better serve the kingdom to bring home a herd of badly needed draft animals. The charges were dropped, and the next day Port headed east to meet Brigham Young, who was returning to the Valley with 1,229 more emigrants.

# Chapter 44

The summer of 1848 the plains were crawling with Mormons. Port caught up with Brigham Young beyond Fort Laramie on the Platte River, leading the largest single company of pioneers ever to cross the plains at one time. There were 1,229 people, 397 wagons, and a huge trail herd of cattle, horses, and mules. After telling Young about the journey to California and the discovery of gold, Port went to work hunting. The company consumed three or four buffalo every day. When fresh meat was available, the people could save their flour and beans, commodities that would be in short supply the coming winter.

The company entered the valley on September 20, effectively doubling the population to over two thousand Saints, making Salt Lake City the largest city west of the Missouri River. Water, timber, and land were declared public property. Parcels of farmland were assigned to individuals based on need and the ability to make it productive. People like Port who didn't intend to farm weren't given farmland.

Brigham Young had a special assignment for Port, placing him on a horse and cattle committee with George Grant and John D. Lee. The emigrants were so busy gathering food and building shelters in preparation for winter that they hadn't built enough fences to contain the livestock. Too many horses and cattle were running loose, the young and feeble becoming prey to coyotes and cougars.

Stray sheep and pigs fell easily and quickly to the predators. Brigham assigned his horse and cattle committee the task of rounding up the strays.

Port and his two co-workers didn't get to work right away. Everyone was talking about the discovery of gold in California, near Sutter's Fort. Almost daily, reports were arriving of the fabulous fortunes being made. It was said a man could earn a thousand dollars in an afternoon. Wading into a stream and picking up nuggets was as easy as walking into the woods and picking up elk droppings. After a month in the gold fields, it was said a man wouldn't have to work again the rest of his life.

To get over the Sierras before the snow became too deep, some men had already left for California, leaving their families and unfinished cabins for the Church to worry about. Brigham Young recognized immediately that the biggest threat to his mountain kingdom was not predators, Indians, crickets, or winter snows, but gold fever. Many of the best men were eager to pull up stakes and head to the gold fields. Young knew many would never return.

There were two things that made the Mormons especially vulnerable to gold fever. First, the gold was discovered by Mormons, men returning home from Mormon Battalion service. There was a feeling in Salt Lake that the discovery of gold was heaven-sent for those who had sacrificed to bring their families west, but the Lord wouldn't put gold in their pockets if they were too lazy to go to California to pick it up.

The second reason was geography. While the gold seekers coming from the United States would have to cross a continent or sail half way around the world to get there, the Mormons were only six hundred miles away, a three-week journey when the mountain passes were not filled with snow. The Mormons were positioned perfectly to get to the gold fields first, with six months or more of easy pickings before the swarms of gold seekers arrived from the United States.

Some began to question Brigham Young's wisdom in settling in the Great Basin. Perhaps the discovery of gold was a sign that the Lord wanted the Saints in California, that Sam Brannan's plea for the Mormons to come to California had been the right thing to do.

Though Brigham Young heard what the people were saying, he did not agree. He told them there was plenty of mineral wealth in the mountains around Salt Lake, but the time was not yet ripe to bring it out. He also predicted the Mormons would make a lot more money selling food and supplies to gold seekers passing through Salt Lake than they would by digging gold.

One afternoon in late fall, Port and George Grant were enjoying a leisurely dinner at the cabin of Catherine Woolley. Catherine was a woman Port had given a big slab of buffalo meat to on the Sweetwater, and she had been inviting Port to dinner ever since.

The conversation covered everything from polygamy to stray cattle to giving food to the Indians. A galloping horse stopped in front of the cabin. It was John D. Lee. He had just come from Brigham Young, who was sick and tired of the stray problem.

"You, Rockwell and Grant, can either round up the strays, the job you have been assigned, or you can go to hell!" Lee said, quoting Brigham Young. "I swear those were his exact words."

"Then I guess we'd better start rounding up the strays," Port said, getting up from the table.

"But how will we know which are strays and which are just let out to graze?" Grant asked.

"The president wants strays, so that's what he'll get," Port said. "Everything that isn't in a fence is a stray."

After recruiting a few men to help, the expanded horse and cattle committee headed to the south end of the settlements, spread out in a wide line, and began moving north, adding every unfenced animal to their rapidly growing herd.

Two days later, Port knocked on Brigham Young's door at five thirty in the morning.

"Sorry to get you out of bed, sir," Port said, shouting so he could be heard above the mooing of hundreds of cows. A yawning Young came to the door in his nightshirt. It wasn't until he stepped out on the porch that he noticed the huge, noisy herd of cattle, horses, and mules.

"Seven hundred and sixty-eight, sir," Port said. "All strays. What do you propose we do with them?"

"Why are they making so much noise?" Young asked, rubbing the sleep from his eyes.

"A lot of milk cows in the herd, sir," Port explained. "They need milking."

"What should we do with them?" Grant asked. There was a long pause. For the first time in the many years Port had known Brigham Young, the Mormon leader did not appear to know what to say.

"Do you want us to leave them here, sir?" Lee asked.

"No!" Brigham roared, becoming his usual self again. "Take them to the open fields down by the Jordan River, until I figure out what to do." He began to step back into the cabin.

"One more question, sir," Grant said. "If the people that own an animal come and want it back, should we give it to them?"

"Of course," Brigham growled. "And stop calling me sir." He marched back into the cabin, slamming the door firmly behind him.

"Yes, sir," Lee laughed, as he and the rest of the men began herding the strays west toward the Jordan River.

Later that afternoon, Brigham Young rode to the stray herd, sheepishly removing his hat and admitting a big mistake had been made. He said he had been answering questions all day such as, "How can we feed our children and calves without our milk cow?" and "How can we get the materials to finish our cabin without a team to pull the wagon?" Young said he was even accused of using the stray roundup as a means to underhandedly increase the size of his own personal herd.

"If you don't want us rounding up strays," Lee said, "then I suppose we are released from the committee."

"Not exactly," Young explained. "The problem of predators attacking strays is still with us. Since it isn't practical to round up strays, perhaps we ought to try to eliminate the lions and wolves that are eating them."

While it was difficult for men to have much enthusiasm for rounding up other people's stray animals, going lion and wolf hunting was an entirely different matter. In a few days Rockwell, Lee, and John Pack had two hundred volunteers to help with the hunt. The timing was perfect, with the winter snow having already driven most of the deer and elk out of the mountains to their wintering grounds in the valley. The cougars and coyotes followed. By March, Lee, Rockwell, Pack, and their men had exterminated fifteen thousand predators, mostly cougars and coyotes but also bears, lynx, bobcats, and a few renegade Indians, some claimed, with a taste for beef.

By spring Brigham Young had an elaborate plan to make a bundle of money selling goods and services to the thousands of gold seekers who would be coming west in the summer. The plan called for money-making endeavors long before the travelers reached the Salt Lake Valley. It included three ferries, two on the Platte and one on the Green River, charging a dollar per wagon at each of the three crossings. Furthermore, a trading post was to be established west of Fort Bridger. Mormon emigrants were to receive lower prices at the post and free passage on the ferries.

Port was assigned to run one of the Platte ferries. He was to leave as soon as the weather permitted. He didn't much like the idea. Not having a family to tie him down, he had been making quiet plans to be the first one over the Sierras that spring on his way to the newly discovered gold fields. But if Brigham Young wanted him to run a ferry, he guessed he would do it.

The first public elections were held in March, so with the predator hunt winding down and little else to do before the snow in the passes melted, Port announced his candidacy for deputy marshal, figuring a badge on his chest would reduce the risk of being shot.

He wasn't sure he had much of a chance of winning, even in Salt Lake. Not only was he divorced, but he was known by all to swear and drink on occasion—qualities Mormons didn't vote for. Still, Port had killed Frank Worrell, scared the hell out of Lilburn Boggs, and attacked and driven off an entire band of Pawnee Indians who had threatened the first pioneer company. Even with a belly full of rotgut, he could out shoot any man in the valley. Port won the election by a handsome margin, becoming the first deputy marshal for the Provisional State of Deseret.

Putting on a silver badge didn't change very much for Port. He was still making plans to operate the ferry on the Platte and eventually run out to California for a few months. The badge just put the law behind him in the event it became necessary to shoot someone who needed shooting.

Law enforcement in Deseret was different from anywhere else on the continent. When the Saints arrived, there were no judges, lawyers, or policemen to meet them. And rather than take time away from farming and building to set up a law enforcement network, the assignment to keep the peace was handed over to bishops and stake presidents. If a man murdered or raped someone, or even if he just stole a mule, he was chased down and captured by the local elders. He was tried before the bishop's court, and if found guilty he was fined, imprisoned, or executed according to the order of the bishop.

Even when the United States sent judges, lawyers, and marshals to Salt Lake, these newcomers found little to do because Young encouraged the Saints to handle their own criminal business. The Mormons didn't seek or want any help from gentile judges, who in turn felt slighted. The result was a never-ending stream of Washington-bound reports accusing the Mormons of criminal outrages.

Port's first assignment as deputy marshal was to ride with eighteen-year-old George Bean down to Utah Valley to see if they couldn't establish some sort of peace with the Timpanogos Utes who didn't want Mormons settling near their traditional fishing grounds on Utah Lake. Bean, a tall, lanky youth, was selected to accompany Port because he had usable knowledge of the Ute language.

Sowiette, chief of the Ute nation, had threatened all-out war on the Mormons if they persisted in trying to settle in the valley around the lake. Bean and Rockwell were supposed to offer trade goods and any other reasonable concessions to soften the Ute stand against Mormons settling in Utah Valley.

It was almost evening when Bean and Rockwell arrived at the camp. Since Bean knew the language best, it was decided he would enter the camp alone, leaving Rockwell free to create a diversion or go for help if necessary.

With Rockwell hiding with the horses behind some brush on a nearby hill, Bean rode bravely into the Indian camp. Before he could explain his mission he was jerked from the saddle. His hands were tied behind his back and he was forced to stand on a buffalo robe that was spread on the ground. Port wasn't sure what to do. Should he charge in, attempting a bold rescue? Should he go for help? Or should he just remain where he was, hoping the Indians would eventually let Bean deliver his message?

For two hours the braves abused Bean, spitting on him, bragging of their victories over whites, and describing what tortures they had in store for the Mormons who were taking their hunting and fishing grounds. Each time Bean tried to answer, he was clubbed to silence. Several times Port was ready to charge in, knowing he was so far outnumbered there would be little chance of rescuing Bean, let alone surviving. But if he went for help and the Indians decided to kill Bean, there would be no one present to try to save the boy. So Port waited, cocking and uncocking his guns, checking the cinch on his horse, wishing desperately to do something, but feeling again that he must wait.

When the braves finished with Bean, they turned him over to the women. Forty squaws gathered around the frightened youth, poking him with sticks. One whipped him. Another tried to jab his eyes.

Port got on his horse and cocked his pistols, deciding it would be better to attempt a rescue now while the boy still had the strength to stand. Just as he was about to dig his heels into the stallion's sides, he noticed that Bean was shouting excitedly at two warriors who had just ridden into camp from the other side. The women made a wide path as the two newcomers strutted up to the captive.

Even though it was dark, Port could see the men clearly in the light of several bonfires. The taller of the two was a young bull of a man, a perfect physical specimen. He was tall for an Indian, muscles bulging from his smooth bronze skin. He walked with the grace and ease of a well-bred horse. He carried his head high, with confidence, like a man who feared neither man nor beast. Port could tell from the faces of the other Indians when they looked at this man that he was respected, even revered by all. He was the Indian equivalent of a Joseph Smith, a natural leader. The other Indian was older, a wise, confident look about him, but a man past his prime.

Both Indians stopped in front of Bean, who for the first time was delivering his message through swollen, bruised lips. The young white man talked swiftly, desperately trying to get his message out before it was too late. He said his leader, Brigham Young, wanted to be friends with the Indians so the two peoples could live together in peace. Bean promised that the white men who came to Utah Valley would be farmers, that they would not catch the fish or kill the game. Furthermore, the Mormon chief promised that if Mormons were allowed to settle in the valley, they would share their food with the Indians, beginning with an immediate shipment of beef.

While the older Indian seemed eager to make the deal, the young chief maintained a skeptical scowl. It soon became apparent that the rest of the Indians were waiting for the young chief to confirm what the older chief had already agreed to.

Port decided the presence of an additional white man might help Bean make his deal. Climbing on his horse, Port reached down and lifted Joseph up behind him, like he had taught the dog to do when crossing rivers. With his hind feet planted firmly behind the saddle, Joseph reared up and placed his front paws on Port's shoulders. Port hoped the novelty of the dog riding with him on the horse would make him appear less threatening to the Indians. He hoped it would at least get their minds on something besides killing white men.

Though he had never met the man, Port guessed the young muscular chief was Walkara, a powerful sub-chief who would become chief of the entire Ute nation when the older chief, Sowiette, stepped down.

After checking his saddlebags to make sure he had the desired trade goods, Port galloped into the Indian camp, calling out to Sowiette and Walkara like they were old friends. Joseph, having had plenty of practice, remained calmly in place, his forepaws still on Port's shoulders.

Port jerked the stallion to a halt at the very edge of Bean's buffalo robe. While Sowiette smiled a welcome to the newcomer, Walkara continued to scowl, at least until Port reached into his saddlebag and tossed the young chief a bottle of valley tan, the Salt Lake equivalent of Missouri white lightning. So as not to offend the older chief, Port tossed a second bottle to the old man. Both Indians began to drink. When Walkara removed the bottle from his lips, he was smiling. Drawing a long hunting knife from his belt, he cut Bean's hands free.

A few minutes later an eager Sowiette and a reluctant Walkara agreed to a conditional peace with the Mormons. While Port joined the chiefs in toasting the agreement, Bean declined.

"I wish you hadn't brought out the whiskey," Bean said, as they were riding away from the camp. "You know how President Young feels about giving firewater to the Indians."

"I also know how the Indians feel about it," Port answered. "They love the stuff, just like I do."

"Looks like it did the trick on Walkara anyway," Bean said.

"I'm not so sure it changed anything with Walkara," Port said, "except get him in a mood to let you out of there with your hair. Walkara's not that easy."

Brigham Young was delighted when Rockwell and Bean reported on their meeting with the two chiefs. "At last we're speaking," Young said. "You made a proposal; they listened and agreed to the terms. It's a big first step."

"I don't think they'll keep the agreement," Port said.

"I can understand that," Young said. "The important thing here is that we are finally talking with them. Now we can invite Sowiette and Walkara to Salt Lake, shower them with gifts, let them know we really want peace, that we would rather be good neighbors than enemies, and that we would rather share our food than fight."

Port had never seen a man so confident in his opinions as Brigham Young. Yet the man was right most of the time, as evidenced by the success of the Mormon settlement in the Great Basin. Port certainly hoped he was right in his dealings with the Utes.

A few weeks later, Port was sitting in the marshal's office, nursing along a bottle of valley tan, waiting for the snow to melt so he could travel to the Platte for his ferry assignment, when an attractive woman in her mid-thirties barged into the room.

Port recognized her immediately. It was Luana, his first wife. Quickly, he corked the bottle, ditched it into one of the desk drawers, and then jumped to attention.

Both had said hello to each other before Port realized he had reacted out of habit. It was no longer necessary for him to behave like an eager-to-please husband around Luana. He dropped back into his chair, motioning for her to be seated too. He removed the bottle from the drawer and returned it to its former place on the desk.

"You look good," he said, sincerely. He knew she wasn't coming to make a social call. "What can I do for you?" He motioned for her to help herself to the bottle, knowing she wouldn't.

"Emily is kidnapped," she said, beginning to cry.

"By Indians?" he asked, suddenly sitting up straight, pushing the bottle to one side.

"No, by two men, Mormons."

"Did Emily know them?"

"She knew one quite well, Hyrum Gates. He was working on an irrigation project. Had supper with us a few times. Went to church with us. Now he's taken our baby to California. He's kidnapped her."

"Did she want to go with him?" Port asked.

"Of course she did."

"Then it doesn't sound like kidnapping."

"She's just a child, only sixteen."

"Did they get married? Were they traveling alone?"

"I don't know who would have married them. His friend, Levi Fifield, was with them. Emily left a note saying they were going to California. You must bring her back."

"I'll do what I can," Port said, standing up.

By the end of the day he had obtained a warrant from Heber C. Kimball, judge and apostle, for the arrest of Hyrum Gates. Port had also talked President Young into releasing him from ferry duty but not without a catch. Young had the uncanny ability to find a practical side to almost any situation.

Brigham Young had mixed feelings about the gold discovery in California. A rush of gold-seeking Saints to California could cripple the colonization efforts in the Great Basin. On the other hand, a wagonload of gold would perform wonders for the fledgling Utah economy. In public, Young preached about the evils of seeking for gold, but in private he began to formulate plans to get some of the gold to Deseret. Sending Lyman and Rich to California with Rockwell was a big first step.

Young proposed a deal. As long as Port was headed to California to find his daughter, he might as well take Amasa Lyman, Charles Rich, and others with him to collect the tithing money from Sam Brannan, do some missionary work, and check out the gold fields. Young knew members of the church were paying tithes to Brannan, yet none of the money had ever been sent to Salt Lake. Lyman had instructions that if he couldn't collect at least ten thousand dollars in tithes from Brannan, the upstart was to be excommunicated on the spot, and a new local church organization formed.

Port was glad for the company, which would make travel through Indian country safer. And now, even if he caught up with his daughter a short distance from Salt Lake, he would still be able to go to California and follow the irresistible lure of the gold fields.

# Chapter 45

On April 13 Porter Rockwell and Amasa Lyman, along with several others, struck out for California. Port guessed his daughter and her abductors were four or five days ahead of them.

Though Port and his companions made good time, averaging nearly forty miles a day, they had not caught up with Emily and her companions by the time they reached the settlement where the Truckee River flowed out of the mountains.

When they learned the pass over Donner Summit was not yet open because of snow, Port knew his daughter couldn't be far away. With Lyman and the remainder of the men setting up camp to rest for a few days, Port set out to find his daughter.

Reno was a city of tents and wagons belonging to Mormons, trappers, gamblers, farmers, Indians, and all sorts of people waiting for the snow to melt sufficiently to allow them into the gold fields. There was no snow in the settlement, however, just on the mountaintops and in the passes.

Port's method was simple. He just stopped people in the middle of the muddy road and asked if they had seen a pretty young woman, about sixteen, with two male companions in their twenties. Since men far outnumbered women in the area, Port figured men on the street would notice a pretty girl like Emily. His hunch was correct. After four or five inquiries he was directed to a grove of Ponderosa pine trees on the north side of the river about five miles west of town.

As Port approached the grove he saw a white pole tent at the edge of the trees. Five yards away, in a sunny flat, a young man without a shirt was chopping wood, his back and shoulder muscles rippling easily beneath the smooth, sweaty skin. Port checked the load in one of his pistols and, after returning it to the holster, continued forward.

The young man straightened up when he saw the approaching rider, still holding the axe in his right hand. With the other hand, he wiped the sweat from his brow. His hair was black and curly, and he was smiling brightly.

"Howdy," the young man said. Port didn't answer.

"Will you join us for supper?"

"Do you usually invite strangers to supper?" Port asked, resisting the urge to like the young man.

"You're no stranger. That white dog, the roan stallion, and the beard to your belly button give you away. You're Mr. Rockwell, Emily's father. I'm Hyrum Gates. Pleased to meet you."

Port stopped the horse and dismounted.

"Emily, you have a visitor," the young man shouted into the tent. A second later Emily stepped through the flap. She was wearing a long blue dress with a white apron. Her long, sandy hair hung loose about her shoulders. She looked more like a beautiful woman than the little girl Port was seeking.

"Oh, Daddy, it's so good to see you," she cried, running to her father, throwing her arms around him.

"I've come to take you home," Port said, finding the words difficult.

"I want you to meet my husband, Hyrum Gates," she said.

"Who married you?" Port asked.

"An elder who asked not to be identified," she said.

"I've come to take you home," he repeated.

"You've wasted a trip then," she said, stepping back, her hands on her hips, a determined look on her face. "I won't go and you can't make me." She was still smiling.

To Port, it seemed like just a few months since Emily was playing tag in the front yard with the other children. It hardly seemed possible that she could have grown up so quickly. He turned his attention to the young man.

"Do you really think it's a good idea to drag my daughter into the gold fields?" Port asked. "Do you care nothing for her safety?"

"Yes, sir, I do," Gates said brightly. "That's why we're not going to the gold fields. We're staying right here."

"What will you do?" Port asked.

"We're going to build a store and blacksmith shop here on the Truckee River," Gates explained. Port could feel the young man's enthusiasm as he explained how his establishment would provide the last opportunity for westbound travelers to put shoes on their stock before heading onto the rocky trail over the mountain. It would also provide the last opportunity to buy supplies before the final and hardest leg of the journey to the gold fields.

Gates explained that his partner, Levi Fifield, who had been in the gold fields the previous summer, had friends there. Levi was already up on the pass, headed for Sutter's Fort. His mission was to offer friends there a partnership in exchange for outfitting the two young men to conduct a trading business on the east side of the mountains. Gates hoped to have the foundation laid and most of the timber cut down before Fifield returned. With the proceeds of the blacksmith-trading venture, they were going to buy a huge ranch on the California side of the mountains, somewhere south of the gold fields. Fifield was going to marry a beautiful Mexican girl, and together they were going to raise their families on the ranch.

Port pulled the warrant out of his pocket and handed it to Gates.

"I have orders to take you home," he said to Emily.

"I'm not going with you," she said.

"I can always tie your hands and feet and throw you over a saddle," Port said threateningly.

"And probably kill your unborn grandson in the process."

"What?" Port asked, taken back by her comment.

"We didn't get married just for the fun of it," she said smartly. "We're going to have a baby, probably lots of them. When your grandson is old enough to talk and wants to know where his father is, will you tell him you arrested his father and sent him off to jail?"

"I didn't know you were expecting a baby," Port said.

"A baby ought to have a father as well as a mother," Emily said, beginning to cry. Port felt awful. "Now will you stay for supper?" she asked.

"Sure." Turning to Hyrum, Port asked, "Do you have a gun?"

"Yes."

"Get it."

"Now?"

"Yes."

"I'm not going to let you take me in."

"Get the gun."

"Why?"

"A man who's going to keep my daughter in a place like this has got to know how to use a gun. Just want to make sure you are properly schooled."

"You're not going to arrest me?"

"Suppose not," Port said, taking back the warrant and throwing it on the smoldering fire. "Don't want any grandson of mine growing up without a father."

"Thanks," Hyrum cried, running into the tent to get his gun.

"When's the baby due?" Port asked, after he and Hyrum had finished shooting their guns and the three were sitting at a table comprised of two rough-hewn planks.

"In a year or two, I suppose," Emily responded brightly.

"You said you were expecting," Port said.

"I am," she said. "I'm expecting to have lots of babies, but that doesn't mean I'm pregnant."

"It doesn't?"

"We've only been married three weeks. It's too early to tell."

"You tricked me," Port said. "I have half a mind to throw you over the saddle and take you back with me."

"You're my father," she said, suddenly getting angry. "You're supposed to help us, encourage us, counsel us—not try to break us up. Hyrum's my husband. I love him."

"As your father I have responsibilities . . ." Port began before Emily interrupted him.

"I'll tell you what your responsibilities are," she said. "Those beans you're eating are the last we have. And we don't have any money to buy more. Levi took it all. If you were a responsible father, you would want to help us."

"Hyrum, my boy," Port said, "you can have her, and may you never win an argument as long as you live." Port reached in his pocket and pulled out five twenty-dollar gold pieces. He handed them to Hyrum.

"I can't take your money," Gates said.

"Nonsense. I'm investing in my future grandchildren or I'm paying you to take a disobedient daughter off my hands or I'm investing in your new business. Look at it any way you wish. Pay me back if you can."

"Oh, I will, sir, from the proceeds of our business."

"Don't call me sir."

"Should I call you dad?"

"No, just Port. That will be fine." The two men shook hands. After giving Emily a hug, Port climbed on his horse and headed back to camp.

Riding along the Truckee River, Port felt older, more tired, less like a notorious gunfighter, more like a grandfather.

But the feeling didn't last long. Two days later Port and his companions were forging through the crusty snows of the high Sierras. At least the snow was crusty in the mornings. By afternoon it turned to slush, fighting a losing battle with the unrelenting May sunshine.

On clear days the men rubbed charcoal around their eyes for protection against the glare off the snow. When the sun was brightest, in mid-afternoon, a man would usually squint through one eye and then the other, taking turns.

They made excellent time all the way to Donner Lake, because others had broken the trail before them. At the lake they saw broken wagons left behind by the Donner Party a few years earlier.

Other gold seekers were camped at the lake, waiting for the snow to melt sufficiently to allow them over the highest and final portion of the pass. No one had gone over yet that year, but it was almost time to try. Every day seemed warmer than the one before.

Port found Levi Fifield camped by himself under a crude shelter of tree branches. Port set the young man at ease by telling him about his meeting with Hyrum and Emily, and how he had given them his blessing and some money. Port invited Fifield to ride with his party over the pass. The young man was glad to have the company of a party of Mormons.

They departed just before noon the next day. They had to wait until the sun began to soften the crust. In the early morning, a man could walk across the top of the snow, but the horses broke through, sometimes cutting their legs.

The party rode single file, Boggs breaking trail the first hour, then another horse or mule moving up front for the second hour. The lead animal worked three times as hard as those that followed, so it was necessary to change the lead frequently to maintain a steady pace.

Port was pleased at their progress. The horses seemed as eager to get to the gold fields as the men. It was as if the animals already knew there would be a long-awaited rest on the other side of the mountains.

The party arrived at Sutter's Fort on May 25. The bustling boomtown reminded Port of Salt Lake the first year the Mormons had arrived, hundreds of people living in tents and wagons. The big difference was that in Salt Lake that first year cabins were going up everywhere. At Sutter's Fort it seemed saloons were going up everywhere. Everyone was talking about gold and the men who had become millionaires finding it.

When Port mentioned to a saloon keeper that his party was going on to Yerba Buena, or San Francisco, the man said they were wasting their time. San Francisco was a ghost town. Every man not confined to a bed or wheelchair had come east to the gold fields.

After some discussion, Amasa Lyman decided to remain in the gold fields, at least for a time. There were many Mormons from whom he could collect tithing. Perhaps he would even run into Sam Brannan. And when not collecting tithing, he could do missionary work. That was fine with Port and the rest of the men, who said a hasty farewell and headed for the diggings.

# Chapter 46

Port and his companions headed up the American River to a huge sandbar where about twenty-five Mormon Battalion volunteers were washing out their fortunes in placer gold. The place was called Mormon Bar. Port soon discovered that Mormonism was probably the dominant religion in the gold fields. There were about 250 from the Mormon Battalion and about 150 more from Sam Brannan's group that sailed to California and those who had come overland from Great Salt Lake City. In addition to Mormon Bar, groups of Saints were working together at Mormon Hill, Mormon Tavern, Mormon Ravine, Mormon Island, Mormon Slough, and Mormon Gulch.

Port learned quickly from his fellow believers that he had better be careful because his reputation had preceded him. The past season several wagon trains of emigrants from Missouri and Illinois had arrived in California, with most of the men now in the gold fields. They knew about Rockwell from the highly publicized Boggs and Worrell shootings.

Furthermore, the Mormon miners told Port that Lilburn Boggs and two of his sons had settled at Sonoma, where they had started several businesses and were as anti-Mormon as ever. Taking the advice that was offered, Port changed his name to Brown, James Brown.

Port paid five dollars for a tin plate and ten dollars for a shovel. Then he began digging and washing the loose gravel at Mormon

Bar. After placing a shovel full of dirt in the pan, he would fill it the rest of the way with water and then slosh it around, hoping the gold would settle to the bottom as he slowly washed the dirt and gravel over the edge. When all the residue was gone, he could see along the bottom a thin film of black sand and gold specks, sometimes a flake or two. Using the blade of his pocket knife, he picked out the gold, wiping it onto his clean handkerchief.

While doing all this, Port was crouched on his heels, bending over the pan. In his enthusiasm to find more gold, hoping he might be lucky enough to find one of the ten-dollar nuggets everyone was talking about, he worked without resting or standing up for nearly two hours. When he finally decided to stand up, the muscles in his back screamed with pain. He couldn't straighten up for several minutes. Like back on the Truckee River, he felt like a grandfather again.

Carefully wrapping up his afternoon's work in the handkerchief, he walked over to a tent belonging to Charles Smith, a Mormon who owned a scale. Carefully dumping the contents of his handkerchief on the scale, he discovered he had earned nearly a dollar for his efforts, and his back still ached. As he left the tent, Port decided there had to be a better way to get the gold out of the California hills. He decided to think about it over a glass of cold whiskey.

The nearest tavern was another tent about two miles downstream. No sign hung over the door, and the only floor was a black bumpy layer of boot-trodden dirt. But from all the shouting and yelling coming from inside, Port knew he had come to the right place.

Though the evening was still early, the tent was packed. Close to a hundred miners crowded up to the bar, which consisted of thick pine planks resting on forty-gallon oak barrels, forming a rectangle. The customers were on the outside, sacks of gold and small drinking glasses in their hands. On the inside, bartenders in gray aprons were filling the glasses and collecting the gold, mostly placer, which the customers poured from leather pouches onto little brass scales. There was a scale about every six feet along the pine plank bar. At any given moment, a dozen or so men were pouring their yellow gold into the scales while the bartenders were pouring what they called San Francisco Gold into the glasses. Everybody seemed happy.

Reaching into his pocket for a silver dollar, Port stepped up to the bar. The closest bartender took his dollar and handed Port a glass of San Francisco Gold. It was a small glass, not much bigger than a hen's egg.

"How about my change?" Port asked, when the bartender turned to walk away.

"You gave me a silver dollar, didn't you?" the man responded, turning to face Port.

"Yes."

"Drinks are a dollar," the man said, turning away again.

Port looked down at the glass, like the whiskey was too valuable to drink. He picked it up, holding it against the light, deciding it contained less than a dime's worth of whiskey. He noticed there was a thin gray film on the glass, and that it was covered with fingerprints. The glass had not been washed recently, if ever.

He lifted the glass to his lips and sampled the contents. It was corn whiskey that had been watered down, perhaps three to one, and contained sugar. A nickel a glass would have been too much to pay.

Port took his time with the drink, not wanting to buy another. He stepped back from the bar, watching and listening. He learned that many of the men in the tent had come long distances, some from as far away as Pilot Hill and Higgin's Point on the south fork of the American River.

Port watched the bartenders taking in the gold nearly as fast as a hundred men could pour it out of their pouches. He compared the way the bartenders were working to the hard work he had performed earlier in the day. They were taking in thousands of dollars per hour, while Port had worked all afternoon for about a dollar's worth of the golden dust. The bartenders didn't even have to bend over. He knew their backs wouldn't be hurting at the end of the shift.

Port also knew that whiskey could probably be bought for about a dollar a gallon in Yerba Buena. Watering it down four to one and adding a little sugar would bring the cost down to thirty cents a gallon, which would fill about twenty-five of those little glasses. In other words, a dollar's worth of whiskey would bring in a hundred dollars' worth of dust or placer.

The next morning Port sold his tin plate and shovel for what he had paid for them a day earlier, saddled his horse, and headed for Sutter's Fort. The next afternoon, after arranging for a Mormon family to keep his horse and dog while he was gone, he boarded a river steamer for Yerba Buena.

Port had never seen a city like Yerba Buena before. It was a city of steep hills, evergreen trees, and cool ocean breezes, even in June. Except for women and children, it was mostly a deserted city. There were few people on the streets, and many businesses were closed. Nearly all of the men had gone to the gold fields.

Whereas the city was nearly empty, the docks at the edge of the bay were clogged with ships. New vessels sailed in almost daily, but none were leaving because there were no crews to handle the unloading, loading, and sailing. When a new ship arrived, it was usually only a matter of hours until most of the crew was marching off to the gold fields, duffel bags over the sailors' shoulders.

Port wasn't too surprised when he couldn't find a barrel of corn whiskey in the entire city. He headed down to the docks, working his way from ship to ship until he found an old, crippled sailor who agreed to sell him thirty barrels of rum made from sugar cane at $1.25 a gallon. He agree to sell Port the rum on the condition Port would carry the barrels out of the ship's hold himself. The Mormon didn't finalize the deal until he had sampled the contents of several of the barrels.

Port couldn't find a large pole tent either, but continued to ask around until he located a big round tent at the old Spanish fort called the Presidio. He purchased the tent for eight dollars.

He didn't have any trouble locating plenty of the little drinking glasses. He purchased two hundred at eight cents each.

Now all Port needed was a way to haul all his stuff down to the dock where the river boats departed and landed. He began to look about for a boy with a wagon but didn't have any immediate success, and it being a Saturday afternoon, he decided to quit for the day, find a room for the night, and get some supper.

He knew there were a lot of Mormons in town, particularly the wives and children of those who had stampeded to the gold fields.

They would be holding church on Sunday. It would be good to worship with the Saints again, and he would probably find someone to loan him a wagon for a few hours on Monday.

At dinner he asked the waitress where the Mormons met for church. She gave him directions to a two-story building on Market Street. But she didn't know the time.

Port was the first one there at nine the next morning. He waited by the door, and by 10:50, sixty Saints had arrived. As he had guessed, most were women and children. There were a few old men.

Everyone had heard of Porter Rockwell, and they were delighted to have such a famous Mormon show up unexpectedly at their little church. It seemed like a thousand questions and handshakes before Port was finally guided to a seat on the stand behind the podium. He would have preferred to sit down in the audience with everyone else, to go unnoticed and just enjoy the meeting, but the San Francisco Mormons would have none of that.

Suddenly, Port regretted having come to church. The brother making the announcements, without any kind of warning, announced that all Sunday School classes and sacrament meeting speaking assignments had been cancelled, so there would be plenty of time to hear from a distinguished visitor. Port looked around. As far as he could tell, he was the only visitor. He felt sick to his stomach. He would rather face an armed Frank Worrell than speak in church.

What these poor Saints in San Francisco didn't know was that their distinguished visitor had never spoken in church before in his life. He had had a one-line part in a play at Nauvoo and had played Satan, a memorized part, in the temple ceremony. But he had never stood up in front of a group of worshiping Saints and delivered an extemporaneous speech—and these poor people wanted to cancel their Sunday School classes so he could speak for an hour or more. Impossible. He couldn't do it.

By now, the opening prayer had been said, the sacrament song had been sung, and the sacrament was being passed. It would be Port's turn to speak in a few minutes. He thought about just getting up and walking out. But he could see the eager anticipation on faces, particularly on the boys' faces. He was a hero to these people. They had been so glad to see him, were so eager to hear him speak. He couldn't just get up and walk out.

He thought about pretending to be sick, too sick to speak. It was true he did feel ill, ever since they announced he was going to speak. Why hadn't they asked him? Surely he would have come up with a good reason to decline the invitation.

The sacrament was ending. His time was running out. How could a man who couldn't even read speak from the pulpit for hours? He couldn't do it.

The sacrament ended, and the brother returned to the pulpit. He talked about Port, the personal bodyguard to the prophet Joseph, the man who avenged the prophet's death by killing Frank Worrell, the leader of the Carthage mob. Port saw tears come to the eyes of some of the women as the old man talked. All the children were listening. In church, that was very unusual. How could he disappoint these good people?

Then it occurred to Port that he might just say a few things about where he had been and what he had done—not really preach a sermon—and then let everyone out early. Maybe he could tell the story about the horse named Sex. No, that wouldn't do.

Suddenly, the brother sat down. Everyone was looking at Port. It was his turn to speak. He looked to one side, then the other. He wanted to get up and run, but the only doorway was in the back of the room. He could feel the perspiration on his forehead. His hands were cold and clammy, and he hadn't even gotten up yet. The people were still staring at him, waiting, some smiling, all eager to hear him.

He stood up and walked stiff-legged to the small oak podium. He took a firm hold, like he was getting on a wild horse. In the event his knees buckled, he wanted to be able to hang on with his hands.

Port remembered being roped in the outhouse on the Big Blue, and realized he was feeling the same fear now. It made him angry. Then he had been surrounded by enemies threatening to kill him. Now he was surrounded by friends, people who loved and respected him. There was nothing to fear but his own silence, and the only way to get rid of that was to start talking. So he did.

"Two years ago, when the first company of Mormon pioneers began crossing the plains," he began, "some of us were attacked by a band of Pawnee Indians." Everyone in the room was listening, hanging on every word, though Port spoke slowly.

"Instead of running away," he continued, "I jerked my horse around, drew a revolver, and charged the Indians. Sometimes people ask if I wasn't frightened. I can honestly say I wasn't half as frightened as I am standing before you today." Some of the people laughed. All waited for him to continue. Someone asked what had happened to the Indians. Port explained how they were so surprised at the charge that they had scattered into the willows.

"I suppose I feel the way I do because I am not a public speaker," he said. "I can handle a gun, ride a horse, and work with men on the open trail. But in front of an audience, I have no skill or training. I hope you will be patient with me today." To his surprise, no one got up and left. All were waiting eagerly for him to continue.

He told about the fledgling church in Palmyra, New York, about when he was a boy and Joseph Smith was translating the Book of Mormon. He described chopping wood and picking berries to help finance the first printing of the Book of Mormon. He told about the Kirtland Temple and the many spiritual manifestations people saw when it was dedicated. He told how Joseph and Hyrum had been killed in Carthage Jail. He told about Frank Worrell's trial and how the Lord had delivered the Carthage mob leader into his hands.

Everyone laughed when he said he missed the shot. He said he was aiming for the belt buckle and missed by about an inch. He told about the sacrifices people had made crossing the Iowa mud and at Winter Quarters.

Port described the Salt Lake Valley and the progress the Saints were making there. He told how strongly Brigham Young felt that the Great Basin was the right place for the Mormons to build their kingdom. Port told the San Francisco congregation to stop paying tithes to Sam Brannan, to hold the money until Amasa Lyman came to San Francisco and then give the tithes directly to him.

He ended by reciting the words from the new song composed by William Clayton while crossing the plains, "Come, Come Ye Saints." He said he would recite the words again after the meeting if someone wished to write them down so the San Francisco Mormons could sing the hymn too. He closed his remarks in the name of Jesus Christ, said "Amen," and sat down. When he looked at his watch, he could not believe that he had been at the pulpit an entire hour.

After the closing prayer, the members flocked around him, asking questions, shaking hands. It was as if they just wanted to be near him. He felt good, still amazed that he had actually given a speech, one that had lasted an entire hour.

He thought he had recognized several of the faces in the audience. One belonged to Agnes Smith, the pretty widow of Joseph's brother, Don Carlos. She was the woman Cora's husband had wanted to marry. Agnes was as pretty as the last time Port had seen her, at Nauvoo four years earlier.

When she came forward to shake his hand, he wanted to ask her why she hadn't married Davis, but decided against it with so many people around. When she invited him to dinner, he didn't hesitate to accept.

They walked down Market Street in the cool San Francisco sunshine. It felt good to be outside, and it felt even better to be with a woman again, especially a pretty one. They were accompanied by Agnes's daughter Ina, a girl of about ten. Some of the edge was removed when Agnes explained she had come to California with her new husband, William Pickett, who was off to the gold fields, seeking his fortune. She had no idea when she would see him again.

Agnes was eager to hear all the news from Winter Quarters and the Great Salt Lake, what all her old friends were doing, which ones had left the Church, which ones had remained, and which ones were in different marriage relationships. She said that even though she still believed in the Church, she was glad to get away from the polygamy.

Port asked her about Amos Davis and why she had not become his plural wife.

"That was his idea, not mine," she stormed. "At first I tried to be nice, being a good friend with Cora and all, but finally I had to just put my foot down and tell him to get lost, or something like that. By then Cora had decided to marry you. How is she?"

Port explained how Cora had gone back to Amos about the time the Mormons left Nauvoo.

"What happened?" Agnes asked.

"Nothing," he explained. "We got along great when we were together. It was just that I was gone a lot. She didn't see much of me, and with the Saints leaving Nauvoo it appeared she would see even less of me. She decided that Amos, since the marriage with you didn't work out, needed her more. So she went back to him."

"Just like that?"

"Just like that."

"That's not very romantic."

"Life is not very romantic," Port said. "At least it hasn't been for me."

"Do you want to marry again?" she asked.

"I haven't thought much about it," he said. "I suppose if I were going to settle down and farm, I would want to marry. I don't know what's in the future, except that I don't think I'll be settling down any time soon."

"Will you return to Deseret?"

"Yes, when the gold rush slows down, but that will be a while, a year or two anyway."

"You ought to marry a woman like me," she said.

"How's that?"

"The happiest day of my marriage to William was when he left for the gold fields," Agnes said. "When he's home he demands three meals a day, too much affection, and all he wants to talk about is making money. I get so bored and depressed I could cry. But when he's gone it's so different. I only cook when we're hungry. I do more with the library committee—we're going to build the most beautiful library. I take Ina places and work with her on her studies—you should see the books she is reading, and she's only ten."

"Do you love your husband?" Port asked.

"Of course I do," she said, "but the flames burn a lot brighter when he only drops in about once a month."

"I suppose if I could find a woman like you, I might remarry," Port said. "The only problem is that I've never heard of another woman like you. I don't think there are any in Salt Lake."

"I'll tell you what," she said, taking him by the arm. "If William happens to drown in the Sacramento River or run off with one of those pretty Mexican girls, you'll be the first one I'll write to."

"Would you stay in San Francisco?" Port asked, trying not to take her too seriously.

"Of course."

"I could only visit you about once a year, never in winter when the passes are snowed in."

"Maybe the flames would burn even brighter," she responded quickly. They both laughed.

For dinner that day Agnes served fresh strawberries and cream, tortillas and beans, and bread with grape jelly for dessert. Agnes said she would have prepared something more formal had she known he was coming, but then again maybe she wouldn't have.

Port liked Agnes. There was an honesty about her spontaneous conversation that made a man feel comfortable, at ease. He wished more women could be that way. Cora had come close, but not Luana.

After dinner they hiked to the top of Telegraph Hill, where they could see much of the bay and some of the ocean. Port concluded that San Francisco was a beautiful place with some wonderful people, particularly Agnes Pickett and her daughter, Ina.

The next day Port used Agnes's carriage to carry his newly purchased cargo down to the docks. The following morning he was chugging up the Sacramento River with enough rum to satisfy a thousand thirsty miners. He had decided to water it down two to one, add a touch of sugar and cayenne pepper, and call it Golden Grog.

At Sutter's Fort, Port spent the last of the reward money he had obtained from Backenstos to buy mules and pack saddles. Loading up his rum, glasses, and tent, he headed up the American River.

As Port rode upstream along the river, there was hardly a place where he didn't see men digging for gold. Some were panning with metal pans, others with Indian baskets. A few had sluice boxes or rockers. Port was glad he was riding a horse leading a pack train, rather than crouching over a pan full of dirt, the cold water sloshing over his hands. He guessed he was going to make a lot more money too.

Without stopping, he passed the tent where he had purchased his first glass of watered-down corn whiskey.

He continued past Mormon Bar to the next mining camp, a place called Murderer's Bar. There being no saloon in the camp, Port proceeded to set up his round tent in an open meadow. Finding an old plank, he gave a boy a nickel to write "Round Tent Saloon" on it. After watering down and flavoring up the rum, he hung up the sign, announcing he was open for business.

Word spread quickly and the men began lining up for Golden Grog at a dollar a cup. Before the day was over, Port found that he could not mix and pour the rum and collect the gold fast enough—at least not fast enough to satisfy the thirsty miners. He could also see that his initial supplies would not last through the end of the week. He needed to head back for more inventory.

The next morning Port found himself a partner, Jack Smith, a trustworthy fellow he had known since Nauvoo. He offered Smith half the profits of the business for running the tent while Port was out on the trail bringing in inventory and taking out the gold.

By the end of the summer, Port had two more partners, the second at an inn he had opened at Buckeye Flat and the third at a halfway house near Mormon Island on the south fork of the American River. He was doing so well that at the end of the summer he gave Thomas Rhodes ten thousand dollars in gold to take back to Great Salt Lake City for Brigham Young to mint into coin. Rhodes, who had been in California since 1847, had organized a special company to carry Mormon gold to Deseret.

Port spent most of his time on the trail, leading his heavily laden pack string of mules to his three businesses. Sitting tall in the saddle, he never felt like trading places with the growing number of men he saw bent over their diggings, always so eager to give him their gold for a glass of rum.

Business was so good that his saloons frequently ran out of rum before he arrived with a fresh shipment.

Whenever he reached the top of the hill above Murderer's Bar with a new shipment, he would blow on a bugle to let Smith know he was coming. Smith, in turn, would fire his shotgun, once up the valley, once down, to let the miners know James Brown was arriving with a fresh load of rum or whiskey. By the time Port reached the round tent, men were already gathering from every direction to give him their gold.

Port often wondered why the men spent so much on drink. He guessed it was probably boredom. The monotony of leaning over a pan of dirt day after day became unbearable to many, and a man simply had to have some diversion. In the gold camps of 1849, drinking and fighting were the two main diversions. Later, gamblers and prostitutes, even preachers, added new choices.

Quite by accident, one afternoon Port discovered a second and very bounteous source of income. He was mixing some rum for Smith inside the Round Tent Saloon when he heard some boisterous conversation followed by shooting from behind the tent. Going to investigate, he discovered that four men were having a shooting match. Each had placed fifty dollars in a pot. The winner was to take all. Their target was a wooden box with a black bull's-eye marked on it, about a hundred yards off.

Port asked if he could join in. The men said he could if he put fifty dollars in the pot. Port returned to the tent for his rifle and money. He was the last to shoot, winning the two hundred dollars by a wide margin.

Port began to sponsor his own shooting contests whenever he was in camp. He put up a hundred dollars, but those shooting against him only had to put up fifty. Some days he would have six or eight men to shoot against, but Port always won, sometimes making four or five hundred dollars a week with his shooting skills.

Not only were the shooting contests an excellent opportunity to earn money, but they were great sport as well. The matches sometimes drew hundreds of spectators. It seemed there was always a new man in camp who thought he could outshoot James Brown, the now-famous marksman. Of course, when the crowds gathered to watch the shooting matches, everyone had to buy a drink or two. Port was making money coming and going.

While his partners ran the businesses, Port made frequent trips down the Sacramento River to Yerba Buena to buy supplies, always visiting Agnes and Ina. Remarkably, Agnes's husband, William, was always gone. Port couldn't understand how a man with a wife like Agnes could stay away so much. Port thoroughly enjoyed the lively conversation, the teasing, and the long walks along the mostly deserted tree-lined streets of San Francisco. He and Agnes became good friends, but as much as they enjoyed each other's company, intimacies were sidestepped on both sides.

Port carefully planned his San Francisco trips to avoid being in the city on the weekends. Though he had been delighted with the outcome of his first public speech, he didn't want to push his luck and risk getting a second invitation to speak. Instead, he avoided church altogether.

In January Amasa Lyman invited Port to accompany him to San Francisco. The apostle was unhappy that in nearly eight months he had only been able to collect four thousand dollars in tithes and offerings, not nearly ten percent of what the Mormons were earning in the gold fields. Partly out of frustration, partly out of duty, he decided it was time to collect the Lord's due from Sam Brannan, who was in San Francisco now. Lyman wanted Port to lend a hand.

It sounded like an exciting adventure to Port. By this time he knew enough about Brannan to guess the money wouldn't be handed over just for the asking. Not only had Brannan been collecting the usual tithing, but an additional ten percent to build a temple for the California Mormons. Not a penny in four years had been turned over to Brigham Young or the Church. Lyman was sure Brannan had used church funds to finance his own, highly profitable, personal business ventures in both San Francisco and the gold fields. The time for reckoning had come.

Upon arriving in San Francisco, Lyman and Rockwell went directly to Brannan's new mansion on Polk Street. To their surprise, they were ushered without delay directly into Brannan's personal office.

Brannan was a good-looking man, well shaved and well dressed. Physically, he looked to Port like he might be a little on the soft side. He was neat and clean, with perfect manners.

"We came for the Lord's tithing," Lyman said, not a man to beat around the bush. Brannan motioned for them to be seated.

"I'm glad you finally came," Brannan said, surprising both Lyman and Rockwell with his warmth. Still, they were not ready to trust the man.

"There are some in the Church here," Brannan said, "who say I would cheat the Lord and keep the tithes of the people."

"That's true," Port said.

"Now you can prove them wrong," Lyman added.

"I fully intend to give the Lord his tithing," Brannan said.

"Good," Lyman responded. "We have come to receive it. How much do you have?"

"Sirs, you misunderstand me," Brannan said. "I said I would turn the money over to the Lord. I will not give it to ordinary mortals like yourselves." It was apparent now that Brannan was playing games. Lyman became angry.

"Are you telling me you will not turn over the tithing unless the Lord himself walks into this room and asks for it?" Lyman demanded.

"A receipt will do just as well," Brannan explained.

"You mean a receipt signed by God in his own hand?" Port added.

"That's exactly right," Brannan concluded. "You bring me God's receipt, and I'll give you God's tithing. It's as simple as that. Now, if you men will excuse me, I have work to do." He got up and walked out of the room.

The next day a church court was called, which included Lyman and local church leaders, and Sam Brannan was excommunicated. While Lyman remained in town to reorganize the local branches, Port returned to the gold fields to tend his prospering businesses.

That spring another Mormon sharpshooter, Boyd Stewart, introduced shooting matches at Columbia. He had heard of the success Port was having and figured he could do as well or better, having never met a man who could outshoot him.

Stewart was good. His offer to attract men to his shooting matches was the same as Port's. He would put one hundred dollars in the kitty, but any man who wanted to shoot against him needed only to come up with fifty. There were plenty of takers at first, but the number gradually declined when there were no winners other than Stewart.

It wasn't long until one of the most-discussed subjects in the saloons was who could shoot best, Stewart or Brown. Men argued over the subject for hours. Whenever someone suggested the name of a common opponent who had fared better against Brown than against Stewart, someone else would come up with another common opponent who had come closer to beating Stewart. Who was the best shot in California, Brown or Stewart? The question remained unresolved through the spring of 1850 and much of the summer. Finally, a shooting contest was set up between the two. The location was Port's halfway house on the south fork of the American River.

Gold seekers came from as far away as Mormon Slough on the San Joaquin River and Rough and Ready on the Bear River to witness the match. While only two men would be shooting, hundreds more would be betting, fighting, and drinking. Word soon spread that the gathering at Port's halfway house would be the biggest whiskeyfest thus far in the California gold rush. The big secret among the Mormons was that it was not James Brown, but Orrin Porter Rockwell, who would be shooting against Boyd Stewart. The prize was one thousand dollars.

Men began arriving at the halfway house early on the morning of the contest. Port had ridden in the previous afternoon. Not only had he checked his weapons but also his inventory of spirits. Even if he lost the shooting contest, this was bound to be the most profitable day of his life. Thousands of drinks would be sold. But he didn't intend to lose the shooting contest. Stewart had a big mouth that needed silencing.

By noon, tables had to be set up outside because there was not enough room inside to serve all the men. The shooting competition began at two.

The rules of the contest were simple. Two identical paper targets were placed on trees at a distance of 150 yards. In the center of each target was a round, black bull's-eye. The shooters took turns until each had fired three shots, one from the standing position, one from the sitting position, and one from the lying down, or prone, position. The judges then measured the distance from each bullet-hole to the bull's-eye, to the nearest eighth of an inch. The three distances for each shooter were then added up. The man with the shortest combined distance was the winner. At 150 yards, scores in the twenties were common.

Thousands of dollars exchanged hands as the whiskey-guzzling men placed their bets. No one kept track of all the wagers that were made, but it appeared Brown was a slight favorite. A few more of the men were willing to bet for Brown than for Stewart. No one, however, gave odds favoring Brown.

Stewart took the first standing shot, missing by nine and one-quarter inches. Port's standing shot missed by an even eight inches. Stewart's second shot scored five and seven-eighths. Port, from the sitting position, scored six and three-fouths. Stewart's final shot missed by only half an inch. To win, Port needed to be closer than seven-eighths of an inch with his final shot.

Without taking his eyes off the target, Port dropped to the ground, finding the bull's-eye in his sights. He breathed deeply, letting the air partway out. Then he held his breath while squeezing the trigger.

When the rifle fired, some of the men near the target cried he had missed the entire target. They could not see a new hole. But when the judges made a close examination, they found a hole in the bull's-eye. Port was the winner by seven-eighths of an inch.

"Double or nothing," shouted an angry Stewart as the men were collecting their bets. "Brown, I challenge you to a shooting contest with pistols. My thousand dollars against the thousand you just won."

Suddenly everyone was cheering and placing new bets. No one had ever seen Brown shoot a pistol, but they knew Stewart was good, probably the best, having won many shooting contests with his pistols.

"I accept on one condition," Port yelled. The crowd became quiet to hear what he had to say. "Since you are the challenger, I should be able to pick the target and the method of shooting." Stewart nodded his agreement.

"Good," Port said. "Each of us will shoot three times at silver dollars thrown over our heads." The crowd roared its approval. Shooting at moving objects was something entirely new. No one had ever heard of shooting silver dollars in the air.

Eager to begin, Stewart offered to be the lead shooter. The first dollar was thrown up. He missed. The second went up. He missed that one too. He nodded for the third one to be thrown. He missed again.

Port stepped forward, drawing his Navy Dragoon from the holster. He nodded for the man with the silver dollars to flip a coin in the air.

The coin hadn't even reached the top of its arc when Port fired. Zing. The dollar changed directions, going higher. Port fired a second time. Again the dollar changed directions. He had hit the coin twice. The crowd went wild. No one had ever seen shooting like that. Some were asking why they hadn't heard of this Brown before.

Port picked up his second thousand dollars of the afternoon and headed for the halfway house to wash the dust from his mouth. He was wrong in thinking the exciting part of the day was over.

Less than an hour later, Stewart climbed on top of one of the tables. He was so drunk he could hardly keep his balance.

"Anybody want to know who James Brown really is?" he shouted. "James Brown is not his real name. I know who he is."

Port hurried out of the tent. He had to shut Stewart up before it was too late. Dozens of drunken miners were gathering around to hear the news.

"That's him, folks," Stewart shouted, pointing at Port, who was racing toward him. "Orrin Porter Rockwell, the Mormon Danite who shot Governor Boggs and Frank Worrell, Brigham Young's Destroying Angel. That's him. I swear it."

Port knew about mining camp justice, how men were routinely hung without trials. He also knew that there were plenty of men from Missouri and Illinois at the diggings, and that his old enemies were more likely to attend shooting matches than Mormons. He knew too that every man within shouting distance was at least partially drunk and would probably welcome a chance to participate in a lynching.

Instead of stopping, Port merely changed directions, running as fast as he could toward the tree where his horse was tied.

"Stop him," Stewart cried.

"Get a rope," someone else yelled, but before any of the drunken horde got around to doing anything, Port was in the saddle and galloping up the trail, the white dog on his heels. Some of the men ran for their horses, but Port was not worried. There was not a horse in the gold fields that could keep up with Boggs on a mountain trail.

A week later Port agreed to guide Apostle Charles C. Rich and a group of homesick Mormons back to Zion. The gold rush had been good to Port. He had made enough money to sustain him the rest of his life. And there was a lot more still to be made. But Port was not a man to push his luck. It was time to pocket his winnings, turn the three prospering businesses over to his partners, and go home.

# Chapter 47

Upon returning to Great Salt Lake City in the fall of 1850, Port saw dramatic changes after an absence of eighteen months. When he left, there had been a few thousand pioneers struggling to build log cabins and plant crops. Now there was a regular community complete with stores, blacksmith shops, and churches. The population had topped ten thousand and was growing daily.

The Mormons were prospering far beyond their earlier expectations. Brigham Young's prediction that the Saints would reap riches from the gold rush by remaining in the Salt Lake Valley had come true.

A steady stream of California-bound emigrants had pushed prices for local commodities sky-high. The going rate for flour was twenty-five dollars a hundredweight, and the Mormons could sell all they could produce. Eggs, cheese, and produce brought similar prices. A good horse or a fat ox team could bring a hundred dollars; a team of mules, two hundred.

On the other hand, items the Mormons needed to buy—like wood stoves, plows, tools, barrels, and wagon parts—could be purchased for a fraction of what these items sold for in St. Louis. In efforts to lighten their loads, the gold seekers had abandoned countless items along the trail from Laramie to Salt Lake. Other items they traded away in Salt Lake for more needed items such as food and fresh teams.

After saying farewell to his companions, having no home of his own to go to, Port headed straight to John Neff's place. He figured that would be a good place to unload the heavy gold he was carrying. He could trust John to keep it for him. Plus, he was eager to see how the Indian girl, Emma, was doing.

Emma was the first to greet Port as he dismounted at the hitching post in front of the house. The Indian girl had changed. She was no longer a thin girl, but a beautiful young woman.

Mountain men had, on more than one occasion, told Port the Shoshones had the best-looking women. Now he believed them. When Neff came outside, noticing Port's admiring glances toward the girl, he said she had no shortage of dancing partners at the church dances—not just young men, but older men with plural wives too.

Emma spoke fluent English now. She began telling Port about all the things she was learning and doing. She could read and write. She had given a talk in church. She sang in a choir. But she was still a Shoshone, she explained, and wanted to return to her family as soon as he could take her. She didn't know yet if she wanted to remain with her people and return to a more primitive life, but she had to see them, to know how they were doing. He promised to take her the following spring.

While conversing with Emma, Port couldn't help but notice John's daughter Mary Ann. He was surprised that she was still at home and unmarried. She was almost twenty-two now and a very attractive young woman—an excellent teacher as evidenced by the progress Emma had made.

Occasionally, while he was talking to Emma, Port would look over at Mary Ann, who would smile and then quickly look away. She was more shy than most women. Perhaps her shyness had prevented her from finding a husband.

The entire family gathered around, eager to hear of California and the gold fields. It took several evenings for Port to tell it all, about San Francisco, Sutter's Fort, the mining camps on the American River, the different ways to wash gold from the sand and gravel, the meeting with Sam Brannan. The only thing he left out was his hour-long talk in church in San Francisco. He didn't want to give the Salt Lake Saints any ideas.

Port told about Indian troubles on the return trip. When the party was camped at the edge of the Humboldt Sink, one night a band of braves ran off with over a dozen horses. The trail led Port and several companions to an Indian village less than a day's journey away. The Mormons waited in the sagebrush until dark and then ran off the Indian herd. When the white men arrived back at their own camp the next morning, not only had they retrieved the stolen horses, but they had added nine Indian ponies to the herd. Anticipating retaliation, the night guard was doubled.

Two nights later, Port woke up in the middle of the night. Noticing one of the guards returning from his post, rifle over his shoulder, Port asked the approaching man if everything was all right. To his surprise, the guard didn't answer. Port repeated the question.

Without a word, the guard turned and began to run away. Port realized the man was not a guard, but an Indian hoping to enter the camp disguised as a guard. Port whipped out his Navy Dragoon and fired three quick shots after the fleeing man.

The next morning they found the counterfeit guard about three hundred yards from camp, dead. His back had stopped one of Port's bullets. He was an Indian dressed in white man's clothing.

That winter it seemed there were Indian troubles everywhere. Part of the problem was the endless stream of California emigrants that had passed through during the last two summers. While the Mormons under Young's strict control vigorously pursued the policy that it was better to feed the red men than to fight them, the California pioneers were more willing to engage the red men in battle. That there were fewer women and children among the gold seekers probably added to their recklessness. Groups of men, without the tempering influence of women, tended to be a lot more prone to get into a good fight. Plus, there seemed to be an attitude that a trip to California was somehow incomplete without at least one good Indian fight.

Port spent much of the winter delivering cattle and blankets to nearby tribes in an effort to establish a more permanent peace.

The policy seemed to be working, at least until April, when a band of about a dozen Utes attacked the settlement at Tooele, west of Salt Lake. The band drove off a large herd of Mormon horses, including about a dozen from a California-bound wagon train that was spending the winter at Tooele, the men building a sawmill for Ezra T. Benson. As deputy marshal, Port was ordered to ride out to Tooele to see if anything could be done to retrieve the stolen horses.

After gathering a posse consisting of both Mormons and California emigrants, Port headed south on the trail of the Indians. A thundershower the previous afternoon had all but wiped out the trail. At the end of the first day, the posse discovered thirty warriors camped on the east shore of Rush Lake. There were no women and children in the group, and no horses either.

Port guessed these Indians had probably been involved in the raid on Tooele, but even if they weren't, they would know which Indians were and where they had taken the stolen horses. Port and his men rounded up all thirty warriors and—when none would volunteer any information on the whereabouts of the horses—began herding them back to Tooele for questioning.

Port thought the horses were probably up in the hills not very far away, and, rather than remain in captivity, the Indians would tell where the stolen horses could be recovered.

Port should have guessed something was afoot when the Indians, all of whom had been walking, began to slow down near the outskirts of Tooele. He should have known they were not as weary as they claimed to be.

Suddenly, at the signal of one of the chiefs, all the Indians began screaming, whooping, and yelling, frightening the horses their guards were riding. The Indians overpowered several of the closest riders, including Lorenzo Custer, leader of the California emigrant train. They shot Custer point-blank with his own gun, killing him instantly. In the meantime, the Mormons were fighting to bring their horses under control. By the time they did and began shooting back, the Indians had disappeared into the oak brush—all but four, who were cut off by the Mormons and returned to Port.

Seeing the white men were angry enough to kill them, the four Indians volunteered to lead Port and his men to the stolen horses. After returning Custer's body to his family at the emigrant camp, Port and his men followed the four Indians south.

After passing Rush Lake, they headed west through the desert mountains into Skull Valley, a sacred Indian burial ground, then north again. They rode all night. Whenever Port asked the Indians where the horses were, they just pointed straight ahead and the journey continued. They rode under a full moon. The Indians were trotting ahead on foot.

At dawn, an irritable Port asked the Indians one more time where the stolen horses were. They pointed beyond a gently sloping hill with an outcropping of rock on top.

Port and several of his men made a wide sweep of the area, looking for horse sign. When all returned, not a single horse track or dropping had been found, though one of the men had flushed out an Indian boy who had been trailing them on foot. The scout had led the boy back to the others, a lariat rope around his neck.

When Port asked the Indians why there was no horse sign, they merely shrugged their shoulders and pointed to the east, a route that would take them back to Tooele, where they had begun the chase a day earlier.

The white men were tired and angry, concluding they had been taken on a wild goose chase. One man suggested whipping the Indians. Another thought they should be taken back to town to stand trial for horse stealing. They could not be tried for murder because the Indians that had killed Custer had all escaped into the brush. Some of the men thought they ought to be looking for Custer's killer, not stolen horses.

Port had hoped that with the help of the four captives he could have secured the stolen horses, thereby keeping the Indians who had killed Custer on foot, making it easier to eventually catch them. But the four captives had led him away from the horses instead, effectively clearing the way for the murderers to reach the horses first. Even if he found out now where the horses had been and which direction the murderers had gone, they would still have too large a lead. His men and their horses were exhausted from the all-night ride. He guessed that by now it would be next to impossible to recover the horses or catch the murderer thanks to the four Indians who had effectively deceived him.

The four Indians were sitting cross-legged on the ground resting their legs, nibbling on some parched corn. The boy was off to one side by himself.

Port drew his Navy revolver, walked up to the four Indians, and fired four times in rapid succession. When the smoke cleared, all four braves were sprawled in the dirt, dead.

One of the men pushed the boy forward, thinking Port would want to shoot him too. Instead, Port returned his pistol to his pocket.

"Let the boy go," he said. "Someone has got to tell the Indians what happened here. They've got to understand they can't just ride into a Mormon community, run off the horses, and kill a man, without paying dearly." The man let go of the frightened boy, who scampered out of sight into the tall sagebrush.

After an unsuccessful hunt for the stolen horses and Custer's killers, Port returned to Salt Lake. He met with Brigham Young, who was concerned over the increasing conflicts with Indians throughout the Mormon settlements.

Young wasn't sure the execution of the four Indians had been the right thing to do. On the one hand, he agreed the shootings would make the Indians think twice before running off another bunch of Mormon horses. On the other hand, the incident could push the Indians closer to declaring all-out war on the Mormons. Young said he would rather see Indians stealing horses than taking scalps.

Young said he was worried about Jim Bridger, who he claimed was selling whiskey and guns to the Indians and encouraging confrontations with the Mormons. Bridger resented the Mormons taking over the rafting business on the Platte and Green rivers. And Old Gabe was furious that the Mormons had established an emigrant trading post, Fort Supply, right in his own backyard. Mormon competition had cost him a lot of money. Young believed the old mountain man was getting his revenge by stirring up the Indians against the Mormons.

"Bridger is telling the Indians we are taking their land and killing their game," Young explained. "We need someone out there telling them we want to be friends, that Mormons have been ordered not to kill the game. We want to share with our Indian brothers. We want to be good neighbors. That's the message I want you to take to them."

During the next two weeks Port put together a pack train loaded with trade goods such as blankets, mirrors, hatchets, pots and pans, sewing needles, cloth, and buttons. Young hadn't approved the purchase of any knives, guns, or whiskey, but Port threw in a few bottles of the latter, just in case.

Port was excited about his new assignment. He would be an ambassador of goodwill, traveling among the Indians just giving stuff away, no strings attached, and delivering a message of peace from the Mormon chief.

Port decided to head north first, through Shoshone country, taking Emma with him to see her family. He hoped that after a short visit she would want to return to her Mormon home with the Neffs, who had grown very fond of her.

On the morning of their departure, while Port was loading the last of his mules, with everyone gathered around enjoying a last few minutes with Emma, Mary Ann announced that she knew the real reason for Port's long beard.

"So he can play Santa Claus to the Indians," she said. "Bearing gifts on his eight tiny mules, spreading a message of peace and goodwill to men."

"Unfortunately, the Indians don't believe in Santa Claus," Port added. "When they see my long beard and hair, instead of Santa, they see a very attractive lodgepole decoration." Everyone laughed.

With preparations finally completed, Port shook hands with everyone present, including Mary Ann, who held onto his hand longer than was necessary and squeezed more than was customary for a woman.

Port wondered if she meant anything by the handshake. She was twenty-two, single, pretty, and sixteen years younger than he was. There were plenty of young men—and older polygamists—interested in her. He concluded that someone so attractive, refined, and educated couldn't have a romantic interest in someone so rough, so old, and gone so much. He wasn't about to make a fool out of himself by pretending there was anything other than a casual friendship between them. And even if she did feel something for him, she would probably change her mind when she learned he had gunned down four Indian prisoners.

Port and Emma climbed onto their eager horses. It was a warm spring day, a perfect day to be departing on a wilderness adventure. After taking the mules' lead rope from Neff and whistling to Joseph, whom he hadn't seen for a few minutes, Port headed his horse north on the heels of Emma, who was already on her way home.

# Chapter 48

The journey into Shoshone country was uneventful except for one brief incident in the mountains two days north of Goodyear's trading post. Emma was leading the way up the tail when a startled badger dove for his hole, under her horse's feet. The horse crow-hopped to one side, throwing Emma off balance. She fell to the ground, cutting her left arm just below the shoulder. The skin was laid back in a five-inch straight line toward her elbow. Otherwise she was unhurt.

Emma didn't whimper or pull away as Port washed the wound with clean water, sewed the skin together with a needle and thread, applied a wad of crushed yarrow leaves, and then covered the cut with a clean dressing. Within an hour they were back on the trail.

About a week later, they found Emma's family with a band of Shoshones near the Snake River. Her mother, a weathered, sinewy woman, wept openly as she embraced the daughter she had thought was lost forever. An older sister showed nearly as much emotion, and two little brothers offered to let her shoot their new bows and arrows. The father and most of the other men in the band were off hunting. Port wondered if they were hunting wild animals or emigrant horses.

The entire village gathered around, the women and girls admiring Emma's cotton dress. They had never seen an Indian in a white woman's dress before.

After unloading his pack animals, Port gave everyone in the village a gift from the great Mormon chief who wanted peace with the Shoshones. Some were reluctant to accept the gifts, not believing a white man would give them something without wanting something in return.

Port spent the next week visiting the Shoshone bands in the area, delivering gifts and his message of peace. Thanks to Emma he knew enough of the language to get by passably well. Without exception, the Indians were surprised and pleased that Port wanted nothing in return for his gifts. One chief tried to give him a young squaw, which he politely refused. Two others gave him horses, which he accepted.

When it was time to leave, Port did his best to convince Emma she should return with him, but she was determined to stay with her people. Apparently, she wanted to see a young brave, who was out hunting with her father and other men from the village.

Port was concerned for Emma's safety, but these were her people, and if she wanted to remain with them, there was nothing he could do. He felt sad leaving Emma behind as he headed east over the Oregon Trail in the direction of Fort Bridger.

Port reached the fort ahead of the year's first wagon train. Old Gabe was home, but offered no warm welcome to the Mormon scout. When Port asked Bridger if he was selling guns and spirits to the Indians, the old mountain man freely admitted that he was.

"Mormons have taken away the rest of my business," he explained. "Guns and spirits is all that's left to keep me solvent. Besides, the Mormons is hogging up the best Indian lands, like a swarm of crickets. Some of the braves want to stop the Mormons, and I can't say I blame them. But they need guns to do it. That's where I come in."

Port was surprised at the man's bluntness, and he assured Bridger he would pass his words to Brigham Young, who was determined to live peacefully with the Indians. After presenting gifts and his message to some of the Indians camped around the fort, Port headed for Ute country, hoping to spread more goodwill. He finally returned to Salt Lake with the winter snows.

There were few Indian troubles that winter, so Port stayed in Salt Lake most of the time. He handled a few deputy assignments and funded a logging venture with John Neff to bring firewood and fence posts out of a nearby canyon, the work to begin in the spring. Otherwise, he just lived the life of a lazy dog.

On Sunday afternoons he could sometimes be seen walking along Salt Lake's wide streets with Mary Ann Neff. She was always eager to hear about his adventures. But the conversation seldom became more personal than that. After the divorce from Luana, Port was reluctant to try his hand at romance again. But he enjoyed being with Mary Ann and did not avoid her.

The lack of Indian problems that winter led Brigham to believe that Rockwell's goodwill mission had accomplished some good. In fact, as spring approached, things were so peaceful that Port arranged to drive a herd of horses to Carson City.

While he was gone, the situation in the Great Basin changed dramatically. It began in Springville one afternoon at the James Ivie farm. While Ivie was digging a new well, a Ute squaw approached the cabin in hopes of trading three large lake trout for some flour.

Mrs. Ivie invited the squaw inside, where the women proceeded to make a deal. A few minutes later the Indian woman left the cabin with three pints of flour, and Mrs. Ivie began preparing a fish feast.

As the squaw left the cabin she was greeted by two companions, Ute braves who wanted to see what she had obtained for the three fish. When they saw the three pints of flour, one of the braves flew from his horse in a rage and began beating the squaw for making such a bad trade.

Ivie crawled from the well to see what was the matter. He saw the screaming squaw run into his cabin to get away from the brave. Ivie stepped in front of the door to prevent the angry warrior from following the woman inside.

Unfortunately, the brave had a rifle in his hand. When the farmer refused to step aside, the Indian raised the rifle to shoot. Ivie grabbed the barrel, and the two men wrestled for possession of the gun until it broke in two pieces, leaving the Indian with the wooden stock and Ivie with the steel barrel. The two men began to swing at each other, but the wood was no match against the steel, and Ivie knocked the red man cold with a blow to the side of the head.

No sooner had Ivie relaxed, thinking the fight was over, than an arrow from the bow of the second brave creased his chest. Renewing his grip on the steel barrel, Ivie lunged forward, delivering a smashing blow to the second Indian before another arrow could be launched. Like the first, this Indian collapsed in a heap.

Ivie was beginning to relax a second time, thinking the fight was finally over, when he was struck from behind with a piece of firewood. Again he tightened his grip on the steel barrel, this time knocking the squaw senseless. She had come to defend her husband.

Having heard the commotion, a neighbor, Joseph Kelly, arrived in time to see the three Indians on the ground and Ivie still holding tightly to the steel barrel, just in case another Indian was lurking nearby. Kelly revived the squaw and the second brave. But the first brave—who had started the whole affair by beating the squaw—was dead.

Walkara, who by this time was having second thoughts about letting the Mormons settle in Utah Valley, flew into a rage. A few wagonloads of friendly Mormons had given him gifts and talked him into a peaceful coexistence. Now, hardly before he realized what was happening, ten thousand Mormons were swarming over his hunting grounds, cutting down the forests for their cabins, driving off the wild animals, and slicing open Mother Earth with their plows. Like grizzly bears, the Mormons became possessive of the land where they lived, putting up fences and keeping others away, especially Indians. Walkara couldn't understand why white men thought they could own a piece of Mother Earth.

Slowly, Walkara had come to think he had made a big mistake in allowing the Mormons to spread over the land. There were too many now. But maybe they would leave, perhaps for California, if the Indians applied enough pressure. Walkara declared war on the Mormons.

There was no official declaration delivered to Brigham Young, just a sudden outbreak in Indian hostilities as Walkara led his braves against Mormon settlements, encouraging his red brothers in other tribes to do the same.

One of Brigham Young's first moves was to issue a warrant for the arrest of Jim Bridger, who was still selling guns and whiskey to the Indians. Young personally handed the warrant to Bill Hickman with orders to go to Fort Bridger, arrest Old Gabe, and destroy or confiscate all guns, ammunition, and whiskey. Hickman was given an escort of 150 Nauvoo Legionnaires in case Bridger offered resistance or Indians were encountered along the way.

Hickman later told Young that Bridger "flew the coop" to avoid arrest. No guns or ammunition were found, but Hickman uncovered a large stock of whiskey and rum.

"No ammunition was found," Hickman said in his report. "But the whiskey and rum, of which he had a good stock, was destroyed by doses; the sheriff, most of his officers, and the doctor and chaplain of the company, all aided in carrying out the orders and worked so hard day and night that they were exhausted, not being able to stand up. But the privates, poor fellows, were rationed, and did not do so much."

Having too much fun to return home, Hickman continued east with his army to the Green River, where there had been a continuing dispute between the Mormons and a group of mountain men over who should have the ferry concession. Hickman resolved the conflict by killing several of the mountain men and threatening similar treatment for the rest if they continued to operate their ferry on the Green River. Abandoning their craft to the Mormons, the mountaineers disappeared into the hills.

It was fall when Port returned from Carson City. About thirty Mormons had been killed so far in the Indian war, and about an equal number of Indians. In October a Pacific Railroad surveying expedition was attacked by Pahvant braves on the Sevier River. The Indians were seeking revenge for two of their companions who had been killed by members of a wagon train from Missouri a few weeks earlier. The Pahvants killed all seven members of the survey crew, plus the leader, Captain John Gunnison.

Gunnison had fought so bravely that the Indians cut out his heart and tossed it from one to another, taking bites of it, hoping the captain's courage would pass on to them.

Finally, in November, winter snows forced the Indians to focus their attention on fighting cold and hunger instead of white men. While the Indians were busy surviving, Young was trying to figure out how to end the war.

As soon as the grass started to grow the following spring, Brigham Young sent George Bean, Amos Neff, and Porter Rockwell south to attempt peace negotiations with Walkara. Young had received reports the chief had wintered near Beaver. Young wanted to propose peace negotiations before the war was in full swing again. He purposely sent a small party of negotiators so the Indians wouldn't feel threatened. The usual pack mule loaded with gifts trailed along.

Port found Walkara near Parowan, trading with a mountain man named Waters. There were thirty or forty braves with the chief, plus an assortment of squaws, old people, and children. While allowing Port and his companions into camp, Walkara was in no mood to negotiate anything, even when Port offered him a bottle of firewater.

Things were different from the year before. Nearly thirty members of his tribe had been killed by Mormons, and now about the same number of fresh Mormon scalps were hanging from Ute lodgepoles.

The next morning Walkara ordered his people to break camp. As the Indians loaded up and headed south, Port and his man accompanied them. Walkara didn't want to discuss peace now, but perhaps with time he would change his mind.

In traveling with the Indians, Port and his companions came to learn the Indians were very poor. They didn't have enough food, blankets, or cooking utensils. They were eating horse and dog meat, mostly horse jerky. When Indians began eating their horses, one knew they were on hard times.

Port and his men accompanied the Walkara band all the way to New Harmony, south of Cedar City, before the surly chief finally agreed to discuss a possible truce with the Mormons.

Walkara invited several smaller chiefs to the meeting in his lodge after dark one evening. Port passed around a little firewater to warm things up, and then he told Walkara the chief was invited to Great Salt Lake City to discuss peace with the Mormon chief.

Walkara said he would not go to the city by the Great Salt Lake. He said Brigham Young would have to come to New Harmony. Bean told Walkara the Mormons would guarantee his safe passage to and from Salt Lake. Still, Walkara refused to go. Brigham Young must come to him. It soon became apparent that Walkara wasn't concerned with safety. It was a matter of face, a power play in which Walkara thought he would be the winner if Young came to him.

The conversation seemed to have reached a stalemate, when the sub-chief Beaverads offered to be the one to go to Salt Lake and receive the presents and anything else Young wanted to offer for peace.

Bean and Rockwell didn't know how to respond. It appeared Beaverads was overstepping his bounds. Only Walkara had the power to negotiate with Young. Walkara was the undisputed chief of the Utes, or was he?

Bean and Rockwell looked at Walkara, seeking some kind of hint as to how they should respond to Beaverads's offer. Walkara's face was stone, telling them nothing. Beaverads repeated his offer. Port could feel the tension building. He placed his right hand closer to his gun.

Suddenly, Walkara drew his knife and struck out at Beaverads's face. The young chief dodged the blade, but not before it opened a gaping crevice across his cheek. Beaverads dove for his rifle with Walkara after him in an effort to inflict more damage with the knife. Port leaped upon Walkara, trying to wrestle the knife away. Bean dove on Beaverads to prevent the young chief from shooting Walkara. The rest of the Indians, and Neff, carefully avoided the scuffle.

When the incident was over, Walkara returned his knife to his belt as if nothing had happened and returned to his place by the fire. Beaverads was steaming for revenge, holding a rag against his bleeding cheek. His lack of action seemed to indicate that he finally understood he had spoken out of turn in offering to go to Salt Lake. Only Walkara could make such a decision. He would remember that in the future.

Since Walkara was firm in his refusal to go to Salt Lake, and because Rockwell and Bean refused to agree to bring Young to New Harmony, a compromise was reached—a meeting at Chicken Creek near Nephi in fifteen days, provided the white men brought plenty of beef cattle, flour, and Indian trade goods. The Indians promised to bring plenty of horses to cover their end of the trading.

The next morning, Rockwell, Bean, and Neff departed for Salt Lake, the first portion of the peace puzzle firmly in place, or so they thought.

# Chapter 49

The following Sunday Port was walking down State Street with Mary Ann, discussing the upcoming negotiations with Walkara. He was leaving with President Young the next day to meet the chief at Chicken Creek, south of Nephi.

"Do you think Walkara really wants peace?" Mary Ann asked. "Or just all the presents you are bringing to the negotiations?"

"He wants the beef and flour," Port said, "but the peace is being forced upon him."

"Could he be planning a trap?" she asked. "Offering peace to get you there with the offerings, then planning to just take everything, after killing President Young and those with him?"

"A man who would slash the face of his own friend without warning is capable of anything," Port answered. "The plan calls for me to ride in first and check things out. If it doesn't look good, Young will not come."

"You could be killed," she said.

"I don't think about it," he said.

"If you were killed I would never see you again."

"You and everyone else."

"I would miss you."

"I would miss you too."

"Port, why do you keep coming to see me and taking me on these Sunday afternoon walks?" she asked, the tone of her voice becoming more urgent. They continued to walk, both looking straight ahead.

"Mary Ann, why do you keep inviting me over and offering to go with me on these walks?" he responded, offering her the first move, not wanting to become the fool with a woman sixteen years younger than he was.

"Because I like you," she said.

"I like you too," he said. Both were silent for a long minute.

"Is there anything more than that?" she asked.

"Yes," he said cautiously. "But since I'm practically old enough to be your father, I hesitate getting more involved."

"I'm twenty-five," Mary Ann said, "hardly young enough to be anyone's daughter. I have three or four gray hairs. Do you want to see them?" She stopped. So did he, turning to look at her. She had never looked more beautiful to him. He was getting nervous. He looked away.

"When I get back from the negotiations with Walkara," he said. "Perhaps we could . . ."

"You might not come back," she interrupted. "Then it will be too late."

"Too late for what?" he asked without thinking and then was suddenly sorry he had made the comment.

"Porter, do you have any idea why I'm not married?"

"Why?" he asked.

"Am I fat?"

"No."

"Am I ugly?"

"No."

"Am I stupid?"

"Maybe that's it," he said teasingly.

"I can assure you I've had plenty of opportunities to marry," she continued.

"I know," he said.

"I love you, Porter," she whined, barely able to get the words out, but once she had said it the rest came easy. "I have ever since the day you brought Emma to our home. For three long years I have been waiting for you to feel the same way about me. I'm tired of waiting. I'm tired of loving a man who doesn't love me back. I'm tired of living on dreams. I want the real thing, and I want it now, before I grow any more gray hairs."

"I can understand that," he said, groping for words.

"I'm not sure you do," she said, "or you wouldn't have let it drag on so long. I can't stand any more of these Sunday afternoon walks. I want you in my bed or out of my life. I want a husband, a place of my own, a family . . ."

"Will you marry me?" he asked.

"Yes, yes, yes," she cried, flying into his arms.

"When?" she asked, pushing away.

He pulled out his pocket watch and looked at it.

"It's almost four o'clock," he said. "President Young eats his dinner at six. If we hurry, we can have him marry us before he eats."

"You mean today?" she asked, suddenly timid again.

"I mean right now," he said. She swallowed hard, nodded her agreement, and placed her arm in his. An hour later they were married by Brigham Young in his new home. The next day Port kissed his bride good-bye and joined Young's peace caravan headed for Chicken Creek.

Conducting peace negotiations with Chief Walkara was no small matter for Brigham Young. His caravan consisted of eighty-two armed men, fourteen women, five children, and thirty-four wagons. His plan was to continue south on his annual visit to the southern settlements immediately following the negotiations. Porter Rockwell, Amos Neff, and George Bean were riding in the twenty-fifth wagon.

The following afternoon, the caravan passed through Nephi, pushing to make Chicken Creek by dark. Port hurried ahead, hoping to make the initial contact with Walkara and determine if it was safe for Young to enter the Indian camp.

It was still light when Port drove the wagon filled with flour among the Ute lodges. Bean and Neff were following on horseback, driving twelve head of steers. Port warned those who tried to take some flour that it wasn't theirs yet.

It was a good sign when Walkara came out of his lodge to welcome the approaching wagon. Had Walkara remained in the lodge, indicating a continuing belligerence toward the Mormons, Port might have recommended Young not enter the camp.

As it was, Walkara seemed pleased the Mormons had brought so much flour and beef, but he offered no warm greetings or handshakes. Port tossed the chief a bottle of watered-down whiskey. Maybe that would warm him up a bit. Without so much as a grunt of thanks, Walkara jerked the cork out and guzzled half the contents of the bottle before removing it from his lips. Port nodded for Neff to bring forward President Young.

The whiskey only made the chief more irritable. Port realized he had made a mistake, but there was nothing to do now but forge ahead. A few minutes later, Young's carriage rolled into camp. It was almost dark now.

Young had brought Dimick Huntington as his interpreter, but Walkara—who was slurring his words by this time—was in no mood to listen. He demanded to know why the Mormons at Nephi were building fortifications if all the Mormons wanted was peace. When Huntington tried to answer the question, Walkara cut him off, demanding to know why the Mormons continued to kill the deer and elk when the Mormon chief said his people would not hunt. When Huntington tried to offer an explanation, Walkara demanded to know why James Ivie had not been punished for killing the Ute brave.

Walkara carried on in a drunken tirade for the next fifteen minutes. When he finally let Huntington get a word in, the interpreter said the Mormon chief wanted to be brothers with the Ute chief.

Then Walkara surprised everyone, at least the Mormons, by saying that if the Mormon chief really wanted to be a brother he would offer Walkara one of his many wives, at least for one night.

"He wants a white woman, one of your wives," Huntington said to Young.

"I could run back to Nephi and hire a whore," Port offered.

"There are no whores in Nephi," Young said. Port knew differently but didn't argue.

"Maybe one of the sisters in the caravan would volunteer," Bean suggested. "Stopping an Indian war is certainly a cause worthy of a little passionate service." Port was the only one who laughed.

"Tell him Mormons do not loan or sell their women," Young said to Huntington, who translated the comment for Walkara. The chief responded by telling Huntington that a man with many wives who would not share even one was no brother to him.

When that was translated, Brigham turned and started walking to his carriage. "I will have war before I will turn our women into whores," he said.

Young had his faults, Port thought, but being a coward wasn't one of them. As Huntington was trying to translate the last comment, two warriors ran to Brigham's carriage and grabbed the horses' bridles. They intended to prevent Young from leaving.

"What's this all about?" Young asked.

"They want peace," Port said. "They need the food."

"What about the white woman?" Young asked.

"Offer him something else, so he doesn't lose face," Port suggested. Young turned back toward Walkara, asking the chief if the Utes needed anything besides beef and flour. Negotiations resumed in earnest. The matter of the white woman was not brought up again. Some of the flour was dispersed among the Indians.

By the time they finished, Young had promised Walkara another wagonload of flour and six more beef cattle. Walkara agreed to stop the fighting and stop selling slave children to the Mexicans, a practice that had concerned the Mormons since first coming in contact with the Utes. On a regular basis the Utes would kidnap Paiute, Pahvant, and Goshute children, which they would take to Mexico to trade for horses. The children ended up slaves in gold and silver mines.

Just when it appeared the negotiations might be finished, Walkara said he had one more request. He motioned for Young to follow him into his lodge. Port accompanied them.

A boy of about nine years was stretched out on a buffalo robe, delirious with fever. He was pale and emaciated. It appeared he had been ill for some time. A young squaw was wiping the boy's forehead with a damp cloth.

"Make boy well," Walkara said in English.

Brigham Young was no doctor, but he knew exactly what to do. Reaching into his pocket, he pulled out a small bottle of consecrated olive oil, the kind Mormons used when blessing their sick. After gently anointing the boy's forehead with the oil and pronouncing a short prayer, Young called Huntington, Bean, and Neff into the lodge. As the five Mormons laid their hands on the boy's head, Young commanded the evil spirits of every name and nature and all sickness to leave the boy. He commanded the youth to become whole again. He ended the blessing in the name of Jesus Christ. Walkara was impressed with Young's confidence in spiritual matters and the forcefulness of his voice. So was Port.

"Will the boy be all right?" Port asked as they were leaving the tent,

"Tonight we risked a continuation of war," Young said, "rather than compromise the chastity of our women. The Lord won't let such an act of faithfulness go unrewarded. The boy will be fine."

The next morning the boy crawled out of the lodge and stood up. He was pale and weak, but the fever was gone.

"We brothers," Walkara said to Young, in English, as the Mormon prophet climbed into his carriage.

While Young's caravan continued south, Port returned home to get the additional goods promised Walkara and to see his bride of only three days.

# Chapter 50

A few weeks later, Port began making preparations for another goodwill journey among the Shoshones, particularly those along the emigrant route near Fort Bridger. As before, he planned to carry the supplies on mules because many of the Indian villages were in places inaccessible to wagons.

He was about ready to leave when word arrived in Salt Lake that an emigrant train from Missouri was at the top of Emigrant Canyon. Silas Boyle, a man in the company, had killed one of the Mormon ferrymen at the Green River crossing. The word reaching Salt Lake was that Boyle was a gunfighter of sorts and had goaded the Mormon youth into a fair fight and then killed the brother with apparent ease. Boyle had tried to draw another Mormon into fighting him at Fort Supply, but the brother was talked out of it at the last minute. There was concern that Boyle would try the same thing again in Salt Lake.

Without telling Mary Ann where he was going, Port rode to the mouth of Emigration Canyon to meet the Missouri company. When he arrived, the wagons had just halted for a noon lunch break. Port had expected Silas Boyle to be a rugged mountaineer of a man. Instead, the tall, well-groomed, well-dressed Missourian was riding in a fancy carriage with polished wood trim.

He looked more like a riverboat gambler than a pioneer. Two matched bays were pulling the carriage.

"I understand you killed a man at Green River," Port said, pulling his horse to a halt beside the fancy carriage. Boyle was on the seat, eating a biscuit and drinking from a bottle of wine.

"I didn't kill a man," Boyle responded dryly. "I killed a Mormon. There's a difference, you know."

"I understand you were badgering one of our men at Fort Supply too," Port said, trying to ignore the first comment.

"He was no man either. When I told the lad how much I enjoyed raping his mother at Far West, he had too much yellow down his back to defend the lady's honor. Never met a Mormon yet with any backbone."

Port had heard it all before and was pleasantly surprised how calm he felt inside. As deputy marshal, his job was to keep the peace, and he knew this man's mouth was too big to allow him to travel safely through the Salt Lake Valley. There would be trouble. Boyle would certainly be killed, but he would probably take some of the brethren with him.

"There are ten thousand Mormons in this valley who would like you dead," Port warned.

"You can't scare me," Boyle snarled.

"I want you to turn around and head back to Fort Laramie," Port said. "You can catch the Oregon Trail from there. Once you reach the Snake you can turn south, joining your friends again on the Humboldt. I can't allow you into this valley."

"I'm not turning back," Boyle growled.

"You're not entering the valley."

"And I suppose you think you can stop me."

"If necessary." The two men were glaring at each other. Port held his reins in his left hand. His right hand was near his Navy Colt. He was ready in the event Boyle tried something foolish.

"Silas, watch out!" someone called from one of the nearby wagons. "You're talking to Rockwell." Men were beginning to walk toward the standoff.

"The famous Orrin Porter Rockwell," Boyle snickered. "How flattering. Brigham Young's Destroying Angel coming all the way up here just to meet me."

"I came up here to save your neck," Port added. "But I'm beginning to wonder if it's worth saving. Now, be a good boy and turn this buggy around."

"I said I'm not going back," Boyle hissed.

"Then let's have at it," Port said, placing his right hand on the butt of his pistol. Boyle folded his arms, making it clear he was not about to get into a gunfight with Porter Rockwell. Port hoped the man was softening.

"According to the rules of dueling and established protocol, the man being challenged has the right to select the weapons," Boyle said. Port had no idea what he was talking about.

"Since you challenged me, sir," Boyle continued, "I choose sabers." Port almost laughed. Boyle couldn't be serious.

The Missourian was serious. He stepped out of his carriage and walked around back, where he opened a long black box that contained two polished sabers. By this time, a large group of men had gathered around, not just Missourians from the company, but also Mormons who were in the area.

Boyle tossed one of the swords to Port, who was thinking he ought to just shoot the puke and get it over with. But the idea of fighting with swords was interesting. As a boy, he and his brothers had spent countless hours fighting with stick swords. Here was a chance to test those skills. He liked the idea of beating Boyle at his own game. Besides, the blessing he had received from Joseph promised he would not be harmed by bullet or blade.

Port felt the edge of the saber. It was sharp. He stepped out of the saddle, removed his gun belt, and hung it over the saddle horn. Remembering one of the favorite stick-fighting tricks of his youth, Port removed a leather glove from his saddlebag and pulled it over his left hand. One of the Mormons led Port's horse away.

Boyle had removed his topcoat, his fighting garb consisting of a white shirt and black trousers. He was not wearing a hat or gloves.

Port was wearing buckskins, a shirt, and leggings. His long hair was in a single braid down his back. He tossed his hat to the Mormon who was holding his horse

Rockwell and Boyle cautiously approached each other. They were surrounded by a tight circle of men. Women and children were watching from wagon boxes. Port noticed that Boyle was holding his sword in his left hand. Port didn't know if that gave the man an advantage or not.

The two men stood facing each other in the middle of the circle, about six feet apart. Boyle brought his sword forward, pointing upward at a slant. Port's sword was pointing down at the ground in front of his boots.

"Touché!" Boyle shouted, bending his knees as he dropped to a rooster crouch, placing his right hand on his hip. It appeared the man was trained in the art of fencing. Port was wishing he had just shot Boyle off his wagon seat.

"Touché," Boyle said again. Apparently he wanted Port to raise his blade to an upright position so they could tap their swords together to begin the fight.

Port had another idea. Instead of raising his blade to meet Boyle's outstretched sword, he began writing something in the dirt with the tip of the blade. While making the marks in the dirt, he was looking straight ahead into Boyle's eyes.

"I have a secret message for you," Port said.

Boyle glanced down at the scratch marks in front of Port's boots. That was all the opportunity Port needed. His gloved left hand shot forward, grabbing the end of Boyle's sword. At the same time, Port lunged forward within striking distance. Though his grip on the end of the sword was like a vise, his arm was loose, moving easily with Boyle's unsuccessful jerks to get the blade free.

At the same time, Port raised his own sword high in the air, bringing it down at a slant with all his might. If Boyle's saber had been in his right hand, he might have been able to bring his left hand up to parry the blow. As it was, Port's blade had a clear path to the side of Boyle's thick neck, slicing through skin, flesh, and bone. Boyle's head rolled onto his chest, then around to the right, like a ball on a string, held up by skin and sinew. Red blood was pulsing from the open neck, turning the white shirt crimson. Port let go of Boyle's blade as the body crumpled to the ground.

Dropping his own sword in the dust, Port turned away from the ugly corpse that had been a man just a few moments earlier. The men in the circle were silent, stunned and horrified. They had gathered for sport. Now this.

Port walked over to his horse and stepped into the saddle. "He didn't know I couldn't write," he said to the man who had been holding the horse. Port galloped back to town in search of a stiff drink of whiskey.

After distributing gifts to the Shoshone camps along the emigrant route, Port led his pack string over the Oregon Trail to the Snake River country. He wanted to distribute the last of his gifts among those Indians, and he wanted to see how Emma was getting along.

He wasn't surprised to find her with a lodge of her own, her belly swollen with her first child to be born later in the summer. Her man, Black Horse, was off on the first summer buffalo hunt.

Emma was glad to see Port and delighted to hear that he and Mary Ann were married. Emma had many questions about Mary Ann and the Neff family. She said she missed Great Salt Lake City and her Mormon friends, but that she was happy where she was, with her own people.

When Port returned to Salt Lake, Colonel Edward Jenner Steptoe had arrived from the east with three hundred troops. Steptoe was the new military governor of Utah Territory. He seemed perfectly happy that Brigham Young remain the political governor.

Steptoe requested a meeting with Rockwell for two reasons. First, the colonel was under pressure from Washington to catch and punish the Indians responsible for the Gunnison massacre on the Sevier River a year earlier. Second, he wanted Port to help scout a new wagon route south of the Great Salt Lake to Carson City. The government was willing to pay Port five dollars a day for his time.

With George Bean for company, Port headed into the west central desert looking for Kanosh, chief of the Pahvants. Port didn't think Kanosh had anything to do with the Gunnison massacre, but he figured the old chief would know who did. Port's plan was to tell the chief that if he didn't turn over the killers, Steptoe and his three hundred soldiers would march into Pahvant lands. There was no telling what damage the U.S. Army would do.

Kanosh was at Fillmore trading with the Mormons when Rockwell and Bean finally caught up with him. When they told the old chief what Steptoe wanted, Kanosh promised to handle the matter himself. He said he would bring the killers to Great Salt Lake City in ten days. After explaining to Kanosh how to get to the marshal's office, Port and George headed for home, speculating the entire way on whether or not Kanosh would keep his word.

Nine days later Port was handling some business at the marshal's office when someone shouted that a band of Indians was coming up the street. Port hurried outside.

It was Kanosh, all right, riding his horse and leading a flock of prisoners on foot. Kanosh was pulling on a long rope that was connected to the neck of the first prisoner, then to the second, the third, and so on. The prisoners' hands were tied behind their backs.

Port began to laugh, anticipating Steptoe's reaction to the prisoners. The first one was an old squaw without any teeth. The next was an old sick fellow. Following him were three little boys, then a blind man, a crazy man, and several more old men who appeared almost too sick to walk. These were the Indians Kanosh hoped to pass off as the ones who had attacked and killed Captain Gunnison and seven armed Americans. Port continued to laugh. He received the prisoners from Kanosh and turned them over to Steptoe, who was furious. After shouting at Kanosh for a full five minutes, the colonel let the prisoners go. He ordered his cook to give each a loaf of bread.

On March 11, 1855, ten months after her marriage to Port, Mary Ann gave birth to her first child, a little girl named Mary Amanda. Two weeks later Port headed west with Steptoe's survey crew, blazing a new wagon trail to Carson City.

The weather was good when the men left Great Salt Lake City, but it soon turned cold and wintry. Harsh north winds buffeted the men for days as they pushed slowly westward along the south shore of the Great Salt Lake

At the western edge of the lake, the wind became so fierce and cold one afternoon that the party members didn't make camp until they had reached some tall rushes. There was too much wind and rain to build fires, so the men just burrowed into the thick rushes and rolled up in their damp blankets.

The next morning one of the men discovered a salt spring bubbling into a fairly large salt water pool. Looking down into the water the man saw what looked like vertical salt statues. Everyone gathered around to look.

The consensus was that Indians, or possibly white men, had been thrown into the pool with rocks tied to their feet. In the heavy salt water the bodies remained upright, but the rocks held them down. With time a thick layer of salt crust covered the bodies. One of the men described the salt statues as "human pickles."

The weather became pleasant, and the survey party made excellent progress. It was a season when the Indians seemed more peaceable. Everyone in the party managed to hang onto his horse and his scalp. Of course, Port still insisted that adequate guards and lookouts be on duty at all times.

Upon arriving in Carson City, Port collected his pay, but instead of returning home, he continued westward. He wanted to see the gold fields, how things had changed. He wanted to see San Francisco again too.

The gold fields were different than he remembered them. The ramshackle mining camps had been replaced with cities and towns or had been totally abandoned. There was still a lot of mining going on, but most of it was commercial now. The tent saloons were gone too. He rode through Murderer's Bar, mostly deserted now, and Mormon Island, where he had won two thousand dollars in a shooting match and nearly lost his life afterwards.

Sacramento had become a large, prosperous city. After arranging to keep his horse in a stable, Port caught a river boat to San Francisco. The next afternoon he walked up the steps to Agnes Smith's front door and knocked.

It took a minute for Port to recognize the young lady who answered the door. In the five years since he had last been there, Ina had changed from a little girl into a young woman. She was pretty like her mother but not happy. She looked troubled. She recognized Port but was not as friendly as he thought she would be. She did not invite him in.

"Is your mother home?" he asked.

"Yes, but she is ill. She cannot come to the door."

"What's wrong with her?" he asked.

"Typhoid fever."

"How bad is it?" he asked, a note of alarm in his voice. People died from typhoid fever.

"The fever part is over," the girl volunteered.

"Then let me see her," he said stepping forward, not understanding why the girl was so cool.

"She doesn't want visitors," the girl said.

"Please tell her I'm here," Port said, "that I've come all the way from Salt Lake to see her. If she doesn't want to see me, I'll leave." The girl left Port standing on the porch as she went to present his request to her mother. Port couldn't figure out why the girl was so guarded.

When Ina returned after several minutes, she ushered Port into the front room. When he was seated, she left him alone. He felt very strange, wondering what was wrong.

A full five minutes passed before Agnes entered the room. She was wearing a hooded satin robe. She was smiling a friendly welcome, and there was more color in her face than he expected. She moved with grace and strength. Apparently she had recovered fully from her bout with the fever, but when she seated herself beside Port, the hood shifted to one side. Port stared in astonishment.

"What's the matter?" Agnes asked. "Haven't you seen a bald-headed lady before?" Port shook his head. He had not seen a bald woman before. He had heard of the fever causing people to lose their hair though.

"I'm sorry," he said. "Will it grow back?"

"The doctor says it won't."

"What are you going to do?" he asked.

"Stay bald, I suppose."

"You look very different," he said. "But in a way you are still beautiful. The look is distinctive."

"Porter Rockwell, don't humor me."

"Let's go for a walk," he said. "Down Market Street, arm in arm. I'll blacken the eyes of any man who stares at you."

Agnes began to laugh.

"That would be very funny," she said. "You with more hair than ten men, and me with none at all." They laughed together but didn't go for the walk.

Port told her about his marriage to Mary Ann and the recent birth of their first child. She said she was happy for him and Mary Ann and was only sorry she had not married Port while she had the chance. She said her husband, William, had taken up permanent residence in the gold fields. She hadn't seen him for over a year and figured they had a common law divorce.

"Have you thought about becoming someone's plural wife?" Port teased, knowing she was opposed to plural marriage.

"You must really feel sorry for me," she said. Port didn't know what to say. He did feel sorry for her, but he knew she would feel worse if he acknowledged the feeling.

"Do you know what's hardest?" she asked.

"No, what?"

"Ina is embarrassed to be with me around other people. She won't admit it, but I know it's so."

"Sure you don't want to go for a walk with me?" he asked.

"No, not today. But I'm glad you came. It's good to see you again. We've been reading about you in the paper." She told him of an article claiming Port had sliced off the head of a Missouri emigrant for no apparent reason, other than the fact the man was from Missouri. Port told her his version of the incident. They continued talking to each other for another half an hour before Port got up to leave. He did not see Ina again.

As he walked away from the apartment, he had an idea. Looking at his watch, Port realized there was still time before the stores closed. He would buy Agnes a wig. He wondered why she hadn't thought of that.

During the next two hours Port went into no less than ten stores. None of them had wigs, and none of the salespeople knew where a wig could be purchased. In a small specialty shop Port found a booklet, complete with drawings, on how to make a wig. He bought it, and a pair of scissors, for fifty cents.

He returned to his room to look at the booklet. He couldn't read the words, but he could tell by the diagrams and drawings that making a wig was a fairly simple process, provided one had plenty of hair to work with. Port spent most of the night pacing the floor.

Early the next morning, he hurried to Agnes's place. Tiptoeing up the stairs, he placed a bulging bag in front of the door. Quickly, he retreated down the steps and hurried toward the docks where the river boats departed for Sacramento.

In the cool morning air, he tried to pull his hat tighter over his ears. But no matter how hard he pulled, his head felt naked and cold. Port prayed no one would challenge him to a fight until his hair had a chance to grow back. He hoped Agnes had the good sense to pick out the gray hairs before she made her wig.

# Chapter 51

Six months later, on January 9, 1856, Brigham Young asked Port to speak to the territorial legislature in Fillmore. Young wanted to bid for the U.S. Mail contract between the Missouri River and San Francisco. Magraw and Hockaday, the gentile firm that presently had the contract, was averaging forty days to carry the mail from Council Bluffs to Salt Lake, and Young wanted Port to testify that the Mormons, under Young's leadership, could cut that time significantly, perhaps by as much as twenty days.

Getting up in front of the legislature was not nearly so difficult for Port as speaking in church. He didn't have to talk about religion or philosophy or any other subject in which his inability to read made him feel inadequate. He was talking about horses and men traveling between Salt Lake and Missouri, a subject he knew as much about as any man alive. He said if there were supply stations every fifty to one hundred miles, stocked with plenty of oats, where a man driving a light carriage could change horses, then a man with a good team could cover 150 miles a day in good weather. Under these conditions the mail might make it to Salt Lake in fifteen days. Another seven days would put it in Sacramento.

The legislature authorized Brigham Young to personally outfit and build the supply stations between Salt Lake and Fort Laramie. Young founded the Brigham Young Express and Carrying Company, soon known to all as the YX Company. Men were called on building missions to construct the supply stations.

In April Port was asked to be guide and hunter for a delegation of local politicians traveling to Washington to pitch the new mail contract. Also in the group were apostles and missionaries heading on church missions. A.O. Smoot was captain.

Assembling for departure at the mouth of Emigration Canyon, on the exact spot where Port had sliced off Silas Boyle's head, Brigham Young blessed each of the men that their missions would be successful.

A short distance east of Fort Bridger, the party came to an abrupt halt as a major blizzard swept in from the north, bringing with it heavy snows and freezing winds that didn't let up for almost three days.

The storm caught the party in the middle of the open prairie, where the men quickly pitched their tents and crawled inside to wait out the late winter wrath. Port didn't sleep as well as the rest, getting up periodically to check the horses. Spring had come early in the Salt Lake Valley, and the horses had already begun to shed their winter coats.

With their backs to the wind and their heads down, the horses seemed to be surviving. But on Port's third trip out of the tent, he noticed one of the animals lying down. He could not make it get up. He noticed that two of the others were acting like they wanted to lie down too.

"The horses are freezing," Port shouted. "Bring me your blankets." The men began to stir. Some complained about coming outside in the storm.

"Bring me the blankets," Port shouted again.

"How will we keep warm?" someone shouted back.

"Put on your coat."

"Never took it off."

In the midst of the howling storm, the men stumbled among the horses, tying on blankets as best they could. If it hadn't been for the wind, the task would have been easy. When the men took off their gloves to tie the knots, their fingers froze. They had no wood for fires. For the remainder of the night, the men huddled together in the tents, occasionally checking the horses, praying for the storm to subside. But it paid little heed.

At first light they stumbled through three miles of blowing snow to the nearest grove of trees. Here the horses found some relief from the relentless wind. The men found all the firewood they needed to maintain roaring campfires for the duration of the storm.

The grove was a mixture of cottonwood and fir trees. While the fir offered the most protection against the bitter wind, the smaller cottonwood branches provided marginal nourishment for the hungry horses.

On the third day, the storm blew itself out and the party continued on its way, wading through the deep snow. But it was May, and when the sun finally appeared, it was high in the sky, reflecting so brightly off the thick snow that the men could hardly see. With black ashes rubbed around their eyes, they looked like raccoons. Still, the May sun was too bright, and by the end of the second day, the party had to halt because half the men were snow-blind and simply could not see to travel.

While the men were recovering, Indians ran off a dozen horses in broad daylight. Port galloped after them on his stallion. He returned two days later with six of the stolen animals.

The party had to wait out two more storms, but by the end of May the men were riding through green grass, eating fresh buffalo meat, and passing emigrant trains almost hourly. They reached the Big Blue in Missouri ten days ahead of schedule.

Except for the Indians stealing their horses near Fort Laramie, there were few problems with the red men, but that was to change quickly.

East of Fort Laramie a cow wandered away from a company of Danish emigrants right into a Sioux camp. Seeing breakfast on the hoof, the Indians quickly killed the cow and proceeded to prepare a feast.

The Danish brother who lost the cow reported the incident to the officer in charge at Fort Laramie, Lieutenant John Gratten, who dispatched twenty-nine soldiers to ride with him to teach the Sioux a lesson. The Indians saw the soldiers coming, prepared an ambush, and slaughtered all twenty-nine cavalrymen.

When news of the massacre reached General William Harney, he marched with several hundred men on the Sioux camp. Upon discovering that the braves were absent, he proceeded with the attack anyway, slaughtering eighty women and children, thus earning his nickname, Squaw Killer Harney.

When Port returned to Salt Lake in November, he was greeted by a new daughter, Sarah, born August 5. Also waiting for him were charges of killing Almon Babbit, the federally appointed anti-Mormon territorial secretary, who was ambushed on the emigrant trail east of Salt Lake. An Indian agent discovered later that the Cheyennes had done it, thereby clearing Port. Increasingly, Port was being blamed for unsolved murders, especially when the victim was not sympathetic toward the Mormons.

Port claimed some land in the west desert, on Government Creek near the main wagon road to California, and some land farther south on Cherry Creek. He was thinking of settling down to a more quiet life of ranching, raising horses and cattle. He started building a cabin so he would have a place to stay when he visited his new land. He had no intention of moving Mary Ann and the two little girls out to the ranch, as there were still too many Indian problems.

That winter the YX Company was awarded the mail contract, its bid coming in thirteen thousand dollars below the Magraw Hockaday bid. Deliveries were to start immediately, with Rockwell carrying the mail from Salt Lake to Fort Laramie, and Bill Hickman handling the route from there to Independence. Hickman wasn't very happy about his assignment. Not only would he be away from home all spring, summer, and fall, risking his life in Indian country, but worst of all there was no serious money to be made, at least not for him. He was a reluctant volunteer.

Port left Salt Lake with the first load of mail on February 8. The journey was plagued by storms, snow, and start-up error— unshod horses, missing harnesses, no spare wheels, and supply station managers off hunting. The mail arrived in Independence on April 11, a journey exceeding forty days.

In May Jon Murdock left Salt Lake with the second delivery. This time the weather cooperated, the station managers were prepared, and the Indians were busy hunting buffalo. The mail reached Independence in a record fifteen days. It appeared the YX Company was going to be a glorious success.

In June Port was carrying the eastbound mail across the open plains beyond Fort Laramie, trying to better the previous record, when he spotted what appeared to be the wagon carrying the westbound mail coming toward him. Salt Lake mayor A.O. Smoot was driving the approaching carriage, Hickman having already abandoned the mission. What surprised Port was that Smoot had company, Judson Stoddard and several others who were driving a herd of YX Company stock along with the carriage.

Port soon learned that in Independence, Smoot had been refused the mail and had been informed the contract had been cancelled. Furthermore, Port learned that 2,500 federal troops were moving west to suppress the so-called Mormon rebellion, unseat Brigham Young as territorial governor, and place an appointed governor in his place. Utah was being invaded by the U.S. Army!

Rockwell, Smoot, and Stoddard hitched the two fastest teams to a light spring wagon. Leaving the others behind to bring the stock, they set out for Great Salt Lake City, 513 miles away.

When they arrived in Salt Lake, Brigham Young and all the church leaders were gone. They were up Big Cottonwood Canyon at Silver Lake celebrating the tenth anniversary of the Saints' arrival in the Salt Lake Valley. Abandoning the weary carriage horses, Rockwell, Smoot, and Stoddard climbed upon fresh saddle horses and headed for Silver Lake.

Upon receiving the news of the invasion, Brigham Young reminded those gathered around him of a prophecy he had made ten years earlier, when he had said, "Give us ten years of peace, and we will ask no odds of Uncle Sam or the devil." Then he added, "God is with us, and the devil has taken me at my word."

A few days later in the great tabernacle, Heber C. Kimball said, "Good God! I have wives enough to whip out the United States, for they will whip themselves."

The invading force, soon to be called Johnston's Army, included eight companies of the United States Tenth Infantry, the entire Fifth

Infantry, and two batteries of artillery, one pulling four six-pound and two twelve-pound howitzers, the other a field battery of four twelve-pounders and two thirty-two pounder siege cannons.

On the Utah side, Lieutenant General Daniel H. Wells commanded the Nauvoo Legion. His orders were to engage the enemy before it entered the valley, using cavalry to harass the army and disrupt supply movements.

Because the Mormons were also waging a public relations war in Congress and the eastern press, Wells had strict orders to avoid killing U.S. soldiers. A few well-publicized killings could turn public sentiment against the Mormons.

Porter Rockwell, Bill Hickman, and Lot Smith were selected to lead the harassment efforts. They were to report directly to Wells and Young. An observation corps headed by Robert Burton left Salt Lake at once, its mission to monitor enemy movements. Rockwell, Smith, and Hickman left a short time later.

Port first saw the army camped in the flatlands of South Pass. The camp was a huge tent city, appearing to approach in size Great Salt Lake City, except that nothing was permanent. Hundreds of tents and wagons were arranged in neat rows, and thousands of mules and oxen grazed in closely guarded herds. Men, 2,500 soldiers and teamsters, were everywhere—a complete army moving across a vast wilderness to put the Mormons in their place.

Five men were with Port, surveying for the first time the mighty army. With their horses staked out of sight beyond the hill, Port and his men had crawled through the tall grass to the edge of the hill, where they could observe the army camp in relative safety.

Most of the tents were in two long rows, facing each other. In the center of the alleyway between the two rows of tents was a long picket line, extending from one end to the other. Port knew the long rope was a picket line because of the grain pans spaced periodically along its entire length. The mules and horses were grazing outside the camp, but Port figured come dark the animals would be brought in and secured to the picket line.

Port had been the victim of Indian raids so many times, it seemed fun for a change to be on the other side. He had clear instructions from Wells not to kill any of the soldiers or teamsters. His orders were to steal and destroy.

Right now his mind was set on stealing a thousand or more mules, which he was sure would be some kind of record. He had heard of Indians stealing a hundred or more horses in a single raid, but no one had ever taken a thousand animals at once.

The plan was simple. Port's men began moving toward the camp immediately after dark. The mules and horses had already been brought in from the meadows and secured to the long picket rope. While Port and three of his men worked their way on horseback to the east end of the camp, the two remaining Mormons crawled into the camp, stationing themselves at each end of the long picket rope.

Nothing happened for about two hours as the soldiers ate, talked, and got ready to sleep.

When the last lantern went out, the two Mormons, armed only with sharp knives, began moving quietly along the long picket rope, cutting partway through the lead ropes of all the animals. The men didn't want to free the animals by cutting all the way through, in the fear the loose animals would wander among the tents and wake up the soldiers. The object was to have each animal secured to the picket rope by only a strand or two of hemp, so they would easily jerk themselves free once the excitement started.

Port and his men waited for what seemed hours, getting on and off their horses, looking at their watches in the starlight, trying to figure out what was taking so long, and wondering if the two men in the camp had been captured or sidetracked with a bottle of white lightning.

The only flaw in the plan was that they had not taken the time to calculate how long it would take two men to cut partway through the lead ropes of two thousand mules. The process took practically the entire night. Eventually the men's knives became dull, and had they not thought to bring replacement knives, they never would have finished the job.

At about 4:30, with the last rope cut through to the last few strands, the two who had accomplished the cutting climbed upon two unsaddled mules and, screaming as loud as they could, kicked their mounts into a full gallop westward along the picket line.

Port and his men leaped upon their horses and galloped toward the tethered mules, firing into the air and yelling. The mules began breaking their tethers and heading west after the first two riders. Port and his men rode along both sides of the picket line, making all the noise they could.

Shouts of confusion and surprise from the tents only added to the confusion. With Port and his men riding between the two rows of tents, the surprised soldiers were reluctant to shoot across the picket line toward the opposite row of tents. In less than two minutes, Port and his men were outside the army camp, herding several thousand mules and horses down the wagon road toward Salt Lake. A rider galloped along each side of the herd in an effort to keep the animals together. Port and the remaining rider stayed in the rear.

Realizing there was no pursuit by the surprised soldiers, Port and his men brought the herd to a halt several miles away from the camp. Some strays had gotten away from the main herd, several with lead ropes caught in brush, and Port thought it would be a good idea to take a minute and round them up.

While the strays were being brought in, Port and the man with him dismounted and climbed into two aspen trees. It was just getting light, and from the top of the trees they figured they could estimate the size of the huge herd. Never had any of the men seen such a large herd of horses or mules. It appeared they had the entire army herd, except for the oxen, consisting of over two thousand mules and hundreds of horses. Port and the men with him would be wealthy if, by chance, Brigham Young allowed them to keep and divide up so many animals.

Port was about to come down from the tree when he heard a strange sound, carried to his ears on a gentle easterly breeze. At first he thought it might be an elk bugle. No. It was an army bugle. It wasn't playing taps or reveille, but the stable call that was sounded every time the horses and mules were grained. Port's first thought was that he and his men had not run off all the animals, that the army was getting ready to feed those left behind in anticipation of pursuing the Mormons.

But suddenly his heart jumped in his throat. Looking down from the tree, he saw a thousand hungry mules looking back over their shoulders in the direction of the bugle calling them to breakfast.

Port and his companion scrambled out of the trees as fast as they could, but they were not fast enough. By the time they hit the ground, the closest mules had turned around and were racing for the oats. Port's horse, and the one with it, pulled away from the bushes to which they were tied and joined the mules. Port and his companion stood in the middle of the road, shouting and waving their hats as 2,000 mules and hundreds of horses stampeded to breakfast.

As the mules galloped by, Port noticed what looked like horses with saddles running with the herd. A few minutes later, as the dust settled, the two men who had been in the lead came running back on foot. They had been changing saddles when the mules decided to head home. Before they could get mounted, their horses had pulled away from them. A minute later the other two men, who had been rounding up the strays, came out of the brush. They were on foot too. They had stopped for a minute to relieve their bladders, and their horses had joined the stampede.

Port found it hard to believe that all six had been dismounted at the same time. He could hardly believe that the greatest horse and mule raid ever had fizzled, that the great success they were celebrating a few minutes earlier had evaporated into thin air. The six men looked at each other in disbelief. Such a thing could not happen, but it had.

"Well, I'm not going back to camp without a horse under me," Port said. The other men echoed his feeling. They hurried down to the Little Sandy about three miles away. Their plan was to hide in the thick willows while monitoring the progress of the army. When darkness fell, they would attempt another raid. They realized the guard would probably be doubled or tripled, and there would be little or no chance of pulling off anything as big or as daring as the night before, but if they could just get enough animals to recover some pride for the ride back to their own camp, that would be sufficient.

By nightfall Port and his men were hungry and irritable but determined to succeed as they marched uphill toward the army's new camp. They approached from the south, where trees and brush were most plentiful. They couldn't risk being discovered in the open without mounts.

They began to hear camp noises long before they could see anything—axes splitting wood, kettles clanking against each other, and men swearing at stubborn mules.

Suddenly they heard a horse whinny, not fifty yards away. Through the sparse moonlight they saw fifteen saddled horses, grazing quietly at the end of picket ropes. Not questioning their good fortune, Port and his men untied all fifteen horses and led the animals down to the Little Sandy and across to the other side. Mounting up, they rode to the main Mormon camp on the Big Sandy to report their adventures and the location of the U.S. Army.

They reached the camp at daylight, coming to a halt before the commanding officer's tent. When Wells finally stepped outside, he had a startled look on his face. He demanded to know where Port and his men had acquired the horses. Port told him the entire story from start to finish. Wells then explained that the horses belonged to a party of Mormon raiders who had left his camp two days earlier to locate and harass the enemy. Thanks to Port and his men there were now fifteen Mormons in enemy territory without horses to ride.

"You got any whiskey?" Port asked.

# Chapter 52

———⧓⊙⧓———

A non-shooting war was in full swing. Colonel Edmund Alexander, who was commanding the advance movement, seemed helpless to defend against the hit-and-run raiders who were stealing his supplies, burning his feed, stampeding his livestock, and frightening his teamsters, who were telling each other stories of bloodthirsty Mormon Danites.

The Mormons, after determining that the army intended to travel down Echo Canyon, started building fortifications along the nearly twenty-five miles of canyon. On both sides were towering cliffs. Men carved trenches on top of the walls and devised a network of small dams along the canyon bottom, where they could collect and release flood waters upon the soldiers. Huge boulders were rolled to the edges of the cliffs, ready to be rolled down on the soldiers.

As Alexander pushed forward, Hickman led numerous attacks, burning five hundred thousand pounds of provisions between Green River and the Big Sandy.

Fort Bridger was burned to the ground. No effort was made to inform Jim Bridger of the action because he was guiding for Colonel Alexander. When Bridger saw the ruins, he called the Mormons robbers and thieves.

Rockwell was ordered to put the torch to Fort Supply, which consisted of more than a hundred log homes, a sawmill, a gristmill, and a threshing machine. The Mormons who were packing to leave were allowed to burn their own homes, if they wished. As the last wagon pulled out of the fort, Port set a match to the stockade, straw, and grain.

Lot Smith captured seventy-five wagons on the Green River and set what the teamsters called a hundred thousand–dollar bonfire. Early October found Port and his men burning grass in front of the approaching army. One morning the soldiers woke up to see Port and his men burning grass within half a mile of the camp. While there had been no shooting thus far, the angry soldiers rolled out the big cannons and began firing at the Mormons, who retreated a short distance and resumed setting fires.

On October 11 Hickman brought word of a huge government cattle herd grazing mostly unguarded near Ham's Fork. Lot Smith and Rockwell, mustering a strike force of about a hundred men, joined forces to try and capture the herd. Without beef to eat, they figured the army would be defeated.

They didn't have any trouble finding the herd, but the fact that it was so poorly guarded, with just a handful of teamsters, made Port suspicious that perhaps a trap had been set, with the herd as bait.

He expressed his concern to Smith as they surveyed the herd from the top of a nearby hill. Smith laughed at the idea, and rather than discuss it anymore, spurred his horse into a full gallop down the hill. Some of the men followed him, but the rest were milling around in confusion. The attack was spread out and disorganized. Port was furious as he galloped down the hill, trying to catch up with Smith, who was already beginning to stampede the vast herd of nearly 2,400 cattle. The teamsters stood by their wagons, watching the cattle go, and making no effort to interfere.

A mile away the cattle were rounded up in small bunches. The plan was to keep some to feed the Mormon troops through the winter and to drive the rest to Salt Lake.

Six of the cattle were killed as they stampeded through rocky gullies and fallen timber. Port singled out twenty of the poorest animals and drove them back to the teamsters, who were still standing by their wagons.

"Here's meat so you men won't starve on the way back to Kansas," Port said, as he turned the cattle over to the teamsters. "When you get to camp," he continued, his voice getting high, "tell Alexander we've stopped playing games. We'll kill every damned bluecoat in his command if he doesn't turn loose the captives."

It was now apparent the army would not make it to Utah before winter. Most of the Mormons went home, including Port, who took a herd of 624 steers with him.

Upon arriving in Salt Lake, he delivered the herd to the church corral, reported to Brigham Young, and then went to see his family. In Port's meeting with Young, the prophet had expressed concern over six Californians he had under house arrest at the Townsend Hotel, a popular gentile hangout.

The men had arrived from California a few weeks earlier with a company of Mormons returning from Carson City. Led by John Aiken, the Californians said they were headed east to meet up with the U.S. Army, where they hoped to set up a gambling tent to separate the soldiers from their wages. The Californians had brought all the necessary gambling paraphernalia with them, and Aiken wore a money belt stuffed full of gold double eagles, six deep the entire length of the belt. The gamblers rode fancy horses with silver-studded Mexican saddles. They wore expensive wide-brimmed Texas hats and hand-sewn shirts and trousers. John Aiken wore pink buckskin leggings. All six were heavily armed.

Young didn't want the gamblers to go to the army camp. Possibly they could be spies, posing as gamblers, but even if they weren't, Young didn't want them taking a firsthand account of conditions in the valley to the enemy. He didn't want them to stay in Salt Lake either, figuring sooner or later they would set up their gambling operation, a vice that to date Young had managed to keep out of the valley. Young admitted that Aiken's golden money belt would be a welcome addition to the cash-poor war effort.

It appeared now that the war with the United States could have a lengthy duration. The earlier hope that public and political pressure would force President Buchanan to recall the troops had evaporated at Mountain Meadows, a remote spot in the mountains of southern

Utah. In early September local Mormons had teamed up with Indians to wipe out an entire company of emigrants from Missouri and Arkansas. Only sixteen children, too young to tell about the massacre, were allowed to survive. As a result, both Congress and the press were now fully behind Buchanan in sending troops to Utah.

Toward the end of November, Young asked Port to escort the Aiken party back to California. Young was firm in his decision not to allow the gamblers to join Johnston's army, and he was equally determined to prevent them from setting up their tents of iniquity in Zion. He agreed to let two members of the party, Chapman and Jones, remain in Salt Lake on the condition they would avoid gambling activities, but John and Tom Aiken, Colonel Eichard, and Tuck Wright, the remaining members of the party, were to return to California. Port and three other Mormons were to accompany the Californians to make sure they didn't "get lost" and end up in the army camp after all.

It being November, and with the Sierra passes already snowed in, Port led the party south along the route he had taken with Hunt and Lathrop to San Bernardino almost ten years earlier. The Aikens were not happy about the decision, but there was nothing they could do about it. They were going home whether they liked it or not.

The party spent the first night in Nephi, Port and his men camping in the public square, Aiken and those with him staying in Foote's Hotel. Aiken refused to camp when hotel accommodations were available.

The next night they halted on the Sevier River, not far from where Captain Gunnison and his survey crew had been massacred a few years earlier. Port figured the local Indians had probably participated in the Mountain Meadows massacre but had returned home by now. He informed the men that from this point on a night guard would be necessary at all times.

Port was surprised when John and Tom Aiken volunteered to stand guard the first night, John the first half, Tom the second. Port was also surprised at how pleasant the Aikens had become after leaving Nephi. They no longer seemed angry at having to go back to California. They seemed cheerfully resolved to their fate.

Port didn't suspect anything was wrong until he felt the familiar tongue on his face in the middle of the night. Quietly sitting up, he pushed Joseph to one side. It was too dark to see very much, the fire having gone out, but he listened carefully. There was movement among the tethered horses. He heard the unmistakable squeak of saddle leather. He reached for his shotgun, which he had left leaning against a tree only a foot or two away. It was gone.

But the Navy Colt, the one he always rolled up in the blanket with him when he was on the trail, was in its usual place. He decided not to sound the alarm until he had a better idea what was going on. With his revolver in one hand and a steel picket pin in the other, he rolled out of his blankets and crawled closer to the horses, hoping to get a glimpse of what was going on. Joseph glided quietly at his side. Port wondered why the guard, who shouldn't have been very far away, hadn't sounded an alarm.

Port heard faint whispering, alerting him to the fact that there were several men among the horses—probably white men. Indians wouldn't be stupid enough to whisper.

Port crawled to where the Californians had made their beds. The men and their blankets were gone. Port realized Aiken and his men were taking the horses. They hadn't given up their plan to meet up with the army afterall. The Californians were probably going to head east to the Green River, then north to the army. To make sure Rockwell and his men didn't follow, they were taking all the horses.

Port was about to sound the alarm that would bring his companions out of their beds when the sudden blast of a shotgun shook the camp and everything in it, filling the air with the bright flash of exploding powder. The gun had been fired by someone standing near the horses. The target was the mound of blankets where Port had been sleeping a few moments earlier. Port realized John Aiken had just tried to kill him. The Californians were more cunning than Port had supposed.

There were voices now, as the Aikens, Eichard, and Wright began to scramble onto their horses. Port charged, yelling to his startled companions what had happened. Before the Californians were fully mounted, Port was among them, swinging the picket pin, firing his Colt. In a few seconds his companions joined in the free-for-all.

When it was over, Port threw an armful of dry brush on the coals from the previous night's fire and puffed them into flame so he and his men could see the devastation more clearly.

Tom Aiken and Colonel Eichard were dead, one with a bullet in the chest, the other with his head cracked open.

Tuck Wright had escaped into the brush with one of Port's bullets in his shoulder. John Aiken, who had been momentarily cornered between the camp and the river, had dropped his heavy money belt and had dived into the water.

As soon as it was light, Port and his companions made a thorough search of the area, but could find no sign of Wright or Aiken. Port strapped on the money belt, which he intended to deliver to Brigham Young, and appropriated John Aiken's large gray mule for his own use. After cooking up a big breakfast of bacon and eggs—giving a good portion of the bacon to Joseph—they broke camp and headed back to Nephi.

To Port's amazement, upon arriving in Nephi he discovered that Tuck Wright was already there, at Foote's Hotel. Wright had wandered into town an hour earlier, his head bleeding and a bullet in his upper back.

Port and his men went to the sheriff's office to get treatment for a few minor wounds. They didn't file any charges against Wright, having already decided they would not risk that man's future to a jury.

The next big surprise occurred late in the afternoon when a battered John Aiken, spattered with blood, staggered into town, finally collapsing on the front steps of Foote's Hotel. He had a small gun in his pocket, but no money.

The next day Port was seen riding through Provo on his way to Salt Lake. There was an unmistakable bulge about his waist, and he was leading a tall gray mule and several fancy horses carrying silver-studded Spanish saddles.

When Aiken and Wright were strong enough to travel they rented a wagon to carry them to Salt Lake, where they intended to join up with their two friends who had stayed behind. The story they told in Nephi was that they had been ambushed by Rockwell and his men who wanted their gold.

A short distance out of Nephi, as Aiken and Wright stopped at a spring for water, they were ambushed and killed, their bodies thrown into the spring.

Upon arrival in Salt Lake, Port had no time to contemplate the Aiken killings. Young had received word that General Johnston had finally caught up with the main army near Fort Bridger and was preparing to push into Utah immediately. Young had already sent 1,300 men to the Echo Canyon fortifications and wanted Port up there right away to evaluate the enemy's readiness for a winter march into Utah.

Port did not find an army preparing for an invasion. Instead, he found a rag-tag bunch of under-fed, under-clothed men on the verge of collapse. Only ten of the 144 horses Johnston left Ft. Leavenworth with were still alive.

The morning Port surveyed the camp the thermometer had dropped to -16 degrees. The discouraged soldiers were huddled around campfires, eating the horses and mules that had been pulling their cannons. Port sent word to Young that not only were the soldiers in no condition to march into Utah, but they would be lucky to survive the winter.

Most of the Mormon troops were allowed to return home. Brigham Young had until spring to decide what to do. But there was no doubt in anyone's mind, that come spring, the U.S. troops would receive new supplies and reinforcements, enabling them to march on Great Salt Lake City.

Brigham Young decided that rather than defend the city against the U.S. Army, he would give the army the city, in ashes. The Mormons began moving south. Wells were covered up. Straw was stuffed under porches and in attics so on the signal from Young the entire city could become ashes in a few hours. The Mormons were ready to torch the city they had taken ten years to build.

On April 12 the new governor, Alfred Cumming, and a delegation of politicians arrived in Salt Lake City. Thomas Kane, the well-known friend of the Mormons from Illinois, had traveled to Fort Bridger in March from his new home in California. He had persuaded Cumming to attempt peace negotiations with the Mormons before allowing Johnston's troops into the valley.

Johnston didn't like the idea. Steaming mad, he was left behind at Fort Bridger, worrying that a bunch of weak-kneed politicians might upset his plans to march into Utah and kick the hell out of the Mormons. He was confident his howitzers would make short work of the Echo Canyon fortifications the Mormons had worked so hard to build.

Upon their arrival in Salt Lake, Cumming and his party were greeted by a delegation of Mormons. While Brigham Young at one time was ready to torch the city and engage in all-out war with the United States, his position was now softened. He gave Cumming the official seal of the territory, and with it the governorship.

The U.S. Government had achieved its primary objective without firing a shot, except for the cannon fire at Rockwell when he was burning grass on the Big Sandy. Young, on the other hand, might have given up the seal, but he was still in charge, and all the Mormons knew it.

President Buchanan granted amnesty to all Mormons who had participated in the skirmishes the previous fall and destroyed government property. The president also agreed that the army would establish its headquarters at least forty miles from Great Salt Lake City.

Johnston didn't like the agreement, but there wasn't a thing he could do about it. He and his troops marched through Salt Lake on July 4 and arrived at their final destination, Camp Floyd, on July 6. That same week Port brought Mary Ann and the girls back to Salt Lake from their temporary home in Provo. Mary Ann was six months pregnant with their third child.

# Chapter 53

———◆———

On July 29 Port purchased sixteen acres from Evan Green near a hot spring at Point of the Mountain, south of Salt Lake, about halfway between the city and the army camp. Forty miles was a long way for the soldiers and their suppliers to ride in one day as they passed back and forth between the city and the camp. Port knew that by the time the men reached the halfway point, they would be hungry and thirsty, especially for something that had a little fire in it. He decided to build an inn.

Port's inn would also be a convenient stopping point for Saints and emigrants traveling to and from Utah Valley and destinations farther south.

Port paid five hundred dollars for the land and took in two partners. Charles Mogo was a brewer, and David Burr was a builder. Construction began immediately on what was to become known as the Hot Springs Brewery Hotel. Upon completion, the brewery was capable of producing five hundred gallons of fine lager beer a day.

While the inn was under construction, Port moved Mary Ann and the girls to Lehi so they would be close to where he was working. He didn't want to keep them at the inn because he didn't want his wife and little girls around the rough element, the soldiers and teamsters, whom he guessed would be his most frequent customers. In Lehi the family was close to a school and a church, surrounded by good Mormon neighbors, and close enough that Port could ride home every night if he wished. There hadn't been any Indian problems in Utah Valley for some time, so he felt his family was safe.

As the number of soldiers at Camp Floyd increased to nearly three thousand, Port's business flourished. So did anti-Mormonism. Salt Lake was no longer a one-religion city under total control of the Mormon Church. The army had hundreds of camp followers, including gamblers, prostitutes, saloon keepers, fortune tellers, preachers, and businessmen engaged in buying and selling goods and services to the U.S. Government.

Almost overnight, dozens of saloons, gambling establishments, and houses of prostitution opened for business. The city that had been practically free of crime a year earlier now boasted a murder a week. The *Deseret News* reported there was more crime in the first eight months of army occupation than during the previous nine years. The police department increased its size by two hundred men.

Bill Hickman and Joachim Johnston started a highly profitable rustling business, sneaking as many as eighty mules a day out of government corrals and herding the stolen animals off to California to be sold. From an economic standpoint, the city was booming, but from a religious standpoint, the city of Zion had lost much of its savor, possibly forever.

For Porter Rockwell, business couldn't have been better. His inn was a hub of activity. Port's reputation alone helped it become a popular gathering place. Both Mormons and non-Mormons liked to brag about having had a square drink with the Destroying Angel. Port was always happy to accommodate.

But while his reputation was good for business, it was also a source of constant worry. On one fall evening he was driving his buckboard home to Lehi and saw a lone rider waiting for him in the middle of the road. The man wore a wide-brimmed hat and a red wool coat. The hat was tilted forward so Port couldn't see the man's eyes. A rifle was balanced across the front of the saddle. Port had never seen the man before.

"What can I do for you?" Port asked, pulling his team to a halt.

"You can make me famous."

"How's that?"

"Are you Porter Rockwell?" the stranger asked.

"That's right. Should I know you?"

"No. I've come all the way from New Mexico on a bet. I've heard plenty about you. Brigham's Destroying Angel, they call you." The stranger spoke easily, his manner confident.

"What's the wager?"

"A friend bet me a hundred dollars I couldn't kill Porter Rockwell," the stranger said as he quickly swung his rifle around, pointing it straight at Port's chest. No more than twenty feet separated the two men.

"Right here in the middle of the road?" Port asked, trying to keep the man talking instead of shooting. "There are no witnesses. Nobody would believe you, least of all your friend."

"He will if I do like the Indians and take your scalp back with me," the stranger responded.

"You've got to shoot me first, and that's going to be tough to do with a rifle that won't fire," Port said slowly, deliberately, his voice high.

"Why won't it fire?" the stranger asked, his voice revealing a hint of uneasiness for the first time.

"There's no cap on your hammer," Port said.

Both men knew that caps occasionally worked loose and fell to the ground. The stranger couldn't remember if he had checked the cap before waving down the famous gunfighter. Quickly, he glanced down. To his relief, the cap was in place.

As he looked back up, Port's shotgun exploded, the double load of buckshot striking the stranger square in the chest. The charge blew the man over the back of his saddle and into a full somersault before he crashed in a heap in the middle of the road. The horse galloped off down the road toward Lehi.

Getting out of his wagon, Port picked up the man's rifle, noticing the cap was still on the hammer. He threw the rifle in the back of his wagon and climbed back up on the seat. He continued his journey toward Lehi, figuring the authorities could bring in the body in the morning.

Later that winter a government teamster named Martin Oats stopped at the inn on a cold, snowy night. Port was just finishing up business and getting ready to head home to Lehi. Oats suddenly pulled a Bowie knife on Robert Herford, the bartender, claiming Herford had called him a thief.

"I'll cut the heart out of any man who accuses me of stealing," Oats growled. Port walked over to see what was the matter. The teamster glanced at Port.

"You're a damned rustler, Mormon," Oats shouted. "You've stolen cattle from me."

"I don't know you," Port said, wanting only to be on his way home to supper. "I have no fight with you."

Oats shook the knife in Port's face, who once again remembered Joseph's promise that he would never be harmed by bullet or blade. Port's left hand shot up, grabbing Oats's wrist and working to twist it until the knife dropped free. Oats grabbed Port's beard with his free hand and began to jerk and push. Port responded by grabbing Oats's throat.

As the two men shoved each other back and forth, Port realized the teamster was a lot stronger than he had thought at first. No matter how hard he tried, Port could not twist the knife out of the man's hand. He was sorry now he hadn't just gone for the shotgun he kept behind the bar. But it was too late for that now. Oats pushed Port up against the wall, and began slamming Port's head against the uneven log surface. Port realized if he didn't do something fast, he would lose the fight, and possibly his life.

He tried to knee Oats in the groin but caught a bony hip instead. Before he could pull his knee away, Port felt Oats's powerful knee crush upwards into his groin. Port felt the strength go out of his arms and legs.

Suddenly, Oats dropped the knife and let go of the beard. Port wasn't sure what was happening until he saw Herford's cocked pistol against the side of Oats's head. Without moving the pistol, Herford kicked the knife across the room. Slowly, Oats backed away. When he started to say something, Herford ordered him to shut up.

Herford and Rockwell hurried an angry Oats into his coat and shoved him out the door. They kept his Bowie knife, however, telling the teamster that if he wanted to come by sometime when he was in a better mood, they'd give it back to him.

Ten minutes later Port left the inn, climbing into his wagon and heading the horses toward Lehi. He noticed that Oats's wagon hadn't left yet.

Suddenly Oats stepped out of the darkness, grabbing one of Port's horses by the bridle. There was a gun in the teamster's hand, but it was pointed at the ground while the man tried to bring the horses under control.

There was no need for words. Port wasn't about to let this powerful man get an advantage over him twice in one night. He remembered the power in Oats's hands and arms. He remembered the anger as Oats had tried to smash his head against the log wall. He knew if the teamster ever got the pistol up in the air and pointed in Port's direction, Oats was a man who could pull the trigger.

Port didn't wait. He drew his Colt Dragoon and fired, slamming Oats on the snowy ground, the heavy body sliding several feet farther away before coming to rest. There was a growing circle of red on the chest. The feet kicked several times, and the head jerked to one side. In a few seconds the body was still, snowflakes beginning to settle on it, except on the red circle of blood, where the snowflakes melted into the warm wetness.

Having heard the shot, Herford came running outside. After Port explained what had happened, the two men lifted the body into the back of Port's wagon. He hauled it to the police office in Lehi, where he turned himself in for killing the teamster. Port was acquitted the next day.

A month later, February 19, 1860, Mary Ann had another child, this time a boy, David Porter Rockwell.

# Chapter 54

By 1860 Port's inn at Point of the Mountain was not only an important gathering place, but a major hub for news. The pony express stopped there for the rider to change horses. The biggest news item that spring was the Confederate attack on Fort Sumter to start the Civil War. The immediate consequence for Utah was the shutting down of Camp Floyd as the soldiers were sent back east to fight the Confederacy.

Everything at the fort was for sale. Four million dollars worth of goods was auctioned off for a hundred thousand dollars. U.S. Government issue whiskey that had been selling for five dollars a gallon a month earlier was bringing twenty-five cents a gallon at the auction. Buildings were sold for five hundred dollars each.

When two thousand rifles were put on the auction block, with Brigham Young the high bidder at six dollars each, the government decided not to sell the rifles and burned them along with tons of ammunition. The Mormons were furious, and there was talk of possible armed conflict between the Mormons and the departing soldiers.

Once the soldiers were gone, business at Port's inn dropped so much that his partners lost interest, and he bought them out. That same year the transcontinental telegraph was connected coast to coast, putting the pony express out of business. Point of the Mountain was no longer an important news center, and without the soldiers and camp followers, a less interesting gathering point.

But just when it looked like there wasn't enough money to keep the inn's doors open, Brigham Young referred a rich California freighter to Port. His name was Frank Karrick, and eight of his mules and a gray stallion, valued at five hundred dollars each, had been stolen. Karrick had tried to follow the trail left by the missing animals, but it had vanished at a crossroads west of Salt Lake.

Port agreed to help Karrick, and without delay they headed to the crossroads. It didn't take Port long to figure out how Karrick had lost the trail. The outlaws had removed the shoes from the animals, thus changing the appearance of the tracks. The two men continued west for two more days, pushing hard, spending upwards of eighteen hours a day in the saddle.

At the end of the second day, Port spotted dust on the horizon. Taking a telescope out of his saddlebag, he saw two men driving a herd of mules and a lone gray horse. Port and Karrick increased their pace, and by evening they came upon the two men, camped on the far side of a swift creek. Port got the drop on them, recovered the mules and horse, and delivered the two thieves to the marshal in Salt Lake.

Karrick gave Port five hundred dollars in gold. Two months later, Port received a gallon of Sacramento's finest whiskey and a silver-studded saddle on the overland stage. Both gifts were from Karrick, who later said he thought Rockwell appreciated the whiskey more than the saddle.

On New Year's Eve that same year, there was special reason for Utahns to celebrate. Territorial governor John W. Dawson was returning to his home state of Indiana after a term of only three weeks.

His short term had been unpopular from the start. Three days after his arrival, the new chief executive accused the legislature of disloyalty to the United States and proposed a war tax on the Mormons to cover the cost of federal troops stationed in Utah. In addition, the new governor vetoed a bill petitioning the U.S. Congress to grant statehood to Deseret.

Salt Lake City was alive with rumors of Dawson's moral degeneration, and how his appointment to govern Utah Territory was a tricky move by top Indiana politicians to get him as far away from their state as possible.

But all this was bearable. Utahns had survived corrupt politicians before. But when word got out that Dawson had made improper advances toward a pretty Mormon widow he had hired as a house keeper, the Mormons were furious. There were ways to handle immoral gentiles who accosted Mormon women. It didn't matter if the man was governor.

Dawson began to worry, realizing too late that he had gone too far. He didn't deny the charges against him. Instead, he locked himself in his quarters, probably wondering about the wild stories his non-Mormon friends had told him about Danite justice, avenging angels, and the swift gun of Porter Rockwell.

It is not known if Governor Dawson had advance knowledge of a *Deseret News* editorial that was already written and set in type on that New Year's Eve. The editorial claimed the governor had qualified himself for the position of chamberlain or eunuch in the king's palace. This was a direct reference to emasculation, a common form of punishment for sex offenders in pioneer times.

Nevertheless, on that cold New Year's Eve, the new governor decided to leave Deseret, joined by his physician, Dr. Chambers. Worried about possible assault on the trail, Dawson hired six ruffians, at one hundred dollars each, to accompany and protect him from the Mormons. The hired guards were Lot Huntington, Moroni Clawson, John Jason, Wilford Luce, Isaac Neibaur, and Wood Reynolds.

In his haste to leave Utah, the governor apparently didn't take the time to check into the backgrounds or sympathies of his hired guards. One would think he would have been suspicious of a man named Moroni offering to protect him from the Mormons. And a quick check of Wood Reynolds would have revealed that this willing bodyguard was related to the woman whom the governor had assaulted. As one observer put it, "The little rooster had hired a pack of hungry coyotes to protect him on his journey."

Upon reaching the Ephriam Hanks mail station at Mountain Dell, about halfway between Salt Lake and Park City, the hired guards began their New Year's Eve celebration by falling upon the governor and severely beating him. It is not known if a knife was used on the governor, as suggested in the *Deseret News*, only that no John Dawson posterity ever surfaced to prove otherwise.

While most Utahns cheered when they heard what had happened to the unpopular governor, Brigham Young did not. In fact, he was furious. For several years no stone had been left unturned in trying to convince the U.S. Congress that the Mormons were responsible, law-abiding people capable of the kind of self-government available under statehood.

Now a group of Mormons had tried to castrate the highest official in the land. When word reached Congress, statehood for Utah would be tabled again—unless, perhaps, the Mormons brought these ruffians to justice and punished them for what they had done to Dawson. Young sent Rockwell on the trail of the ruffians.

Port began a search that lasted several weeks but had no apparent success. Lot Huntington and Isaac Neibaur had been caught by Port a year earlier driving a herd of stolen mules to California. The rest of the boys who attacked the governor did not have criminal records.

After Port had brought Huntington and Neibaur back to Salt Lake, Huntington thought Bill Hickman had been the one to point the law in their direction. Huntington challenged Hickman to a gunfight in the streets of Salt Lake.

Next to Porter Rockwell, Hickman was supposed to be the best gunfighter in the territory, but he could not whip young, fearless Huntington. When it was over, both men lay wounded in the street.

Then eight hundred dollars suddenly turned up missing from a Salt Lake stable, and Sam Bateman informed Port that a valuable mare belonging to his good friend John Bennion had been stolen while Bennion was attending to tithing settlement at his bishop's home in West Jordan.

Bennion's son, Sam, and some friends had followed the tracks as far as Draper, where residents had seen Lot Huntington, Moroni Clawson, and John Smith heading west on the wagon road to California. Huntington was riding the stolen mare.

Warrants were issued for the arrest of the three men, and Port, accompanied by a posse, set out after them.

It was already dark when Port and his men reached Camp Floyd. They learned the three fugitives had passed that way earlier in the afternoon, and guessed they would be spending the night at Faust's Mail Station, twenty-two miles further west.

Rather than put up for the night, Port and his men abandoned their weary horses and piled into a stagecoach, trying to catch a little sleep as the driver pushed westward through the night.

They arrived at Faust's Mail Station about 4:30 in the morning. After hiding the stagecoach, Port and his men surrounded the mail station, concealing themselves behind sagebrush and rocks, waiting for the dawn. They knew the men they wanted were inside because the stolen mare was in the stable.

By the time the sun came up Port and his men were nearly frozen from the January cold. They had to wait another two hours before the front door finally opened. The station owner, H.J. Faust, stepped outside, closing the door behind him.

Faust was surprised when he saw Port waving to him. In the brief conversation that followed, Faust said the three wanted men were at that very moment eating their breakfast and would soon be coming outside. Port sent Faust back inside to tell the men to come out with their hands over their heads.

After what seemed a long time, Lot Huntington appeared in the open doorway—tall, handsome, arrogant, twenty-seven years old. His hands were not above his head as Port had ordered. In fact, the young outlaw totally ignored Port and his men and sauntered confidently to the stable. There was a cap and ball pistol in a holster on his hip. He paid no attention to a shout to surrender.

No shots were fired as the bold outlaw entered the stable and saddled his horse, the stolen mare. Port ran to the front door of the stable, where Huntington and the horse would have to come out.

Huntington continued to ignore the posse, even as he began to mount. As his leg completed its swing over the back of the saddle, his free hand reached for his gun. Port barked a final warning, but before Huntington could get a shot off, Port's Colt, loaded with buckshot, blasted away.

Eight balls entered Huntington's stomach and chest, knocking him out of the saddle. On the way down his leg caught in the poles of the cedar fence, causing him to hang upside down, warm red blood steaming in the frosty morning air as it ran over his face and onto the ground. Huntington was dead by the time Port reached him.

The other two men came out with their hands up, and were taken back to Salt Lake, where they reportedly were killed by police when they tried to escape.

# Chapter 55

In the summer of 1862 Thomas Kane helped Port get five short-run mail contracts with the U.S. Government. His wagons began making weekly deliveries from Brigham City to Logan, Cedar City to Santa Clara, Cedar Valley to Gardiner's Mills, Nephi to Manti, and Salt Lake City to Alpine. After expenses, the mail business netted Port an annual income of $2,100, making him one of the wealthiest men in the territory.

The men who drove Port's mail wagons were heavily armed, with at least one double-barreled shotgun loaded with buckshot and one or two pistols. Since the end of the Utah War, Indian troubles had been increasing, particularly along the northern emigrant route and in northern communities. The Shoshones were responsible for most of the attacks.

The northern emigrant route along the Humboldt River to California had been mostly abandoned because of Indian troubles, with most California-bound emigrant trains and the U.S. Mail now taking the southern route directly west of Camp Floyd to Carson City.

Port always had a word of advice for west-bound visitors at his inn. "Keep your eyes skinned," he would say. "Especially in canyons and ravines. Carry a double-barreled gun loaded with buckshot. Make at times a dark camp. Never trust to appearances in Indian country. Avoid white Indians especially. Avoid the direct routes."

One writer estimated that of the approximately four hundred whites killed by Indians between 1840 and 1860, 90 percent died west of South Pass in Shoshone lands. The Indians saw their best lands being filled up with settlers. They saw endless streams of California and Oregon-bound emigrants slaughtering the buffalo, elk, and deer.

Many Mormons were getting weary of giving almost daily handouts to increasingly ungrateful Indians. More and more Mormons decided that an occasional fight was better than daily feeding. The Mormon missionary effort among the Shoshones came to a standstill.

Because of reports of white men riding with Indian raiding parties, some government officials suspected Mormon involvement in the attacks on emigrant trains. What these critics failed to notice was a corresponding increase in attacks against Mormon travelers and settlers, though the bulk of the hostilities still focused on non-Mormons.

About this time a party of young men from Springville was returning from Carson City when they found themselves surrounded by a band of hostile Shoshones. At the time it was customary among Mormon men to let their hair grow long. Only gentiles enjoyed closely cropped hair. In fact, when young Mormons tried to look more like the gentiles by cutting their hair, the practice was preached against from the pulpit.

The young men returning from Carson City had gone against counsel and had cut their hair short. As a result, they had difficulty convincing the Shoshones they were Mormons. It wasn't until one of the braves ripped open the front of William Huntington's shirt and saw the young man's Mormon temple garment, that the Indians believed the men were Mormons and allowed them to continue their journey in peace.

Rockwell frequently warned travelers to be particularly cautious of white Indians. Outlaws and bandits were finding it increasingly convenient to pose as Indians, thereby passing the blame for their crimes to the nearest Indian tribe. One white woman reportedly stolen from her emigrant company by raiding Indians was raped by five men, shot, and left for dead. When found, she lived long enough to say that all five of her attackers had been white men.

In a particularly brutal attack on a company at Cold Springs near the Sublette Cutoff northwest of Salt Lake, a five-year-old girl was captured. Her ears were cut off and her eyes gouged out. Then her legs were cut off at the knees. She was forced to walk around on the stumps as she bled to death.

Whites reacted by killing Indians, sometimes women and children. White retaliation was often against friendly bands because they were the easiest to find. When the army left Camp Floyd to fight in the Civil War, Indian troubles increased. In Cache Valley travel became suicidal. Indian-white relations were at an all-time low. Yet emigrant trains continued to pour in from the east. Brigham Young appealed to President Lincoln for help.

On July 12, 1862, Colonel Patrick Edward Conner, with seven companies of his third regiment of California volunteers, left San Francisco to clear the plains from Carson City to Fort Laramie of raiding war parties. Earlier that season twenty-three men had been killed on the Humboldt.

Conner and his men entered Camp Floyd right after the name was changed to Camp Crittenden because its namesake, former Secretary of War John B. Floyd, had defected to the confederate cause.

Rumors had been circulating in Salt Lake that Conner was going to station his men in the city in violation of the agreement of 1858, which required the army to keep its troops at least forty miles from the city. There was also a rumor that Porter Rockwell had been riding through the streets of Salt Lake, offering to bet anyone five hundred dollars that Conner didn't have the salt to bring his men across the Jordan River located a mile or so west of the city.

When the feisty Conner heard this news, he ordered his men to roll up their tents and follow him across the Jordan River, into the city, and to a gentle hillside within cannon range of Brigham Young's house. The camp became known as Fort Douglas. The month was late October.

In early December Conner sent Major Edward McGarry with a detachment of men to the Bear River ferry to engage a band of Shoshone warriors who had stolen some stock in the area. The major captured four braves near the crossing and sent a fifth to the Indian village with a message that if recently stolen animals were not returned immediately the four prisoners would be shot.

When the Indians ignored his ultimatum, McGarry ordered the Indians be tied to the long ferry rope. He lined up his firing squad, which pumped fifty-one rounds into the captives. The *Deseret News* commented that either the soldiers were very poor shots, or the Indians very tenacious of life.

The executions whipped the Shoshones and Bannocks into a fervor of hostile activity, even in winter. The Mormons in Cache Valley were banded together, unable to do anything but defend themselves. Travel in small groups was out of the question.

Port had to place a second man, a guard, on each of his mail wagons. Still, attacks were frequent and sometimes successful. A thousand dollars was stolen and two men killed on his Brigham City to Logan run.

In January word reached Salt Lake that a number of hostile chiefs, including San Pitch, Bear Hunter, Sagwitch, and Pocatello, had assembled several hundred braves on the Bear River north of Logan. The report said the Indians had built breastworks and dug rifle pits in a small canyon overlooking the river, and they were challenging the white men to come and fight them.

Conner wasn't familiar with the area, so he hired Porter Rockwell as guide. The colonel didn't particularly want a Mormon guide, believing the Mormons were too sympathetic toward the Indians, but he had no choice. None of his men was familiar with the Bear River country, whereas Rockwell knew the exact location where the Indians were fortified.

Port marked his *X* on the federal payroll book once again. His pay was five dollars a day, plus expenses. Marshall Gibbs issued warrants for the arrest of the renegade chieftains, but when Port delivered them, Conner said he wouldn't be needing any arrest papers because he didn't intend on taking any prisoners.

The plan was a simple one. On January 22, forty foot soldiers followed by two howitzers began marching north from Salt Lake.

Three days later four cavalry units led by Conner and Rockwell moved out, traveling at night only, hiding by day in settlers' barns. They hoped that when the Indian scouts saw the forty men on foot, the red men would remain in their fortifications, thinking they could win easily against forty soldiers. The Indians wouldn't find out about the cavalrymen until the battle had begun.

Traveling at night in January was no easy task for the men with the horses. Many got frostbite during the first night's journey of sixty-eight miles. Most of the men led their horses in an effort to keep warm. Port was wearing his heavy buffalo coat.

The Californians were tough, uncomplaining men. Most were eager to engage the enemy, even in winter.

Port's respect for the volunteers increased with each mile of snowy road.

The plan worked. Thinking they had only a forty-man infantry to contend with, the Indians waited for the approaching soldiers, continuing to strengthen their fortifications.

There were about seventy-five Indian lodges in the ravine, some made of brush, but most of wagon canvas. The canyon opened up on a flat by the river, giving the Indians a clear view of the approaching enemy. The head of the canyon disappeared into the foothills, allowing a handy escape for the Indians, should that become necessary. Both side approaches to the canyon were steep and rugged, providing difficult access for an approaching enemy, especially with snipers placed on the ridgetops.

The squaws had dug steps up and down the ridges and constructed willow rifle rests at strategic locations to increase their braves' accuracy.

Shortly before dawn on January 29, the cavalry passed the foot soldiers at Franklin, the nearest Mormon community. The mounted soldiers, under the command of McGarry, pushed their horses into the icy river. When companies K and M reached the west bank, a sniper's bullet critically wounded one of the soldiers. Dismounting, the troopers scampered for cover behind bushes and rocks, while some of the men hurried the horses back across the river so they could carry the approaching infantry across.

At sunrise a chief on a spirited pony appeared on the top of the breastwork. He waved his lance at the soldiers as he raced the pony back and forth. Other Indians waved scalps of white women on the ends of poles, trying to taunt the soldiers even more.

The troops charged just as the infantry reached the river. The soldiers had instructions to save their ammunition until they reached the top of the embankment. With the battle begun, McGarry took some of the men to the north in an attempt to circle the area and attack the Indians from above.

The Indians had been waiting for this day a long time, and they didn't waste any time. The volunteers began to fall like flies. Conner was sick. Wounded and dying men lay everywhere. Many were suffering from frostbite and exposure in the sub-freezing temperatures. Unable to push into the withering fire of the Indians, the soldiers holed up behind bushes and rocks as the Indians picked away at them. Those trying to remove the wounded were shot too.

For about an hour it looked as if the Indians would be victorious. Then McGarry suddenly appeared behind the Indians to the north, with a clear field of fire from above. When McGarry and his men opened fire, the rest of the men below were encouraged, and they charged up the canyon.

Caught in the crossfire, the Indians panicked. Some tried to escape into the forests above. Others headed for the river. For the soldiers, the battle became a turkey shoot. With dozens of their companions already killed or wounded by the Indian sharpshooters, the soldiers didn't let up, even when they discovered there were nearly a hundred women and children running in confusion across the battlefield. With enthusiasm, they remembered Conner's order that there would be no prisoners.

Port climbed upon the breastwork to watch the slaughter. Initially, he had fired at the Indians when it appeared they might whip the California volunteers, but when McGarry crashed in from the rear, changing the tide of the battle, Port had ceased firing. He knew the slaughter would be horrible without any help from him.

Some excitement came in watching the running and shooting matches with the armed but desperate braves, but when there were no more warriors left to fight, the soldiers began turning their attention to the women and children. Port was sick. Still, he stayed.

He noticed a group of women at the bottom of the draw. He wondered why they were crouching. They were doing something with their hands under their robes. Then he remembered Jim Bridger telling him that the squaws of some tribes, when taken captive by an enemy, would shove sand inside them so the enemy would find no pleasure in raping them. Port guessed that that's what these Shoshone women were doing, knowing they would soon be at the mercy of the California volunteers. Some of the women were carrying babies. Several older children were standing among the crouching women.

The scouting reports as relayed to Port hadn't indicated the presence of so many women and children. Had that been known, the battle plan might have been different, Port thought. Perhaps there could have been orders not to harm defenseless women and children. Port wondered if Conner had known about the women and children and just hadn't said anything.

Just when Port figured the battle would start winding down, two soldiers waded into the group of crouching women, smashing them with rifle butts. One young woman began running up the hill toward Port. There was something familiar about the way she moved, the way she looked.

The two men ran after and caught her, throwing her on the ground. One of the soldiers pulled up her dress and fell upon her. Port looked away, wishing he could interfere but knowing if he did the action would be considered taking sides with the enemy.

When he looked back, the man had gotten off the woman. Apparently the sand inside her had spoiled his fun. The soldier grabbed his rifle and, pushing the barrel against the woman's abdomen, pulled the trigger. The woman screamed, trying to roll away from the soldiers. The men were laughing as the second soldier fell upon the bleeding woman in an effort to rape her again, even as she was dying.

Port had had enough. After making sure his rifle was loaded, he raised it to his shoulder. Again, Port thought he recognized something familiar in the woman's scream. Could it be Emma? Pushing the thought from his mind, he took careful aim with his rifle, hitting the first man in the side of the head, the second in the heart.

After taking a quick look around to make sure he didn't have to defend himself against someone who might have seen him, Port ran down the hill to the bleeding woman. At first he couldn't tell if it was Emma, the face was so twisted in agony. Then he saw the scar on her left arm and remembered the wound he had sewed up.

Port dropped to the ground, pulling her head onto his lap, brushing her hair into place, holding her close, calling her by name. She did not respond, though her screaming had ceased. A minute later she was dead.

Port raised his face toward the gray sky and offered a tearful prayer. He asked why life had to be so cruel, why the volunteers had to come from California, why the Indians had to raid emigrant trains, why the Mormons had to settle on Indian lands, why the mobs had driven the Mormons from Nauvoo. Where did it all begin? Where would it all end? Who was to blame? At least the two men who had killed Emma wouldn't be killing anyone else.

When Port stood up, the shooting had stopped. He thanked God the battle was finally over. He wanted to bury Emma, but the ground was frozen. He stretched her out straight on the ground, facing east. He straightened her clothing as best he could, covering the ugly wound and as much blood as possible.

While the soldiers rounded up horses, gathered up the loot consisting mostly of guns, ammunition, and wheat, and looked after their wounded, Port headed back to Franklin to see about getting wagons and sleighs for the dead and wounded. He had to keep busy, not think about what had happened. He needed a drink of whiskey.

Before dark, Port returned with ten sleighs to bring the wounded soldiers to Fort Douglas in Salt Lake. As the sleighs were being loaded, Port mentioned to Conner that he was going back to Franklin to get more sleighs to carry the wounded Indians into town, where the Mormons could care for them.

"That won't be necessary," Conner said. "There are no wounded Indians."

Nearly four hundred Indians were killed, including ninety women and children, making the Bear River battle the largest slaughter of human life in the history of the American West. Port saw forty-eight braves in one gruesome pile. One warrior had been shot fourteen times.

Fourteen California volunteers had been killed, including two right at the end of the battle when their companions thought danger had passed. Forty-nine were wounded, and seventy-nine had frostbitten feet. Most of the men had gotten their feet wet in crossing the river.

The spoils included 175 horses, seventy lodges, one thousand bushels of wheat, and large quantities of powder and lead.

Several months later, Conner was promoted to brigadier general, but he was no hero to the Mormons, who had known many of the slaughtered Indians. The general feeling in Utah Territory was that a show of strength was necessary to turn back the increasing tide of Indian raids, but the indiscriminate slaughter of women and children had been uncalled-for and unnecessary.

Upon arriving in Salt Lake, Port headed for the nearest saloon, hoping four or five square drinks might help him forget Emma.

# Chapter 56

The Bear River battle didn't mark the end of hostilities with the Shoshones. On April 11 Lieutenant Francis Honeyman was jumped by a raiding party at an adobe house where he was staying near Pleasant Grove. The enthusiastic officer opened fired on the Indians with his howitzer, killing most of his own mules in the process. The seven that didn't get killed got away with the Indians, none of whom received a scratch.

The next day Port accompanied Conner to Pleasant Grove to investigate the damages and attempt to trail the Indians while the tracks were still fresh. Conner was angry that Port was nursing along a bottle of Valley Tan, but he didn't say anything because Port led him to where the guilty Indians were camped in Spanish Fork Canyon. In a battle that lasted most of the next day, thirty-two Indians were killed, and dozens of horses and mules were recovered, including those lost by Honeyman at Pleasant Grove.

Like at Bear River, the California volunteers were not content just to win the battle. There were no women and children to harass, so they scalped twenty-seven of the dead Indians. Riding through Utah Valley that evening, they displayed the scalps on the ends of their rifle barrels. Two months later, the eastern Shoshones sued for peace, signing a treaty at Fort Bridger.

Not long after Port returned home from the Indian wars, Mary Ann delivered her fifth child, a little girl named Letitia. Her oldest daughters, eight-year-old Mary and six-year-old Sarah, loved to unbraid and comb their father's long hair, now streaked with silver. In June an eastbound stage was attacked just west of Lehi. The driver and Rockwell family friend Wood Reynolds were brutally killed. When Port arrived at the scene, their naked bodies were full of arrows and bullet holes. Reynolds had fought bravely. The Indians had cut his heart out and eaten it raw, hoping in the process his courage would be passed on to them.

Reynolds had spent a lot of time in the Rockwell home. Mary Ann had treated the young man as she would her own son. When the raiders could not be found, Mary Ann insisted on moving back to Salt Lake, where her family would be safer. Port boarded up the Lehi home and moved his family to the fourteenth ward neighborhood in Salt Lake City.

Since the Bear River battle, Port had felt a growing urge to be by himself, to get away from people, especially soldiers. It was time to have his own secluded ranch where he could raise fine horses and cattle undisturbed. He was fifty. It was time to slow down. He wanted no more of the exciting, sometimes violent life that had consumed much of his time.

He went back to Skull Valley, where he had started building a cabin years earlier. The place, located on the west slopes of the Sheeprock Mountains at the head of Government Creek, looked even better to him than before. He filed on 640 acres. His grazing stock would range over a much greater area.

Though Port wanted only to be left alone, he was constantly hounded by reporters who wanted to interview the great gunfighter. Some of the writers were local boys, some were from back east or across the ocean. Each one asked Port how many men he had killed. He always evaded the question by saying something like, "No more than needed killing." But specific numbers always appeared in the articles, starting at about forty and working gradually upwards, until a writer named Richardson set the notch count at 150.

"Hell, if I had that many notches in my gun," Port laughed, "I wouldn't have anything left to hold in my hand."

The poor writer was unfortunate enough to run into Port on a Salt Lake street a short time after the article appeared. Port told Richardson he was about to make the number 151, and that he would kill any writer who published any such falsehoods about him.

On September 28, 1866, Mary Ann died, two weeks after giving birth to her sixth child. It was hard for Port to let her go. Mary Ann was all he had ever wanted in a woman. He was in no mood to find another wife, but with six children he had to do something, especially with him gone as much as he was. He solved the problem by hiring a housekeeper, Christine Olsen.

Two months after Mary Ann's death, Port closed the inn at Point of the Mountain. He purchased an acre of ground from Wells Fargo and Company for $7,500 on Second East between South Temple and First South Streets. He built the Colorado Stables, from which ran his mail routes.

Dividing his time between the mail business and the new ranch, Port was finally ready to settle down. Without the inn, it was harder for reporters and other unwanted visitors to find him. He enjoyed the increased privacy of his new life. But even with all the change he continued to miss Mary Ann.

There were welcome distractions. One afternoon he was at Faust's Mail Station waiting for the eastbound stage. Wells Fargo had hired him as a special shotgun guard from Faust's to Fort Bridger. He was supposed to guard a box containing forty thousand dollars in gold.

As soon as he could see the dust in the distance, Port knew something was wrong. The stage was ahead of schedule, and the horses were running too hard. As the coach drew closer, he could see the driver whipping the horses.

A few minutes later, as the excited driver pulled the foaming horses to a halt, he shouted the stage had been robbed by a lone gunman west of Government Creek. The stage had stopped when the driver saw a man lying in the middle of the road, thinking the man needed help. Once the stage was stopped, the man jumped up, pointing a shotgun at the driver and guard. After they had thrown down the cash box, the bandit hurried them on their way. They didn't see a horse or any accomplices.

After stuffing his pockets full of bread and dried beef, Port hurried to the stable to saddle his horse. Faust urged him to wait for a posse, but Port thought that would take several days, and by then the trail would be cold. This was probably the biggest stagecoach robbery in the history of the territory. Port couldn't risk letting the trail get cold. A storm or a good wind could wipe out the tracks in a few hours.

Fifteen minutes after the stage arrived, Port was heading west at an easy gallop. He didn't feel fifty anymore, but twenty. The excitement of the chase did that to him. Life was suddenly very simple. All he had to do was find the gold and bring it back.

Port didn't have any trouble locating the exact spot where the robbery had taken place. He found the square indentation in the dust where the cash box had hit the ground. He found boot tracks leading to a nearby draw where a single horse had been hidden.

Port followed the horse's trail south for two days, eventually ending up near Cherry Creek, north of the Sevier River. From the top of a rocky hill, Port saw the horse that had made the tracks. The animal was picketed in a small meadow beside a creek. A lone man, presumably the bandit, was sleeping under a juniper tree. There was no sign of the cash box.

Just to be sure he had the right man, Port carefully made a wide circle around the camp, making sure he could not be seen. No tracks led away from the little meadow, and only one set, the trail he had been following, headed in. Port was confident he had found the bandit, but where was the gold?

Port realized the man might have hidden the box somewhere between the holdup location and the meadow. That the man was sleeping in the middle of the day, appearing in no hurry to go anywhere, seemed to indicate he did not have the gold with him.

Port did not see any point in taking the bandit in without the gold, so he waited, out of sight, letting the bandit think he had not been followed, that his trail across the desert sands had disappeared.

Port picketed his horse in a tiny meadow a good mile upstream, where he was sure the bandit would not find it. Then he returned with his canteen and food to the rocky hill.

Port figured he would have to wait two or three days. At the end of the fourth day the man seemed perfectly content to stay right where he was. Once, the bandit had walked to the top of the hill where Port was hiding and looked off to the north, as if to see if a posse might be coming. Port remained hidden.

On the fifth morning, with enough food for only one more day, Port cut his ration in half so he would have something to eat on the sixth day. From then on he would be without food. He rationalized the situation, thinking about the growing thickness he had noticed around his waist in recent years. This would be an excellent opportunity to get trim again. He would call it the bandido stakeout diet.

In addition to foolishness, Port had a lot of time to think about Mary Ann, the Bear River massacre, his new ranch, his mail business, his family, his religion, his life of violence. But while he thought, he watched and waited.

On the seventh day the bandit walked a short distance from camp and commenced digging beside a juniper tree. By this time Port was sure the man had ditched the gold somewhere along the trail. But now it appeared he had been wrong.

After a few minutes of digging with a strong stick, the man reached into the hole and pulled out a heavy black cash box, the kind Wells Fargo used to carry gold and other valuable cargo.

Port glided down the hill, careful to keep out of sight as the bandit broke the box open and began to count his bounty. He hadn't quite finished when he felt Port's pistol in his ribs.

The bandit was a young man, handsome, with black curly hair and a smooth complexion. Port expected the robber to get angry. Instead, the young man started to cry, as if the bad luck that had just befallen him was too much to bear. In seven days he had laid elaborate plans for spending the money. Now, Port had smashed his dreams.

Port made the poor young man load the gold on the horse and then lead the animal upstream to the meadow where Port's horse was tethered. The two began the long journey home. After getting his tears under control, the young man had little to say, other than that people called him Tex.

Port took his prisoner and gold to his newly completed cabin on Government Creek, where his hired man, Hat Shurtliff, was staying. After a hearty supper of beefsteak and fried potatoes, Port asked Shurtliff to keep an eye on the prisoner while Port got some much-needed sleep. He curled up under a blanket, with a gun in his hand and the cash box under his head.

Port fell into a deep sleep, and eventually Shurtliff did too. When they awakened, the young bandit was gone. Quickly, Port checked under his head. The gold was still there.

Returning the gold was the top priority, so Port made no attempt to follow the young outlaw. Bidding farewell to Shurtliff, he headed for Salt Lake.

Riding along the dusty road, the heavy cash box tied behind his saddle, the thought occurred to Port that if he didn't return the gold, no one would ever know he had it. He could just say he lost the outlaw's trail out in the desert somewhere. Shurtliff could be trusted never to tell. With forty thousand dollars in gold, Port would never have to work again. No, he finally decided he was too old to start a life of crime. But this was only one crime. No, he didn't want to be a thief, not even for forty thousand dollars.

Wells Fargo was delighted to receive the gold but wasn't willing to pay Port to go after the bandit. Actually, Port was in no mood anyway to return to the desert and try to pick up Tex's trail.

A tired Port returned to the Colorado Stables to see how the mail had been moving in his absence. Everything was fine. He walked into the back room and poured himself a square drink. "Wheat," he mumbled before stretching out on the cot and going to sleep.

Two days later the manager of the local Wells Fargo office sent a message for Port to come to the office. As Port entered, the manager handed him a telegram. Port looked at it and handed it back.

"I don't read," he said.

"I forgot," the manager responded. "It's from Fort Bridger, from a man named Tex who says he stole forty thousand dollars in gold from us. Said Rockwell stole it from him. 'Rockwell has gold,' it says. Also that 'Shurtliff will verify.' "

Port remembered his thoughts about keeping the gold and wondered how he would be feeling now had he kept it. Probably not very good. It felt good to know he had done the right thing.

# Chapter 57

Late one summer night in 1870, Port dismounted in front of the Colorado Stables, returning from a week's stay at Government Creek. One of the men inside said there was an urgent message from the housekeeper that Port hurry home. Fearing something might have happened to one of the children, he climbed back on his weary horse and hurried home.

He was greeted at the door by Christine Olsen, the housekeeper. He liked Christine. She was a young woman, in her early thirties, never married. She wasn't particularly attractive, nor was she homely. But looks were all that was average about Christine. She had more energy than a wolverine, treated Port's children as if they were her own, and was very intelligent. Along with the usual washing, cleaning, and cooking responsibilities, she helped the children with their schoolwork, made sure they all had music lessons, and helped referee their neighborhood battles. And she found time to read to them every night before or after prayers. While Christine would never replace Mary Ann, she had become a second mother to Port and Mary Ann's children.

Even before they spoke Port knew he no longer had to fear that something terrible had happened to one of the children. He could tell by Christine's relaxed, happy countenance that nothing serious was wrong, unless she was hiding something. He followed her into the kitchen.

"How are the children?" he asked.

"Fine. They're all asleep and had you come ten minutes later, I would have been in bed too."

"I wouldn't have come so late," Port said, "but there was a message at the stable that you needed to see me immediately."

"That's right," she said, seating herself at the table, looking down at her hands as she rubbed them together. Her face was no longer happy. Port sat down opposite her.

"What's wrong?" he asked.

"Mr. Rockwell," she said, her body shaking with emotion, "you are going to have to find another housekeeper."

"Am I not paying you enough?" he asked. He had always thought the seventy-five dollars a month he gave her, plus room and board, was a generous income.

"No, I do not need more money," she said, tears welling up in her eyes.

"If you are overworked, I can hire someone to help you, a cleaning lady, perhaps," he offered.

"No, that isn't it."

"The children. You are having trouble with the children."

"No. I love the children as if they were my own. You know that."

"Then why do you want to leave?" he asked.

"I don't."

"Isn't that what you said?"

"Mr. Rockwell," she began, fighting to keep control of her emotions. Her hands had become fists. "I'm almost thity-five years old. I want a family of my own before it's too late."

"Has someone been courting you?" he asked.

"No, not exactly," she said. She turned her head toward the window. "I always thought the right man would just come along and sweep me off my feet. But I've realized lately that it's not going to happen."

"If you leave, where will you go?"

"There are several good homes where I could move in as a plural wife. I could have my own family that way."

"Is that what you want?" he asked.

"I want a family of my own," she said. "And I don't see any other way."

"Have you told the children?" he asked.

"Heavens, no. You are the only one."

"How will you tell them?" he asked. She began to cry.

"I don't know," she sobbed.

"You have been their mother for four years," he said. "If you go, to them it will be like losing a real mother. The girls especially will be heartbroken."

"If I don't do it now," she cried, "it will only be harder later on. You must try to understand why a woman wants her own family."

"I think I've got the answer," Port said, suddenly standing up, walking over to the door, turning around, and marching back. Her sad eyes followed him. She couldn't imagine what he was thinking.

"Let me be your man," he said brightly. "Then you wouldn't have to leave, and you could have your own babies."

"Mr. Rockwell, I hope you are not proposing anything indiscreet," she said.

"Christine, I am proposing marriage. I also propose that you call me Port." He sat back down at the table. There was a look of disbelief on Christine's face.

"Are you serious?" she asked. "You wouldn't be teasing me?"

"I've never been more serious in my life."

"But after Mary Ann passed away I thought you had decided never to remarry."

"I did decide that."

"Why are you changing your mind?"

"Because of you," he said, getting up again, beginning to pace the floor. "After Mary Ann died I just never had the desire to court another woman. But with you it's different."

"How's that?" she asked.

"You moved into my home and have become the mother to my children. How could I not love you?"

"Your feelings are the result of my involvement with your children," she said. "But can you love me as a man loves a woman?"

"I've been selfish and foolish," Port said thoughtfully, "thinking a woman like you could be happy just taking care of my children for seventy-five dollars a month. I just didn't realize you needed more than that. Tonight you opened my eyes and my heart. Will you marry me?"

"I might," she said, overwhelmed at the possibilities of what was happening but still hesitant.

"I'm almost sixty, and I drink too much," he said. "But I have a good name, a strong testimony, and plenty of money." They both laughed. Port sat back down at the table. They looked searchingly into each other's faces. They weren't strangers, having been involved together with the children and home for four years.

"Could I ask a personal question?" she said, a note of hesitation in her voice. She looked down at her hands.

"Can't think of a better time," he said.

"You said you are almost sixty," she began. "And I said I wanted to have children of my own. You're not too old to, I mean, can you still . . ." Port began to laugh.

"An old stud doesn't ever forget how," he said. "He just slows down, and some say that's an advantage. There's still plenty of lead in this old pencil. It won't be my fault if you don't have children. In fact, I can tell you right now you'll have to learn to get by on less sleep when I'm in town."

"Port," she said, "then you're sure you can really care about me as a woman?"

"I suppose I have loved you for a long time," he said, "but never realized it until tonight. The question I have is, can you love me too?"

"I can, and I do," she said.

"Then it's a deal? You'll marry me?" he said, reaching across the table to shake her hand.

"Yes," she said, not taking his hand, "but I think a kiss rather than a handshake would be the appropriate way to conclude the matter." They leaned across the table and kissed.

"Should we tell the children now?" she asked.

"Why not?"

As she hurried upstairs to wake the children, Port leaned back on his chair and looked up at the ceiling. He felt good, better than he had felt in years. And he hadn't had a drink all day.

# Chapter 58

Port's marriage to Christine resulted in three daughters, Irene, Elizabeth, and Ida Mae. Irene died at birth.

Except for a brief mission with George Bean to the Indians near Fish Lake, Port's life was focused almost entirely on his family, the ranch at Government Creek, and the mail delivery business headquartered at his Colorado Stables.

Utah was changing, growing up, becoming more civilized. With the coming of the transcontinental railroad, emigration in covered wagons and handcarts had stopped. While there were still Indian problems in Montana and Wyoming, the red men in the Utah Territory had pretty much resigned themselves to getting along with the whites.

Bill Hickman had published a book that had gotten him excommunicated from the Church. Also excommunicated was John D. Lee, a loyal pioneer Mormon who was finally caught and convicted for his role in the massacre of an emigrant company at Mountain Meadows twenty years earlier. He was executed at Mountain Meadows by firing squad. Port couldn't understand why the Church would abandon Lee. He didn't understand all the talk about needing a scapegoat. Friends were supposed to stick together.

In August 1877, Brigham Young died. A month later Port was arrested for the murder of John Aiken. He posted bail of fifteen thousand dollars, and the trial date was set for October the following year. Port met with some young lawyers who offered to prepare his defense. He wondered how they could possibly understand the events and pressures of 1857 that led to the Aiken killings. They'd probably laugh if he told them how his dog Joseph had licked his face to warn him of danger.

When the lawyers started asking questions, Port's response was, "Wheat, wheat in the mill." They didn't know what that meant, and Port was in no mood to explain. He left the law office, having agreed to answer their questions at some undetermined future date.

The following June, Port attended the famous pioneer play *The Old Homestead*, which was being performed before sold-out audiences. Thespian Denman Thompson was playing Joshua Whitcomb, the starring role. The play was the theatrical highlight of the season.

Port had two tickets to the performance, but when he went by the house to pick up Christine, she wasn't feeling well, being three months pregnant with their third child. His oldest daughter, Mary, had already decided to go in place of her stepmother. Port had no objections. Mary had grown into a beautiful young woman. He was proud to have her ride with him in the carriage and sit with him in the theater. Best of all, she was proud to be with him too.

The play was good, but Port enjoyed most the conversations with old friends before, after, and between scenes. When the play was over, he took Mary home. When he stepped inside to see how Christine was, she was asleep on the sofa, so he headed back downtown, stopping at a tavern on the corner of Main Street and First South.

Seeing no one he knew, Port drank by himself, muttering "Wheat" or "Wheat in the mill" every time he finished a drink. He returned to Colorado Stables around midnight.

Port felt ill as he unharnessed the horses. Still, he gave them a quick rubdown, and, after turning them into their stalls, he poured each a gallon of oats so they would have plenty of spirit the next morning.

At the tavern he had thought a lot about his dog Joseph. Port remembered how Joseph would lick his face to warn him against danger in the night. He missed Joseph. He thought that tomorrow he would look for another dog, one he could train to lick his face when danger was near. Maybe he would let it ride behind his saddle when he crossed the Jordan River.

As Port closed the stable door, the night air felt cold. He began to shiver, wondering how the air could be so cold in June. Entering his office, he sat on the bed against the wall, removed his boots, and rolled up in a wool blanket.

He slept for several hours. When he awakened he was colder than before. One of the hired men brought him another blanket, but the chills continued, followed by waves of nausea.

Port stayed in bed all morning and much of the afternoon. He was always cold, unable to hold down any food or drink. Finally, in the late afternoon, he sat up with a start, announcing in slurred words that he had been ill long enough, that he intended to find him a new dog. He started to pull his boots on but then suddenly lurched backward onto the bed. Orrin Porter Rockwell was dead.

The coroners gave the body a close examination, finding no evidence of poison or injury. They determined the cause of death was heart failure. Finishing their work, they stepped back to contemplate the naked remains of the Destroying Angel, the bodyguard to two prophets, the gunfighter who had become a legend in his own time.

"The amazing thing," one of the coroners said, "is that there's hardly a mark on him. Here's what's left of a man who fought mobs and Indians and chased outlaws for forty years. He has no bullet or knife wounds. That's truly amazing."

"The thing I find amazing," the second coroner said, "is all that hair. I've never seen so much on a man. I wonder if he ever cut it."

"I asked his wife if she wanted us to trim his hair before the viewing," the first coroner added. "She said definitely not, just to wash it."

"Did you ask her why?"

"Yes. She said he believed the long hair protected him from harm—bullets and knives and such."

"Do you believe in such nonsense?"

"Do you have a better explanation for the lack of marks on this man's body?"

"No."

"Neither do I."

# About the Author

Until someone else steps forward, it appears *Storm Testament* series author Lee Nelson is the only man in modern times to kill a bull buffalo from the back of a galloping horse with a bow and arrow.

No, Lee is not a lunatic bent on suicide, but a best-selling author intent on gathering authentic research. Digging through dusty journals, starting fires without matches, even chewing on raw buffalo is part of Nelson's research in writing historical/adventure/romance novels unparalleled in authenticity and originality.

Lee was born high in the Rocky Mountains in Logan, Utah, later graduating from high school in California. After studying at the University of California at Berkeley, he served a mission for the LDS Church in Southern Germany. Lee has a bachelor's degree in English literature and an MBA, both from Brigham Young University.

Lee Nelson has over thirty published books, including ten historical novels in the *Storm Testament* series.